DAISY TATE

The Happy Glampers

HarperCollins*Publishers*

HarperCollins*Publishers* Ltd
The News Building
1 London Bridge Street
London SE1 9GF

First published as e-book serial in 2019
The paperback edition 2020
1

A catalogue record for this book
is available from the British Library

This novel is entirely a work of fiction.
The names, characters and incidents portrayed in it are
the work of the author's imagination. Any resemblance to
actual persons, living or dead, events or localities is
entirely coincidental.

ISBN: 978-0-00-831300-5

Typeset in Minion Pro by Palimpsest Book Production Ltd, Falkirk, Stirlingshire

Printed and bound in Great Britain by CPI Group (UK) Ltd, Croydon CR0 4YY

MIX
Paper from
responsible sources
FSC
www.fsc.org **FSC** C007454

This book is produced from independently certified FSC™ paper
to ensure responsible forest management.

For more information visit: www.harpercollins.co.uk/green

For Jorja and Grissom

'Cake!'

Everyone cheered as Charlotte slid the very last cake they would ever eat as university flatmates onto the table. She dropped a shy curtsey and stood back, watching as they plunged their forks into the huge lemon drizzle. No plates. No serviettes. No 'you firsts'. Just pure, unadulterated, last-day-of-uni bliss.

She'd miss uni. She'd miss her friends. These last three years had been the first time in her life she'd felt as if she mattered. As if all of her silly hopes and dreams might have a splash of validity. London, she worried, could very well prove her parents right. That taking a 'useless degree' in art history would land her one job and one job only: cleaner.

'Ohmigawd, Charlotte. This is ah-mazing!' Izzy's mid-Atlantic accent cranked west as she sang out, 'I'm surfing my *nirvana waves!*'

'Izz. Your bit's at that end.' Charlotte always made one end gooier than the other because Freya liked it fluffy, Izzy liked it gooey and Emily said she didn't really give a monkey's so long as it looked and tasted like cake.

Her eyes jumped from friend to friend as conversations

pinged all over the shop. Everywhere but on the question of when they'd meet again. Did they care as much as she did that their 'household' was splitting up? It was a bit late in the day to fret about whether or not her role as 'The Organizer' was the only reason they adored her. She'd almost slavishly taken to the role, taking charge of any and all pragmatic concerns – finding housing, creating cleaning rotas, always ensuring there was loo roll. Three short years ago they were strangers. Today? Today they were the most mismatched gaggle of girls she'd ever had the pleasure of calling her very best friends.

'This is cardiovascular disease on an epic level,' Emily said through a mouthful of icing. 'And I never want it to end.' The future Dr Cheung was too busy waiting for Izzy's cackle of delight to notice how pleased Charlotte was at the back-handed compliment. If there was a way to preserve this moment in time – capture it in a jar, press it into a scrapbook, dangle it from a charm bracelet – she would do it in an instant.

'C'mon girlie,' Freya pointed at the empty chair beside her, her Scottish burr exaggerated by the rolling of the *r*. 'Would you park your wee bum for once?'

Charlotte sat, pretending she didn't care that they were devouring the cake like heathens, missing the fact she'd spent that little bit extra on the lemons, added a half-cup more drizzle, precious pence spent that she could barely afford on her student grant, because that's the way her friends liked it best, but, as ever, she was unable to stop herself from beaming. She basked in the glow of their approbation. Relished that they loved it every bit as much as they had when, just a week into uni and shy as a dormouse, she'd made one for them in their very first student accommodation.

'Nummy!' Freya swept her wavy, pixie cut to the side and grinned at Charlotte. 'Promise me we'll meet up in London and eat cake?'

'No!' Emily put up a hand. 'She's mine. I refuse to let her leave. I claim you as my baking bitch for the duration of med school.' She took a decisive bite as if the matter was settled. Emily had a way of drawing lines in the sand.

They all turned to Izzy, waiting for her to stake her claim on Charlotte. She looked up when she felt the group's eyes on her. 'What?'

Emily patted Izzy's cheek. 'Bless. What's our little Izzy going to do out in the big wide world without all of us to look after her?'

'Dunno.' Izzy shrugged, that bloom of mystery surrounding her as it always did when she dodged their questions about the specifics of her life. 'What are any of us going to do?'

Chapter One

Whatsapp Group: Happy Glampers

Charlotte: Hello Girls! I suppose it's Ladies now. So pleased you've received the invites for my fortieth. I can't believe it's so soon! This is a test message, really. Techy things aren't my forte. Oh! And as a small favour, I doubt you'll be running into anyone else who's coming, but you girls (sorry, ladies) are the only ones invited to stay, so . . . secret squirrels?

Charlotte: *taps on microphone to make sure you can hear me* LOL. Freya? Emily? Are these the correct phone numbers? Or does WhatsApp take a few days to get up and running?

Charlotte: Emily! So sorry to have used your work mobile. No wonder you ignored me! I hate to think I might've interfered with one of your surgeries. Sounds like the NHS is running you ragged. Has this message come through? Do say if I'm becoming a pest. Freya? Are you out there or have I got the wrong number? x Charlotte

Freya: Sorry, Charlotte! Monty put my phone in the wash last week, the numpty! Am using Stone Age tablet until I can wrestle phone off one of the children. Was it the first bank holiday or the second? We're a definite Yesx4 xoxoxxF

Charlotte: Oh, wonderful! Not about the phone, obviously. It's the SECOND May bank holiday. I'm so pleased you can make it. Bank holidays seem to get booked up so quickly! As you know, families and plus ones welcome. I'll get one of the children to help me forward a map and the rest of the details for Sittingstone. Any more questions just throw them my way. x Charlotte

Emily Cheung: Sorry for erratic communiqué. Story of my life. Like my new scary doctor name? The patients love it. Lotte (still okay if we call you Lotte now you're a married mother of two?), I just googled Sittingstone. It appears to be out of doors. Or are we staying in the castle?

Freya: Emms, you eejit! Didn't u read the INVITE? IT'S GLAMPING (SOZ FOR THE SHOUTING . . . CAN'T FIGURE OUT HOW TO TURN OFF ON THIS GERIATRIC BEASTIE!) XOXOXOX

Charlotte: Oh, dear. Glamping's not a problem is it, Emms? I have been assured all of the yurts are done up to the highest level.

Emily: Like, indoors, highest level? Or still outside but pretending to be inside? #chinesepeopledontcamp

Freya: EMMS! SHOW SOME GRATITUDE. WE EXPECT NOTHING LESS THAN FULL SOPHISTICATion from you Charlotte. (Hey! Lower case!) x F

Emily: Plus ça change.

Freya: What's with the Francais?

Emily: Charlotte! I've been in touch with Izzy. Can she come too? She's going to be here. (Praying you say yes as I already told her and she's really excited.)

Charlotte: Izzy!!!!!!!!! I haven't seen her in years! Gosh. A proper Bristol Uni girls reunion. Absolutely. xx Charlotte

Freya: Wait. What? Izzy's here? *faints in disbelief* xF

Charlotte: There's a bell tent that will be just perfect for her. Does anyone know if she's eating meat again? Is there a plus one I should know about?

Emily: You know Izz. Expect the unexpected.

Chapter Two

Bunting. Charlotte could've kicked herself. How could she have forgotten the *bunting*? It definitely wasn't in the car. She'd checked three times on the way to Sittingstone. The same three times she'd pulled into lay-bys to 'check directions'. Her children hadn't commented that the Land Rover's satnav was in the front of the car rather than the boot. Hopefully they wouldn't notice the slight edge of pink round her eyes. Yes, it was all there bar the bunting. The cool boxes, the wellies, the cake. The same placid smile, the same pale pink lipstick and, of course, the same sensible, ash-blonde mum do she'd had three hours earlier when Oliver had ripped her world in two.

A real stalwart, her hairstyle. Not so much the husband.

At least he'd offered to drive to West Sussex separately to give her some space to absorb his news. Although, what better way to avoid seeing her normally composed exterior crack into fractals of disbelief? Absence worked a treat when Oliver wanted to prevent a scene.

As if she'd ever cause a scene.

He really should know her better by now.

So she started the car, followed the signs, and sped along

the motorway as if she could outdrive the fact her marriage might not last the day.

An hour later, as the Discovery crackled over the gravel at the entrance to the Sittingstone Estate, Charlotte's heart lifted. The castle was every bit as wonderful as it looked on the internet. The stone structure soared up into the bright blue sky with full Tudor Gothic grandeur. The remains of the first castle – a fortress, really – was a stunning tumble of stone over by the lake, whilst this one – the family seat – dominated a small hill. A truly resplendent calendar house. One pane of glass for each day of the year, fifty-two rooms, seven entrances and four, very grand, storeys. There were sprawling lawns, a blooming rose garden and lashings of wisteria shifting in the light breeze like . . . bunting.

Her wedding ring caught the light as she turned the car down the long, shaded avenue signposted for the glampsite. Ridiculous, oversized thing. Had she been so blinded by its beauty all those years ago that she'd been unable to see what her future held? Worse perhaps. She hadn't wanted to see it. If she'd just opened her eyes she would have noticed the horrid predictability of it all spooling out in front of her. Too many golfing weekends. A *pied à terre* in London. An affair with a junior partner. It was all so obvious it was almost gauche. How *could* he? And to find out on *this* weekend. The one solitary weekend she'd hoped to show off her life to her dearest friends.

She glanced into the rear-view mirror to the back seat where her children remained blissfully unaware of any discord. Perhaps she shouldn't have agreed with Oli when he'd decided, for the pair of them, that bothering the children with the 'whole silly mess' would be the wrong thing to do.

Fair enough for the weekend, but they weren't innocent babes in arms. They were young adults. Young adults who knew having an affair was the wrong thing to do.

She looked into the mirror again. Two bent heads. Two sets of noise-cancelling headsets. Hardly a word passed between them the entire journey. Perhaps they already knew. Perhaps, like Oli, they too had tired of her. Bundling them into the car today, you'd've thought she was slinging them into Guantanamo rather than putting them up in a five-star yurt. She was doubly horrified to catch Oli slipping them fifty quid each to play along.

She glanced at her children again, completely oblivious to the estate's glorious setting. One weekend with her friend's children rather than their mates, she silently groused. Was that so big an ask? To *talk* with someone for a change? Play a board game instead of devoting all of their attention to their phones?

Before climbing down from the car, she guiltily closed the search engine on her own phone. Googling her husband's not-so-new fancy woman in lay-bys probably hadn't been the best way to salve her wounds.

After one more scan in the boot for the bunting, Charlotte's eyes fell on the shiny new shoebox. A ridiculous pair of cream-coloured canvas Diors that Oli had given her for 'being so reasonable.' She hadn't been able to bring herself to put them on. In all honesty, she didn't want a pair of completely impractical shoes, even if it was her fortieth. Technically, she'd tick that box tomorrow, but he'd suggested she treat the entire weekend as her birthday, seeing as he'd cast a shadow on things.

Shadow? More like an apocalypse, obliterating sixteen

years of her very nearly perfect life. Other than that? He was right. A jolly birthday weekend was exactly what she needed. What else could crush the urge to lash out at him with his pointless shoes and ask him over and over again, *Why? Why, when I've been so true to you?*

She left the shoes untouched. The Charlotte Mayfield she'd taught herself to be kept the peace, put on a brave face, and didn't – *wouldn't* – spoil it for anyone else. Later, quietly and privately, she'd sift through the wreckage and see what was left. Then, perhaps, she'd wear the Diors through a particularly fetid puddle.

She tapped on the side door and gestured for her son, Jack, to open the window.

'Darlings. How 'bout you pop out and give me a hand unpacking the boot?'

Charlotte's blond, blue-eyed son – a picture of his father if ever there was one – looked at her with a stony expression. '*Mum*. I'm *knackered*. I've been at school. *All. Week.*' He abruptly changed tack (another Oli trick). 'You do it best anyway. We'd only get it wrong.' She looked across to where her daughter Poppy sat staring out of the opposite window, avoiding her gaze and looking glum. Nothing.

'You're right. It'll be easier on my own,' she chirped, too brightly. 'You two can have a wander around the site, how about that?' Jack rolled his eyes and Poppy continued to ignore her. Charlotte pushed down the knot of anxiety in her stomach. She'd absolutely adored being a mother when they were little. The only time she'd felt pure, unconditional love, and the hope that she had a chance to give her children the childhood she'd only dreamt of having. Teens, it turned out, were harder to please.

Charlotte felt the knot surge up into her throat where it threatened to erupt into a sob. She took a deep breath, easing it back down into place. There was a party to organize. Something she was very good at, despite the lack of bunting.

So! She began loading up her arms. Anytime now her friends would be arriving and she'd be taking her first stab at behaving as if everything was perfectly perfect. Friends she'd admittedly lost touch with over the years but, if she was being really honest, Freya, Emily and Izzy were the closest friends she'd ever had. And they were *her* friends rather than the guests who came with Oli's stamp of approval. That was a bridge she wasn't quite ready to cross.

Cake tins up to her chin, she headed towards the 'Starlight Tucker Tent'. The vast open-sided kitchen and lounge area didn't, as advertised, have a view of the sky, but she supposed landed gentry could call their idyllic glampsite features whatever they fancied. The plus side, she supposed, of being born to 'shoulder the burden of their forebears'.

Burden or not, the Sittingstone Glampsite was everything she'd hoped it would be. Three yurts, a pair of bell tents, and the tree house. The air smelt of warm meadow grass. The sky was a pure, deep blue. She couldn't have asked for a better bank holiday weekend. Apart from the whole adulterous-husband thing.

Relishing the unexpected cool under the canvas-roofed structure, she unloaded her tins onto the butcher's block made out of an old cable spool. If they'd been alive, or invited, her parents would've howled with derision. *Cast-offs from the sparky? Get off!*

Charlotte gave her head a little shake. Her parents had been masters of mocking the haves on behalf of the have-nots.

Though they'd been gone some five years now – her father from a heart attack, her mother not long after when pneumonia forced her to pick between alcohol and antibiotics – she could still hear their commentary about her own life choices, the thick Sheffield accent piercing right through to the quick of things. *Serves you bloody right for thinking you were better than everyone else.* Which, of course, stopped her from pulling out her iPhone and triple-checking the status on her Ocado delivery.

Instead she marched purposefully back to the Land Rover after commandeering a rather fetching lavender-coloured wheelbarrow called 'Felicity' and continued to unload the car.

A while later, Jack sloped into the kitchen and waved his phone at her. 'Muuuum. Dad's texted.'

'Oh?' She'd thought he might back out entirely. Leave her to save face on her own.

'He's checking out the pub up in the village. "Taste-testing the local brew".'

'Oh! Right. Well.' That was something. She popped the sausages she'd picked up from her favourite farm shop in the pristine, empty refrigerator.

'Muuuum. There's nothing to do here.'

'Of course there is, Jack.' She reached out to give him a hug, but he'd already walked away to examine some board games tucked up on a high shelf. He'd outgrow his father in a year or so.

He dropped the boxes onto a table with a despondent groan. Monopoly and the like had clearly outgrown their lustre. Goodness. If Charlotte had been brought to a place like this for a bank holiday weekend at their age she would've thought she'd died and gone to heaven! Her children were behaving as if they'd been asked to weekend in the bowels of purgatory.

'How about going down to the river?'

'Pffft.' The 'no clue what fifteen-year-old boys liked to do' variety. 'I wish this place had clay shooting. Or quad bikes. Why didn't you pick the Alps or something *interesting* for your birthday? Did you know Jago's mum and dad booked, like, a whole island in the Caribbean for their wedding anniversary?'

'How lovely.' Perhaps Jago's mum and dad were happily married and not bothered about silly messes like mistresses who may or may not be pregnant. That little gem had slipped out in the end. When Oli was telling her just how little the affair had meant and how much he'd like for them to find a way to make their marriage work despite the pregnancy.

Despite the pregnancy!

He'd back-pedalled. Said he wasn't sure, really. Or was it that Xanthe didn't know if she was going to keep it? The roar of blood in her brain had made it difficult to hear.

Xanthe.

The name tasted of bile. And inexplicably gave her the giggles.

'*Mum!* I'm *starving.*'

Charlotte's daughter Poppy, the definition of a blossoming English rose, dramatically collapsed onto one of the benches at the far end of the tent, clutching her stomach. 'This place is like, a total wilderness! Can you make me a toastie?' Her eyes lit on the tins. 'Is that cake?'

'Cake's for tomorrow, duck—' she tripped over the Yorkshire-ism and landed on a rather garbled 'darling'. 'How

14

about a biscuit?' She opened up a tin of homemade custard creams. Poppy made a vomit face.

Always nice to know her efforts were appreciated.

She checked her watch. Nearly three o'clock and still no Ocado delivery. 'Here.' She rustled in one of the cool boxes. 'Why don't you have an apple?'

Jack made a face. 'There's a tuck shop or something by the car park. They'll have something good.'

Charlotte protested as Poppy dived into her handbag. Hadn't their father just given them bribe money? When her daughter unearthed a twenty and clapped her hands she looked away. At least she had the money to spare. But would she always?

What if she and Oli couldn't iron everything out and carry on as normal? What if he chose this possibly pregnant lover over the family he claimed to adore? It was common enough. Regretting it when it was far too late to make amends. She had tacked on that last bit. It was nothing Oli had actually said, as such.

Tomorrow, of course, was the big 'do', but tonight was her night. Simple, straightforward, outdoor fare with the small handful of friends she had invited. She looked out to where a handful of picnic tables were dotted round a huge fire pit.

How could she have forgotten the *bunting*?

She'd laid it out in the mud room along with . . . what had she laid it out with? The children's wellies, Oliver's linen jacket (the one without the red wine stain, yes, she'd double-checked). The same one in which she'd found the receipt for a lingerie set from Coco de Mer in a size ten (she was a twelve to fourteen), the pile of picnic rugs (with waterproofing because you never really could rely on the weather), Oli's iPad. His new

15

one, which had pinged with a message just as she'd set it down. *Hello darling, just wondering if you'd managed to escape the horrid . . .*

Another tendril of Charlotte's confidence drifted off in the breeze.

Would she be able to play happy families all weekend?

She decanted some strawberries into a rather lovely china bowl. An antique from the looks of things. With a chip. Oli would hate it.

Anyway. The strawberries were perfect. And that counted for something.

'How do I look?'

Emily did an awkward twirl in front of Callum. From the look on his face, he didn't need to say a word. The khaki skort and plaid shirt combo exemplified the precise aesthetic she'd fastidiously avoided for some two decades, now. Earthy lesbian. Thank you very much outdoor wear.

Her normal attire was easy. Scrubs, or something black. Callum was trying not to laugh. They both knew she looked like an idiot.

'You, look like someone who'd rather do anything other than camping.'

If she were being really honest, it was little short of a miracle that Charlotte had managed to cleave her from the hospital. Not that she made a habit of being *dis*honest, she simply wasn't big into girlie weekends. There was always so much *talking*. And *feelings*. Definitely not her thing.

But! These women were about as close to a crew as she had. Not that they'd been in each other's pockets since uni. Apart from Izzy, she'd let the friendships . . . drift. Yes.

Drifting would be a good way to describe it. She didn't *not* want to be friends. She simply didn't include any time in her life to *have* friends. Which was why Callum, a man gifted with actual social skills, was the perfect person to accompany her to a fortieth birthday party where she'd swat at insects, not flush loos, and eat carcinogen-covered food with friends she hadn't seen for at least a decade and might not actually like any more.

Callum's quirked eyebrow meant he was still waiting for an explanation about the Chinese distaste for outdoor activities.

'Fifty years of enforced labour do that to a people.'

He laughed. 'I suppose it's the same as my people.'

Emily blinked and asked in her best innocent voice, 'The people of Edinburgh don't go camping?'

He pulled off his scrubs top, then basket-balled it into the laundry bin. 'My mum is permanently scarred by childhood exposure to midges and my father prides himself on being the most immaculately dressed man Nigeria has ever produced. I think we can agree, Emms –' he did his own version of a catwalk strut and twirl – 'this apple did not fall far from the tree.' He pulled a shirt out of the closet and held it up for Emily to inspect. 'Will this impress?'

She nodded her approval. 'Very Crocodile Dundee.'

He feigned disappointment. 'I was going more for the Bear Grylls look. Now, who are we communing with again?'

She held up fingers to represent them. 'Freya Burns-West. Scottish. Arty. *Very* woke. Husband is a living saint.'

'Why?'

'You'll see.' She held up another finger. 'Charlotte Mayfield. Organizer extraordinaire. Want your place to look picture perfect? She's your woman. Two point four kids. House in the country. Amazing cake-maker. And Izzy Yeats.'

Emily stared as Callum wriggled into a pair of fitted, cream-coloured trousers that were entirely inappropriate for the great outdoors. Maybe that's why she was so drawn to him. He just seemed so *comfortable* being him. The gayness. The braininess. The inability to pick a special someone and get on with life like the rest of the adult world.

Callum slid his belt on and nodded. 'Right. So, we've got a happy homemaker and an arty tree-hugger. You're the brainy, over-achieving, too narky for her own good because you're actually very lovely wunderkind . . .' Callum smiled when she punched him in the arm. 'Which one's Izzy?'

'Another housemate.' Emily paused, uncertain what to tell him about the woman she counted as her soul mate. 'She ran a surf camp in Hawaii for the last ten years. Just moved back. C'mon. Move it. We're going to be late.'

Eventually he'd tease more out of her. But for now? The fact she owned a skort should be proof enough these women meant the world to her.

Chapter Three

'Monty! Stop laughing. What does Charlotte want?' Freya caught her husband's giggles so badly she had to pull into a lay-by. The children, of course, were in a world of their own in the back seat. Ah, to be a Gen Z tween.

Monty put his fingers up in air quotes. 'Last-minute bunting.'

Freya snorted. Bless her wee cotton socks. Only Charlotte Mayfield would answer an 'anything we can pick up?' text with a request for last-minute bunting.

'C'mon then, woman,' Monty commanded in his best imitation of her accent which always came out *Braveheart*-y. 'It's her party . . . If she wants bunting, she gets bunting.'

Still giggling, she pulled back onto the country lane winding towards Sittingstone lightly asking the question that always made both of their smiles freeze in place. 'Have you got any dosh?'

Monty shot Freya a look. One that read, *I thought you were the one bringing cash*. Bloody great. Why was the overdraft always looming up at them?

She actually knew why. Sort of. Bringing home the bacon was her job. Allocating it was Monty's. Lately, there hadn't been quite so much bacon. You'd think with their back-grounds (working class) and their lifestyle (modestly aspirational), they'd be fine. From the expression on Monty's face, they definitely weren't.

'I've got a bit in my bag,' she rummaged around in her purse as they drove into the picture-postcard village. 'I've got some cash, I was supposed to bank it after I shut the shop, but most of the actual banks are closed in Camden now, so—'

Her admission sucked another lungful of oxygen from the car. Money was neither of their favourite topics.

'Well, I'm sure Charlotte will be eternally grateful,' Monty deftly smoothed over what could have easily become a fight. 'She's always liked things just so, hasn't she?'

Though she was loath to admit it – *girlfriend loyalty* – Monty did have a point. On their handful of weekends with the Mayfields, back when the children were actual children, Freya often felt as if they were participating in a tableau. Picnics on the lawn complete with china. Pony rides for the children when the apple blossom was at its fullest. Sunday lunch with Oli triumphantly entering their large dining room carrying a vast rib of beef, talking up Charlotte's Yorkshire puddings as she hung up her polka-dotted pinafore and joined them. Beautiful visions to be sure, but . . . Freya had never been entirely convinced that Oli brought out the best in Charlotte. Gone were the dreams of running a café/gallery for up-and-coming artists that Charlotte had envisioned when they'd first moved to the country. In their place was a cardboard-cutout corporate wife and mother . . . *och*. She was being mean. Dreams changed. She should know.

At least Charlotte had her picture-perfect family. Even if

it was with Oli. And tomorrow there'd be enough free, swish booze to make idle chitchat with the corporate-first, fox-hunting, Brexiteer, *Telegraph*-reading social set of theirs a bit easier to stomach. Not that she tarred everyone with the same brush, but . . .

'There's a spot, love.' Monty pointed to a free space. His voice and body language were back to normal now.

Awww. Monty might not be Jeff Bezos, but his heart was always in the right place, and money wasn't everything, right?

'Right everyone!' Freya pulled the car alongside the village green and prayed the double-yellow lines didn't come with a lurking traffic warden. 'Ten minutes to find bunting!' They spread out – one child per adult – and scoured the village for bunting. There was an artisanal butcher's, a baker's, two charity shops with some rather sparkly frocks in the windows, about nineteen tearooms and a pub. No bunting. If Freya had her sewing machine she could make some, but . . . alas!

Just as they were about to pile back into the car, Monty spotted Oliver standing outside the picturesque pub, his phone to his ear in what appeared to be an agitated conversation. He looked up briefly and caught sight of them when Monty waved exaggeratedly at him. Freya didn't think Charlotte's husband looked very pleased to see them, but Oli briskly ended the call and headed over to them, his furtive look transformed into a broad, if not entirely sincere, smile.

'Hallo, chaps! You've caught me bang to rights!' Oli flicked his thumb towards The Golden Goose. 'Told the wife I'd do a little recce. Wouldn't be a trip to the countryside without an excursion to the pub, now would it! Lovely to see you both.' Oliver gave Freya a kiss on both cheeks and clapped

Monty in one of those bear hugs that ex-Sandhurst types like him were fond of giving.

'Charlotte will be thrilled you're here, Freya, and the . . . ah . . . children . . .'

Freya helped him out. 'Felix and Regan.' Monty's hand slipped onto her shoulder and gave her one of those 'here we go' rubs.

'Of course, how could I forget! Look, why don't you pop in for a quick pint with me, Monty. Let the wives and sprogs get reacquainted, eh?' Oli dropped Monty a conspiratorial wink.

'Splendid idea!' Monty beamed, as Freya popped on her own false smile. How lovely to nip back to the 1950s in the blink of an eye.

'Frey, could you make sure when you unpack the car you're extra careful with my camera equipment?'

Freya shrugged Monty's hand off her shoulder. Traitor.

He dropped his voice as Oli tried to engage the children in an awkward 'what have you been up to for the past five years' conversation.

'I should probably pop in for a swift one, shouldn't I? Keep the old boy company.'

Old boy? Who kidnapped her husband and turned him into Boris Johnson?

'Yes. Or . . .' Even she could hear the passive-aggression as she continued, 'You could come with your family to the glampsite where our hostess awaits and help unpack the car.'

'Yes. Or . . .' Cue Monty's *'I know it's not ideal, but I'm with the kids all week and even though it's Oli, it'd be nice to talk with a grown man once in a while'* voice. 'You could see this as a thank-you for putting up the shelves in the shed *and* remembering to pack your onesie even though you forgot to put it on the list.'

She forced herself to acknowledge it wasn't a dig. Monty was, after all, the son of a builder and home all day so he was the person to put up the shelves. And, yes. She'd promised to help with packing but she'd been late getting back from the shop. As usual.

He pulled her left hand into his and began to trace round her wedding ring, an antique emerald and diamond number they'd spotted on a rain-soaked walk during a weekend in Gloucestershire that ended up being more romantic than miserable. It was the night the twins had been conceived. Three years later, they managed to officially put the ring on her finger.

'Just one quick pint,' Monty said sincerely, then, 'It'll give you and Charlotte a chance to catch up properly.' Puppy-dog eyes. Puppy-dog eyes pointedly dipping down to her handbag.

He always got her at moments like this. She wanted to be cross. She *was* cross! But . . . it wasn't like he made habit of it, and they *were* on holiday . . . oh, hell. She dug one of the three twenties she'd earmarked for petrol out of her purse and gave it to him. 'Go on then.' Monty pulled her in for an untidy kiss, but was heading towards the pub with his back to her as she shouted after him.

'Just the one! And don't come back half-cut. We've got things to do!' she said a bit too starchily. Particularly for someone who never got a telling-off for coming home from work smelling just the tiniest bit of cheap pinot grigio.

She watched as he and Oliver clapped one another on the back as if *they* were actually long-lost friends, ducking one after the other beneath the rose-framed doorway of The Golden Goose. *Humph.* She believed they'd be back after one pint as much as she believed in the Tooth Fairy.

Right. Onwards and upwards. She didn't need to be minted, but a bit more money would help. Help to pay with the PGL trip that was coming up for Felix, in his last year at primary school. It would mean so much to him, but two hundred quid was a lot of money right now. Help fix the downstairs loo that never played ball despite (or because of) Monty's efforts. Help them edge away from the relentless stream of bills that had them constantly teetering on the financial edge these days . . . and just like that she was choking against a fresh swarm of feelings bottlenecking in her throat.

Och away, darlin'. It's no' life and death, is it?

Her mother's voice had a way of appearing at times like these. When things threatened to overwhelm her. Freya was having a bad year, was all. If her mum were still alive, she'd be the first to remind Freya that money wasn't everything. That people don't time their deaths. That fortieth birthday parties didn't have to be all bells and whistles. Having her mum's wake on the same day hadn't been all bad. They'd plumped for St Andrews in the end as her mum had always joked that the wakes 'up the road' had much better sand-wiches than the ones scrabbled together at the church hall, so . . . There'd be other birthdays. Other moments. This one, for instance. Freya shook her head, picturing as she did all of the negative thoughts physically leaving her head just as the grief counsellor had advised. Out of sight, out of mind.

This weekend was about Charlotte and friendship. Friendship she was certain Charlotte needed. As charmed as it looked on the outside, there was something off about her connection with Oli. Something off about Oli.

Anyway, a fancy, catered reunion with her besties from the carefree days of uni was exactly what she needed. Cake and a campfire. What more could a girl ask for?

A husband who would dust off his law degree and do something with it.

Some actual free time to make art that mattered.

Children whose parents could afford school trips.

She thunked her head against the steering wheel.

It didn't feel very progressive of her to make art no one would buy or for Monty to put on that old suit of his to go out and make some proper dosh at a city law firm knowing it would suck the very lifeblood out of him. She'd taken on the role of household earner long ago – by choice. The fact she was maybe, possibly, failing at it, wasn't any fun to be around any more and was missing the bulk of her children's actual childhood was ... *bleurgh*. Maybe there was something to be said for the 1950s.

'Mum? Are you okay?'

Regan, her little worrier, stuck her head between the two front seats. Felix was still engrossed in one of those doorstop fantasy books of his.

'Yes, darlin'. Just got a little something in my eye.' She made a show of trying to extract an invisible speck before rubbing her hands together and singing out, 'Right, my beloved offspring! Let's get glamping!'

She breathed in a huge lungful of sun-saturated wildflower meadow and cow poo, ignoring the little twist in her heart that the scent always brought.

The wafty, pungent aroma of home.

She pictured her brother Rocco getting 'the girls' in for the afternoon milking session. Her dad still helped, but at seventy-something and just a wee bit more absent-minded than he'd been since Mum had died, Rocco had started filling in the gaps until, over the Easter hols, it had become very clear he was running the farm on his own. The fact that their small farm had yet to be eaten by some big nameless, faceless conglomerate or turned into so-called affordable housing, well . . . *thank god for big brothers.*

She waved her foot in front of the rear sensor and watched the hatch open like some sort of *Star Wars* portal. Charlotte's quirkily wrapped present sat atop a jumble of duffel bags, Monty's camera bag and last-minute panic packing.

She carefully set the camera gear to the side, praying Monty's latest craze, Instagram 'portraiture', would finally bring some cash in. More than likely, the equipment would end up in the loft with the rest of his 'sure things' when yet another inspiration hit. Sure. He was busy with the kids, juggling the household finances and being the family chauffeur, but surely he could see it was time to start eBaying some (all) of his rejects. She'd have to find a more delicate way to suggest as much. Last December, after squeezing past the home-brewing kits, the cheese-making equipment, and the empty beehive in a vain attempt to find the Christmas tree decorations, she'd told Monty that the loft should be renamed The Attic of Unfulfilled Potential. He'd not spoken to her for the rest of the week. He was a sensitive little bear, her Monty.

She scanned the area for Charlotte. It was doubtful Emily had arrived yet. Not with her workload. Freya was still a bit shell-shocked Izzy was coming. And nervous. It had been ten years since she'd seen her last. At her and Monty's wedding. She wished they hadn't bickered, but who ran off with the bride's toddlers to drop Pooh sticks in the river without telling anyone?

Okay. Fine. There was a part of her that would always be a bit funny about the fact Monty dated Izzy before her. Clarification. Monty and Izzy had hit all of the bases. Done it. Had actual sex. Hopefully enough time had passed that it would no longer be weird that one of the most beautiful women in the world had seen her husband's penis. Sure. It had been actual years prior to Freya's access to said penis, but still. Yup. Feeling extra grown-up now. She'd definitely moved on. That's right. Moved on from the fact that her blue-eyed, Poldark-esque husband and one of her best mates had had sex. With each other. In the nude.

As she turned, something caught her attention. Was that . . . ?

It looked like a drunken hedgehog.

They were nocturnal, so what was it doing out here in broad daylight? Surely, it wasn't . . . was it?

Yes. It was definitely lurching around. Dehydrated? Starving?

Freya grabbed Monty's Pearl Jam hoodie from the pile of clothes he'd stuffed into the back of the car and scooped it up into the thick cotton.

'Kids!' She beckoned for them to come out. 'We've got a medical emergency here.'

Freya held the hedgehog's tiny little face in front of her own and cooed, 'It's okay, darlin'. We've got you.'

A premonition jolted through her.

Babies.

It was technically too early, but . . . *climate change*. She gently tipped the hedgehog over and exposed her stomach. It looked swollen. She traced her finger along the creature's tiny pink feet, then atop the soft white arc of her belly. 'Do you have some hoglets growing inside you?'

'She's pregnant?' Regan looked as if she'd found a treasure chest.

Freya secretly wished her daughter would become a vet. Between the mice, the budgies, the runaway tortoise, and, of course, Dumbledore, the family Labradoodle, Regan was definitely the family's number-one animal lover. Maybe a proper summer at her family's farm would do the trick.

'Should we ring the RSPCA?' Her daughter's delicate fingers hovered above the hedgehog's spines.

'Yes. Definitely. Unless they have a wildlife clinic here. Felix, love. Can you grab Dad's woolly hat, please?'

Her gangly son tripped on his way to the back of the car. Poor lad. All limbs and no coordination.

'She's soooooo cute!' Regan lightly brushed her fingers along the hedgehog's spines.

'I'm pretty sure she's pregnant.'

'Can we call her Persephone?' Felix asked.

'We can call her whatever you like, darlin''

'This is great,' Regan cooed. 'I love it here already.'

And just like that . . . the long weekend stretched before Freya as a place of wide, joyful possibility.

Izzy couldn't move.

C'mon Yeats. Get out of the van!

An overwhelming instinct to turn round and head straight back to the airport hit so powerfully it made her light-headed. Why was she doing this, again?

'Mom?' Luna whispered from the back seat, puppy firmly nestled in her lap despite Izzy's entreaties to keep him in his newly purchased crate. 'They're staring at us.'

Freya and Charlotte were, indeed, staring. Well. Smiling. Waving. Beckoning. Wondering why the hell Izzy wasn't running towards them like a lunatic and joyously screaming her head off like she would've back in the day.

Get a grip, big breath in and . . . she flung the car door open, ran towards her friends, arms wide open and shouting at the top of her voice. '*Aloha*, ladies!' She threw in a whoop. Ten years in America taught her a whoop always helped.

They countered with some British-style whoops. A bit perplexed. A bit delighted. Mostly uncomfortable.

Bless. Despite the jitterbugs, it was great to see them. If she kept making a big show of things, it'd be no big deal. *Same ol' Dizzy Izzy.*

'Hey hey, girlies!'

As the space between them diminished, Izzy just managed to keep her game face on. Charlotte looked like a proper grown-up now. Blonde, in good shape, and immaculately put together with a splash of . . . Stepford Wife wasn't exactly right because Charlotte was too damn sweet, but . . . hmmm. She'd have to think on that. As usual, Freya was pulling off something mere mortals couldn't. An asymmetrical pastel-striped skirt, a camouflage tank top sporting a skunk sitting on top of a landmine, and a pair of Converse. As she got closer she clocked a few more crinkles round her eyes, a proper divot between her brows, and just a hint of the softness that came with the passage of time. Like, she could talk. Should she stick with the plan to blame her own eye crinkles on Hawaii or ruin everyone's weekend with some blunt honesty?

Before she could decide, she was enveloped in one of Charlotte's trademark hugs. Charlotte held onto her for just slightly longer than most people would; the type of hug that reminded Izzy of the three years Charlotte had been big sister and mother all rolled into one. Izzy breathed her in, her familiar scent filling her nostrils: expensive hair product mixed with Miss Dior.

Izzy took a step back and gave Charlotte a proper *wow! look at you* scan. Pretty as ever. A tiny bit stressy, but Charlotte had always been a bit *gah!* whenever there was an event on the horizon.

Freya stood awkwardly to the side, curling one of her purple-dipped curls round her finger. When Izzy opened her arms wide, Freya stepped into them, giving Izzy that astonishingly familiar '*I hate you but I love you too*' hug that meant she still hadn't got over the fact she and Monty had done it. Ah well.

Izzy put Freya out of her misery and stepped back. 'You both looking amazing. Not aged a day.'

They protested and Izzy pretended she hadn't been lying.

The women were standing in front of a rather impressive selection of wheelbarrows. Every colour of the rainbow, the barrows were bedecked with hand-painted flowers and names. Mabel. Ruth. Esmerelda.

'Look what we've found!' They parted as one and revealed an Isabelle.

'Awwww, girlfriends! You shouldn't have.' Izzy pressed her mountain of coils back from her face and went to stuff her hands in her back pockets, only to remember she had dressed up for her friends in one of her two maxi-dresses rather than wearing her go-to cargos.

'Your hair looks nice,' said Freya.

Izzy lifted her hand self-consciously to the coif. Kind, but no one was fooling anyone. She looked like a train wreck. The years of surfing had kept her fit, but the last couple of years? Ugh . . . She couldn't even go there. 'Where's Emms?'

'Not here yet.' Charlotte's mouth looked as though it wanted to keep on going and say something else. Oooo-kay . . .

Eventually Izzy had to fill the silence.

'I can't believe I'm not last!' Izzy was always last. 'Does that mean I get a prize?'

Freya rolled her eyes in an *oh lordy, look who hasn't changed at all* way. It was a wonder it had taken this long. Freya had been the least tolerant of her messiness. Her lateness. Her general inability to pin herself down. The fact she'd got a starred first for her degree despite not having appeared to have studied all that much. That had particularly annoyed Freya.

Charlotte, on the other hand, had always treated Izzy as if she were a wonder. Her poet mother. A childhood of flitting from one academic hotspot to the next. Dining with royalty one day and living on beans the next. *Your life sounds so romantic.* Until this very moment, Izzy hadn't realized just how much she'd missed her.

A sudden urge swept through her to throw herself at Charlotte's feet and beg her to make all of the incredibly difficult decisions she still had yet to make. Charlotte would choose well. Charlotte would choose impeccably. Emily was helping the best she could, but she wasn't exactly well equipped in the sensitivity department. Charlotte was. She would know which tack to take. Which path to follow. Like marrying Oli, for instance. That had panned out well. City lawyer. Country life. Beautiful children. Hiring super-fancy glampsites for her fortieth. From what Emily had relayed, everyone still thought Oli was a bit of a wanker, but on the whole? Charlotte's life was just as she'd planned. Perfect.

Behind her, she heard the van door slide open. The enormous canine fur-ball that was Bonzer ran between Izzy's legs, his voluminous puppy fluff tickling her calves as he settled himself in front of her. One ear up. One ear down. Fur the colour of an apricot. And the biggest, brownest eyes in the universe. He'd break the ice. Everyone loved a giant puppy.

'Izzy?' Charlotte's hands fisted, except for her index fingers which were pointing at Bonzer. 'Ummmm . . . is this a *dog*?'

Except maybe Charlotte?

'We left our dog with a pet sitter,' Freya said pointedly. *Well, bully for you.*

Explaining was always an option. She could pour her heart out. Detail the Amazonian effort it had taken to leave Hawaii, come back to the UK, find a school for Luna, a van, a puppy. But she'd get flustered and leave bits out, fuelling yet more 'typical Dizzy' eye-rolls. So she smiled and said nothing.

Charlotte, on the other hand, fell over herself apologizing.

'I'm so sorry, Izz. I thought I said on the WhatsApp that there were no dogs. Remember? They have some health and safety issues here and Oli's a tiny bit allergic.' Charlotte pinched her fingers close together, as if doing so would make the dog evaporate and all of the awkwardness that came from not having seen one another in over a decade would *poof!* disappear.

Izzy flashed Charlotte her apology grin. The one she used to use when Charlotte reminded her she forgot to get tea bags. Or to Freya when she'd neglected to take out the rubbish. Or Emms (plus a fluttering of eyelashes) when she hadn't strictly finished one of her term papers and maybe, kind of sort of, needed just a leeeetle bit of help. They always moaned at her. They also always forgave her.

Was that why she'd come back? So she could be with people she knew would take her in no matter what? Screwing it all up over a puppy simply wasn't worth it.

So she smiled, boofed her forehead with the heel of her hand and made a goofy face. 'Girl, you know what I'm like with fine print! I never exactly got on the WhatsApp thing because of changing phones and countries. Tell me what I gotta do to make it up to you? Sing? Dance? Bake cakes? You probably already did that, didn't you? I'll be your birthday slave all weekend.' She put her hands into prayer position and made sad clown eyes until, finally, they laughed.

'I'm so sorry, but he can't stay,' Charlotte's eyebrows templed in a way that suggested she understood the pickle Izzy was in, but matters were out of her control. 'The manager was very insistent. I had to sign a disclaimer.'

'Really? It's just . . . I'm not asking for me, it's more . . .'

Everyone turned as the world's most beautiful child ran up alongside her.

'Mom?'

Her daughter, Luna, slipped her hand into Izzy's and looked up at her, those bright blue eyes of hers still a bit of a surprise each time she saw them. A bit like a Siamese cat's. Sapphire brightness against silky smooth skin. Just a shade or so lighter than her own. Luna was her very own flesh and blood and yet, every time she looked at her afresh . . . goosebumps.

Izzy turned to face her friends. How to introduce the daughter she'd never told any of them about except for Emms who was really letting the team down by not *being* here.

Freya's jaw had dropped open. Not a cute face. A bit like Edvard Munch's *The Scream*.

Subtle.

Charlotte, on the other hand, smiled warmly.

Thank you.

'Well, who do we have here?' Charlotte squatted down, introduced herself to Luna, and shook her hand.

Izzy knew she could rely on Charlotte. 'This is Luna.'

'Luna! That's a beautiful name.' She looked back up at Izzy, 'Sooo . . . I guess there's been a bit more than surf camp in your life since we've seen you last.'

'Yup. Just a little.' Understatement of the year.

Where on earth was Emily? She'd always been better at telling Izzy off for things than Charlotte had. Charlotte had never been any good at telling anyone off for anything. Which was very likely why her children had no respect for her and her husband was having an affair, but that was another matter.

Izzy held the puppy up. 'Are you absolutely positive the puppy can't stay?' She waved his paw at them.

'Izz. Sorry, it's just that . . . Oh, this is terribly awkward . .'

The last thing she wanted to do was upset Izzy's newly discovered daughter. Charlotte could feel a little bit of her self-possession slipping away. Her friends were bound to see through it, of course. A true friend wouldn't need X-ray vision to tell she was barely holding it together. It had been years since they'd all lived together, but she knew she wasn't fooling anyone. Freya had definitely noticed something was up. Since she'd arrived, she kept pointedly making reference to their husbands. *Did you know our* husbands *are at the pub? What will our* husbands *make of this yurt, these olives, those cows?* Maybe not the cow part, but she wished Freya would stop pressing the point that the two of them were married. To *husbands.* How on earth was she going to get through the weekend?

Time to have a grown-up talk with Izzy away from little girl ears.

She smiled at Izzy's daughter. What was she? Nine or ten? *Such* pretty blue eyes. So, like Izzy, but she must look like her father, too. Whoever he was. Charlotte knew there was no point in asking Izzy about the father outright. She'd never liked being pushed on personal details. They'd just have to wait until Izzy was good and ready.

Such pretty eyes.

Charlotte had always loved blue eyes, especially Oli's. Light blue like a perfect summer sky, she'd once thought. Lately, today especially, they seemed cooler. Chilly. Like ice.

Right. On to this talk. 'Luna, if you like, the children are around somewhere . . .'

Freya helpfully jumped in. 'My children have got a hedgehog they're looking after until management bring down a little house for it. Perhaps you'd like to join them, Luna?'

Luna looked up at her mother with a pleading expression. How Izzy ever said no to that face was beyond her. Perhaps she didn't. 'Can I stay here with Bonzer? We'll sit in the car.' Luna stroked the puppy, which licked her hand.

Izzy raised her eyebrows at Charlotte's micro 'please can you just do this' look, then smiled softly at her daughter. 'No, Booboo. It's a beautiful day, no one is sitting in the car.'

She gave her daughter a hip bump, pulled her incredible mane of dark, coiled hair away from her face and kissed Luna's forehead. 'Why don't you go check out the hedgehog? They don't have those in Hawaii.'

'Felix and Regan would love to meet you,' Freya added. 'My two. They're twins!'

Charlotte could see that Luna was clever enough to know she was being moved on so the grown-ups could talk about 'the situation' without her.

'C'mon. I'll show you.' Freya put out her hand as Luna, clearly intrigued by the prospect of a brand-new mammalian discovery, gave in and took it. 'Charlotte?'

Her cue to sort out the problem. This one she could handle. Unlike the wayward husband problem. That one would have to wait.

Before Izzy could blink, she found herself handing Bonzer's lead over to Sittingstone's estate manager.

'Bye bye, bud. See you soon.' Izzy nuzzled the puppy.

'Any news on the hedgehog house?' Freya had just jogged up to their little group and given them all a full report on the hedgehog, a need for tweezers (ticks) and an assurance that Luna was as transfixed by the little creature as the rest of the children were. And by 'rest of the children', she meant hers. Charlotte's children, just that little bit older than the others, had been seen sloping off to their bell tent arguing about charging points.

'We should have one kitted out for you in the next hour or two,' the manager said. 'The dowager countess has a thing for hedgehogs, so we've got loads round the estate. Normally we've got a few in store, but this one's caught us a bit early.'

'Mmm,' Freya nodded deeply, then mouthed '*global warming*'.

Izzy stifled a laugh. Same ol' Freya. Bless. She'd have to triple-check the recycling rules before she threw anything away. That. Or torture her like she and Emily used to back in the day. The *fuss* over an uncomposted banana skin. Good times. Simpler times.

The manager gave Bonzer a '*let's see now*' look. One that suggested he had the hedgehog situation under control, but puppies? Not so much.

'Are you sure it's okay?' Izzy held out her hand for the lead.

'Positive,' said the manager, who had insisted several times everyone call him Whiffy instead of Peter. Something to do with how he'd always 'smelt of the countryside' as a kid, and nowt had changed other than that he lived down South where the weather were a bit fairer.

'It's for his own safety.' He crouched down and gave the puppy's head a scrub. Izzy was vaguely mollified when Bonzer gave him a big sloppy lick on the face and Whiffy laughed.

'Breed?'

'Erm . . . designer dog?' Or mutt. All in the spin, she supposed.

'The rescue charity said he's a mishmash of Lab, collie and some sort of enormous mystery beast. I'm guessing that's why his paws are so huge. Pyrenean mountain dog?'

They all studiously examined Bonzer. His white eyebrows quirking left, then right, then left again. 'The woman said he was the product of a "secret liaison".'

Freya's eyes shot to her as if she'd been giving them some

code about Luna. Izzy herself was the product of a secret liaison, so . . . no judgement in this camp.

'When did you move back again?' Freya asked. 'Long enough to get a puppy, obviously.'

'Monday.' Izzy held up her hands. 'I know. We're doing this all a bit ass-backwards, but . . .' She shrugged. 'I thought Bonzer might help us both settle in once we get to the cottage.'

'Cottage?' Freya's eyebrow shot up.

She'd forgotten Freya's insatiable appetite for details.

Cool your jets. It's been ten years. Plenty of water under the bridge. More water to come.

'The one I inherited. It's in Wales. Welsh Wales.' She swiped the air between them. 'I'll fill you in on everything later. Right now I just wanna make sure this little guy is going to be all right.'

Bonzer nestled his head into Whiffy's hand then looked up at him, a picture of doe-eyed innocence. Everyone went, 'awwww', then threw guilty looks at each other seeing as they were meant to be saying goodbye.

Whiffy grinned at Izzy. 'Don't you worry. His accommodation will be posher than what you lot are in.'

Charlotte bristled.

Whiffy held up his hands. 'Not like that.' He laughed. 'A kennel's a kennel. It's just that it's up at the main house.'

'You mean the earl and countess are in residence?' Charlotte shook her hair a bit to make it look as if she didn't really care, but Charlotte, Izzy now remembered, had never been particularly good at pretending.

Whiffy looked down at Bonzer. 'They'd love a little guy like this. Mad about puppies, they are.'

Izzy threw Charlotte a panicked look.

Whiffy saw the exchange. 'Don't worry. Lord James and Her Ladyship are away this weekend. Greece, I think. They won't be anywhere near the kennels. The dowager countess is in.' He dropped them a cheeky. wink. 'She does love an evening stroll to the kennels. Not sure I'll be able to keep her mitts off this one.'

'Well, if that's the case, then maybe it's better if we keep Bonzer. I've got the van and—'

'Nope. No. Sorry, madam.' Whiffy really did look sorry, but he took a step back from her all the same. 'You really don't want to see a longhorn cow protecting her calf against this little guy.' Whiffy gave Bonzer's head another scrub, then lifted him into the back of his utility truck. The women waved goodbye. Bonzer's expression read as all of theirs had when their parents had left them to 'get on with the magic of learning' that first day of uni. Half bewildered, half 'you can go now'.

Devoid of her puppy and child, Izzy gave the site a proper scan. It was lush. Stunning, really. That seemingly effortless combination of whimsy and class. The Brits were brilliant at baronial elegance.

Her eyes settled on a nearby yurt. The first time she'd ever gone camping was with these girlies. Emily had had a hissy fit after her first insect bite and had slept in Izzy's van. Not that there had been much room in it. Charlotte had decanted near enough their whole house into the thing. Freya had been the truly useful one. Fire-starter. Tent putter-upper. Arbiter of just how long the five-second rule really lasted when a sausage dropped off a stick into the sand. (About thirty seconds if anyone was asking.)

'Are you all right, Izzy?' Charlotte reached out to take the backpack Izzy was holding looped on her arm.

'Absolutely. More than.' Izzy smiled. She wasn't here to mope. She was here to party! 'This place is amazing.'

Charlotte beamed. 'I'm so glad you like it.' She tucked her arm in Izzy's and pointed towards a bell tent. 'I can't wait to hear all about what's brought you back home.'

All in good time, Izzy thought. This was great. Being home again. She loved the UK. She loved her friends. She loved life. All in good time, but not tonight. First, she wanted absorb all of this. The fire pit, the kitchen tent, the smattering of benches and picnic rugs that were all so fabulously British. Everything was just so, except . . . 'You know what would make this place absolutely perfect?'

Charlotte and Freya leaned in.

'Bunting!'

'Wait! Stop the car.'

'I thought we were late.'

Emily pressed her hands to the dash. 'Oh, gawd. Just look at it all.' Emily thought she might throw up a little. It was all so twee! She loved kitsch, but she did not do twee. In fairness, she thought there'd be bunting. Bunting might've tipped her over the edge.

Emily arched an imperious eyebrow at Callum and did a refresher course. 'Okay. Charlotte's the hostess with the mostest and it's her birthday.'

'Am I right in guessing she's also the world's biggest fan of Emma Bridgewater?'

Emily shrugged. 'Probably. She's the nice one. The nicest.' They were all *nice*.

'Freya. Erm . . . She drummed her fingers on her lips. 'Freya is our resident eco-politico-do-gooder. Married to Monty. Don't recycle in front of her. You'll get it wrong.'

'She sounds a right barrel of laughs.' Callum mimed turning the car around and making a break for it.

'Less annoying than she sounds. She's a weird mix of practicality and creative idealism. Or was anyway. It's difficult to dislike someone who once made a dress entirely out of cornflakes then tried to donate it to a homeless shelter.'

Callum laughed appreciatively. 'Sounds like the sort of person who should've stayed in Bristol.'

Emily shoved her chunky fringe out of her eyes. Good point. But London was a bit like Oz back in the day. Going to uni then moving to London was simply what you did. Their lot anyway. Except, of course, Izzy. 'I think the plan was to be some sort of couture artist, but she has a shop in Camden now.'

'Selling?'

Clothes that were a far cry from the unbelievably beautiful dresses she had once made out of flower petals, but . . . daisy-chain tutus weren't exactly everyday wear. 'Slogan T-shirts.'

Callum looked at her blankly.

'You know. The kind that say "Don't Hate Me Because I'm a Unicorn" or "hashtagI'mWithHer".'

A smile lit up Callum's face. 'You should have one that says "Glamping Queen".'

He laughed so hard the car lurched and ground to a halt.

'Listen, mate, if I get the slightest hint that there are nasty insects or a compost loo anywhere near this so-called "glamorous" bell tent we're in, you're taking me to a Hilton.'

41

'Well, someone's certainly looking forward to seeing her nearest and dearest girlfriends of days gone by.'

She was. Oh, she definitely was. And she also really wasn't.

'Just as a point of interest, they might also think you're my boyfriend. Just go with it.'

She ignored the pointed look and unfurled her index finger towards the glampsite. 'Onward, James.'

Fuck it.

Was there nothing that would stop the hounds of insecurity baying at Freya's door? At least Charlotte had finally given her a job. Chopping. Chopping was good. These would be the best carrot, pepper and celery batons the world had ever seen.

Tuning out Izzy's oohing and aahing as she peered into all the cake tins, Freya selected a glossy red pepper and chopped it in half in one fluid, surgical move. It felt good. But not good enough. Were there enough crudités here to pound out the jealousy she was still feeling over Izzy and Monty?

Logic dictated she should be grateful. Logic seemed to be taking a bit of a holiday.

Sure. If Izzy hadn't brought him home and had Very Loud Sex with him over that fortnight, she and Monty never would have met. He'd been unceremoniously dumped but had still popped up at the odd party because Izzy had pronounced him good fun if not boyfriend material. When their paths had crossed again at that massive anti-Gulf War march, *kismet*, Freya had thought. *Kismet.* But the truth was, fate had nothing to do with it. Her cupid was Izzy.

She chopped so hard she gave herself a crick in her neck.

Idiot. Monty loved *her*. He'd chosen *her*. They had two chestnut-haired, blue-eyed children to prove it. Their lives were *exactly* what they'd hoped for. They didn't need nods from the couture houses or an Amal Clooney-esque track record of human rights triumphs to know they were still in love. That had been the original plan, but . . . life. At least they were still doing their bit for the planet.

Chop.

Just because, unlike Charlotte, she and Monty had done everything the wrong way round, didn't mean she needed to be insecure about it.

First came love. They'd got that part right. Then came the double-wide baby carriage. Then, once they'd given in to Monty's father's extremely unsubtle offer to pay for a reception at their local in Gloucestershire, marriage.

In the lead-up to their wedding, the twins had been toddlers. Two year olds into everything. It all began to flood back as if it were happening right now. The endless stream of nappies. The panic about primary schools. A ridiculous need to prove to all of their friends that they were still up for throwing one hell of a party. The bone-crushing fatigue.

Freya had had no energy beyond caring for her children, making on-trend T-shirts and getting her family's bills paid. There hadn't been extra energy for rolls in the hay. Or money for a nursery or a nanny. Monty had told her it didn't matter. The job at Human Rights Watch would've paid less than it would've cost to hire someone to look after the kids, so . . . Looking after them at that juncture hadn't meant to be permanent, more . . . a means to an end. Only there didn't seem to be an end. Maybe Izzy's reappearance was a sign that change was afoot. Of good things to come? Or a harbinger of doom?

Chop.

It came to her clear as day. Monty was going to leave her. No wonder he'd run off to have a pint with Oliver. She'd hollered instructions after him as if he were a teenaged boy, not a man. If she were in his shoes, *she'd* run away. With Izzy, for example. Now that she was back. Izzy was beautiful. Carefree. Freya was the opposite of carefree. She was . . . pernickety. A bossy, pernickety, purveyor of so-so unicorn T-shirts.

Chopchopchopchopchopchopchopchopchopchop.

'All right there, woman?' Izzy sidled up to Freya and hip-bumped her at just the wrong moment. Freya was about to snap at her when Izzy leant in and gave her a kiss on the cheek. 'So good to see you. You look bloody brilliant. Still keeping Monty on his toes?'

. . . and breathe.

'Brilliant T-shirt, Frey.' Izzy pointed at it with a slice of red pepper. 'Love the skunk and grenade motif. Is that a Banksy-inspired take on conflict? A "war stinks" kind of thing?'

Prickles of frustration crackled through her. The T-shirt was one of her favourites. And, yes, it was inspired by Banksy. Not that she would ever admit as much. 'I thought it was a bit more subtle than that. More along the lines that the artist's role in nonviolent protest is critical to bringing about change.' She sniffed.

'It's cute.' Izzy plopped the dips into a pair of glossy green bowls without waiting for Charlotte's decision.

Typical Izzy. Just ploughing ahead and doing whatever she wants, no matter the consequences!

'It's very . . . evocative,' Charlotte said. Which was kind, but not really the ego boost it was meant to be because, in a million-zillion years, Charlotte would never be caught dead wearing one of Freya's T-shirts. Except, perhaps, the unicorn range and even then—

'*Emily!*' Izzy's scream brought Freya's maniacal chopping to an abrupt halt.

Charlotte clapped her hands. 'Oh, *good!* I was beginning to think she wouldn't make it.'

Izzy took off like a gazelle, arms wide open, as Emily peeled away from the fancy convertible she'd arrived in, instantly falling into her role as The Girl Who Hates Group Hugs.

Freya followed Izzy, noticing – as she left the tent – Charlotte swiftly rearranging the dips before she, too, headed towards the car park.

'Enough!' Emily wailed as they surrounded her and bombarded her with the very things she hated most, kisses and hugs. 'Get *off!*'

Through her cries of protest, they all vied to be heard, 'You look amazing!' tangled up with, 'How long was the drive?' 'Who's the hottie emptying the boot?' And '*Jesus wept*, are you wearing a *skort*?'

The familiarity of this, the *silliness* of it, stripped a layer of defensiveness from Freya's heart. Her insecurities were obviously playing silly buggers with her. Everything was as it appeared. Izzy was no threat to her marriage. Oli was as good a husband as any. And Emily was secretly loving this.

'*Get off me you heathens!*'

See? Nothing had changed at all.

Once she'd shaken everyone off, bar Izzy, who was draping

her arm over Emily like a feather boa, Freya got a proper look at her.

'Crikey, Emms. You've not aged a day!'

Emily gave a nonchalant shrug. She looked like Lucy Liu with a fringe. Long, inky-black hair. Pitch-black eyes. Not a line in sight, nor a lick of make-up. The women all beamed at each other and, for a moment, the years fell away and they were all twenty-one again, the world at their feet.

Emily made a show of assessing each of them before abruptly unleashing that sly-dog, hard-won smile of hers. 'Well, thanks very much, ladies!'

'For what?' Charlotte looked perplexed.

'For telling me we didn't have to dress like Ray Mears.'

Laughing, Emily clapped her hands together with a decisive crack, then brandished two condensation-covered bottles of fizz that she'd pulled from her shoulder bag. 'Let's get this pre-party party started!'

Chapter Four

When supper was finally ready, the children descended like locusts, making Charlotte's efforts feel worthwhile. She'd always loved the hubbub of happy children. Even hers had cheered when Izzy revealed some genuine American marshmallows.

The children, having devoured most of the marshmallows, started to disappear from around the fire which, until food was put in front of him, Monty couldn't seem to leave alone. Or Oli, for that matter. As if he who made the largest fire would come out as top man. Why on earth was Oliver still trying to prove he was the alpha male when he so obviously was? Charlotte's concept of what made a real man snagged on the thought. Perhaps the fact Monty had enough pride and self-confidence to be a stay-at-home father *did* make him the stronger one of the two. She would bet any money in the world Monty wasn't running around behind Freya's back.

'Oof! *Charlotte.*' Izzy rubbed her flat-as-a-pancake belly. 'That was amazing. Still hostess with the mostest!'

Hostess with the mostest secrets, Charlotte thought, giving herself an invisible pat on the back for not succumbing to the growing urge to tell her friends that her charming husband sought his carnal pleasures elsewhere. It had been on the tip of her tongue all evening.

'Tomato sauce, Emily?' *Did you know I've not had sex with my husband since Christmas?*

'Pimm's, Freya?' *The last time I tried to make love with him, he pushed me away.*

'Izzy, do have the last bit of burrata.' *How's life as a single mum? Do you think I'd take to it?*

'Anyone care to finish these off?' Charlotte held out the scant remains of their supper. A pair of odd-shaped sausages, a bit of over-charred potato with chorizo and some wilted salad leaves.

'Would you look at that?' Freya tipped her head towards the fire pit where Monty was now sound asleep on a broad slab of oak, tucked beneath one of the lovely National Trust rugs Whiffy had brought out. He was hugging his camera bag like a teddy bear. 'Stamina of a gnat.'

Charlotte watched Freya examine her slumbering husband. It was difficult to read her expression. Half loving, half '*oh, please*'. Their banter was as bright as ever. Maybe a bit more bossy on Freya's part, but . . . she *was* the breadwinner in the house, and if Charlotte's home was anything to go by, the bill payer had free rein to comment on the failings of the non-earning person. Perhaps that was where she'd gone wrong. Literally making herself valueless.

'He lasted longer than Callum.' Emily flicked her eyes towards the yurt where her boyfriend had disappeared after announcing he was exhausted after a 'savage week on the ward'. Mind you, Emily hadn't actually introduced him as her boyfriend. Just said, 'And this is Callum, the hospital's answer to Dr Kildare.' The two of them seemed to have a little joke at this, which was sweet . . . but he did seem a bit . . . theatrical. 'He seems lovely. Your Callum.' Charlotte pushed the remains of the cheese tray towards Emily.

'Ha! He's definitely not "mine".' Emily picked up a grape and stared at it. 'The man does as he chooses.' When she realized everyone was looking at her with raised eyebrows, she qualified. 'As do I. Obviously.'

'Amen to that.' Freya sat up straight. 'I find a lot of the mums at the school treat me *very* differently to the other mums, but that they simple *adore* Monty. Make a huge fanfare out of things he does – like getting the children to school on time – that the other mums get tuppence for. When I point it out? They all flock to his defence.'

Emily gave her a sideways look. 'I was just saying we're our own people. Open and honest. Nothing to make a big deal about.'

Izzy gave Emily a stagey nudge. 'Yes. It's good to be open and honest with the people we love, isn't it?'

Emily's eyes narrowed. 'Why, yes, Isabelle. It *is* good to be open and honest with the people we love.'

Freya snorted, then pretended she hadn't. 'Are you two still doing that weird "saying meaningful stuff in front of us without spelling it out" thing?'

'No,' they both said tightly.

Freya drained her wine glass and extracted herself from the picnic table, announcing an urgent need for more Sancerre.

Charlotte gave Emily and Izzy a curious look. Were they hiding things? Not that she was judging. She'd been hiding things all night.

As if on cue, Oli strode out of the kitchen tent where he'd been muttering away on his mobile.

He shut off his phone and sauntered over towards the women. Charlotte noticed that his natural swagger was exaggerated to the point of outright arrogance by the amount of booze he'd put away, both at The Golden Goose and here.

'Here she is, the birthday girl. Well done, darling. Did the meal transport you back to the good old days as expected? Burnt bangers and charred burgers hit the spot for everyone?'

Charlotte squirmed. What an odd way to make her feel good about herself. Mocking her Northern simplicity. She was certain the tzatziki had covered up any dryness the burgers might have suffered on the grill. And the griddled potato and chorizo had been devoured. Putting in that touch of sherry *had* made a difference.

'Have you lot had Charlotte's Yorkies? Best thing to come out of Yorkshire, if you ask me.' Oli just missed covering up a belch. 'Apart from Charlotte, of course.'

'Your wife can rustle up a *MasterChef* meal on a hotplate. I've seen it.' Freya gave him a curt nod and handed him the bottle and the corkscrew. 'Here. Why don't you make yourself useful?'

Charlotte caught the glint of a challenge in his eye. 'Of course!' He grunted as he deftly extracted the cork and handed Freya the bottle with a pointed, 'The perfect little woman, my Charlotte. Maid in the living room, cook in the kitchen and whore in the bedroom, right love?' He leant back and barked a solitary ha!, pleased with his own daring. Charlotte failed to hide her cringe, her eyes darting round the table, hoping no one noticed the sharp look Oli shot her when his joke fell flat. How quickly he must have forgotten how, just a few hours earlier, he had been pleading her, with actual tears in his eyes, to forgive him. Take him back. Continue to love him and keep their family whole. It was the only thing he wanted, he'd said. *She* was the only thing he wanted. Somehow, she wasn't entirely convinced that was true.

'You're a lucky man to have your very own K-Midd,' Emily said, holding out her glass for more wine. 'The power behind the throne.'

'And the brains.' Izzy gave Oli one of those '*just try and contradict me*' looks she'd learned from her mother. Charlotte had always been a bit intimidated by Izzy's mother. As, she supposed, she had been of Oli. Which was an awful thing to realize. Maybe she should have refused his offer to try and work things out. Instead of accepting gratefully, she could have nodded benignly and said, 'I'm afraid you've made your bed, Oliver. Now off you go. Lie in it.' As if she'd ever have the courage.

Freya was about to say something else but Charlotte gave her head a quick '*please don't*' shake.

She knew she should be grateful to her friends for attempting to burst his little bubble, but all she could feel was the hot embarrassment of shame at the situation, at Oliver, and mostly at herself. How had she managed to end up like this? No self-esteem, no respect, and – potentially – no husband.

'Well, this is all lovely, the old gang together, thick as thieves like always.' Oliver put the emphasis on 'thick' and Charlotte felt the colour rise to her face. She'd never embarrass *him* in front of his friends.

Oli yawned and stretched. 'Wonderful as all this is, how about some coffee, and possibly a nightcap, Charlotte?' His request felt suspiciously like an order, but desperate to end this particular horror show, she was about to acquiesce when Freya made a 'no you don't' cluck.

'Sit back down, Lotts. It's your birthday.' She shot a look at Oli then said, 'You're to be waited on hand and foot this weekend. Sit.' She climbed out of her spot on the picnic bench and playfully, but firmly, admonished Oli. 'Lavish your wife with affection.'

Charlotte flushed again. Oli didn't take to being told what to do, and getting him to lavish anything on her other than disapproval at this point was as likely as Elton John turning up and bashing out 'Happy Birthday to You'.

A tinny-sounding tune vibrated in Oliver's pocket. Charlotte thought it sounded a lot like Justin Timberlake's 'Sexy Back'. He tugged his phone out, quickly silenced it, then shoved it back in again. Was it *her*? Was that their song? She almost wanted to laugh. Filthy and annoying. A bit like him.

He turned towards the tree house, mouthing, 'Business. Sorry.' Her friends stared at Oliver's retreating figure with ill-disguised horror.

'Not to worry,' she said in too high a voice. 'He's always a bit like this when he's working on a big deal.' It wasn't a lie. 'Besides,' she tacked on as brightly as she could, 'if he didn't work so hard, I wouldn't get lovely treats like this.'

She waved her hands expansively at the scene around them, at the detritus from the evening; then, as if Oli had snipped the marionette strings that held up her wrists, her hands dropped to the table top with a small thud.

*

Freya caught eyes with Izzy. For once they could agree on something. Oli was being an arse. The splinters of hurt splicing through Charlotte's cheery demeanour as her husband disappeared up into the tree house were painful to watch.

It was a super-big 'ouch' in an evening that had been increasingly filled with Awkward Oliver Moments. Not that he'd been anything less than charming in his trademark way. A bit of locker-room humour, a bit of bantz and teasing in that slightly juvenile, slightly bullying public-schoolboy way of his.

Everyone's awkwardness spoke volumes. None of them had ever really taken to Oli. Apart from Charlotte, obviously, so they'd all made allowances. Laughed at his terrible jokes and tried to ignore his privileged egotism. When he'd proposed, they'd all figured if the nicest human in the world loved him, then he couldn't be all that bad. Hidden depths and all that. But this time there was something else at play, something more . . . cutting.

'Guess I'd best clear up for the big day, then.' Charlotte half stood. 'Perhaps bring Oli up a coffee.'

The three women exchanged brief 'WTF' looks with each other and all rose to help.

Izzy picked up the stray food platter while Emily cleared up the unused cutlery. Freya shooed Charlotte away from the stovetop coffee percolator and made a show of topping up Charlotte's wine glass whilst lavishing her with praise about the glampsite, the meal, her outfit. When the coffee was ready, Freya ran it up to Oli but didn't bother waiting for him to answer the door. The soft murmuring tones she'd heard before she'd knocked hadn't sounded anything like a business call.

Once they'd sat back round the picnic table, an awkward silence settled around them, which Freya was the first to break.

'Are you sure you're all right, hen?' she asked Charlotte quietly. When Freya reached out to touch her hand, Charlotte looked as if she was about to break. A kind word or a hug could push her over the edge. 'I'm absolutely fine. Oli's just had a few too many, that's all.' She popped on a bright smile.

Freya wasn't convinced, but! As Monty would say, it was her party, so no point pressing if she didn't want to talk about it. 'Let's sort out this bunting crisis, shall we?' Freya started folding little 3D dresses, robins and hearts out of the unused serviettes.

Izzy plucked a serviette off the pile. 'Show me?'

'Give us a stack.' Emily made pincing movements with her hand until Charlotte handed her some of the polka-dotted napkins, then took some for herself.

Under Freya's instruction, the women listened, learnt, folded. 'I'm just going to nip out and find some twine or string for these,' Charlotte said. When she came back from the car where she had indeed found a ball of green twine, her eyes were rimmed red.

Izzy was officially fuming on Charlotte's behalf. What a bastard. How *dare* he make Charlotte feel small? Her mother's poet voice came to her, rich and strong: *The instinct of man is to oppress.* It was why Izzy's mum had never married. She'd always said she didn't care if the caged bird sang. The free one did, too. And without fear of a blanket being thrown over its head.

Izzy looked up to the tree house where a battery-powered lantern lit up the windows.

How had Oli gone from the husband she'd last seen at Freya and Monty's wedding – a bit grabby, but still proudly boastful of Charlotte and their little ones – to a man who barely bothered disguising his lack of respect for her. And her mates, for that matter. As if they were B-grade guests versus the A-listers invited for 'the real do' tomorrow.

Charlotte had been so ridiculously in love when they'd married. A true Cinderella story, with Jimmy Choos standing in for glass slippers. They'd all been thrilled for her, if not slightly perplexed that she wanted them to be her bridesmaids in lieu of her new set of friends. Except for Freya, they'd not really stayed in touch. Either way, they'd all been excited. Perhaps it had been the promise of a swanky reception. It definitely hadn't been the dreadful, flouncy, lavender brides- maid dresses. Freya had tried her best to zshuzsh them up, but Charlotte's mother-in-law had put a shockingly swift end to 'those shenanigans'. Charlotte's mother-in-law was a society girl from a bygone era. There were rules. They were meant to be obeyed.

Perhaps that was what had happened. Too many rules.

Izzy wasn't very good with rules. But she was good with loyalty, and she wanted to put a smile back on Charlotte's face.

Freya moved the huge pile of serviette bunting to the side, throwing a quick glance over at Monty who was still sound asleep. 'And you're absolutely sure there's nothing we can do to help tonight?'

'Honestly, most of it's taken care of,' Charlotte insisted. 'Oli's booked caterers, servers, everything. We've even sorted things for the vegans.' She gasped and paled. 'Oh, Freya. I didn't force you into eating meat tonight, did I? I know we did a few vegetable kebabs, but I kept pushing everyone to eat the sausages.'

'Not to worry.' Freya gave one of her Mother Earth smiles. 'We did go veggie for a bit, but now we get boxes from an organic farm out in Berkshire. Grass fed, free range, massaged on a daily basis. That sort of thing.'

Charlotte cleared her throat. 'It really was lovely of you all to make the effort to come early. The big do was Oli's idea, but mostly I wanted to see you girls. Catch up on your news.'

'Which perfectly leads us to the question on everybody's mind,' Freya said, rather grandly.

Emily glanced behind her, as if the question was tiptoeing in from the darkness, waiting for the perfect moment to pounce. 'What question?'

Poor Emms. She hated questions. Her mother relentlessly peppered her with them. It had been the only reason Emily had been allowed a phone at uni. So that her mother could send texts demanding updates on her daughter's academic progress and promises of sexual abstinence. Polar opposite to her mum. There'd been times Izzy had been quite jealous of Emily and her mum. There'd been times when she'd been jealous of each and every one of them. Even Little Miss I'm Still Jelly That You Shagged My Husband sitting across from her. Freya topped up her glass again. Maybe she should slow down on her one-woman attempt to drink all of Oli's fancy wine.

'Right! What's this question of yours then, Freya?'

Freya sat up straighter, as if psyching herself up, then asked in one of those 'not at all casual but meant to be' tones, 'How did Luna come into your life, Izz?'

'The usual way.' She almost pointed to her lady garden, but as Charlotte was there she made a bulging tummy gesture instead.

'And the father is?' Freya's eyes jumped between hers and Emily's, rightly suspecting that Emily already knew.

Emily shrugged. She was the best liar.

Izzy was less gifted, so she threw Freya a smattering of facts. 'He was a surfer. Surprise surprise. We met in Morocco. He was a bit of a player. I found out I was pregnant after he'd left to chase some waves in Bali and . . . that's about it.'

Freya, strangely, looked rather relieved. As if the fact that Luna was the product of a one-night stand in Morocco had settled a bet she'd made with herself.

'Do you know his name?' Charlotte asked, just a tiny bit horrified.

'Course! It's a bit dorky, though. Sounds much better in his accent.'

'Oh!' Charlotte clapped, her eyes softening. 'He's foreign. I always thought that would be so exotic. To have a husband with an accent.'

'And his name is . . . ?'

'Alfred.'

'Oh!'

The table fell silent. Like she'd said. Dorky.

'Did you ever see him again? The father?'

She shook her head no. She had actually. From a distance. At a surfing festival on Maui, where pretty much everyone but her and Alf had been in their twenties and high as a kite. He hadn't seen her. Or Luna. One look at those eyes and he would've known. They were his. All his. If she'd known then what she knew today, she just might have braved it, but . . . regrets and all that.

'I think he's back in Denmark. Not a hundred per cent sure.'

She was. She'd googled him. Once a year she let herself, on Luna's birthday. Her way of checking in. It had taken a few years, but he was back in Denmark, behaving like a responsible adult. Just as her own father had when her mother had shooed him out the door to return to his wife and children in Sweden. Anyhoo . . .

She faked a massive yawn. 'Ladies, I am afraid I am going to have to turn in. I still haven't shaken the jet lag, so if you don't mind?'

They all said they didn't, though it was easy to see Charlotte and Freya wished she'd told them more. Just before she got up, she felt Emily's hand creep into her lap and grab her hand for a quick squeeze.

The gesture spoke volumes. *I love you. I'm glad you're here. One day you're going to have to tell them.*

Soon enough she'd tell them, but tonight? Tonight she was totally happy to let everyone think she was the same ol' Dizzy Izzy.

Chapter Five

Emily flushed the toilet and called out to Izzy who was brushing her teeth. 'I can't believe how *civilized* this feels. Flushing!'

She joined Izzy at the long, low butler's sink, turned on the tap and smiled at Izzy's reflection in the mirror. It was good to see her looking every bit the surfer girl she had emblazoned in her memory. Neither of them were Facebookers or Instagrammers, so her imagination had gone to some very dark places.

'You all right?'

'Mmm,' Izzy said, after spitting out her toothpaste.

'You know she doesn't mean it, right?'

'Who?'

'Freya. The narkiness.'

'Oh,' Izzy said, then, 'Yeah, I know.'

She finished brushing her own teeth then gave her face a quick wash.

Emily didn't like it when Izzy fell silent. When it came to expressing what they really felt, neither of them were talkers, but Izzy was the queen of babbling on about anything and everything. Like a toddler. Not talking about anything at all? Not a good sign.

It had to be The Other Thing.

After they'd walked back past the kitchen tent where Freya and Charlotte were herding their children away from the cake tins, Emily grabbed Izzy in a loose headlock.

'You. Me,' Emily said to the big ball of curly half-fro in her face. 'Talky talky.'

Izzy squirmed against her, then nuzzled into Emily's neck and made purring noises. That was more like it. The Izzy she knew and loved. 'I don't wanna!'

Emily shook her off. 'We have to. For Luna.' She felt like a bitch for adding that part, but . . . needs must and all that.

Izzy's shoulders slumped. The gesture of defeat felt like a sucker punch. It wasn't like Emily *wanted* to have the talk. Or be the grown-up. She was as rattled by everything as Izzy was.

'Tomorrow? Later? We can meet in London. Talk then. Once I've got all of the paperwork together,' Izzy pleaded.

'Isn't it in the van? I thought you said you had everything with you.'

Izzy shrunk another few centimetres. 'Most of it. I just . . . C'mon, Emms. I don't want the girls to accidentally see. Or Luna.'

Both good points. Even so. Emily jabbed at the air between them. 'You're not leaving here without the two of us coming up with a proper plan.'

'I *have* a plan. It's a good plan.'

'It's *not* a good plan. Nor does it seem to involve Alf.'

Izzy fuzzed her lips. 'Why should it?'

'He's the father of your child, idiot.'

That got Izzy's back up. 'He doesn't even know her!'

'So maybe now's as good a time as any to change that. Go for a weekend. Take a city break.'

'Yeah, right. Oh, hi Alf! Remember that night on the beach ten years ago with the girl with the big hair? Look! We made a mini us. Copenhagen's brill! Should we go see the mermaid?' She looked out towards the castle. 'Besides. There'd be no one to look after Bonzer.'

Emily's shoulders scrunched up to her ears in frustration. 'What's up with the elephant puppy, anyway?'

'Luna's pretty wobbly about things.' She held up a hand so Emily would let her finish. 'About leaving Hawaii. Starting in a new school. Not knowing anyone. I decided we needed a comfort dog.'

The two of them were going to need a damn sight more than a dopey-faced therapy puppy if things didn't go according to Izzy's so-called plan.

When they reached Emily's yurt, Izzy gave her a kiss on the bonce, filling Emily's nostrils with that crazy almond vanilla scent of hers. 'Night night, Dr Cheung.'

Emily made a show of wiping off the kiss and waved goodbye without looking back.

When she got into the tent and began to undress, she shivered. It was chilly enough that, for the first time in a long while, she actually wanted a good old-fashioned cuddle.

Easing the quilt out of Callum's fist, Emily curled up next to him. After an evening playing board games with Luna, then on to an intense-looking 'what do you do' talk with Monty, the man deserved a prize. Though he was clearly asleep, he pulled her into a tight, snuggly embrace.

He was a great snuggler. She mostly hated the whole body-against-body thing. The *heat* bodies generated. But if, like now, she was facing out and had the bulk of their very large bed as an escape zone, it was actually all right. When Izzy had crawled into her bed back in uni it had driven her bonkers. On a number of levels.

She let herself be tugged in close to Callum. Feel the steady thump thump of his heart against her back.

Why hadn't she just come out with it when she had the chance?

Told them Callum was just a mate.

Because. That's what she did.

Once she overcame thousands of years of Chinese tradition and told her parents . . .

Ping!

Swear to god her mother had a sixth sense. She tugged the phone across to her.

Listen. Mr Chang from next door has cousin visiting from China. Hunan Province. Tall. Good idea for you to come for Sunday dim sum.

She flipped the phone over and took a deep inhalation of cotton, canvas and earth. It was quite cosy, this. Snuggling with someone with all of that fresh air circulating around them.

Good bed. Soft sheets.

The quiet.

It was really, really quiet.

Almost quiet enough to hear the skittering of a field mouse.

Instantly, Emily was wide awake again.

God, she hated camping.

As they hung their tea towels on the Aga, Freya got the sense Charlotte wasn't quite ready to go.

'Everything all right?'

'Yes! Of course,' Charlotte said unconvincingly. 'Why do you ask?' She swiped at the perfectly clean counter with a J-cloth.

'Nothing really. I just . . . I kind of got the sense that everything might not be tickety-boo with Oli.'

Charlotte looked physically ill. 'What? No. Everything's fine. I'm just being a bit funny about turning forty.'

'Don't be daft. You look as young as you did the day you got married.'

Charlotte's smile faltered.

Ah. It was definitely about Oli. Freya felt that bloom of solidarity that came from discovering she wasn't the only one wading through the magical wilderness of a long-term relationship.

Charlotte's laugh fell flat. 'Perhaps I'm just a bit worried about tomorrow.'

'Why?'

'Ohhh. You know . . .' She threw Freya a quick glance then set about refolding all the tea towels. 'My in-laws are coming and all of our friends. I mean . . . obviously *you're* my friends, but these are more Oli and his family's group. Some of the children's friends and their parents. They can be a bit cliquey. High expectations always make me a bit edgy.'

'Is this party meant to be for you or for Oli?'

Charlotte threw her a sharp look. 'For me, of course. We'd hardly be camping if it was Oli's party.'

'Well,' Freya said, 'I think this place is amazing. Anyone would be hard pressed to find a better venue.'

'Oh, believe me they do.' In a very un-Charlotte-like move,

she began ticking things off on her fingers. 'So far this year, we've been to all of the Soho House venues – private rooms. Babington House. Twice. A château in France. A snowmobile trek to see the Northern Lights with two nights in an ice hotel. Oh. And a weekend at a country estate in Ireland.' She pulled a small handkerchief out of an invisible side pocket and fretted at its scalloped edging. 'My children didn't want to tell their friends. About the glamping. In truth, they didn't want to come at all. Oli had to bribe them.'

'Oh, Lotte.' Freya pretended not to notice Charlotte swiping at her eyes.

How awful.

Sure. Freya sometimes had rich people envy, but at this moment? She wouldn't trade places with Charlotte for anything.

Freya felt an unexpected rush of love for Monty. He might be shit with money, living in a bit of a dream world most of the time with his harebrained schemes for their future (perhaps they should move to the Isle of Mull one day and set up a retreat for burned-out tech entrepreneurs and teach them how to live mindfully), but he was an amazing father and her family loved each other. Not one of them would ever have to be bribed to spend time together. Monty always instilled respect into their kids. Years ago, when Regan was four, she'd had a particularly foul tantrum when Freya had been trying to get out of the house to work. Monty had made Regan FaceTime her on her way to the tube and sing 'The Apology Song'. It wasn't a real song. Monty had made it up. They'd also bought her a Tunnock's Snowball and put it on her pillow after making her toad-in-the-hole for supper. Her faves from home.

She couldn't imagine Oliver ever doing the same for Charlotte. She made a silent vow to try and not kick Monty tonight when he began to snore.

'Hey,' Freya brightened at a memory. 'I forgot to say, Rocco sends his best.'

'Your brother?' Charlotte's features softened.

'The one and only. We rang him on the drive down. I mentioned we were seeing you and he starting dredging up memories from the summer you came up and worked at the fruit farm with me. Remember that?'

'Of course, I do. It was a brilliant summer.'

Freya squawked, 'Hardly! We worked our fingers to the bone . . . oh, wait. You got upgraded to the café, didn't you?'

'Farm shop. I did the displays,' Charlotte said, as if it had happened yesterday. 'And your brother dropped us off and picked us up every single day.'

'Oh, yeah. I'd forgotten that. He's a good big brother.'

'Yes,' Charlotte looked lost in a world of her own. 'Very nice.'

Freya grabbed a couple of Charlotte's brilliant homemade biscuits then took a torch out of the 'general use' box.

Charlotte hadn't moved.

'You sure you're okay?'

'Perfect.' Charlotte gave her hand a quick squeeze then shooed her on. 'Never better.'

Charlotte had nearly cracked. Told Freya everything. She'd virtually tasted the words in her mouth.

Oliver's having an affair. He wants us to stay married. Push on through. I don't know if I can. I don't know if I want to.

And that was the problem, wasn't it? She didn't know what she wanted. Plenty of women forgave their husbands for indiscretions. Even Beyoncé. There were others, of course, who didn't. But could you ever move on from betrayal?

She had no money of her own. No job. Nowhere to go. No friends to turn to – not on her doorstep anyway.

Oh, it was an impossible situation, and not one she'd imagined having to contend with on her birthday. Not anytime, really, but it did seem particularly unfair to find out now. Her mother would've wept with laughter. *Shows you, Little Miss Fancy Britches. Always thought you were too good for your own kind.*

Yes. She had been shown. And now she needed to decide how to proceed. She tiptoed up the curved stairwell to the tree house, even though the place was still blazing with light. Perhaps Oli hadn't been taking a call from *her* after all.

She quietly opened the door and looked across to the huge king-sized bed where Oli was skimming through messages on his phone, that telltale smile playing on his lips. The one that said he was in the mood. Her heart lifted. Maybe he really had meant it. About keeping things going. Wanting the best for their marriage. He looked up when she closed the door behind her with little more than a click, met her inquisitive gaze and said, 'Oh. It's you.' As if he had been expecting someone else.

'Hello, darling. Chilly out. Oh, good, you got your coffee.'

His eyes flicked to the bedside table then back to his phone. 'Your friends were pretty lairy tonight,' he said. As if they'd trashed the place. 'Especially . . . who is it? The Scottish one. She likes her sauce.' He mimed glugging a bottle of wine, which was rich given the fumes he was emitting. 'You'll keep an eye on her tomorrow, right? Make sure the staff don't top her up too often?'

An instruction. So many of their conversations were actually lists of instructions. What was wrong with him? He wasn't even *trying* to be different. This wasn't the behaviour of a repentant man. A husband desperate to make amends. All of her hopeful thoughts that they might be able to go through this marital . . . calamity . . . fluttered to her feet.

She wondered if Oli's lover was the same as she had once been. In complete awe of him. The power. His physical presence. The *confidence*. It was his confidence that had really swept her off her feet. He was still every bit as handsome. Every bit as charismatic. Every bit as much in love with her?

She reached out to him, her heart lurching up into her throat as she asked, 'Darling, do you think this will all work out?'

'What? The party? So long as your mates behave themselves, I've got it all in hand. Don't you worry your pretty little head about it.'

Then he rolled over and turned out the light.

In that moment, Charlotte resolved to tell her friends everything.

Chapter Six

Sleep might have helped. So would flinging her phone into the fire and watching it melt away into nothing.

As things stood, Charlotte wasn't in the best frame of mind to host a birthday party.

Calling it off was out of the question. Too many wheels in motion. The caterers, for example, would be arriving any time now.

Almost involuntarily, her thumb flicked her phone from the home page to Instagram. Cyber-stalking, it turned out, was rather addictive.

Xanthe was terrifically young and beautiful. No surprise there.

Xanthe had well over two thousand followers, could ski, scuba, and loved a quality organic facial.

Xanthe – she thumbed a bit further down the page – also went out to nightclubs where her husband doled out kisses like lollipops. She looked happy and comfortable. As if it were perfectly normal to have another woman's husband plant kisses on her dewy young cheek.

Charlotte pocketed the phone and stared helplessly at the yurts where her friends peacefully slept away.

As certain as she'd been that she must tell them what was really going on, morning brought with it the dawning realization that if she were to veer off script now she might lose what little traction she had in her marriage. Putting on 'a good show' was paramount to the Mayfields. And today, which came complete with the full complement of in-laws, would be no different.

Mostly because everything seemed one step removed from reality. As if discovering her husband was a cheat had dropped triple-glazing between her and the life she thought she'd been living.

She remembered the advice that some of the older wives at the law firm had given her in the early days of their marriage; giving her the lowdown on what being a 'seasoned wife' meant, and what was in store for Charlotte when Oliver became the youngest partner in his firm. Don't complain about supper drying out in the oven. It will happen frequently. Never moan about the long days. Those billable hours were keeping her in Chloé and Stella McCartney. And most importantly, don't fight about the affairs. It was simply how it worked. *That will never happen to me*, she had thought.

The affairs, she'd learnt that night, had tiers. The secretaries slept with the junior partners. The junior partners slept with the senior partners. The librarian slept with everyone.

She took a sip of her tea and watched, through the steam, as the morning sun edged its way from the woodland into the large meadowscape where, soon enough, she'd be celebrating her birthday.

Forty years old. She'd got her first party-planning job the year her mum had turned forty. They'd not celebrated. *Quelle surprise*. Forty. So much more grown-up sounding than thirty. Thirty had sounded full of possibility. Forty sounded . . . forty sounded a bit flat, if she were being perfectly honest. A crossroads.

Charlotte's gaze shifted. Freya's makeshift bunting had grown dewy in the night, causing quite a few of the cranes' wings to droop, but, if the weather report was anything to go by, the string of origami serviettes would be shifting in a light, sun-soaked breeze by the time the party was under way.

The whole idea that she was throwing a birthday party suddenly seemed completely ridiculous.

This morning when she'd come down to put on the coffee, she'd foolishly looked around expecting something, *anything*, to be sitting out in the kitchen waiting for her. A card. A simply wrapped gift. A flower. But no. There had been nothing except a list of chores written in her own hand.

For all she knew, Oli had had to bribe the rest of their friends to come as he had the children. Veuve Clicquot and Michelin-starred amuse-bouches standing in for fifty-pound notes.

. . . deep breath in . . .

All she had to do was get through the next twelve hours. Twelve hours of smiling, greeting, nodding and, perhaps, if she dared, testing just how strong the bonds of her old friendships were.

Charlotte smoothed her hand across her spreadsheet, willing the detailed layout to act as a balm. Here was her day, laid out before her in black and white, with the odd yellow highlight (she really would have to stay on top of the Watlington boy's peanut allergy, seeing as how Oli had insisted on a satay-based canapé and there was no guarantee his mother would remember his epi pen or that the catering staff would make an announcement).

Welcome drinks.

Nibbles.

Games for the children.

The hog roast.

Cake.

She pored over the sheet until she could see it with her eyes closed, then, as if someone had flicked a switch, the day began.

Her phone buzzed. It was a text from Oli. *Bacon sarnies ready soon? Need to run into town to get something.*

Someone, more like.

Well, she thought, her thumb hovering above the Instagram app, happy birthday to me.

'What did you say?'

Felix glanced nervously over his shoulder. Felix didn't do conflict. 'Ummm . . . Dad's taking a bath so he told me to ask you?'

Freya was in danger of turning into a bobble head she was nodding so violently. 'A bath. I see. Well, that's bloody rich, isn't it?'

'I suppose so?' Felix had never known a bath to be an activity of conflict before. 'Ummm . . . can I have some money?'

Freya felt the hot rise of anger at her throat. 'And he told you to ask me for money?'

Why did Monty do this? Send the children to her for money so she'd have to be the one to say no. She'd told him she only had forty quid and that they needed it to fill the car seeing as they'd already used the electric charge on the hybrid. Bloody London traffic!

'Jack says there's a shop and they've just put out scones and sausage rolls.' Felix scuffed the dirt with his trainer. 'I'm hungry.'

Freya did a quick calculation of the change that might've fallen to the bottom of her handbag and came up empty. 'I'm sorry, darlin'. Charlotte's making breakfast. We can't afford fancy extras.'

Felix looked crestfallen, but tough cheddar. Waking up to not one but two 'You've exceeded your overdraft' texts from the bank hadn't set the morning off in quite the whimsical, escape-to-the-country vein she'd been hoping for. Bloody Monty and his bloody largesse. Oli should've been the one footing the micro-distillery gin tasting at the pub, not her broke, wannabe portrait-photographer husband who had yet to pull his camera out of the very expensive case he'd begged her to buy him for Christmas.

Felix's tummy growled.

Her son never asked for anything apart from books. She turned away so he wouldn't see the screwy face she made when she was fighting off tears. This was ridiculous, having to count the pennies for a bloody pastry. How on earth had things become so bad she'd turned her own son into a modern-day Oliver Twist? Or, for that matter, flew into a rage because her husband was taking a bath.

'Sorry, love. I . . . can you just hang on a few more minutes? Charlotte's making bacon sandwiches. You won't starve. First-world problems, remember!'

Rather than reply, Felix plopped down on the picnic bench, heaved his latest library book up onto his lap, threw a look of sheer longing in Charlotte's direction, then cracked the book in half with a sigh and began to read.

Freya strode over to the bath-house and was about to bash the door in when her fresh-faced husband flung it open with a big old goofy smile on his face. The one that had won her over that very first time Izzy had brought him back to Holly House.

Monty wiggled his eyebrows. 'Wanna get jiggy with it? I've not let the water out of the bath.'

Seriously? Was he *mad*?

'Montgomery Burns-West. You are treading on remarkably thin ice.'

He feigned being hit in the heart with an arrow. 'What? I can't proposition my fair wife for a morning shag?'

'Not when the overdraft police are riding my ass, no.'

Monty looked genuinely hurt. There was no glory in it. Why did she always have to be the bad cop? Unexpectedly, he pulled her to him, his wet chest saturating her top. 'It's all right, love. I know things are tough, but we'll get there. Dreams are worth fighting for, right?'

They were, but . . . Freya thought of her Camden shop, and the oh-so-witty T-shirts that no one seemed to want; the dream of sustainable fashion that had now turned into an endless compromise of her ideals and lots of bounced cheques.

She found herself responding to his kiss until the butter-flies began, then pulled away. A kiss and a cuddle wouldn't fix the overdraft. Nor would fighting about it. She stuffed her tug-of-war mood into the darker recesses and told Monty she was going to help get breakfast ready. Today was about Charlotte. Tomorrow would be about facing facts.

*

'Charlotte, you've converted me!' Emily mooched up to the fire, a quilt slung over her shoulders, and inhaled deeply. She hadn't slept this well in months. Years maybe. 'That bacon smells amazing. Is there coffee as well?'

Charlotte turned around, tears pouring down her cheeks.

'Shit. Crap. What is it? I don't need coffee. I don't need bacon. Fuck. Are you okay?'

Nice one, Emms. Yes. The weeping woman is perfectly fine.

'Sorry, yes. No. There is coffee. I mean . . .' Charlotte didn't even bother swiping at her tears. 'Oliver's having an affair.'

Emily looked round in a panic. Where was the lemon drizzle crew when you needed them? She wasn't equipped for this. There was the doctor's bedside manner thing, but she'd had training for that. Professional distance came much more easily than the whole warm-and-fuzzy thing.

That. And Charlotte wasn't a patient. Charlotte had held her hair up when she'd thrown up after an overzealous margarita night. Charlotte had helped her make models of organs out of jelly for her anatomy class. Charlotte still liked her enough to invite her to her fortieth birthday party, despite fifteen years of bunking off invitations to meet up.

'Here.' She grabbed an origami crane from the bunting and pushed it into Charlotte's hand. 'Wipe your face. He's coming.'

With the swiftness and expertise of a Hollywood actress, Charlotte snapped open the crane, swept the serviette across her face and turned to her husband with a soft, practised smile. 'Hello, darling. Did you sleep well?'

Izzy fought the lure of sizzling bacon and waited until Oliver had walked out to the meadow, car keys jingling in his hand

and phone to his ear, before joining Emily and Charlotte at the campfire. Her karma was off kilter enough without having to play along with more crap jokes and wife-belittlement. Maybe he was heading off to get Charlotte a present. A big one. 'Hey, lay-deeez! Top of the morning to you!'

Emily jerked her head towards Charlotte who was weeping into the bacon sandwiches. 'Izz. *Do* something. *Say* something.'

Oh, bums. Charlotte was crying. So why had Oliver just walked away as if nothing was going on?

'Ummm . . . Happy birthday!?'

'Thank you, Izzy. That is kind.' Sniff. Wipe. Charlotte gave her head one of those quick shakes a person performed when they were hoping to look perfectly fine. It wasn't entirely successful. 'Bacon sandwich?' She hastily loaded some bacon into a crusty roll then handed it to her.

Izzy took it and made a show of it being *mmm-mmm, delicious*, while Charlotte and Emily stared at her.

Wait a minute. Emily hadn't spilled the beans about why she'd come back to the UK, had she? She'd *promised.*

'Emily! Did you—'

'No,' Emily said through gritted teeth. 'This is about Charlotte. Charlotte who's got lots of *feelings* today.'

'Charlotte Mayfield!' Izzy planted her hands on her hips. 'You aren't being funny about turning forty, are you? You look amazing. Gorgeous. I want to be you when I grow up. Forty's the new black.' She kept spluttering platitudes until Emily cut her off.

'Oliver's cheating.'

Ah. She hadn't expected that.

Then again, the man had felt her up at his own wedding.

'Sorry. Sorry, girls.' Charlotte swept away some tears then gave a slightly hysterical laugh. 'Honestly. It isn't about that. Well, it is, but . . . I'm just going a bit mad is all. One minute I was frying bacon, happy as can be. The next I was bawling my eyes out and telling my least emotionally available friend – sorry Emily, you're lovely, but we both know you're not equipped for these sorts of histrionics, are you?' Emily nodded. It was fine.

'I've been like this for hours.' Charlotte was on a roll. 'All night actually. One minute I can't bear the sight of him and the next I'm absolutely, positively sure I want nothing more than to devote my life to making our marriage better. He said he wants it to work. *I* want it to work. And then . . . all of a sudden . . . I don't! It's like being on one of those – those . . .' She looked up to seek the best word, tears dripping off her chin.

'Waltzers?' offered Izzy. They'd once made Charlotte go on one and she'd never seen a human more pale.

'Yes.' Charlotte nodded. '*Just* like that.'

Clearly the memory hadn't faded.

'Okay. Right. Well, first of all, the man's an idiot.'

Charlotte offered Izzy a forlorn smile through her tears. 'Her name's Xanthe.'

Izzy scoffed. 'That's a stupid name.'

'It's Greek, actually. She's a junior partner at his law firm.' Charlotte almost sounded wistful.

'So? Anyone can become a lawyer. *Monty's* a lawyer.' They threw each other guilty looks. 'No offence to Monty.'

'She's very pretty. Especially in a bikini.'

'You've seen her poolside?' Emily looked appalled.

'Instagram,' explained Charlotte.

They all nodded and quietly thought on the complex world of cyber-stalking.

'She also might be pregnant.'

'Oh!' Izzy said in her upper register. That made things more complicated. 'Ummm . . . Is there a plan?'

'No, you na-na. She's only just found out,' Emily said.

'Muuuuum! I'm starving.'

Charlotte's son dropped onto a bench where he was clearly expecting to be served as Charlotte hastily wiped her face with . . . was that Freya's origami bunting?

'I'll get a tray of sandwiches up in a minute, darling. Why don't you go over to the kitchen tent and see if you can't find the ketchup and brown sauce?' Charlotte looked and sounded like a modern Doris Day. How did she do that?

'Brown sauce?' Jack made a vomit face. '*Mother.*' He shuddered.

Charming.

He pointed at Izzy. 'Why's she got one then?'

Doubly charmed. Izzy resisted giving him a slap round the back of his head and telling him to pull his socks up because his mother had just found out his dad was a lying, cheating bastard.

'Because she's a guest, darling.' Charlotte gave Izzy a sorrowful look. 'With low blood sugar. It's a condition.'

Gosh. Charlotte told a fib! Izzy tried to figure out the best way to look as if she had a condition when Emily cut in. 'Go. Ketchup. Brown sauce. It's your mother's birthday.'

Wow. Guess no one had given Emily the memo about telling other people's children what to do. Even so . . . Jack obeyed her.

'Okay, Lotte. What do you want us to do?' Izzy whispered as soon as he was out of earshot, noting that Oli, the bastard, still hadn't left yet.

Charlotte ran her index fingers under her eyes to swipe away invisible mascara stains.

'Well, there's no plan really. Yes,' she said abruptly straightening her spine. 'There *is* a plan. It is to do nothing. Oliver reckons we'll get through this. Just an early morning wobble is all. I shouldn't have said anything. I'm being a silly goose.'

'What? About your husband having an affair?'

Charlotte nearly lost her composure.

'No, of course not. He's said he's put a halt to it. That the pregnancy isn't for sure. Most likely a lie to get him to choose between the two of us. That's what all of these phone calls are for.' She vaguely gestured out towards the meadow where Oli was, once again, jabbering away on his mobile. He caught Charlotte's eye, pointed at Izzy's sandwich, then at himself.

Dickhead.

'It'll be just a moment, darling. Izzy's got low blood sugar!'

Izzy did a little wobbly knee move to make it look true.

'Is that what you want? To carry on?' Emily asked her.

'Yes.' Charlotte clapped her hands together decisively. 'Now. If you two wouldn't mind keeping this under your hats, I'd really appreciate it. Sorry, I didn't mean to create such a fuss—'

Freya marched up to their group, mouth already open in 'I'm about to give a speech' mode. One of the children had probably messed up the recycling bins or some equally heinous crime.

Emily's eyes silenced her.

Emily was a powerful ally in a crisis.

'Can I tell Freya?' Izzy was horrid with keeping secrets. Most secrets, anyway.

'Tell me what?'

'Oliver's having an affair. Shit. Sorry, Lotte. And she's preggers. Crap. Is that all right? Fuck. My bad.'

Emily glared at Freya as if it was her fault Izzy had spilled the beans.

Freya's open mouth dropped even further. Izzy was tempted to close it for her.

'Charlotte wants her party to go ahead as planned.' Izzy handed the rest of her sandwich to Freya. If she was eating, she wouldn't be able to embark on a diatribe against Oli.

'Fucking bastard,' Freya said, stuffing in an errant piece of bacon.

Okay. That hadn't worked.

'She wants to work through it. Stay with Oli,' Izzy said. *Meaningfully*.

'Oh.' Freya swallowed. 'I mean . . . marriage is tough.' Her eyes flitted to Monty who was horrifying the children with a pretend striptease with his towel only to reveal he was actually wearing shorts. *Goofball*. He was everything Oli wasn't in a father figure. Which, of course, made him endearingly lovable despite all their problems.

'So . . . the plan is?' Freya took another bite of bacon sandwich. Hopefully, to keep the sea of commentary at bay.

Charlotte began crisply shifting perfectly fried bacon onto a serving platter covered in rosebuds. 'The plan is to forget we ever had this discussion. It's all a bit embarrassing really. I'm so sorry I—'

'No,' Emily cut in. 'You have nothing to apologize for.'

'That's right. Absolutely nothing. This is your day.' Freya nodded along.

Izzy clicked her heels together and gave Charlotte a sharp salute. 'Party pixie reporting for duty!' Izzy took the tray from Charlotte and tipped her head towards the tent. 'I'll round up the children. Freya, are you good with helping Charlotte sort out whatever she needs to make this the happiest fortieth ever?'

Freya stuffed the rest of the bacon sarnie into her mouth and swiped her hands together. She was ready for action.

'Right,' Emily nodded in a style usually reserved for black-and-white war films as a squadron of mismatched soldiers were about to embark on a make-or-break mission. 'We have three hours to make this place look exactly the way Charlotte wants it. Ready or not, girlies. Operation Happy Glampers is under way.'

Chapter Seven

'Charlotte! *Darls* . . . Happy Birthday! Twenty-one again!'
And so the charade begins.

'Jessica! So glad you could make it. Treena! What a lovely frock. Is that Rixo? Thank you so much for . . . oh! For me? You really shouldn't have. Oli's just over there, by the champagne. Ha ha! You know what he says. A day that begins with bubbly is never a bad one!'

The effort was exhausting. Was this what her mother had felt like during her final days with the oxygen mask? Constantly taking those small sips of air in the vain hope the torture might end.

Oli was long back from his mystery errand looking roughly the same as when he'd wandered off, bacon sandwich in hand, phone to ear. Only this time it was glasses of fizz and lipsticky kisses that were occupying him. No added layers of guilt as far as she could ascertain. Perhaps, as Izzy had suggested, he had been off getting her a present.

The only truly good part of this, Charlotte thought, was having Freya, Izzy and Emily here. They were doing a remarkable job. Steering people this way and that. Checking up on her but not looking too sympathetic. Too much sympathy would crack the very thin veneer of normality she was desperately clinging on to.

'What? We're not up at the proper house?'

Charlotte's attention shot to the car park where, amidst the hubbub of their other guests, she couldn't miss her mother-in-law's distinctive voice.

Verity had grown up in Rhodesia – when it was still Rhodesia – in a sprawling home overflowing with staff. She'd met and married Nigel shortly after they'd both matriculated from Oxford (classics for her because 'she had to do something' and law for him).

After a stint in New York where Nigel had made a rather tidy sum in real estate, they moved to their Sussex home where, Verity was fond of saying to anyone who would listen, their 'crumbly old manor home had given them no choice but to hire in a gardener, housekeeper and an odd-jobs man.'

Charlotte had always had the distinct feeling that Verity included her on the staff list. She had, after all, been 'one of the staff' when she'd met Oli. It struck her that perhaps one of the reasons Oli had been so enchanted with her was because he finally had someone who thought he was perfectly fine as he was. Better than that. Amazing. His mother was incredibly demanding. Where her parents hadn't had any expectations for her at all, Verity wanted her son to be Nigel but better, and never shied away from reminding him that the reason Oli and Charlotte lived in a very nice house was because Nigel had bought it for them. For their wedding, in fact. Her parents had given them an Argos gift token. She bristled on Oli's behalf. The economy was quite different to what it had been back in the day, and making the squillions Nigel had was nigh on impossible unless you were an outright crook. As things stood, Oli did very well. Even if he did agreed with his mother about just about everything Charlotte could improve upon. Very well indeed. Her heart softened for her husband. Affair aside, he worked incredibly hard. And he did love his family. Perhaps all that bravura was masking a little boy still trying to attain his mother's approval. Which made his affair a blip. A painful one, but something they could move past.

'Darling!' Verity swept in. 'Don't you look sweet in that little . . . that's not Zara, is it? I'm sure I saw one of the other girls wearing the exact same one. My *goodness*.' Verity gave her a dry peck on the cheek then pursed her taupe lips as she scanned the area, her eyes stopping and stalling at Freya's serviette bunting. 'It all looks so—'

'Wonderful!' Charlotte's father-in-law, Nigel, bustled his wife out of the way, planting the obligatory kisses first on one cheek and then the other. He always smelled of pipe tobacco and leather, though she'd never seen him come in contact with either. 'The place looks ripping. Hope you don't mind, love, but Verity didn't want to mess with the hoi polloi on the bus so we've got a driver in tow. You wouldn't mind sparing him a sandwich or something, would you?'

Charlotte didn't get a chance to answer as a second stream of guests from the Sussex Schooner, as Oli insisted on calling it, arrived from the car park. They all seemed quite jolly for so early in the day. It was only just noon.

'Brilliant idea with the champers, doll.' A friend from Oli's golf club purred into her ear as she went through the motions. Kiss. Kiss. Half hug. Smile. 'Is that Zara? I have the same one! My goodness. It's all very *rustic* out here, isn't it?'

'That's what I was saying, darling!' Verity had a knack for pouncing on moments to prove she'd been right. 'Look at you! Now, *that's* what I call a party frock.'

Whether Charlotte wanted it to or not, the flow of people coming off the bus swept her into the role of hostess for a party she'd not entirely wanted to have.

She looked up and smiled at the long strings of decoration above her. At least she had her bunting.

An hour later she felt as if her head was spinning. Perhaps she should've eaten something before letting all of those leather-aproned serving staff fill up her glass. She went into the kitchen to get a glass of water and escape the sun for a moment, only to find Poppy curled up in a corner of a sofa, thumbing away at her phone.

'Hello, darling. Everything all right?'

Poppy's eyes shot out to a crowd of teens playing Giant Jenga. Jack was clearly the ringleader, egging everyone on to have a go. Freya's two were a short way off showing Luna how to play Connect Four.

Poppy looked back at her phone and shrugged.

Charlotte examined the group a bit more closely. She was sure she recognized a couple of girls from the children's boarding school. Ella and Maisie, was it? She'd definitely seen Maisie's mum. A rather brisk woman who never bored of letting everyone know how terrifically busy she was with her organic energy ball business now that Nestlé were interested in snapping it up.

'Isn't that Maisie out there? And Ella? Don't you want to be with the group?'

Poppy's mouth screwed up tight to the left-hand side of her mouth. A nervous habit that Verity regularly tried to discourage. Charlotte preferred not to mention it as she'd always found her own mother's rebukes doubled her humiliation and her need to seek comfort from it. Nail biting had been hers.

'They're having enough fun without me there to ruin it.'

Oh. Now this didn't sound good.

Charlotte sat down beside her, resisting the urge to pull her into one of the cuddles they'd so enjoyed when she was a little girl. Poppy had become a big fan of *space* since she'd started at this new boarding school that Oli had insisted would be the making of them.

'I thought the three of you were friends.'

'No, Mum!' Poppy spat. 'We're *not* friends. Typical you. Seeing what you want to see instead of seeing exactly what's in front of your face! Can't you see they're only nice to me because of Jack?'

When she saw the dismay on Charlotte's face, she crumpled as quickly as she'd roared. 'I'm sorry, Mummy. I don't mean to shout at you on your birthday.'

This time Charlotte did put her arms round her daughter. Stiff shoulders and all. The poor love. Feeling she was playing second fiddle to her brother. How awful. Who knew if it was true? Girls could be so difficult at that age. So complex.

She'd hated being a teen. All of the changes that had come with it. And not just the physical ones. The new schools. New cliques. New friends to invent when she needed to escape her parents' flat. She'd been so dreadfully shy and her school had been particularly awful. Bullies. Truants. Gangs. Charlotte had always thought of the life they gave their children as a godsend. Not a well-heeled copy of her own.

Poppy eventually ducked out of the hug, loosening yet

more hair out of her thick, fishtail plait. She looked more little girl than blossoming thirteen-year-old. 'I'll be fine, Mum. Don't worry. I've probably got my period coming or something.'

She tried to protest, but Poppy held up a hand that distinctly said *No*, grabbed a couple of canapés off the counter and slipped away into the crowd. She was right. Now wasn't the time. Just as it wasn't the time to tell Oli she was up to the challenge. She wanted to raise their children together. For their marriage to work. She wanted her family. Even if it meant constantly treading water to keep it.

Charlotte cringed as the calls for a speech grew louder. It had been mortifying enough opening her presents in front of everyone. The gifts had been lovely, of course. Freya's lace-edged serviettes made from Irish linen were beautiful. There'd been no need to confess they were seconds. Izzy had bought her a delicate necklace with a starfish on it. Her favourite sea animal. And Emily had given her a Brora cardigan she already had plans to move into for the autumn. Together they had bought her membership to the Royal Academy of Arts. She'd nearly wept at the thoughtfulness. It had been so long since she'd been to a gallery. Oli found art appreciation tedious at best.

Amazing to think how many years it had been since they'd properly seen one another and yet how perfectly her friends still knew her.

She stared at the gifts on the table. The children had given her a handbag she knew for a fact her mother-in-law had selected because it was bright blue, a colour Charlotte had never favoured. Poppy had tucked a couple of her favourite sanitizing gels into the side pocket, which was thoughtful. The rest of the gifts were . . . nice. She wasn't ungrateful, but couldn't help feeling that the guests had been generous in the way one might be to a maiden aunt who only came down from her poky cottage in the Lake District for Christmas. A spiralizer. A leather-bound journal. Quite a few organic soaps and lotions. She already had the book on *hygge* and was fairly certain she'd seen the Christmas ornaments at one of the school's silent auctions a year or so back.

It was extraordinary how little the people she saw every day of her life *knew* her. Was it because there wasn't much to know? She always agreed with Oli. Rarely put her foot down about anything as one of the school governors. She was the tea-maker, really. Had no opinion on current events. What little news she was aware of she read in *Waitrose Weekend*. Not exactly a paper with its finger on the world's political pulse.

Perhaps it was *her* fault Oliver had strayed. Xanthe did seem terrifically interesting, if her Instagram posts were anything to go by.

Her eyes moved over to the small velvet box placed in prime position on the gift table. It was from the jeweller's in Sittingstone village, so his errand this morning must have been to collect it. She didn't know whether to feel hurt it had been so last minute or pleased he'd remembered at all.

The sapphire earrings Oliver had chosen were lovely. Beautiful, in fact. But clip-ons? It was his mother who didn't have pierced ears. She'd had hers done since she was a teen. And, again, she had never really been one to wear blue, so . . .

'Speeeeeech!'

Oliver stood up, shushing the crowd in that 'All right, already. I'll give you what you've all been waiting for' way of his. They never wanted *her* to say anything, thank god.

'Charlotte,' he began loftily as the crowd leant in and the waiting staff topped up everyone's glasses.

The children weren't anywhere to be seen, save Poppy who, worryingly, was wandering back towards that little nook she'd appropriated in the kitchen tent. At the edge of the crowd, Emily, Izzy and Freya had all lined up and were each holding one of her handmade cakes. It looked like a *Bake-Off* presentation of Charlotte Mayfield's Greatest Cake Hits. Those *girls*. Until this very moment, Charlotte had thought she'd invited them out of misguided sentiment, but honestly? She'd asked them to come because she wanted people who knew *her* at her party. The Charlotte who adored art. The Charlotte who couldn't enter a room without giving it a tweak or a rejig so that it looked just so, and would then appreciate that she'd done as much. The Charlotte whose hopes and dreams they'd supported rather than dismissed as silly when there were other, Mayfield-shaped hopes and dreams to fulfil. She saw now she was drowning in a quick-sand of upper-middle-class beigeness. Perhaps she'd known that, without their help, there wasn't a chance on earth she'd be able to claw her way out and find herself again.

'What can I say about my wife of over fifteen years?' Oli took her hand and stood back, appraising her as one might a newly purchased heifer.

'That she has the patience of a bloody saint!' a red-faced man shouted out. Karl, was it? One of the chaps who propped up the bar at their local. What on earth had he done to warrant an invitation? She'd not so much as said hello to the man.

'That's a good start,' Oli laughed congenially. He always could play to the crowd. 'It's astonishing to think this beautiful creature here is forty. It seems like only yesterday she was but a naive Yorkshire lass with nothing more than big dreams in an even bigger city—'

'Oi!' shouted Izzy, nearly losing her grip on the carrot cake. *Oh dear.* 'I think you'll find an *art history degree* hardly makes her Dorothy in Oz!'

Charlotte squeezed Oli's hand. He squeezed back, mistakenly thinking she was on board with being portrayed as a modern-day Eliza Doolittle. When had his hand stopped becoming a thing of comfort? Yesterday morning? The first time he'd sided with his mother rather than his wife? This very moment?

She pulled her hand free.

'Absolutely right, Izzy. And of course there was the party planning. Back in the day she would've had us celebrating properly up at Sittingstone Castle, but this clever one insisted all the cool kids were keeping it *au naturel*!'

No she hadn't. She'd done no such thing. Charlotte was about to correct him when she caught him sending a pointed look at Freya's bunting which was now, unfortunately, a bit worse for wear.

People laughed, but didn't look as if they were entirely sure they knew why.

He carried on smoothly, 'Regardless.'

Indeed.

'Charlotte is, as I said, from ooop North. When I met her . . .'

. . . Oli had been covered in red wine that one of the legal secretaries had thrown at him after he'd made a sexist remark.

Not that Charlotte had known that then. He'd told her the girl was cross because he wouldn't go home with her.

Oli smiled ingratiatingly at Charlotte, then the crowd. 'My girl here needed a bit of softening round the edges. With a few curative pointers from myself and my family,' he lifted a glass to his mother who sent an adoring look in return, 'we now have supper instead of dinner, bread instead of teacakes and, my personal favourite, a proper cup of Earl Grey in the morning instead of that—'

'Eh, laddie! I object to that! A person's from where a person's from and no one should try and oppress them for it!' Freya's broad Scots rang out despite Monty's feeble attempt to shush her. Charlotte had forgotten what champagne did to Freya's accent.

Amidst the murmurings of 'bloody Scots' and 'never miss a chance to wave the Saltire', Oli soldiered on. This was his crowd and he knew it. 'So here she is, over fifteen years on. All grown up and properly civilized. She makes a mean Sunday roast. Her Yorkies are the envy of Sussex—'

'Seriously? Her Yorkies?' Emily, who hated the limelight as much as she did, was indignant. 'How about her brains? Her efficiency. Her UN-like diplomacy?'

A few people called out 'hear-hear', but not enough to decrease the humiliation. Or Emily's sotto voce, '*Bloody wanker.*'

The children appeared at the edge of the group, clearly keen to see what the hubbub was about.

Oh, when would this *end*?

Undeterred, Oli carried on as if no one had said a word. 'Thanks to Charlotte's fortitude, we've got two gorgeous children who, hopefully, take after their mother more than they do their monster of an old man.' He pulled a face, beaming when the protests flooded in.

Charlotte did her best not to flinch when he put his arm around her shoulder and lifted his glass. 'I'm going to wrap this up so all of this attention doesn't go to her head. Wouldn't want her running off and finding someone else's shirts to iron, would we? To Charlotte. Happy Birthday.'

As the crowd dutifully echoed the toast and drank, Charlotte watched in horror as Freya marched with the fixed determination of someone who may have had slightly too much to drink to the front of the group and lobbed her beautiful, buttercream, triple-chocolate devil's food cake directly into Oliver's face.

Chapter Eight

Freya drained her water glass and shot another sheepish grin at the girls. At least the catering staff had finally left. Mea culpa-ing with an audience was – *och*. She'd screwed up. Plain and simple. Even if the children had found it hilarious. And the *look* on Oli's face! Blinking priceless. Not that it was clever or funny to throw Charlotte's beautiful birthday cake into her husband's face in front of all their friends and family. No. It wasn't funny at all. She swallowed her giggles and tried again. 'Charlotte, I am so, *so* sorry.'

'Please.' Charlotte rigorously scrubbed at the chocolate icing on her skirt, 'Don't apologize.'

'Can I help? Run up to the tree house and get you something else to put on?'

'No. Please. Just . . .'

Charlotte's refusal to look at her sent Freya back a few steps. Maybe she really had meant it when she'd said she wanted the marriage to work. Maybe she just hated a scene.

Izzy pulled her knees up to her chin on the nearby bench and mouthed a quick 'nice one, babes.' Emily, who'd already given her a very awkward high five, whispered something to Callum who gave her a nod then wandered off towards their yurt.

Grrrrr. Why had Freya let that bloody man rile her so much? All she'd had to do was listen to his crass speech like a good girl and then later, when everyone had left, tell Charlotte she'd thought him very rude.

Indignation surged through her like a tsunami.

No!

Oliver was an adulterer. Then he adds insult to injury by telling everyone Charlotte would be little more than a gutter-snipe if he hadn't gone all Henry Higgins on her? Happy fucking birthday, o wife of mine! Monty wouldn't *dare* talk about her like that in front of her friends. *Especially* if he'd just confessed to having an affair.

She rinsed another sponge out and handed it to Charlotte. 'I'm so sorry about how much cake ended up on you.'

Oli had flung it on her, blinded as he'd been by the devil's food.

'Not to worry, Freya. Honestly.'

Her tone was softer, but Charlotte still wouldn't meet her eye.

She'd already offered to pay for any dry cleaning. Would've promised to cover costs for the weekend (or at least the fizz) if it wouldn't have meant remortgaging the house. She'd pull her heart out of her chest if it meant Charlotte would forgive her. Should she drop to her knees and beg? It had worked the time she'd borrowed one of her dresses back at uni and accidentally ripped it on a blackthorn bush during a rather unfortunate conga-line incident. Emily had taken great delight in plucking the greenery out of her bum.

This wasn't about a dress. It was about humiliating

Charlotte's husband and, by extension, Charlotte, in front of all their friends and family. Freya felt awful. Would fall on any sword. Make any amends. She wanted Charlotte to know just how much she valued her friendship. Somehow, she didn't think a Sunday roast at The Harvester would work as well as it had back in the day.

Oh, *tarnation*. As her mother used to say. Freya quickly crossed to the refrigerator and relished the hit of cool as she fought the sting of tears that inevitably followed when she remembered she couldn't ring her mum any more.

She stuck her finger into a bowl of guacamole and sucked it off as she peeked under the tinfoil-covered plates. A few canapés. Some pork. A *lot* of pork. Surprise surprise. Half the crowd had been crowing about how energetic they felt since they'd gone vegan.

Her mother would've found it hilarious. The cake thing. Cheered her, in fact. Not gasped in horror as most everyone else had done, apart from Izzy, who had cheered then quickly peeped 'kidding' when she realized no one else had.

The only good thing to come of it was Oliver's departure with the rest of the guests. Oh, he'd pretended to laugh it off. Claimed it had all been part of the plan. But he'd been fuming.

'Here you are, Charlotte.' Monty popped an enamel mug onto the spool table top. 'A nice cup of tea for you. Two sugars as you've had a bit of a shock. Anyone else for tea?'

No one said anything. They'd all had a bit of a shock.

'Love,' Freya pulled Monty to the side. 'If I scrounge together some money, what do you think to taking all the children to the pub for tea?'

Chips. If they kept to the child-size portions and he only had one pint . . . or better still, tap water! 'Umm, OK.'

94

'You've got enough? To cover that and a bit of petrol on the way back, right?' His expression said 'your call babe'. Maybe . . . the forty quid was earmarked for petrol, but if they kept it cheap and cheerful they could scrimp on fuel. It wasn't like they needed a full tank to get home.

She glanced across at Charlotte. Emily and Izzy were assuring her the skirt would be fine after a dry clean. *Oh, lordy.* She should give Charlotte a twenty immediately.

She'd give Monty her card. The one earmarked for extreme emergencies. She hadn't checked the balance for a few months, but if memory served there were still a couple hundred quid left before it was maxed out.

When she dug out the card and told Monty he was to stick to a ten-pound *max* budget, he gave her a solemn nod. 'I'll try and keep the kids busy with some card games or something as well. Give you girls some time together to . . . errr . . . sort things out.'

'If Charlotte will even speak to me again.' What on earth had she been *thinking*? Smashing a cake in the host's face in front of all his friends and family?

She swiped at a couple of escapee tears.

Monty pulled her in close. He smelt of whisky she hadn't remembered seeing circulated. Bums. Would he be able to drive?

He tucked a curl behind her ear. 'Talk to her. She knows what you did came from a good place. Hey! Why don't you help her come up with a plan? You're good at plans.'

She gave a doleful nod. She was good at plans. Freya nestled her head into the sweet nook between Monty's chin and shoulder. The man definitely had his plus sides, and this was one of them.

She pushed back from Monty's chest when she heard giggling. Was that . . . *Charlotte?*

She turned round and saw Izzy stomping around, waving her hands about as if she were in the middle of some grand oratory.

Oliver. Had to be.

Oh, lordy. Izzy was re-enacting it already? Before she could launch herself across the room to stop her, Emily got up and re-enacted Freya's role. With a real cake. Carrot from the looks of things.

'Ooo! Easy!' Charlotte held out her hands. 'We want to keep at least one!' She saw Freya was watching. 'C'mere you.' She patted the seat next to her then, when Freya had sat down, whispered, 'Thanks for having my back.'

Thank god for Izzy and her ability to make something funny sooner rather than later. When she wanted to, Izzy was like eucalyptus. She had a magical way of clearing the air. If only Freya could do the same.

'Nom, nom.' Emily dunked a tortilla into a bowl of guacamole that Freya had unearthed from the refrigerator. She well and truly had the post-party munchies. 'Anyone seen Monty? I'd have thought they'd be off to the pub by now.'

Callum, whom she suspected had been trying to convert Monty all day, had valiantly offered to go to the pub as well. 'Leave you girlies to your bonding.'

'He's still rounding them up, I think.' Izzy finally took a bite of the carrot baton she'd been waving around for ages. Did the woman ever actually eat a square meal? 'Ohmigawd. I'm sorry, Charlotte, but I can't help reliving Cake-gate over and over. Hi-lar-ious!' She cackled. 'Did you see Oli's mum? She looked like she was going to have an aneurysm!'

They all laughed except for Freya, who abruptly stood up from the table and started clearing the plates away.

Izzy made an oops face. 'My bad.'

Emily patted her head then got up and joined Freya at the sink.

'All right, woman?'

'Totes. *Super* totes.'

Which, of course, meant no.

Emily companionably bumped her out of the way. 'I'll wash if you dry.'

'Why don't you dry?'

'Boring,' said Emily. 'Now. Why don't you tell your nice Auntie Emms what's wrong.'

Freya threw a quick look over towards Charlotte who was trying to turn a serviette into a crane. 'I just feel such a numpty that I lost it like that.'

Emily had forgotten the fragility of Freya's bravura. Sometimes it seemed indomitable. Others? You could pop with a pin.

'You were epic. I wouldn't have had the guts to do it.'

'You drill inside people for a living. You definitely would've have the guts to do it.'

'Nah. They're unconscious.'

Freya blew a raspberry. 'I was drunk. It was stupid. I was just so . . . so angry with him. Humiliating her like that. My father never would've even *dreamt* of making my mum feel that way. Nor would Monty. And I'm *much* more difficult to live with than my mother.'

Emily thought she'd let that one lie.

Freya swiped at a plate with her tea towel. 'I wanted him to feel as small as he was making her feel.'

Emily handed her another plate. 'If that was the goal? I would say you achieved it. In spades.'

The hint of a smile appeared. 'And it wasn't too awful?'

Emily shook her head. 'As I said. Epic. Bolshie. If not a little bit fuelled by the cray-cray juice.'

And then, at last, Freya began to laugh.

'Knock knock!' Monty clomped into the kitchen in his walking boots. Izzy smiled at him since no one else did. Poor Monty. Being a man at this particular moment wasn't really working in his favour. 'Sorry girls. Still getting the children together. Ummmm . . . I can't seem to track down Luna.'

'Isn't she with the rest of the children?' Freya asked, narrowly avoiding being brained by the Monopoly box she was trying to pull down from the high shelf.

'I'm sure I saw her recently,' Charlotte called from the sink where she was dutifully washing up her mug of tea.

Emily said something about seeing her as well. They chattered away, putting their hands to their eyes and scanning the vast wildflower meadow beyond the tent. It really was a huge field.

An hour later, Izzy could barely make out the words coming out of people's mouths. They hadn't been able to track down Whiffy. No one else seemed to be about. No surprise seeing as it was the bank holiday weekend, but . . .

Izzy stemmed a pathetic whimper. She knew she shouldn't be panicking, but . . . where was Luna? Her sweet, beautiful, *raison d'être*.

She'd checked everywhere. In the toilets where she'd found

Charlotte splashing cold water on her face. The car park where Monty and Freya were having one of those gritted-teeth talks with terse gestures. In her tent. The children's tent. Under beds. By the river. The tree house. Oli had left his things strewn about the place. She wondered how Charlotte put up with it, being the neatnik she was.

Not that it mattered. Tidy. Messy. Loud. Quiet.

All she wanted was her daughter back in her arms.

Panic overrode everything. As if the pendulum had swung directly from happy-go-lucky straight to worst nightmare ever.

If anything, *anything*, happened to Luna she'd not be able to live with herself. This felt worse than her inability to get her mother to Switzerland even though she'd begged. Soared past not contacting her father 'to bond' as her mother's will had stipulated and then, of course, being too late when they'd finally tracked her down. A chill poured through her. Was she wrong not to have let Luna's father know he had a daughter? If she'd let him know, would he be here now? With Luna? Holding her in his arms, keeping her safe. She couldn't imagine a world without her little Loony Tune. Her Booboo. Her joy.

She began calling out Luna's name, only pausing long enough to suck in enough air to do it again.

Charlotte pressed a torch into her hand.

Callum took hold of her elbow and steered her towards the long track that led up to the village. He put his big hand on the small of her back when Emily joined them, and assured her they were going to do this together. Systematically. They'd find her daughter. No matter how long it took.

Luna wasn't meant to go first. Izzy was. That's what this whole move had been about. To ensure Luna would be safe. And here she was, falling at the very first hurdle.

Freya hadn't remembered just how *long* the drive was.

She glanced ahead at Charlotte whose two children were lagging behind her, each of them staring at their phones, only occasionally remembering to call out Luna's name.

'Mum?' Regan whispered.

'Yes, darlin'?'

'Is this my fault? I mean . . . I was with her last.'

A protective fire flared in her chest.

'Absolutely not,' Freya said, solidly cupping Regan's face in her hands. 'This is not your fault.'

'Are you sure?' Regan's head crinkled in the same way she knew hers did when she asked Monty whether or not he'd had a chance to file the taxes. 'If Izzy wants to shout at someone, I think she should blame me.'

She pulled her daughter in close and dropped a kiss on her silky hair. 'It's not your fault love. It's no one's fault.'

Just like it hadn't been anyone's fault when her mum had gone in to check on the bull over the Christmas holidays last year. They'd told her time and time again not to go into his stall, no matter how much he looked as if he wanted a cuddle. Aberdeen Angus bulls weighed nearly a tonne. Her little bird of a mum had always been such a softie for the cattle. The number of calves and lambs who'd spent the night warming in front of the stove in their kitchen . . . Her mum would've done anything for them. Just as Freya would for Monty, Regan and Felix. They were her *family*.

*

Charlotte's phone vibrated against her hip. It took Jack doing a 'Gah! *Mum*. Are you, like, going to answer that?' to get her to connect the dots.

All she'd been able to hear were Izzy's raw shouts of appeal to her daughter ringing out across the fields. The naked strains of fear were painful to listen to. Please god let them find Luna quickly. Watching Izzy career into panic mode from her usual unhurried, hippy self had been disconcerting to say the least.

She answered the phone.

'Yes. Good evening. I'm looking for the birthday girl.' Charlotte stared at the phone. The voice at the other end was very posh. She'd said *gehl* instead of girl. It wasn't her mother-in-law. Although . . . a chill ran down her spine. Many of Oli's parents' friends sounded similar. Had something happened to Oli on the way home?

'This is Charlotte Mayfield speaking,' Charlotte said primly. Just as uptight as Oli sometimes accused her of being.

'Yes. Good. Venetia Brockley here.'

'Lady Brockley?' Charlotte stopped dead in her tracks.

'Well.' There was a sniff at the other end of the line. '*Technically*, it's Lady Venetia, but we mustn't let ourselves get muddled up with technicalities so deep into the weekend, must we?'

Venetia's voice was like cut glass, but strangely friendly. A bit like Princess Margaret, Charlotte couldn't help thinking. Or, at least, the actress who played her.

'Yes? How may I help?'

'It's the other way around, dear. If you wouldn't mind making your way up to the house, I'm quite certain I have something of yours.'

Chapter Nine

The Dowager Countess of Sittingstone, Lady Venetia, or 'plain old Venetia', as she insisted everyone called her, turned out to be a dead ringer for Joanna Lumley. A Joanna Lumley who enjoyed gardening, raucous dinner parties, and had no interest in being sent off to moulder in some London ladies' club by her globe-trotting, eco-warrior son, whose latest plan was to set up Sittingstone as an Airbnb.

Charlotte thought she was wonderful. There was something so very confident about her, and yet she seemed incredibly approachable. She bore no air of competitiveness. As if she, too, had once been humbled and, like a phoenix, risen from the ashes. Charlotte longed to have just one solitary ounce of that strength. To rebuild herself from nothing.

She shook her head. Pure fiction. The woman just had one of those auras.

'An Airbnb would be amazing,' Freya gushed, then quickly corrected herself at Venetia's narrowed eyes. 'I mean. Obviously, it is much better as a private home.'

They all oohed and aahed at the grand entrance hall that could've been straight out of *Downton*. Towering oak columns. Marble flooring. Enough portraits to fill a gallery. Family, Charlotte guessed, from the tight set of most of the men's eyes.

Charlotte was still shocked Venetia had let them in the front door, ragtag bunch that they were. She kept a hand pressed over the most persistent of the chocolate-cake stains on her skirt. Oli would've been horrified.

'Thank you *so* much.' Izzy blew her nose again, her daughter clamped to her side like a limpet. 'I don't know how I can ever repay you.'

'Don't be ridiculous. Best Sunday evening I've had in yonks. Do come in, dear.' She beckoned to Felix who was still standing just outside the door, angling one of those enormous books of his up towards the porch light. 'Yes. That's right. And close the door behind you. We wouldn't want any more escapes, would we?' She cackled gleefully and cuddled Bonzer close to her, pretending to give him a sip of her martini. 'Gorgeous little beastie you've got here. The child, too. Lucky for both of them I'm drawn to the kennels of an evening. There's nothing more curative than a trip down to the hounds at sunset with a martini in hand.'

'Sounds bloody good to me,' Monty said. No one acknowledged him. Poor Monty.

A short retelling of 'the great discovery ensued' once they'd all been ushered inside. Luna, it transpired, had never got her turn to play Giant Jenga and, not knowing anyone, found a bottle of water, a pocketful of biscuits and had set off down the long lane to find Bonzer. After briefly getting lost in the stables – Izzy gasped at this point – she'd eventually tracked down Bonzer in the kennels.

Venetia smiled at Luna, '. . . and there she was. Fast asleep with this adorable little scrub of a pup. They both looked so angelic I couldn't bear to wake them. Apologies,' she stage-whispered to Izzy who, now that she had her daughter back, seemed fine with the fact that Lady Venetia had waited until Luna had woken to call.

'I'm awfully sorry to have imposed,' Charlotte apologized. She seemed to do a lot of that. Apologizing. Perhaps she should take a leaf out of Freya's book and, not necessarily fling cakes about, but . . . be less remorseful for things she hadn't actually done.

'Nonsense!' Lady Venetia tinkled her jewel-weighted fingers at Luna. 'I think this delightful girl has the right idea. Puppies over people. I'm very much in the same camp. Adults are such a ruddy bore and children aren't always that much better.' Her eyes swept across to Charlotte's two who were not so subtly taking Instagram photos on their phones. Heat poured into Charlotte's cheeks. She'd be getting a rash at this rate. Perhaps a few boundaries for the children would be in order once they got home.

Venetia allowed Luna to take the puppy when his wiggling spilt the remains of her drink.

'She's a rather good-looking little thing, isn't she?'

They all turned and gazed at Luna.

'She is a beauty,' Izzy agreed. Crème-caramel skin. Piercing blue eyes. The same smattering of freckles across her nose that Izzy had endlessly tried to scrub away when she'd been the same age.

She flushed when she realized Venetia was watching her and not Luna. 'This one the father?' Venetia tipped her head in Monty's direction.

Izzy couldn't help it. She laughed. *As if.*

'Oh, that one's mine.' Freya held up her hand, pointed at her ring finger, silencing Izzy's cackle with a well-aimed glare.

Never going to let that one go, are you girlie?

Venetia noted the exchange of looks. 'So, you've all known one another for some time then?'

'Yes. Bristol University. Graduating class of 2000.' Freya began babbling as if she'd been given a truth serum. They all squirmed as she launched into a rather meticulous explanation as to how they'd all met, stayed in touch for a few years after uni, but then drifted off in their own directions, going on to explain that even though she and Monty had had children *before* they were married, they were *definitely* married now and the two lovely children just over there . . . ? Twins! Yes. Fraternal. *Obviously.* Not the two on the phones, no. The bookish-looking ones. *They* were Monty and Freya's children. In fact . . . they hadn't even known Izzy *had* a child until just yesterday. Had they?

All eyes turned to Izzy.

WTF? Had Izzy missed the 'Dirty Laundry Cocktail Hour' memo?

'Wonderful!' Lady Venetia looked utterly delighted. 'So this is a reunion?'

'Yes! *And* a celebration,' Freya did a little presentation swirl with her hands after sending the tiniest of guilt-laced apology smiles at Izzy. 'It's Charlotte's birthday!'

Charlotte looked as though she wished Freya would put a sock in it.

'Wonderful. Yes. Luna here was telling me all about it.' Her eyes twinkled. 'I hope you've been spoilt rotten,

Charlotte.' Lady Venetia looked across at Callum, who was running his fingers atop a velvet cushion as if it were a Persian cat. 'This one's yours?'

'Oh, goodness, no. Not mine.' Charlotte threw an apologetic look at Emily.

'Charlotte's husband's gone off in a strop. I mean, rightfully so,' Freya strode straight into the deep end . . . but in a stage-whisper so that the children, if they were paying attention, would know it was a bad thing – the cake, the crappy speech, the infidelity.

Emily started scanning Freya as if looking for an off button.

Charlotte looked as though she wished she were anywhere but here.

Izzy prayed for a way to make it all stop.

'Well, my goodness me!' said Venetia with an air of cheer that suggested she hadn't had this much fun in donkey's years. 'What a lovely time to repair to the library for an après-sundowner. Fizz suit, seeing as we're celebrating? We can find something suitable for the children unless they want to head over to the kennels with Whiffy.'

Thank god for Lady Venetia.

When yet another round of martinis was circulated, Freya ignored Emily's glare. This wasn't talking out of turn. This was *explaining*. She folded one leg meaningfully over the other and persisted. 'What I'm trying to say, Venetia, is that I don't think Charlotte should go back at all. She should put the children in the car and go.'

'Right,' Emily countered. 'So . . . in this great plan of yours, where exactly is Charlotte meant to go?'

Freya's mind fuzzed for a second. *Well, home of course.* And then, *Charlotte doesn't have a family*. 'Fine. She should kick him out. File for divorce.'

'Isn't it up to Charlotte what she decides?'

'Izzy, just because your mother had extramarital affairs, doesn't make it right,' Freya intoned.

Everyone sucked in a sharp breath.

Lady Venetia took a sip from her champagne flute and said, 'In my experience, it really is the woman's choice.' She nodded at Charlotte as if she were a judge passing a decree in her favour. Perhaps there was a splash of Betty Boothroyd in there, too.

'Okay.' Freya back-pedalled. The extra dose of bubbles was screwing up her *'what is right in this situation'* versus her *'what is right for Charlotte'* compass. 'I'm just saying, Oliver shouldn't be the one getting sympathy because of a bit of well-deserved public humiliation.'

'He was embarrassed,' Charlotte explained to Venetia. 'He's not used to being made a spectacle of.'

'Nor are you!' Freya was indignant. Where had Charlotte's spine gone? She knew she was a pleaser, but c'mon! Oli had been properly out of order. Speaking of Charlotte as if she were nothing more than his skivvy.

Venetia tutted. 'As the resident geriatric, might I offer the suggestion that there is no need to make a decision straight away. Men, in my experience, don't ever entirely know what they want.' She smiled at Monty and Callum, who both held up their hands in a 'you go on ahead' move. They knew when they were outnumbered.

No, Freya silently fumed. Charlotte should *do* something. Not sit back and take it.

As if everyone read her mind, suggestions began to fly about as to What Charlotte Should Do.

'She could slowly poison him.' Emily primed an invisible syringe.

'Public humiliation? I mean . . . beyond the cake thing,' Izzy said.

'Gaslighting?' offered Callum with a wicked laugh.

'I'm right here.'

'Course you are, Lotte,' Freya said, her mind still reeling with ways to take Oli down a notch or seven.

'I'm *right* here,' Charlotte repeated. 'Please stop speaking about me as if what I think doesn't matter. Do you have any idea how humiliating this is?'

Everyone froze.

Freya wanted to kick herself. Hard.

Charlotte was right, of course. Who were they to tell her what to do? It wasn't as if Freya's marriage was a bright and shining example of perfection. Debt up to their eyeballs. The bickering. The jealousy of Izzy that she couldn't seem to shake, despite some fifteen years of proof that Monty was hers, all hers. Mortification took over where indignation had begun. She was spouting off when she should've listened. If she hadn't been so touchy about being around rich people all day and quaffed Veuve Clicquot like it was water, none of this would've happened.

'I'm sorry, Charlotte. I—'

Charlotte held up a hand. 'I know. Just . . . please. Can we talk about something else?'

Lady Venetia stood up, glass aloft. 'I propose a toast.'

Everyone awkwardly pushed themselves up from the deeply cushioned sofas and chairs and raised their glasses.

The last time a toast had been proposed, it hadn't gone particularly well.

'To Charlotte. May her friends long continue to celebrate her . . . no matter what she decides.'

To a chorus of hear-hears, Freya drank deeply. It wasn't often she was the one being put in her place. But Lady Venetia was right. Friends supported friends. Even if it meant watching them return to a philandering, pompous ass. He was Charlotte's philandering, pompous ass and it was her decision to make. She shot a guilty look in Monty's direction. She would definitely try to be more supportive about the Instagram-portraiture phase. Particularly if it took the edge off their overdraft.

'Night Mum.' Poppy gave Charlotte a quick, fierce hug then scuttled off to her yurt.

'Night, night darling,' Charlotte called after her, her heart warming as, for the first time in what felt like for ever, Poppy acknowledged her with a little wave.

'Night, Mum.' Jack whacked an arm round her shoulders and planted a kiss on top of her head. 'Glamping's pretty cool. Nice one.'

She smiled up at her son and wiped an invisible bit of toastie off his chin. He'd be shaving soon. Her little boy.

He wished her a good night and ambled off to bed in that leggy, easy-natured manner of his. He was so very much like his father.

Now that Whiffy had safely returned them to the glamp-site (with two spare bottles of fizz from Venetia 'just in case'), Charlotte was quite persuaded that she *didn't* need a plan. Not yet anyway.

After the champagne toast (which really *had* made it feel as though it was her birthday), Venetia had steered everyone to the huge kitchen and put Freya in charge of a production line making piles of toasties. Poor Freya. She probably would've mopped the entire mansion if she'd been asked. Venetia had then taken Charlotte on a turn round the fairy-light-bedecked rose garden and chirpily explained that she too had been stepped out on by her dearly departed husband. A man against whom she seemed to hold no grudge.

Amid the budding roses, Lady Venetia had turned to her and said, 'Love comes in many forms. It's not all about fidelity so long as there is respect. My husband dallied on more than one occasion. But he would never, *ever* embarrass me in public. That was our agreement. I loved him, I supported him, I also made sure I lived the life *I* wanted to. The same as any other marriage, just slightly more . . . complex. And that's what it boils down to, isn't it darling? Making decisions about the life or lifestyle we'd like – then living it without remorse or shame.'

For the first time in years, Charlotte felt as though she had been seen. She hadn't married for money. She'd married for love. But she did wonder how her life would've turned out if she'd fallen in love with Freya's brother, say. *Rocco.* Tall, strong, a smile that lit a girl up from the inside out, but a man who would never woo her in Michelin restaurants, take her on city breaks in Barcelona . . . go on golfing weekends.

Perhaps that was where she'd gone wrong. She'd been so blinded by the perfect aesthetics of the life she and Oli shared, she'd forgotten to examine the man with whom she'd be spending it. Little wonder when her own upbringing had been so . . . small. Parents trudging through life as if they were its prisoners. A cramped council flat. No appreciation for . . . anything really, other than *Corrie* and a cheap take-away. When she'd left home she'd been desperate to create a beautiful, calm, conflict-free life and give her children the same. It was why she'd never once invited any of the girls home with her over the holidays. She'd been too ashamed. How perfectly ironic that the weekend should culminate in her friend smashing cake into her husband's face.

Izzy waved a hand in front of Charlotte and grinned. 'So. Tell us everything.' She wanted all the details of the rose garden stroll.

'What? About Lady V?'

'Oh, it's Lady V now, is it?' Emily put out her fist.

Charlotte patted it and said, 'Oh, it was nothing really. I'm most likely too far away to consider it, but . . .'

'Consider what?' Izzy pinched a single crisp out of the big bowl Freya had put out for everyone (mostly Monty) in a last-ditch effort to sop up Lady V's largesse. He'd wandered off for some star-gazing with one of the bottles instead of taking the hint.

'Well, she seemed very keen on the ideas I gave her for her honey.'

'Her honey?' Emily looked confused. And a little grossed out.

'She's got bees.' Izzy made a buzz-buzz noise.

Charlotte smiled at her then explained, 'I suggested a better way to present it in the shop.'

'Shop?'

Had Emily actually seen anything of the glampsite?

Izzy pointed out into the darkness. 'The one in the car

park? The thing that looks like a wooden bus shelter with weird local artwork and, like, two pots of honey with labels from the 1970s? Horrid store-bought sausage rolls on the first morning? No? No memory?'

'She suggested I have a go at redesigning it,' Charlotte said after Emily gave them all a blank look.

'You should go for it, Lotts,' Freya called from the refrigerator, a bit more timorously than normal. 'You were brilliant that summer up in Scotland at the fruit farm.'

Before Charlotte could say she actually quite liked the idea of building the tiny little shack into a micro-business (that's what Lady V had suggested calling the venture, a micro-business of her own), the conversation veered off to a madcap story Callum had heard about a beekeeper in the centre of London, but Charlotte didn't mind. Being given the compliment about her ideas for packaging the Sittingstone honey was every bit as good as coming along and 'consulting'. Imagine! Charlotte Mayfield: micro-shop stylist.

It might not be her café/gallery dream, but it wasn't as if she'd added anything to her CV in the past fifteen years. At the very least, it was a chance to make good on her promise to try and do something for herself, even if it would involve a bit of a commute.

She wove her fingers together and stared at them, her engagement ring occasionally glinting against the fairy lights. No matter how appealing the idea of making her own money was, she was simply too busy being CEO of her own family to take on anything more. Particularly if she and Oliver were going to stick to their guns about putting their marriage back on track.

Either way. It was nice to have been asked.

She selected a couple of crisps and watched as her friends listened to Callum's story, then belly-laughed when he hit the inevitable punch line. Callum didn't seem to have stories without one.

This was what she had wanted. What she had pictured. Being part of something, even if she felt, as she had back in uni, a bit on the periphery.

Seeing Izzy so closely bonded with her daughter, watching Freya claim Monty as her own, even though he was still incredibly, embarrassingly drunk, and then, of course, the ever-chivalrous Callum taking off his coat and draping it across Emily's shoulders when he saw she was shivering. This, when her own husband had stormed off over a bit of cake in the face.

Freya scooched in beside her and whispered, 'You all right, girlie?'

'Yes,' said Charlotte.

'Forgive me?'

'Of *course!*' Now that a bit of time had passed, she was actually a tiny bit grateful. It wasn't as if she would ever have been brave enough to fling a cake at Oli, but . . . They squeezed hands beneath the table. It was so *comforting* to have real friends of her own.

'I can't believe we just had champagne with a dowager countess.' Emily laughed. 'At a *glampsite*.'

'You mean the *castle* at the glampsite,' Izzy corrected, as she drew her fingers through Emily's long dark hair. Twenty years on and Izzy still couldn't keep her fingers out of it. She was the only one Emily never batted away.

'Did you see the way she dragged that chair across the drawing room so Regan could see that painting of a hare?'

Freya had shifted gears. 'I was praying she wouldn't put her foot through it. It must've cost a fortune!'

'I'm sure she could afford a replacement,' Callum said lightly. He dropped a kiss on Emily's head then wished everyone goodnight.

They all waved him off.

'We still have some cake left. Shall we eat it, too?' Charlotte was gratified when everyone dissolved into fits of giggles. Jokes had never been her forte.

Freya hunted down some candles. Emily found a knife and Izzy kept throwing protective glances in Luna's direction, though she'd long been fast asleep on the sofa. Bless. Charlotte would've most likely done the same.

'Here we go.' Freya carefully slid the lemon drizzle onto the cable-spool table top . . . candles in place, already alight. Everyone did that little inhale and shoulder-jiggle thing that meant they were excited to eat cake.

Charlotte looked at her friends. Emily, righting one of the askew candles. Izzy, sticking her finger in another one and covering the tip of her finger in melted wax. Freya, adjusting a bit of frosting with a knife so that the cake looked just so.

'I'm so happy you've come to my birthday party! You really are wonderful.' It was out before Charlotte could stop it. *Sugar.* Why did she say things like that? Set herself up for disappointment.

'We're happy, too, Lotts,' Izzy said, with a solid, yes-it's-true nod, her mouth parting into that wide, open smile of hers.

The others nodded. Smiled. Bumped against her shoulder.

It felt like one of the birthday candles had lit up deep inside her heart. They cared about her. She hoped they'd meet again. She doubted they'd meet again. But something very lonely inside of her knew that staying in touch with these women was essential if she were going to, in the words of Lady V, 'live her life without remorse or shame.'

'Shall we blow out the candles?'

'Only if you've made your wish.' Izzy dipped another fingertip into the wax then pressed them together.

'Let's *all* make a wish,' Charlotte suggested. 'Just like in the old days.'

'Great idea.' Freya crossed her fingers and looked up to the heavens. 'I could do with a bit of Lady Luck.'

Truthfully? Charlotte didn't have to wish. Everything she wanted was right here round the table.

'Ready? On, one . . . two . . . threeeee!'

Chapter Ten

And just like that the long weekend was over.

Emily cradled the tin of vegan carrot cake that Charlotte had insisted she take.

'You're sure you're going to be all right?' Emily asked.

'Of course. And all the better for seeing *you*.'

'Thanks for this.' Emily tapped the cake tin. 'I'll bring it to the nurses' station tomorrow. They'll die of shock. I never do anything nice.'

'The glamping wasn't too awful?' Charlotte clearly knew what a stretch it was.

'I complained the whole way here.' Now that she'd survived it, she might as well confess. 'I've not slept so well in years!'

Charlotte gave her arm a squeeze. 'Thanks for coming. It meant a lot.'

'Right. Ummm . . . if you ever need to escape to the big smoke . . . uhhhh . . .' She lived in a box room, it wasn't as if she could have guests.

'I know you're busy.'

Charlotte had always been good at absolving her. They finished off their goodbyes with a quick peck on either cheek.

'Ready to hit the road, woman?'

Emily nodded and followed Callum to the car park, wondering whether she might, one day, be truly honest with her friends. Her heart did a little flip as she caught a last glimpse of Izzy and Luna trickling flower petals from one of Charlotte's birthday bouquets into one another's hair. They were the obvious reason she'd come, but seeing Freya and Charlotte again had been more of a bonus than she'd anticipated. She should stop being such an ice queen. Being nice had its benefits.

'C'mon, Emms. There's a long, hot shower, a face mask and a new box set of *Grey's* calling my name.'

'You big girl!'

'It's why you love me.' He gave her a knuckle-duster then ducked into the car. 'That and my impeccable taste in flatmates.'

She grinned. He was, of course, spot on.

'Call if you need to,' Freya said meaningfully. '*Anytime.*'

'All right.' Charlotte gave the counter a swipe.

'Promise?'

'Promise. Now give me a hug. It looks like Monty's ready to hit the road.'

Freya gave Charlotte a big hug and a kiss. 'Call me.'

Charlotte blew her a kiss then headed off to find her children.

Leaving Charlotte without a pragmatic solution had been tough, but she'd insisted she needed time to think. Make up her mind on her own. Poor love. Oli had her well and truly brainwashed. Freya gave Monty's shoulder a kiss before inching the car back onto the motorway.

'What was that for?'

117

'Just because.'

'Ha!' Monty barked. But he left off the usual retort. *There's always something.*

The weekend had been great in the end. Okay. They'd spent too much money, eaten like pigs, drunk too much, and seeing Izzy again had unleashed the green-eyed monster a bit too ferociously, but . . . everyone had their wobbles.

She genuinely did hope they'd meet again. Another ten years would be way too long. Maybe she should invite the gang camping for their annual foray to Wales this summer.

She smiled as she pictured Emily swatting away a fly as if it were an incoming land mine. Maybe Wales could wait. Besides. Living up to the high thread count, the open-air Aga, the endless supply of champers versus a grassy field on the Welsh coast where there was no escaping the sea fleas? She didn't fancy her chances.

'Right everyone, homeward bound!'

'All right, Booboo?' Izzy waved a final goodbye to Charlotte then reached across to give Luna's knee a pit-pat. She was touching her more than she usually did, pulling her in for slightly claustrophobic hugs . . . she knew they were too tight because Luna would push her away and look at her like she'd lost the plot. Last night had scared the hell out of her. Izzy had lived her entire adult life without a mother, and the thought of missing so much as a single day with Luna . . . bah. She couldn't go there. Not now.

At least she was back in the friend-loop now.

Maybe not so much with Freya. She should've cleared the air. Told her she'd always been jealous of Freya's upbringing. The loving family. The cool older brother dropping her off at term time in his beat-up old Land Rover and picking her up again at the end with a tin of shortbread from her mum. They all seemed to love each so easily. Like breathing. She thought of her mother's last, exhausted breaths. Maybe breathing wasn't so easy after all. She should've cornered Lady Venetia. Asked for some words of wisdom.

'Mom! Are you going to sit there or drive?'

'Drive, baby.' She swept the back of her hand along her daughter's cheek. 'Let's get this show on the road.'

Charlotte waved them all off, one by one, giving a different reason to each as to why she was hanging back. The truth was, she wasn't entirely ready to go home.

It had been so lovely being surrounded by friends whose only purpose in coming was to wish her a happy birthday.

She sat at one of the picnic tables, ignoring the wheelbarrow-loads of things, piled just outside the kitchen, that she still had to pack into the car. A text pinged on to her phone. No doubt another appeal from her children to *Leave now, Mum* that they had been sending from the Land Rover where they were embroiled in a fight for the front seat.

The site was free of most of the signs that they'd been there. The fire pit was cleared. All of the picnic tables back in place. Woollen blankets all tightly rolled and nestled into the large willow whip basket.

The girls had helped her with a final swoop, eventually popping the dew-soaked serviette bunting into the recycling bin now that it had served its purpose.

She scanned the site again, soaking it all up. Superimposing the bunting she could now picture sitting on the worktop in the boot room as clearly as if she were looking right at it. Suddenly the bunting didn't seem very important at all.

It was friendship that mattered. Not things.

She gave herself a bit of a hug, willing the gesture to keep that tiny flicker of possibility alight in her heart.

They would meet again, she promised herself. They would definitely meet again.

Chapter Eleven

[Text message from Freya]
999!!!! Just got off the phone w/ Charlotte. Oli wants divorce. She doesn't sound great. We're off camping in Wales at the weekend. Convinced Lotte to join us. Any chance you girls want to come along too? There for a week and a bit. A friend in need, ladies ⛺

[Emily]
Wot? The ass. Does she have friends with her? (Is Izzy on this loop?).

[Freya]
We're the friends, idiot. You & Izz in the loop. Will send postcode for campsite. It's easy to find. Drive to Wales, reach ocean, see tents. Will text more deets asap.

[Emily]
Soz. Have back to back surgeries until the end of time. What do you people have against hotels? Surely Charlotte doesn't want to drown her sorrows on an airbed.

[Izzy]
Oliver's an idiot. Van acting up. Maybe next weekend?? How long you staying? Xx 🖐

[Freya]
MONTY! Pull your effing socks up! The car won't pack itself!

[Freya]
Soz! Obviously intended for Monty.

[Izzy]
Is wild camping like a rave? Are children allowed? Will have to sneak Luna in even if non-age-appropriate. Have negotiated a truce with van. Will aim for day trip over weekend. Looney has school until then. ☺

[Emily]
Have begged Evil Nemesis Surgeon to cover. No joy. Sorry girlies. Not looking good.

[Freya]
BYO pillow, Izz. Our car will be stuffed to the hilt. BYO tent if you have one. If you want anything beyond lukewarm, cheap plonk bring that, too. ()@£&%)!! Monty bound to forget ice. *deep breath* Emms – please come. I promise to paint your toes. You do remember this is about Charlotte's husband being a total plonker, right?

[Emily]
☺ Will try. No promises. Just read weather report. Major suckage incoming from Ireland. Still time to reconsider and meet in London instead.

[Freya]
Monty???? WTF? Hurry. Up. No sex for a week – not even a BJ if you aren't back in five.

[Emily]
Freya. Please. There's only so much we want to know about your private life.

[Freya]
My humiliation is complete. 😂

Charlotte shook away the cloud of washing-up bubbles and stared at her rings.

She should leave soon if she was going to beat the traffic to meet up with Freya. She also should've packed. Should've baked a cake. Packed a hamper. It was very unlike her not to be prepared. It was also a very unusual day. Her very first as an about-to-be-divorcée.

Oli had waited until she'd gone downstairs to start his packing. A strange courtesy considering he hadn't really left much to the imagination when he'd explained why he'd been 'forced to do this.' As he spoke the words – not *in* love any more, fenced-in, someone with more drive – Charlotte wondered if the buzzing in her head would ever stop.

It had. But the new sounds were every bit as bewildering. Step, step, step from the chest of drawers to the suitcase.

This as she'd gone through the motions down in the kitchen, getting some breakfast together for the pair of them. Breakfast. As if it were just another day. Scritch, scritch went the hangers as shirt after shirt came out of the wardrobe. He'd taken an awful lot of toiletries, judging from all the clatter coming from the en suite. The methodical cadence of it all had put her in a sort of stupor. One she'd best snap out of now that 'Xanthe and the baby were his priorities'. And the children, he'd hastily added. Charlotte, of course, had now officially been dropped off the list.

She stared at the rings again.

What did one do in this scenario?

Take them off straight away, or feign, as she had the past couple of months, that everything in her life was perfectly perfect?

What a fool she'd been. Believing Oliver wanted to make a go of things.

At least she was getting out of this wretched house for a bit of perspective. It had been her pride and joy when the children were young and she'd bustled about like Doris Day. Now it was little more than a show home for a beautiful but meaningless life.

She glanced out the window to where Oli's car had been, chiding herself for having been so *acquiescent* about the whole thing. She'd just sat there and listened. Accepted everything he'd said, as if it would be sheer madness to express any sort of opinion about the fact he'd pulled the grenade pin on her life.

She tried to channel her friends to see if that would help. Freya, Izzy and Emily were all so different but each of them seemed to possess a core strength she herself lacked.

If she had been more like Freya, she would've made a proper show of things. Thrown something. Strode out to the recently relaid stone patio after Oli announced his 'slight' change of heart and, one by one, dropped the rings into the well with some sort of pithy comment about how they were most likely blood diamonds anyway. Heaven knew he'd sucked *her* dry.

Emily would've quirked an eyebrow and said, 'Get out your chequebook.'

Lady Venetia might very likely have done the same. Charlotte made a quick note to ring her to say she wouldn't be coming into the shop this week. Part of her still couldn't believe her birthday glamping trip that had reunited her with her besties from university had brought her the most unexpected of presents. A new friend and mentor, Lady V. It was a proper shop now. The Sittingstone Larder. There was a part of her that wanted to be there right now. Pour the mounting pressure-cooker of unspent emotion into making it even better, but in her heart she knew what she needed most was to see her friends.

After Oliver had finished his speech (rehearsed, from the sounds of it) she'd sat and nodded and, when he'd finished, offered to make up the guest room with fresh sheets, only to end up sleeping there herself as Oli found the room too draughty.

She scrubbed at a plate, suddenly furious with herself for not having left him on her birthday. After the whole mess with the cake it had taken Charlotte well over a fortnight to get back into his good books. As if a bit of wayward butter-cream had wreaked more havoc in their marriage than the fact that her husband had impregnated his law firm's most active Instagrammer, the ludicrously named Xanthe.

CheekyLawGirl if she was going for full accuracy. Not that Charlotte had been cyber-stalking her. Much.

She stared at the wrinkled pads of her fingers, then turned them over. She would keep the eternity ring. That was for the children and it wasn't their fault their father had a change-able heart.

Poppy had gone to the South of France (Cannes!) for language submersion, and Jack was in Namibia for she wasn't entirely sure what sort of 'formative cultural experience'. But would either trip prepare them for parents en route to a divorce? *En route* . . . Poppy's *français* would definitely come in handy. A mother who sat listening to her husband devalue the last fifteen years of their lives together as 'non-progressive' would not.

A question she'd asked herself with increasingly regularity popped into her mind. *What would Lady Venetia do?*

She'd keep busy, Charlotte thought to herself. Exactly what she'd been trying to do in transforming The Sittingstone Larder. Once a bit of an eyesore, it was now the very first, bunting-clad piece of magic that visitors to Sittingstone Estate's glampsite laid eyes on. Gone was the akimbo shed; in its place was a gently greying Sussex barn that Whiffy had found stacked up in bits in one of their much larger barns and carefully rebuilt. They still sold Lady V's honey, of course. Charlotte had tweaked a few of her own recipes into 'glamp-cakes'. There were other items – largely designed for forgetful packers or those who might want to bring a gift home to remember their weekend by. Jams, preserves, pickled onions, cheeses (hard and soft). The village bakery had started making some particularly delicious rolls (sausage and bacon), which the Londoners in particular seemed to be mad for.

Though it had all been a great success, Charlotte could see where she'd gone wrong now. Rather than truly seeing her time at the Larder as a means of expanding her own world, she'd used it as the perfect way to avoid the truth. Her marriage hadn't stood a chance of weathering the storm.

Now, she supposed, it was time to find if she could.

Before her children returned home, she would need to acquire a spine. Particularly for her poor little Poppy, still stinging from a rather bruising year settling in at boarding school. Oli had brushed Charlotte off when she'd suggested, perhaps, taking Poppy out of the school and keeping her home for another year. As usual she'd demurred, but perhaps now they were getting divorced she would get a bit more say in these things. Or less. She supposed it was up to her how that worked.

She would love to see an end to Poppy's almost permanently locked bedroom door for endless hours on social media. She hoped she wasn't being bullied on one of those . . . what did they call them? Platforms. A shudder jolted through her. Sounded too much like the setting for a public hanging.

Perhaps she shouldn't have waited for Poppy to come to her. Since when did a child ever volunteer information? It was down to the parent to chisel it out of them. Charlotte had let Oli take the lead in so many things, she'd virtually forgotten it was completely possible to act of her own free will.

Either way, she supposed Oli did have a point regarding the timing of his announcement that he was destroying her life. Breaking his news whilst the children were away gave her time to 'draw up a party line'. (His suggestion.) There was still the August holiday in Italy with the Pickerings to consider. They'd pre-paid a breathtaking sum for the villa. He wouldn't want her to miss out on their last holiday as a family, he'd said.

His thoughtfulness knew no bounds.

Her rings glinted under the LED lighting they'd installed over the sink. Oli had thought the one tiny window would be sufficient, though this particular corner of the kitchen was always a bit of a cave, even on a bright summer's day like today. When his mother had deigned to wash a teacup a few years back and deemed the area a black hole, workmen had appeared the next day.

She put away last night's wine glasses. Delicate crystal stemware matched to the wine. A Chablis that Oli had been given by a grateful client. He'd picked it out for them last night because he hadn't been convinced it was 'up to' sharing with guests, even though it had had excellent reviews. Back at the sink she stared at last night's dinner plates, this morning's breakfast plates, the egg and coffee cups. All roosting on top of the drying rack. It looked like an Instagram photo.

In one swift move she swept the entire lot onto the hard, unforgiving floor.

So, this was what Old Mother Hubbard felt like.

Freya shook the contactless payment device as if it were one of her children's piggy banks. This, in lieu of closing the shop, going home and murdering her husband. Seriously? Monty couldn't find one measly pound to put in the shopping trolley so he wanted *her* to go to the shops? She was at work. That thing that kept them out of debtors' prison?

She tapped out a text. *Sofa cushions. Trouser pockets. Bottom of the laundry basket. Felix's bed. The spotty mug with the pens in it.* When she finished she slammed the phone down so hard her solitary customer yelped.

'Sorry.' She made a lame flexing gesture. 'Didn't know my own strength. Anything I can help you find? Unicorns are just over there.' She pointed at her most popular line, as if the woman couldn't actually make her own way around the shop. It was hardly vast.

When she'd signed the lease some fifteen years ago, it had felt huge. Like a dreamy, brick-lined Aladdin's cave. Her very own blank canvas, glowing with limitless possibility.

'Are there any of the raccoon T-shirts left?'

Freya's mouth stretched back into an apologetic wince. 'Sorry. We're off camping tomorrow and I didn't get another run in.'

The young woman hauled her dreadlocks over her shoulder, interested. 'What festival are you going to?'

Freya laughed. As if. Buying tickets for her entire family to go to a festival was not an option. 'Just camping.'

The woman's half-hearted smile faded before it'd had a chance to catch purchase.

Freya soldiered on. 'Sorry about the shirts. You know how it is. End of term. Sports days. Flute concerts.' She'd actually missed both. Monty had taken videos. 'Anyway, we love camping, with or without the face painting.' She was losing the girl fast. 'Any interest in the unicorn range?'

The woman glanced at the door as if targeting an emergency exit. 'Not really.'

She took her chance to flee when a gaggle of Japanese tourists bundled in. They looked as if they were from one of those futuristic films that Felix adored, all candy-floss-coloured hair in quirky ponytails and jet-black, razor-sharp bobs. Giggly and raving about something one minute, dismissively silent the next.

They looked at the walls more than the T-shirts, which was a shame.

The previous lessee, a joss-stick vendor who'd decided she'd rather live in Bali where 'the energy just spoke to her', had painted the interior gold. When Freya had finally got some time and money together a few years later, they'd all bundled in on a Monday and got to work. The exacting plan Freya had drawn up – immaculate white walls with painted anthropomorphized animals 'wearing' the T-shirts – had almost instantly degenerated into one of those wacky painting scenes reserved for rom-coms. Dabbing one another on the nose. The ear. The hair. Until, inevitably, it had ended up as a paint fight. She'd been furious at first then, as ever, Monty had made it fun and she'd decided to keep the paint-splattered interior. When Monty had taken the children to the zoo the following day, she had tactically accented an area or two to heighten the Pollack-esque effect.

She didn't need to know Japanese to absorb the fact that the shop needed rejuvenating. Fresh paint. A new presentation style. Gallery lighting rather than the filament bulbs they'd all been obsessed with back in the day. Lighting she should have installed in the first place because she had always hoped, one day, to ease out the money-spinning T-shirts and start showing her own more high-end designs. Designs she simply didn't have the resources to make any more.

The Japanese squad headed towards the door. 'The #Impeach hoodies are half price!' Freya called out.

They left without a second glance.

She should've moved to the shop opposite the Amy Winehouse statue when she'd had the chance. The rent was astronomical, but the footfall would've had her back in the black in no time.

She stared at her empty shop, then dropped her head into her hands and moaned as another 'where is . . . ?' text popped through from Monty.

One week. It was all she was asking for. One week without being responsible for anything other than enjoying her family. Lazing about by the seaside. Eating burnt sausages. Foraging for seafood suppers. Board games in the tent if it poured down with rain. They were, after all, going to Wales.

The empty shop was soul-destroying. Particularly after Charlotte's text from last week. How, after only two months of 'dabbling', Charlotte had managed to turn Lady V's 'micro-business' into the talk of West Sussex . . . Charlotte was glowing in the *Waitrose Weekend* article, even if it did look as though Venetia had forced her into posing alongside her. If Freya had any money, she'd ask Charlotte to her shop and get her consultancy advice. Wonder Woman sleeveless vests weren't really bringing home the bacon any more. Had she lost sight of her customer base? Had she lost sight of everything?

Blanking the piles of T-shirts that needed stock-taking, the invoices that needed tending to and the lack of customers, Freya glared at her mobile, willing Monty to make good on something – for both of their sakes. She knew he did a lot of juggling between looking after the kids and her and, of course, the finances, but maybe it was time they had a proper sit-down and talked about moving on from Instagram portraiture. It had yet to reel in a solitary pound coin with which he might then be able to do the ruddy shopping.

Just last night, Freya had pulled Monty down to the bottom of the garden and not so subtly suggested he start pulling his discarded projects out of the loft and putting them on eBay. Regan could benefit from extra violin tuition judging by the last week's concert, Felix's school trip kept rearing its ugly head on the ParentPay website. She didn't want her children to go without because their father might fancy making probiotic yoghurt again. *Or because you can't face up to things either*, whispered the little voice in her head.

He'd started to say something about his parents and she'd cut him short. No loans. He was a grown man. It was time to start behaving like one.

Her assistant Fallon flounced into the shop in a cloud of tonka bean and myrrh, fresh from a flirting session with the chap who sold upcycled 'art' a few shops up the cobbled lane.

'OMG. Total tomb in here. It's buzzing everywhere else.'

Freya resisted making a narky comment about hubcap sconces. 'Just nipping out for a second.'

'I thought you wanted to stock-take.'

'Back in a mo.'

She wove her way through the crowds, past the four-hundred-odd competing vendors, and made a quick stop at her guilty pleasure, the Himalayan Coffee Man stall. (Guilty, because she'd given Monty a right earful about spending money on ridiculously overpriced coffees the other day.) Her pace slowed as she reached Camden Canal, found a bench and pulled out her phone and started bashing out an email. They were off camping tomorrow and they would have fun if it killed her.

M – if you can't find pound, please could you finishing packing? Most stuff in roof box already . . . These for back of the car. NB: leave room for dog.

Sleeping bags (airing in Regan's room)

Inflater thingy that plugs into car (shed)

Tent pegs (Think they somehow got mixed up with Christmas decorations, check red box by tree stand)

Ground cloth

Fly sheet (the waterproof thing that goes on top)

Folding camping chairs (not the blue one, it's broken)

Playing cards

Spatula (the one that gets right under the pancakes)

Cool boxes (air please, and if there's mould in them make sure you wipe with the non-toxic spray not bleach)

Get children to pack BEFORE they hit Netflix otherwise no bargaining chip.

One onesie each – but not the ones Nanna B gave them this last Christmas. xxF

Freya stared at the email before pressing send. It didn't read quite as jauntily as she'd hoped. Frankly it was downright bossy, but she knew how Monty's brain worked. Attention span of a gnat when it came to things like packing. Her mind drifted to her feminista tank-top collection. One slogan in particular pinged out. *I'm not with him, he's with me.* It hadn't been selling all that well either. Was she crushing Monty with the weight of her dreams at the expense of his? She looked at the phone again and tacked on a quick:

PS – make sure you take a portrait of yourself! Fxx

*

'I don't want to go to school!' Luna pushed her bowl of cereal away, her accompanying wail leaving no doubt as to how she felt about the matter.

'C'mon Booboo. There's rules about this sort of thing.' Izzy shifted tack. 'Can't have you turning out a surf bum like your old moms, eh? Anyway, I've gotta go out and find a new way to keep you in Honey Nut Loops, yeah?'

Luna pulled Bonzer up onto her lap, her little eyebrows scrunching up tight. 'I liked our old life.'

Izzy had too. Once.

'I know Looney. But life comes in all different shapes and sizes and we're trying on a new one. C'mon. Bonzer loves walking to school.'

'No he doesn't! He hates it too.' Izzy's daughter blinked away her tears, the tightly cuddled, increasingly large Bonzer masking the bulk of her expression. 'The other kids won't make friends with me.'

Izzy's heart contracted. *Sugar.*

She knew that feeling. Thanks to her own mother's wandering ways, she'd been in more than her share of new schools. She'd played the chameleon to make things easier, hence the weird accent. It had worked to an extent, but she hadn't wanted that life for Luna. It was one of the reasons why she'd set up the surf school. Best-laid plans and all that.

She gave her head a scrub, trying to clear away yesteryear so that she could focus on the here and now.

School.

Mrs Jones, the head teacher at Luna's new school, had seemed lovely; an experienced, Welsh earth-mother who'd welcomed Luna with open arms.

'You can tell the other pupils all about what Hawaii is

like. I don't think we've ever had a child who's lived on an island in the Pacific before, how exciting!'

Izzy had convinced herself that the wonderful Mrs Jones and Luna's equally nice teacher would make everything all right, while she went about the increasingly urgent task of finding a job.

Izzy swept her daughter's curls to one side and planted a kiss on her forehead.

'Sometimes it takes a little while to make friends, Booboo. They'll love you every bit as much as I do.' They wouldn't. 'Just give it a bit more time.'

'One of the boys laughed at the way I said tomato at lunch time,' Luna sniffed, burying her head in Bonzer's ample fluff.

Song lyrics wafted across Izzy's brain, 'You say tom-ay-to, I say tom-ah-to . . .'

'He's probably just jealous. You're a world traveller and he probably hasn't even been to Cardiff.' She resisted the temptation to hurl insults at the little blighter. Mocking her daughter. How very dare he?

'I don't wanna go.' Luna's bottom lip was still projecting into the room but Izzy could sense her daughter's resolve waning.

'Here baby. Why don't you wear this?' She handed her a ratty old tutu. Luckily it fitted over the insipid grey uniform.

Luna tugged it on then gave her hand a squeeze. They still held hands. Izzy was already scared for the day when she might not want to any more. 'Are we poor?'

'Poor? Us? No. Why do you ask?' They weren't actually. They were simply living . . . thriftily. It was important. She'd been given a couple of unexpected gifts in life – a savings account she hadn't realized her mother had been keeping for her and, of course, Ash Cottage from the father she'd never met. Izzy tried not to think about how long the money her mother had left her would last, but it wouldn't be for ever. She'd never been one to think about the future. Other people did that. She was more of an in-the-moment kinda gal, but this time there was no getting away from it: she'd have to get a job.

'Some of the kids were saying because we moved from Hawaii to here it must mean that we're poor.'

Izzy looked out of the window and laughed. Today was a rare sunny day. Apart from the insanely beautiful May bank holiday with Charlotte and the gang (chocolate cake would never be the same again), they'd pretty much enjoyed grey, drizzly, British seaside weather every day.

Her daughter was still looking at her expectantly.

'I can see where they're coming from, Booboo. Hawaii was pretty amazing, but they've got castles here. And . . . umm . . . other things. We're good. Don't you worry about that.'

'Then why did we move?'

It was a good question. And one she really didn't want to answer.

'To be near friends.' It wasn't entirely a lie.

'But . . . Auntie Emms lives in London and Freya does too and Charlotte's getting divorced.'

Izzy squatted down and swept her daughter's hair away from her eyes. 'You don't miss much, do you? Look, just because Charlotte's getting a divorce doesn't mean we aren't going to see her again. In fact we'll probably see more of her.'

'Good.' Izzy grinned. 'Bonzer likes her.'

'Loons.' Izzy held up her hand and showed four fingers.

'School breaks up in this many. If you finish the rest of the week, how about we jump into the van and drive up to meet Freya and Charlotte on their crazy wild camping trip?'

Luna's blue eyes lit up instantly. 'Really? Can we bring Bonzer?'

'Of course we can!' Izzy crossed her fingers behind her back, desperately trying to remember if Freya had said he was welcome. His incarceration at Sittingstone Castle had led to meeting Charlotte's new mentor, Lady Venetia, but losing Looney for the two hours before the dowager countess had discovered both child and dog asleep in the castle kennels had scared the living daylights out of her. No chance she was going through that again. If the worst came to the worst, she'd stick Bonzer in a pair of cargoes and vest and pretend he was her husband.

'Yay!' Luna jumped up and down, her long, coiled hair flying around her head like a whirling dervish.

'Right, time to get dressed!'

As Luna ran upstairs to her room, Izzy spied the letter she'd tucked behind the fruit bowl, away from little girl eyes. Every time she caught a glimpse of it she shrank a little, knowing the longer she ignored it, the worse things might be. Or better. There was always a possibility.

She looked around her at the cottage, its patches of peeling plaster, its lack of central heating, the damp that seemed to permeate the whole house even though summer had well and truly arrived.

It hadn't even occurred to her to sell it as, apart from a small savings account, this was all she had left of her mum (and dad), but how on earth could she have known it was going to be like this?

137

She should've sold it the second she found out about it and moved to Bristol instead. Tantalizingly close, just across the mouth of the Severn River, and yet, oh so far.

She'd been so busy the past few months. Packing up what she could afford to bring on the plane. Selling or Craigslisting the rest. Answering the barrage of emails from Emily as best she could. Wishing Nr Cardiff was Nr-er to Bristol, or that Cardiff wasn't so insanely far away from London. Why couldn't her parents have had an affair in Brighton? Bloomsbury. Paris, even. They'd both been artistic types. What was the allure of Nr Cardiff?

Who knew? Her mother's tastes had always eluded her, and too late Izzy had realized the millions of questions she should have asked her before she'd died. At least her father had thought of her in his will. She'd done her best to make the flint stone cottage seem the tiniest bit like their simple but perfect beach house they'd left behind in Hawaii, all the while trying to ignore the growing fear that the mould she smelt (and saw) was toxic.

That. And, of course, The Other Thing. She nudged the letter out from between the bowl and the wall, eyes glued as it fell open, the name of the hospital and the department in bright blue lettering at the top of the page, glowing like a neon sign.

Oncology Department

She could hear Emily's voice in her head, 'Deal with it. Now!'

Bonzer batted at her chest. It was like he knew.

Izzy shoved the letter in the pocket of her cut-off jeans. She'd look at it later.

*

'Wait. What? *Who?*' Emily was properly regretting taking Callum's call. His love life was definitely not an emergency. The fact he wanted her to move out, however, was.

'A *boy*-friend.' Callum said it really slowly, as if she were a thicko. Then, 'He's called Ernesto. He's Spanish.' Callum made a trill of his tongue wrapped up with a click of the fingers and an *Olé!*

'*Bueno*,' she said flatly, then, 'I thought you were in Vienna today.'

'Yes indeed. We met at the Regenbogen parade. He's a musician. That's why we need your room. So he can set up his studio.'

Puta madre. Trust Callum to have his 'some enchanted evening' with Barcelona's answer to Moby. If she'd gone on his EuroPride Tour with him as requested, she'd very likely not be in this mess.

'You'll like him,' Callum gushed. 'I can't wait for you two to meet.'

As he yammered on about the perfect place in Soho to eat because he thought meeting at the flat would be awkward *all things considered*, she shook the phone, praying something, *anything*, would magically change the fact that Callum was dumping her by FaceTime. Why couldn't he have text-dumped her like a normal person? Not that it was really dumping seeing as they were only friends, but . . . even so . . .

She stomped down the road to her appointment. How was she going to find somewhere new to live by the end of the month?

There was always her parents' place. The basement 'granny flat' was kept in pristine condition for her inevitable return to care for them in their dotage like a good little spinster daughter.

'Soo . . . you need me out by the end of July? If I'm working and packing, how much time does that leave us for Brighton?'

Callum put on his apology face. It needed work. 'About Brighton . . . Ernesto's never been and with only the one room booked—'

She made a screeching noise. 'No. Please. I get it.' Emily didn't need Callum to spell it out. Boyfriend trumped flatmate. Ex-flatmate. Whatever.

'You okay, Emms?'

Oh, now he cared.

'Brilliant. I'm on my way to a meeting. Better go.'

'Emmzzzz. C'mon, baby. I know there's some hurt going on in there.'

'What do you want me to say? You've met me. I'm not going to cry. I don't have feelings.' She had loads of feelings. She just didn't want to show them.

Maybe she'd go and see Izzy.

Emily thought about their last text exchange.

Emz! Reeeeeeks of mould in here. There're big, dark stains on the ceilings.

　Any chance you could come out with a Petri dish or something sometime? It'd be a shame to die before . . . you know . . . it's time to die. Love to Callum. xx

A shudder ran down Emily's spine. *Euuurgh. Wales.* Thank god 'gay time' moved at an exponential rate of knots and the standard two-year relationship could be boiled down to a fortnight. She would stay in one of the on-call rooms.

Callum's whole 'I've met the love of my life' thing would blow over soon enough.

'Got another call coming in. Have a great time! Kisses to Ernesto!' No one in their right mind would've thought she sounded sincere.

'Thanks, doll face! Love you!'

'Yeah.' Whatever.

Emily rammed her phone into her backpack and stomped to the sky-blue terraced house in the middle of the pastel-painted block. She'd have to build up to ringing her mum about the flat. Right now she had other worries.

She pulled her hair into a ponytail before taking the handful of steps up to the slightly chipped, sunny yellow door. She took a couple of breaths before she triple-thumped the knocker with a bit more reverb than anticipated, stepping back in a ridiculous attempt to make it look as though someone else had pounded it and she'd only just shown up.

Her parents would be mortified if they knew about this. In all honesty, *she* was mortified. Which is why she'd told precisely no one. She'd only been to two sessions and they'd been so long ago she was pretty sure this one would count as starting again.

'Emily!'

Noomi held the door open wide and beamed at her. Noomi was a beamer. Something to do with her Icelandic heritage and lots of oily fish, she supposed. That or the fact she made her living by hugging people.

'Don't be shy. Come on in.'

It wasn't shyness that was holding her back.

Noomi beckoned for her to come in. 'It's a half-hour session today, right?'

'Ummm.' Emily tripped as she entered the doorway. *Skillz*. 'I'm pretty sure it was the full hour.'

'Of course. Sorry.' Noomi thunked her forehead then ushered Emily through a cloud of mint-and-grapefruit-scented air into the Victorian tiled corridor. 'I'm such an airhead.'

Yes. She was. Emily was beginning to wonder if she had a thing for airheads. Well. Not airheads exactly. People who were connected to the more . . . *elemental* components of being a human. Like feeling comfortable in their own skin. The way Callum was. And Izzy. Was that why she'd looked at the brochure she normally would've thrown away and booked an appointment? To one day realize that deep-seeded desire to be hugged and not instantly go rigid with an all-consuming discomfort. Sometimes Emily wondered if she'd been doled out extra helpings of back-off vibes when she was born. Even as a little kid she'd preferred a wide arc between her and the other kids. My space. Your space. And a big fat empty area in between the two.

'Right, Emily,' Noomi led her into the room kitted out with an abundance of soft furnishings and natural light. 'Was it just the cuddling today or was it half cuddling half coffee and connect?'

'The former.'

'Good! Excellent. Shall we get down to it?'

Noomi invited her to sit down and said they'd start with a 'back hug' to ease into things. She walked behind Emily, knelt down and slowly closed the space between them, touching first one arm, then the other as, cell by cell, Emily felt herself stiffen.

Chapter Twelve

'You sure you're all right to drive?'

Charlotte glanced across at Freya just long enough for the car to drift into the next lane and yet another volley of horns to sound.

Freya's grip on the door handle tightened as Charlotte pulled the car back into the fast lane behind Monty. The choice of lane had been thoughtless of him, given the fact Charlotte was suffering great emotional distress. 'You can just say, Lotts. I'm happy to take a turn at the wheel.' Not that she was sure she'd do much better, given her own emotionally charged state.

'Maybe if we hold fire on the rest of the Oli questions till we get there?'

'Of course. Whatever you want.' Freya swallowed down a lump of guilt. Not launching into Monty between London and the Oxford services had taken near enough all the will-power she possessed. She had long ago vowed to follow her parents' lead to never, ever, have a free-for-all in front of the children. As such, once she'd ensured everyone had had a wee, had unearthed the children's reusable drinks bottles from the cool box (un-aired and smelling of bleach) and waved Monty and the kids off before finally jumping into Charlotte's car, she had an almost biological need to tear apart someone else's husband in a vain attempt not to feel so alone.

Charlotte, on the flipside, appeared to be experiencing an entirely different breed of shell shock. The kind that didn't involve fielding 'how low did he go?' questions from Freya.

Another lump of guilt followed the first. Rather than shredding husbands to bits, Freya had wanted to be the friend who offered that jewel of advice. The one that would provide a beacon of hope to Charlotte in this, her darkest hour. Proof that Freya still had the capacity for insight and compassion when all she really wanted to do was paper-cut her husband to death with the year's worth of unpaid council tax bills she'd just discovered. She fretted at a hangnail. Who tidily stuffed overdue notices under the cutlery tray anyhow?

Someone with something to hide.

The betrayal she was feeling was on a par to discovering he'd slept with someone else. Courtesy of the unpaid bills, their own home could now be beyond their financial reach.

'Did you see the piece about the Sittingstone Larder in *Waitrose Weekend*? I thought the photographer really captured the place brilliantly. Lady Venetia was such a natural,' Charlotte said after a few moments' silence.

'Yes!' Yes, Freya had. She'd become a loyalty cardholder so that the magazine came free along with a café latte. She'd bought an 80p cabbage as well, so hadn't felt a complete freeloader. 'Wonderful. I absolutely loved it.' And she had also been tooth-grindingly jealous that she didn't have a dowager countess swooping into her life in her time of need. 'You looked brilliant. I can't believe how many products you've got in the shop now.'

Charlotte flushed and waved her off. Freya nodded back to the heavy traffic. It was as if the whole of Britain were heading to Wales today. The whole of Britain minus Emily and Izzy, who still had yet to say whether or not they were going to come. They had to. If she fell to bits, who would look after Charlotte?

'It was silly really.' Charlotte, despite the protestation, sounded proud. 'Lady Venetia insisted I be in the photo as well, but it should've just been her.'

'What? Why? You did all the work.'

'Sure, but—'

'But nothing, Charlotte. It was your brain, your creativity and your hard work that turned that scruffy little shed into something the Waitrose crowd would flock to, not her. I'm sure she's absolutely fab, but don't you go thinking just because Oli tore your self-confidence to bits that you need to give Lady Venetia the credit for the Larder. That's all you.'

Charlotte gave Freya's knee a pat. 'Let's talk about you for a bit, hey?'

'Me? What for?' Freya sat up straighter. Had she been too obvious about not wanting to be within screeching distance of Monty? Or was it that Charlotte genuinely wasn't up for talking about herself right now? *Crumbs.* She wasn't doing a very good job of pushing her own troubles to the side. If only she hadn't lifted up the cutlery tray to find that special spatula she used for pancakes. She'd found it all right. Along with the damning evidence that Monty hadn't paid the council tax in a year. This, despite knowing they were behind on the mortgage to a gut-churning level. She'd have to sell at least an extra two grands' worth of T-shirts if they wanted to pay the big red number at the bottom of the bill. She pictured the requisite number of T-shirts flying out the door with Camden's monied weekend crowd. Positive imagery had been another suggestion from her grief counsellor. As if picturing a vase filled with tulips on Valentine's Day or a shop stuffed with customers could make up for the fact that the one thing she wanted she couldn't have. Her mother back, alive, at the end of the phone, offering her some advice on what to do. Shouting at Monty wouldn't change the fact her designer dream was becoming a nightmare.

'Everything all right with you two?'

'Course. Absolutely fine. Ticking away nicely.'

'Liar.' Charlotte poked her knee then immediately began apologizing. 'Sorry, I didn't mean that. I was just trying to be – well, sticking my foot in it really. I should never try to be funny. I'm not funny.'

'What? Of course you're funny,' Freya fibbed, wishing not talking about Oli didn't mean talking about her instead.

She resisted flicking through the radio channels to find a distraction and flopped back against the leather climate-controlled seat with a fuzz of the lips. 'Anyway. You're right. I am a liar. Much nicer than being called the household Himmler.' She ran her hands along the seat. She'd had no idea they could cool as well as warm.

Charlotte looked horrified. 'Who called you that?'

'Monty.'

'Well, that's not very nice. Or funny.'

'Vell, I kan be vvvery ex-akting!' She could. If Monty became capable of reading a simple list, she wouldn't have to be.

Charlotte indulged her horrible German accent with a laugh and said something about men never seeing the why behind the request. 'There are ramifications for everything,' Charlotte said, as if she knew the fight had started because Monty had tossed a pair of red socks in with the children's white school shirts. 'Men seem to resent the fact that women can see the flaws in their behaviour before they do.'

'Zose are verrry vise vords, meine Freundin.' They were as well.

Freya had been furious when Monty had uncharacteristically lashed back. Told her to back the hell off and let things be; if he'd wanted his life micro-managed he would've stayed back home in Gloucestershire. At least he'd refrained from pulling out the lowest of blows. That she was turning into his mother, the architect of Monty's resistance to making the family's dreams come true. With his older brother following in his builder father's footsteps, Monty's mum had been over the moon when he'd become the first in the family to attend university. Ever since he'd matriculated, his mum had regularly hounded Monty about his unfulfilled potential. The blame for this, in her eyes, fell firmly in Freya's lap. Apparently it was her fault that he'd done human rights law when she'd steered him towards corporate. Definitely her fault he'd not made a go of the micro-brewing, the cheese-making, or the yoghurt. No, she didn't want Monty to fall back on being a tradie because he could. What she wanted was for Freya to take a back seat so that Monty could fulfil all his mother's dreams.

Yes, that particular argument always ground some rather uncomfortable grains of truth into her craw. Today even more so, seeing as she was squirming in a quagmire of contemporary feminist ideals and an old-fashioned desire to have someone else be in charge. Like, for example, her husband.

Oh, Monty.

If she were going to turn into anyone, she'd far rather turn into her own mother, a woman who'd never been fazed by empty bank accounts, enormous workloads and no chance of finding a pot of gold at the end of any rainbow. Her mother simply accepted that this was the life she had chosen when she'd married a dairy farmer. She loved him, so she loved the life. End of story. Freya was beginning to worry that her love for Monty wasn't as robust.

'Well, for the record I think you're much more like . . .' Charlotte chewed on her lips as she sought the perfect person and smiled when she came up with, 'Lady Venetia. A woman who knows what she wants and goes for it.'

Despite the inaccuracy of the comparison, Freya was stupidly pleased. 'Honestly, Charlotte. I'm not trawling for compliments.' She was a little.

'I'm not trying to butter you up,' Charlotte insisted. 'How many women do you know who would invite someone – *last minute* – on their annual family camping trip when their marriage fell to bits over poached pears and Armagnac.'

'Is that when he did it? Over *pudding*?' Freya knew Oli was a selfish git, but honestly. Trust him to wait until she'd served him an entire meal and the blinking *digestif* before pulling the plug.

Charlotte didn't register the question. She swept a French-manicured hand through her hair and glanced up into the rear-view mirror. 'Your children are going to think I'm a proper disaster. Between the chaos at Sittingstone and now this . . .'

'No they won't,' Freya said darkly. 'They live with Monty and me.' Perhaps they could both do with not talking about their lives for the next five hours. 'Have you got any snacks?' She twisted round in the seat. 'Sorry. I was running about putting the remains of the packing together this morning and didn't eat anything.' Once her blood sugar was up she'd be fine.

'Yes, sorry. I forgot to say I picked up a few things while I was waiting for you at the services. There's a bag just behind me and some more things on the back seat.'

Charlotte tipped her head towards the back seat where three brand-spanking-new Waitrose cool bags overflowed with all sorts of delights. Behind her seat, as promised, was another bag that appeared to have all of the crisps ever made in it.

Freya gave a delighted laugh. 'Did you clear out the whole of the services?'

Charlotte threw her an embarrassed smile. 'I'm not entirely sure what happened to me this morning. One minute I was in the kitchen, the next I was in the car realizing I hadn't really prepared anything, so when I got to the services I may have gone a bit OTT.'

Wow. An unprepared Charlotte. This was bad.

Freya had a dig around in one of the bags.

'Hula Hoops! I haven't had Hula Hoops since the kids were wee. Ha!' She flopped back against the seat and pulled open the packet. She adorned a few of her fingers with the cylindrical snacks then grinned.

'Oh my goodness. Freya. Look.'

Freya followed Charlotte's finger to their car where, if the hand gestures were anything to go by, Monty, Felix and Regan were having a boogie. It looked fun. Freya couldn't remember the last time she and the children had had a singsong on the way to school. It was all 'did you remember to do this?' and 'don't forget to tell the headmistress that.' *In-struk-tions.*

Maybe Monty had a point.

As fast as she could, she blurted, 'It was the council tax bill actually. Monty told me ages ago he'd sorted the direct debit and . . .' She threw her hands up in the air trying to decide whether or not to also admit to being scarily behind on their mortgage. 'We're in quite a state of arrears, it seems. Instead of screaming at him like I wanted to, I was very, very bossy about how we loaded up the car, then when we'd finally got the kids and the dog in, my brother called and . . .' She fuzzed her lips and conked her head against the window.

Charlotte's voice dropped an octave. 'Your brother?' And then it went high-pitched. 'Is Rocco all right?'

'Yes, absolutely. Rocco's fine. He's always fine. A hero, really. Best big brother ever. Needs a girlfriend who doesn't mind that he smells of cow poo, but other than that . . . It's Dad, really.' She hoicked round, pulling the seatbelt out and away from her as she retucked one of her flipflop-less feet (dirty) up onto the (cream) leather seat so that she could sit side-on to Charlotte. She'd wipe it off later.

'Is your father all right? It must've been such a blow to him, losing your mother like that.'

It had been a blow to all of them. 'He's not really. Rocco thinks he has dementia. I think it's grief, but if I even *begin* thinking that Rocco's right, I'll start blubbering and I don't want to be all red-eyed when we arrive. Monty'll think I've been weeping about him.' She glared at the car in front of them, where the gestures had become more wild. 'The jobby-flavoured numpty.'

150

Charlotte threw her a look. 'Do I want to know what that means?'

'No,' Freya grinned, imagining the words coming from Charlotte. 'I don't think jobby-flavoured anything should ever enter your far more civilized lexicon.'

Charlotte made a noise as if that was probably a good idea, then tipped her head to the side. 'That's a lot to have on your plate. Fingers crossed, Rocco's just being overprotective. As for you and Monty, are you all right? Financially, I mean.'

'No.' Instead of feeling horrible about the admission, Freya felt strangely relieved. Honesty. With a friend. How novel.

'I'm sorry. That's tough. Anything I can do?'

'You could share your divorce lawyer with me,' Freya joked, then before Charlotte could ask if she meant it, waved the comment away. 'Kidding. Anyway, I shouldn't be dumping all of this on you. It's not like you haven't had a crap time as well. For what it's worth, I hope you drain him dry.'

Charlotte made a difficult-to-pin-down noise. 'It's more the children I'm worried about.'

'You've told them already?'

'No, I had thought we might . . .' Her mouth stayed open, as if she was going to explain what it was she actually thought, then shook her head as if she didn't trust herself. 'We're waiting until they get back from their school trips.'

Freya, who had zero expertise in this department, offered Charlotte a Hula Hoop. She said no, thank you, then gracefully changed the topic. 'How would you like a shop consultation? You're obviously the expert on the shirts and things, but, it seemed to help out at Sittingstone if *Waitrose Weekend* is anything to go by.'

Though she'd already thought of asking her, Freya balked at the suggestion.

She'd always had a fiercely protective need to run the shop on her own. When she'd decided to do a degree in art and textiles, her family had said they'd support her in every way they could but financially – mostly because they couldn't – and she had translated that into a blinkered intensity to prove to them their loving support had been worth it. But now, with the business clearly struggling and, according to Rocco's call this morning, milk prices dropping again, why did it feel so humiliating to say, *yes, please. I need all the help I can get*?

Izzy popped into her head again. People were always giving things to Izzy. Loved doing it, in fact. And Izzy always accepted with a huge smile. As if she couldn't believe her luck. Maybe it was time to learn how to start accepting offers of help instead of pushing them away.

'That would be amazing, Charlotte. Thank you.' She dug round in the bottom of the Hula Hoop bag and came up empty.

'Have some more crisps,' Charlotte urged. 'There's every flavour under the rainbow, including . . . prawn cocktail.'

Freya made a rapturous sound of delight. 'Oh, you are a legend. You won't tell Monty, will you? He'd not let this go. Not after my crusade on E numbers.'

Charlotte turned an invisible key in front of her lips and threw it away with a smile. How nice. To have someone entirely on her side. Suddenly she was ravenous.

'I'll do them.'

Emily's registrar looked at her in shock. No one volunteered to work the entire duration of their kyboshed holiday. 'What? All of them?'

'Yeah. Why not? Sign me up.' She pretended she was hunting for something really important on her phone and reread Izzy's text. It wasn't *strictly* urgent, but it was worrying. Izzy was reaching out. As it was a rare event, Emily's instinct was to pretty much come running. And it did sound like an actual problem.

She had the time now that Callum had flung her to the wolves.

She glanced down at the schedule the registrar was merrily filling in.

'Wait. Sorry. Keep that bit free. I'll work from today to Thursday and let you know tomorrow if I can do the rest. Let's get all of these hips *replaced!*' She put her hand up as Noomi had suggested. *Initiating physical contact gives you control of how far it goes.*

The registrar went in for a fist bump as she went for a high five. It was all very awkward.

They both pretended it hadn't happened. He tapped his tablet. 'Thanks, Dr Cheung. You're a life-saver.'

'That's the guys up in cardio – I'm just the *joint* saver.' She dropped an invisible mic and mimed saying *Boom!*

The registrar stared at her for a moment, a poster boy for all exhausted, thirty-something, NHS medical practitioners, then scuttled away. Fair enough. She was being weird. She would've run away, too.

She headed towards one of the on-call rooms and flopped down on the bed. She'd go and see Izzy on Friday. She would. Definitely. It'd make up for not seeing Freya and Charlotte. She'd yet to master being empathetic for someone else's shit life when she was actively engaged in wallowing in the crapitude that was her own sad excuse of an existence.

That. And she had to find a way to move back into her parents' house without dooming herself to a life of constant remorse. *Yes, Ma. You're right. I should've stuck with the violin. And the piano. Physics club. Oxford. Cambridge. Harvard. Princeton.* All of it. She should have done it all and hadn't, because fulfilling even a handful of her parents' dreams had been hard enough. Then again, they'd been right about the doctor thing. She loved it. Maybe they'd be right about living with them and finally learning how to play mah-jong with her 'aunties'.

She picked up her phone to text the registrar and tell him she would work for ever.

Another message pinged in from Izzy. A photo of a black splodge.

Gah! She should go. If she didn't, she'd very possibly be dooming her best friend and child to death by toxic mould.

That sort of negligence eclipsed sulking about having to move back in with her parents.

She tapped out the text and pressed send. She even put in a hug emoji. Noomi would be very proud.

Chapter Thirteen

Freya gave the chilli a distracted stir as she stared out at the ocean. Arriving at the sparsely populated campsite had been like entering their own nook of heaven. She had absolutely no idea how the whole of Britain didn't know about this sheep field by the sea. Not that she was going to start advertising it. One deep breath of the sun-warmed, tangy air and she felt the tiniest of layers of her 'real-life problems' ease away. The tents were up. Monty had been surprisingly good about helping to unpack the car, organizing the fire, setting up the tripod which she never seemed to manage on her own and, as ever, keeping the kids entertained while she and Charlotte sorted out their makeshift kitchen. The wind wasn't too strong tonight, but there had been 'weather' predicted.

'Ready, Mum?'

'Yes, sorry darlin'. I was away with the fairies. Here you are. Take that extra bowl over to your brother, would you Regan? Chilli, Monts?' Freya held the ladle above the flame-licked pot. 'The tripod worked a treat over the fire,' she said when he didn't answer.

'What a lucky wife you are, eh? To have such a handy husband.' Monty kissed her cheek, took one of the battered tin camping plates they'd bought as newlyweds and drifted off after Regan and Jack who were sitting at a wooden table in the old lambing shed.

How lucky, she thought, to have such a selective memory. All right, fine. *Yes.* He had been handy putting up the tent. A big burnt-orange number the twins were beginning to balk at sharing with their parents. He'd unpacked the rooftop storage case and helped Charlotte with the gargantuan tent she'd bought at one of those outdoor shops near the Brecon Beacons. He had also started a truly excellent campfire. All of which he'd done *after* the game of squirt guns had fallen apart when Felix had tripped over a log and broken one of the arms off his glasses. Another forty-odd quid down the drain.

She wondered if this skill – the selective memory – was how he managed to be at peace with himself. That. Or he was doing what she was. Stupidly hoping against hope she would sort herself out and earn some more money. In moments of brutal honesty, she knew she'd be better off designing pants for Sainsbury's. A reliable salary. A pension. Nice benefits if she included the staff discount. Maybe she should give Gok Wan's people a call. She'd taken a textiles course with one of his minions back in the day. She thought of her shop and then . . . failure. Maybe she should read that book about how to fail? Freya felt the familiar sickening knot in her stomach. She didn't feel particularly ready for that reality yet.

'Here, Freya.' Charlotte pulled the tinfoil-covered garlic bread out of the fire. 'Why don't I bring this over to the shed and you sort yourself out. No more serving everyone, all right?'

'Thank you.' She meant it.

'No,' corrected Charlotte with a wag of her finger. 'It's me who should be thanking you. This is bliss. Just what I needed. Perfect place to blow away the cobwebs. France and Namibia have their lures, but I think the children are missing out.'

Somehow Freya doubted that compost toilets and a bumpy old sheep field would have quite the appeal of Cannes and dune-surfing in Africa, but you never knew. Charlotte seemed to be enjoying it. Charlotte took the bowl of chilli and wrapped the garlic bread in an oven mitt Freya didn't remember owning, then went over to join Monty and the children.

She pressed her hands against her lower back and stretched, taking a moment to soak it all in. Almost ten o'clock and the sun was still yet to fully set. The campsite was basically a field belonging to a farm that abutted the sea. They'd discovered it one hot summer when the shop had been doing really well and Monty, fed up with trying to entertain toddlers in a sticky, sweaty London, had packed them all into the car and headed west. At that juncture, all the advertising the site had was a cardboard sign with an arrow and the words Earthly Delights. Monty had taken it as a sign. Freya had made a run of T-shirts when they'd got back featuring the arrow and the sign, and added in a tent. They'd sold well for a bit. Londoners only wore camping-related items ironically and the economy had been about to crash, so unicorns took over from there.

It was such a beautiful site she was surprised the elderly owners – Allun and Olwyn Collins – didn't want to keep it to themselves. Apparently the grazing wasn't up to much. Once they took off the first cut of hay in May, there wasn't much chance of a second cut, so they'd done what all farmers did: tried to make some money out of it another way.

Allun had since passed away, but Olwyn still ran her sheep and the campsite, never booking in more than five or so families at a time. Her sons dealt with any big problems these days but, like many farmers, weren't much for chitchat. Silently loping in and out, fixing things, but not hanging about for fanfare or praise at a job well done. Just like her brother.

They'd not seen Olwyn yet, but, if it was like every other year, she'd appear at some point. No doubt with a couple of bottle-fed lambs in the boot of her battered old Defender for the twins to cuddle. She and her boys were always tinkering away with some little addition or another. The hedge, planted back when the twins were toddlers, had thickened up now. The tent was less likely to blow away as it had that first year. A huge old stone sink with a hose attached had appeared a few years back. Stumps as replacements for the canvas chairs that *always* blew away appeared the next. This year it was a pizza oven. The children's eyes had lit up when they saw it, then dulled when they heard Monty had forgotten to bring along the frozen dough that Freya had marked up for the trip in the freezer. The children were less cross about it than she had been.

Freya walked round the hedge so there was nothing between her and the sea.

It was windy, yes. But the seaside often was. A good old blast of sea air felt strangely curative. A hint of the scents of St Andrews, she supposed. The gorgeous sunset didn't hurt either.

She scrubbed a hand across her face. Why couldn't the man follow a simple list? Each and every item Monty had deemed excessive (forgotten), or hadn't been able to fit in the car (forgotten) or actually admitted he'd forgotten was burbling like poison along with the rest of the stew of frustrations that seemed constantly on the boil in her gut. No wonder she'd been losing weight. This latest one, though. This latest one had actually taken her breath away.

How could he have neglected to pay the council tax for *an entire year*? They didn't have that kind of money to pay back. Sure. It was tip-of-the-iceberg stuff and she shouldn't be having a meltdown about it, but the problem wasn't the tip. It was the actual iceberg. The mortgage they'd frozen over a year ago when her business rates had been ratcheted up into the stratosphere. A freeze their bank manager had indicated was due for a thaw. There were the school trips, her business taxes, Regan's violin needed updating, the utility bills. The artisan coffees . . . Food. Funnily enough, with two brand-new teenagers and a husband who all ate like wolves, they were big on food in their house. 'We'll sort it,' Monty had said with that encouraging smile of his. And by 'we' he meant Freya.

As the sun dipped below the horizon, she was hit with a swift and merciless fear that she simply didn't have it in her to dig them out this time. Sure. Monty could've told her about the council tax, but if there'd been money in the coffers, it wouldn't have been an issue. Perhaps he didn't tell her because he knew how she would feel. Like a couple of chickens with paper bags over their heads. There would have to be changes. Big changes. And for the first time ever Freya wondered if it was actually Monty who'd backed the wrong horse on the marriage front . . .

'Would you like a marshmallow?' Regan held open the pack for Charlotte. 'Mum's coming in a minute. After she's had her shower.'

Freya had begun doing that after the first night. Serving dinner, wandering off to the sea 'for a quiet moment', going for a shower then making a bit of a show of being tired and ready for bed when she came back and realized they were all still up.

Charlotte was worried. Normally Freya vented. Quiet Freya was concerning.

'Charlotte?' Regan shook the bag of marshmallows, immediately pulling Dumbledore the dog out of his fireside snooze and into a state of high alert. 'Mrs Mayfield?'

'Charlotte, please. Call me Charlotte,' Charlotte said, all of a sudden realizing she wouldn't actually *be* Mrs Mayfield that much longer. Would she keep the name or go back to her maiden name, Bunce? 'Thank you. Not just yet. You go on ahead,' Charlotte teased at a loose string on one of the embroidered flowers on her skirt. Alliums, the shop assistant had said in an authoritative way that had reminded her of her mother-in-law. A woman used to having whatever she said accepted as gospel. Perhaps that came with the name. A 'Verity' was hardly going to be a wilting flower, was she?

She half rose to retrieve the mini sewing kit she always kept in her cavernous handbag then, remembering she had no one to be exactingly perfect for anymore, yanked the cotton free. Or was this hemp? She did try to hit all of Freya's briefs when shopping. Local, Fairtrade and organic were the flags Freya had always waved. She thought it best not to mention the fact that she'd noticed the T-shirts she'd bought from Freya's online shop had come direct from Bangladesh, something she'd once sworn she would never do. Charlotte had no idea about sourcing these things, but she was sure Freya would've counterbalanced with a good deed. Like opening a school. Or sending books. Heaven knew they must have stacks of them lying about, the way Felix tore through them. She wasn't entirely sure she'd ever seen her own son voluntarily reading a book.

Monty loped over from the shed, camera looped round his neck. Monty never seemed to plain old walk anywhere. Running, loping, striding. He was full of verve. Shame it hadn't translated to the paperwork that Freya said he'd neglected to do. Charlotte would have loved to offer Freya some financial help, but with things being so up in the air on her side, and knowing how proud Freya was . . . Besides. She'd yet to receive the email that Oli had promised would be coming her way from his lawyers. It'd be interesting to see what that had to say.

'All right there, Lotte? Mind if I take a quick snap?' Monty took the picture without waiting for an answer. 'Enjoying your de-luxe camping chair?'

'Loving it.' She was actually. She ran her hands along the durable, reinforced stitching and gave him a toothy grin. 'Look.' She moved her hands like a show model. 'It even has side pockets!'

She'd bought it from one of the camping outlets that Freya kept none-too-subtly pointing out once they'd pulled off the motorway. She should've cottoned on earlier when Freya went into an elaborate story about last year's camping excursion and how the children had grown so much they'd spent half the night elbowing one another in the face. A cue, she realized, to remember she didn't own a tent. After she'd found a sleeping bag (on special offer), Freya had actually cheered and crowed, 'That'll show him', when she'd settled on a tent that was full price. Is this what almost-divorcées did? Buy insanely expensive, startlingly pink, two-bedroom – with additional central cooking/living area – tents on their husband's debit cards?

Charlotte made a visor out of her hand (Monty had yet to turn off his head torch) and smiled up at him. 'I may never leave.'

'Good,' Monty gave her shoulder a squeeze.

'May I?' Monty gestured to the stump beside her and pulled a tin of lager out of his windbreaker.

'Please.'

He cracked the can open then furtively glanced about. 'While the cat's away . . .' He waggled his eyebrows then took a few long gulps, as if he'd been dreaming of this moment the entire day.

'Lotte . . . just for the record, anything Freya says goes for the both of us, but I want you to know from me that I think Oliver has well and truly lost it. The plot I mean.'

'Ohhhh . . .' Her smile faltered. 'That's very kind, Monty, but you don't have to say that.'

'I know. I wanted to. The man's an idiot. Anyone in their right mind would be falling over backwards to keep you happy.'

Charlotte was finding herself quite drawn to Monty. Not in a sexy way, obviously. More . . . a strange sort of admiration for his relentless optimism. Perhaps if he put a bit more energy towards keeping the family finances in order . . .

Again, he drank deeply. 'Is, ummm . . . how do you think Freya's getting on?'

'Oh! Well . . .' What did one do here? At home she would've lied through her teeth. 'I think she might be a bit upset actually.'

Monty scrubbed his hands through his hair.

'Yeah. Ummm. I think that might be my fault.'

Charlotte didn't say anything. She often found this was best. 'You know I love her, right?'

Charlotte sat upright. 'Of course, Monty. No one's doubting that.' Except, perhaps, Freya.

'Good. Good.' He kept on nodding, staring at the fire, his mind catching up with his body, perhaps. The two didn't often seem to work in tandem. Like a puppy. 'I should probably get a job. Help her out. Time just seems . . . well, you look after two teenagers. It's like your life is eaten alive by chauffeuring them everywhere and PE bags and whose laundry is or isn't done, you know? And tied to the oven and the dishwasher! I mean, they never stop eating. Any of them!'

Charlotte nodded. She knew. She also knew how little credit someone who was 'just' a housewife or house-husband received for the endless ream of details and chores. Some days she thought of herself as the family CEO. Others, a mere skivvy.

Monty swiped at the air. 'I shouldn't complain. Freya shoulders a lot, you know. I probably shouldn't say anything, but the shop isn't doing as well as it once did. And with her mum dying and her brother looking after her dad and all . . . did she tell you about the milk prices?'

Charlotte shook her head no, but Monty didn't need to explain they were bad. It had been all over the news lately. Small family dairy farmers were going out of business at a shocking rate.

'It's a lot for her to deal with.' He rubbed his own neck, as if the weight of it all had landed on him as well. 'I suppose I could always hang up my proverbial pinny and get a proper job. Building trade's looking up again. My brother's just taken on a couple of new guys, but that's out in Bristol, so . . .'

As complicated as their lives sounded, Charlotte's thoughts drifted back to Rocco. He used to drop Freya off at term time. Stay the night sometimes. He'd always reminded her a bit of a cartoon lumberjack. One with a warm, inviting smile. His eyes were green to Freya's dark brown ones. Like the heather, he'd joked once. Since then she'd never been able to look at heather without thinking of him.

'It'd mean more laundry duty for both of us, but do you think she'd be up for that? Me getting a job?'

Freya would probably sob with relief. 'I think it's something you'd be better off discussing with her. I mean, not that I'm not happy to talk.'

Monty flashed her one of those cheeky grins of his and laughed. 'Yeah. Course. I suppose I just look up to Freya so much, I thought I'd test the waters with someone I know she respects. I just . . . I want her to be proud of me but I haven't found the window of time to find my niche yet, you know? That place where I can turn this into this.' He pointed to his head then rubbed his fingers together across some invisible money. 'Any road . . . I shouldn't be dumping on you when you've got . . . well . . . things.'

'We've all got things, Monty.' Big or small, everyone had things.

After he'd retrieved the football that Dumbledore had nosed into the sink, fetched Regan a hoodie, then produced a hay-fever tablet for a violently sneezing Felix, Monty plonked himself back down on the stump next to Charlotte.

Charlotte handed him the bag of marshmallows, which he waved off. 'You know,' she said, 'you are absolutely brilliant with the children.'

He looked across at the twins who'd abandoned their game

of footie and were setting up a game of chess in the lambing shed. 'They're pretty fab, aren't they?'

'Very much so. And a lot of the credit for that goes to you. Maybe teaching's something you could consider.'

His brow scrunched up, as if he were genuinely thinking on it, then shook his head. 'Freya would kill me if I said I wanted to go back to uni again.'

Excuses! Then again, she'd wanted to set up a shop from the day she'd been married and had that ever materialized? It had taken Oli destroying their marriage for her to so much as consider doing something along those lines, so . . . Charlotte cleared her thoughts of her own marriage and tried to channel Freya. What would Freya want most from Monty, apart from a million pounds? Something he could actually give her.

'What about . . . ?' She pierced a marshmallow onto a stick. 'Have you ever considered treating your wife the same way you treat your children?'

'Ha! I don't really think she'd be up for a water-balloon fight.'

It wasn't quite the direction she'd been heading, but who knew? Maybe she'd been jealous. 'Have you asked her?'

'No.' His sunny features briefly clouded then lifted. 'She'd go on about the mess and there'd be the reminders to avoid smashing Felix's specs and, god, you know Freya. She's usually so busy doing stuff she never has time for messing about.'

'Maybe it'd be nice for her to have a reprieve every now and again. What if you and the children were to chip in a bit more so that she'd actually have the time to find out if she likes it?'

She'd often wondered if Oliver was blind to the millions of things she'd done to keep the household in order, or if he simply didn't care. If he had wanted to go out, he'd wanted to go out *now* – oblivious to the fact there were still nappies to change, bottles to fill for the babysitter, and who knew what else left to do before she could so much as think about getting herself ready to go out of the door. Perhaps she'd been the one to draw the line. Made *those types* of chores her own so that she felt she had at least some value. Had Freya made too much of an art of sweeping into a room and grumpily tidying it up whilst her family got on with the business of living? More than once Charlotte had wished she'd been the one guiding a laughing Poppy along on her pony or learning how to use the Wii with Jack.

She tried a different tack. 'Maybe it goes deeper than that.' Charlotte rotated her marshmallow so it wouldn't slip off the stick. 'Perhaps she doesn't feel as though she's part of the gang.'

Monty looked shocked. 'She's part of the gang! She practically *is* the gang! We'd be nothing without her.'

'Does she know that's how you think of her? Or do you think she's lodged herself into the role of She Who Must Be Obeyed?'

Monty's lack of an answer was answer enough.

She pulled her marshmallow out of the fire and tipped it towards him. 'Want to share?'

They ate the marshmallow in silence then, after Monty had toasted another and they'd eaten that too, he nudged her with his elbow.

'You're a wise old duck, you know that Lotte?'

She felt a silly puff of pride. 'I try my best.' It wasn't that great an insight into life. But it was a start.

Monty clapped her on the knee, stretched, yawned, then crushed his can in his hand. 'Right then! I'm off to see if I can get these children of mine to finally learn how to play poker!' He galloped towards them, singing some pop song or other.

Perhaps she should've been sharper with him. Emily would've launched straight into him. Given him a proper tongue-lashing. Of course he should get a job. Of course he should feel badly if things were as bad as Freya was intimating. Then again, from what Monty had said about the business not going so well, perhaps all of the blame might not be entirely his?

Oh, she didn't know. Monty was obviously very much in love with his wife, but Freya was stuck on the fact that he'd betrayed her trust and the bills they faced sounded serious.

If Oliver had broken down after Freya had smashed him in the face with her birthday cake and told Charlotte he still loved her, or had a water-balloon fight with her, would that have been enough to stitch their marriage back together? Build something stronger?

She suddenly, urgently, began to will Monty to do something tangibly helpful so that Freya could forgive him and the pair of them could move on. She wanted their marriage to succeed. Needed it, even. Perhaps it had been a good thing she'd come along. Served as a bit of a buffer between the two of them so tensions didn't escalate past a point of no return. There were, after all, the children to think about. She pulled a guilty face though no one was looking. Both of her children would be heading back to boarding school in the autumn. It was how all the Mayfield children had been raised. They'd sent Poppy off a bit early, but she was very bright and Oliver had thought having her traipsing around the house on her own wasn't for the best. Charlotte hadn't wanted to send her. Said it was too soon and that perhaps it might be nice for the pair of them to have a special mother-daughter year.

Oli had laughed and said no one wanted a child who stayed tied to the apron strings.

Why was it she seemed incapable of putting her foot down with that man?

Because he paid for everything and was posh. It was that simple.

Well! Just because she was raised in a Sheffield council flat didn't make Oliver a better person than her, did it? She was simply going to have to . . . dig deep, or whatever it was a girl did to churn up a bit more self-worth. Her children were hardly going to want to live with a milksop. Her children were her family now. From here on out, she would refuse to let Oliver and his 'Mayfield Ways' take that from her.

She pulled out her phone and sent Poppy a text. In French, as recommended by the course tutors, so as 'not to jar the students out of their immersive experience'. A minute or two later she received a selfie in return. Poppy and her best friend Willow, moodily – Gallicly? – chomping into opposite ends of a rather large baguette. She sent a message to Jack as well, in English, but didn't expect to hear back. He'd gone a bit surly as of late. Most of his mates were off to Eton or Winchester and, the truth was, he simply didn't have the academic leanings for either.

'Hey!' Freya appeared zipped up tight in her onesie, Uggs on her feet and her hair corkscrewing out at odd angles. She looked around, gauging whether or not she needed to launch into her ooo, ohhh, so-tired routine.

'Everyone gone to bed?'

'Poker lesson.'

Freya's eyebrows shot up, then dropped. Her brow crinkled. 'Everything all right?'

Charlotte felt as though she should be asking Freya the same thing. 'Absolutely. Better than all right.' Charlotte meant it, too. She'd just decided to grow a spine. 'Yes I am.'

Whatsapp Conversation: Izzledizzle to Emmzzz

Izzledizzle to Emmzzz: Yahooo! You're coming! Luna ecstatic. Me too, obvs. Wot have you booked a hotel for? You're coming here, right?

Emmzzz to Izzledizzle: Not staying in cottage full of deadly mould even if it is your mother's love shack. I'll book for you and Luna, too. My treat. She eats grown-up food, I presume?

Izzledizzle to Emmzzz: Yes, she's not lost that many teeth! Looks super cute! Natch. #TotesPrejudiced

Izzledizzle to Emmzzz: Been googling. There's a castle down the road with rooms! How cool would that be?

Izzledizzle to Emmzzz: And a Premier Inn just off motorway. They take dogs. Not the castle.

Izzledizzle to Emmzzz: Just stay here at the cottage. Luna and I aren't dead. Yet. *mwah ha ha ha haaaaa*

Emzzz to Izzledizzle: You're sick.

169

Izzledizzle to Emmzzz: That I am.

Emily conked her head against the wall. Hard. Trust Izzy to find the funny side.

Izzy was trying to read Emily's expression, but it was difficult. After the taxi driver had dropped her off and they'd had one of their exceedingly awkward hugs, weirder this time because – for the tiniest fraction of a second – Emily had leaned into it, Emily had on her neutral face. She had yet to leave the doorway, her dark eyes travelling along the ceiling of the cottage.

'Well . . . what do you think?' Izzy held her hands out and twisted side to side, a bit like Luna did when she'd said something clever and was waiting for a reaction. Izzy had sent Luna outside with Bonzer to practise his newly acquired trick of rolling over. She didn't want Luna to get freaked if Emily was freaked. Then she would freak and it would all be very bad.

'It's a death trap waiting to happen.' Emily wasn't one to mince words.

'Seriously? C'mon. You haven't put anything in a beaker or . . . whatever. Did you bring a microscope?'

Emily smirked at her and pointed at her rather swish but compact Burberry handbag. 'Yes. I brought two.'

'Ha ha.' Cow. Lovely cow. But seriously. She'd brought her daughter here. Emily could at least fake it a little. 'Hey! Did you know there's an actual village called Mouldsworth?'

'I did not,' Emily said distractedly.

She was staring at the rather unseemly dark splodges that Izzy had clocked advancing across the ceiling from the windows. Maybe it was pretty bad and she'd just gotten used to it. Like the leaking roof in their rental in Hawaii. She hadn't had the energy to move and, as they were a bit behind on their rent those last few months before the business sold, she'd decided bugging the landlord would be a bad thing. She and Luna had made a game of it. Dodge the bucket.

After a few more seconds inspecting, Emily made a call. 'Izz. You can't stay here.' She said it in a voice that went straight through to Izzy's 'this is actually happening' department. As much as she hated the place, denial kicked in instantly.

'I'll scrub it off. It'll be fine.'

'No. You can't. Experts have to do that, otherwise you'll be practically mainlining the spores. You've probably already . . .' Emily took a step forward onto the swirly 1980s pub-style carpet then realized what she'd done and ducked back into the doorway. Izzy stared at the carpet forlornly. It probably should be ripped out, but her mother had written a poem about it. Published it in her final collection.

'Listen, Izz . . . for you? Toxic mould is the last thing you should be around.'

'We don't know if it's toxic.'

Emily huffed. An obvious display of her frustration at Izzy's persistent need to be optimistic. 'Izz. Mould is bad. Chances that that gunk up there is the toxic variety? I dunno. But even the normal stuff could mean asthma, pneumonia, reduced lung function. It can cause irritation in your eyes, skin, nose—'

'Stop! I get it. What about Luna?' Izzy already knew what she was up against. Luna was who really mattered here.

'Same. Worse maybe, because she's still growing. Would you like me to tell you about the neurological implications of toxic mould?' Emily asked in that fake happy voice of hers that was a portent to doom and gloom. Izzy didn't but Emily told her anyway. 'Mycotoxins like to kill neurons in the brain. That means confusion, dizziness, hallucinations, tremors. And that's just the beginning.'

Oh.

Emily continued her singsong-y lecture on all the things that would start to go wrong unless she were to get the situation sorted. Izzy slumped onto the sofa.

She'd had similar lectures. Ones that she *and* her mother before her had done their best to ignore. Swelling, skin irritation, pain. Scaliness. Izzy and her mum had scoffed at that one. They had African blood coursing through their veins. They were the *queens* of moisturizing. *Scaliness.* Bah.

Izzy ran a finger along the fuzzy edging of the faded peach and cream sofa. The one her mother had stretched out on forty-odd years ago when it would've been new, or near as, no doubt reading poetry aloud to her Scandinavian lover. Izzy wondered what her own Scandinavian lover was doing now. Still chasing waves? Or, now that he was forty-odd, perhaps he'd changed. The website bio didn't give away much, other than that he worked at the family boat-building company. Did he hate it as he'd feared? Or was he properly settled back in Copenhagen with a beautiful wife and a pair of blonde, blue-eyed children who were destined for great things. She teared up a bit. This was precisely why she never thought about him. The man had wanted freedom, not a child. In between torrid sessions of lovemaking he'd told her he craved independence like air. That surfing was his escape from an upbringing that threatened to nail him to Copenhagen and the family business for ever. So, when she'd found out she was pregnant, she'd told him she'd met someone else and they'd gone their separate ways. Him none the wiser about a child born to shoulder a rather different set of burdens.

'Is there mould in the bathroom?' Emily poked her in the thigh.

She nodded and batted Emily's hand away.

'The bedrooms?'

'Yes,' she snapped. 'And the kitchen. Happy?'

Emily looked as though she was going to say something but Izzy beat her to it. 'Yup. As usual, Dizzy Izzy has made a complete hash of everything. C'mon.' She did the 'bring it on' beckoning gesture. 'I can tell you're desperate to say I told you so.'

Emily sat down beside her, trying not to look as repulsed by the sofa as she was by the ceiling. 'Look, Izz. I'm not trying to be evil or bossy or tell you what to do, but . . . you can't live here. Not until you get professionals to sort it, anyway.'

Izzy bit down on the remains of her scowl. She knew. It was just . . . it had taken so much energy to get here in the first place and now they'd have to leave? What was the universe trying to tell her? That she had been wrong to come back? She stared at her fingers, willing the whorls and lines to turn into oracles and point her in the right direction.

Suddenly she couldn't bear being in the little cottage any more. It wasn't cosy, it was cramped. It wasn't twee. Or picture perfect. Or anything like a chocolate box. It was a cheap, two-up, two-down terraced house in Nr Cardiff that had missed the regeneration memo. A postage-stamp garden for Looney and Bonzer. If four squares' worth of paving stones counted as a garden. Bonzer would probably take up all of the floor space in the lounge once he was fully grown. Whenever that happened. Next week? The one after?

'Should we go and find a hotel?' This wasn't Emily being smug. She was trying to help.

'Yes,' Izzy said, then, 'But!'

'But what?' Emily's eyes narrowed. She knew when Izzy got an idea it was difficult to deter her. Emily knew her very well for a friend she rarely saw.

'I think it should be near the girls. Freya and Charlotte. They wanted us to come camping, right?'

'I am not camping.' Emily got up from the sofa and balled her hands into grumpy little fists on her teensy-tiny hips. Emily was hilarious when she was being belligerent. How could someone so petite be so fierce! 'It's out in the middle of god knows where. I doubt there'd be a dog-friendly anything out there.'

'There's bound to be an Airbnb or something.'

'Fine.' Emily glared at her. She hated Airbnbs. Less control over germs. 'And if you think I'm riding out there in that sorry excuse of a van of yours, you have another think coming.'

Izzy smiled. There was the Emily she knew and loved. The one who leaned into hugs – even fractionally – and then freaked out.

'Right then! I'll get me and Looney packed and ready to go.'

'Charlotte?'

She put the book down, using a dandelion Regan had given her earlier as a bookmark, and was shocked to see the sun was already setting. She really had been miles away. 'Sorry, Freya. What can I do? Washing up? Chopping?'

'No. Not a thing. Done it.' Freya had increasingly been in two modes as the week progressed. Frantic or asleep. Frantically scrubbing up dishes. Chopping up kindling.

Cutting apart sausages. And then, abruptly, she would sort of – pffffzzzt! – short-circuit and go to bed.

'I just got another text from Izzy and Emms.'

Charlotte couldn't tell if Freya was happy or angry about it. She chose a neutral response. 'Oh, good! How are they? Did they sort out that mould problem? It sounded horrid.'

Freya shook her head. 'Doesn't look like it.' She chewed on the inside of her cheek. 'They're driving up. Tonight. Emily said she's hunting for a hotel but I know for a fact she won't find one.'

'Why not?'

'There aren't any. It'll take them another hour or so.' She scrubbed a hand through her hair and gave Charlotte a forlorn smile. 'How many more people do you think you could fit inside that tent of yours?'

Two and a half hours, and one rather dramatic arrival by tow-truck later, Emily, Izzy, Luna and an astonishingly large Bonzer were in situ. Izzy, of course, came running at them like a rubber starfish – all limbs and smiles and 'hey, girlies!' This, whilst Emily went straight to the van the driver had unceremoniously deposited at the edge of the field and produced one very large, very clanky box. 'Time to get this party started!'

Freya, who'd been undecided as to whether or not she was entirely pleased with the turn of events, was suddenly flooded with relief. The back-up team had arrived.

Chapter Fourteen

'Right everyone!' Freya clapped her hands until she had the entire group's attention. A feat, considering the children were on sugar highs and Monty was knee-deep in an instruction manual on how to download the footage from the mini time-lapse camera he'd taped to the top of one of the windbreaks to chronicle their holiday.

'Here's the plan for today!'

Monty shouted, 'Boo! I thought the whole point of camping was that there were no plans. Isn't that right kids?' He tried to start a 'No plans, no plans' chant, but Freya shot him a look and the children knew better than to side with Monty when Freya unleashed The Look.

For once, it was rather pleasant being She Who Must Be Obeyed, because this time she wouldn't be telling anyone off. When Izzy, Luna, Emily and Bonzer had arrived the night before, that elusive cure-all she'd been trying to plumb from deep within her had finally surfaced. Me-time. Not alone time as such, but she had to get her head around her insanely overdrawn life, and having her girlfriends to bounce ideas off – or at least listen to her vent – seemed critical if she were going to sort herself out. With no money to pack her family off to a hotel, or a theme park, or anywhere else for that matter, she'd been absolutely floored when Charlotte had said she would like to give Freya a belated fortieth by doing just that.

As uncomfortable as she was accepting hand-outs, Freya had been twisting into an increasing tailspin all week, her failures and Monty's accumulating like tiny little daggers.

It seemed too generous a gift seeing as all she'd given Charlotte were some linen napkins. Pukka, but . . . not quite on a par with paying for her whole family to have a play-day. After Charlotte intimated that she could do with some girl-friend time every bit as much as Freya could, Freya relented.

Charlotte's first suggestion had been for a spa day. But Freya loved it here at the beach, so when they thought up a few options for the children, Charlotte had gone Grouponing. The gesture felt like a lifeline. A friend who could see she was cracking at the seams throwing her a suture kit in the nick of time.

One day. One entire day alone with her and her girlfriends. They needed it. Charlotte's life was in crisis. Freya's life was in crisis. Izzy's sounded pretty up in the air. Even Emily seemed a bit unsettled. Something about things not working out the way she'd thought with Callum. Which, Freya had to admit, hadn't come as much of a surprise. Not that she would ever *ever* broach it with her, because Emily could be so damn uptight, but Callum had been rather . . . *fashionable*, and there was always the thing that had niggled away at her: that maybe just maybe Emily might want to be looking at people of another persuasion?

Anyway. She pictured wine. She pictured snacks. Smelly cheese the children would never eat. There would be giggling. They could talk openly and honestly without worrying about

Monty appearing at exactly the wrong moment. A full twenty-four hours of purging the bleurghhh. Then everything would be fine and they could all go back to their real lives without having a mental breakdown.

'You lot,' she pointed at the children and Monty as if she were a drill sergeant, 'are going on an adventure today.'

'Oh, Mum . . .' Felix wilted onto one of the stump stools. 'If it's one of those seashell things, I've got, like, only twenty-seven chapters before I'm done.' Felix held up his book. It was a wonder the boy's arms weren't bulging with muscles from the weight of the things.

'Unh-unh! No whining. I think you're going to like this. Ready girls?' Izzy was sniggering behind her. Izzy loved a surprise but could rarely keep one. 'On . . . onetwothree!'

The girls popped out from behind her in the sequence they'd practised in the shower block.

'Paintballing!' Charlotte sprayed them all with invisible paint pellets.

The children cheered.

'Off-road Segway tour!' Emily used motorcycle movements instead of Segway movements, but it still elicited a whoop.

Monty was as wide-eyed as the children. He'd wanted to go on a Segway tour for years. Literally. Since they'd been invented.

'And . . . drum roll please, girls.' They all obliged. 'The longest zip wire in the Northern Hemisphere!' Izzy put her hands in the air and raced round the group, making a vrrr-rrooooom noise, then abruptly pulled her arms down and cradled her ribcage. She must've pulled something surfing. It was the second time Freya had seen her do that.

Oblivious to Izzy's moment, the children and Monty were literally jumping up and down with excitement.

'Hey wait!' Monty quirked his head to the side and asked Freya, 'Isn't all of that stuff further up the coast?'

'Yes.' Freya nodded gravely. 'Much further.'

'Sooo . . . won't that take for ever? Getting up there, paint-balling . . . Segway tour . . . feeding and watering the children. You sure you're happy trusting me with them for all of that?'

Well. That was a loaded question.

He flicked his thumb to the children who were busy discussing just how cool a turn of events this was. 'Won't they be a total nightmare tomorrow? We won't get back until well past midnight and you know what Regan's like if she doesn't get her requisite ten hours.'

'Not a problem.' Charlotte crossed to Monty and pulled out her phone. 'Look. I've got you all booked into a log cabin up by the zip wire.' Charlotte quickly continued, 'Since my own children aren't here to spoil, I hope you don't mind me splashing out on yours.' Monty didn't. 'There's a café on site that does takeaways. There's also a mobile pizza truck—'

The children tuned back in at 'pizza truck', whooped and immediately began negotiating toppings.

Charlotte continued over the din, 'There's a small shop if you need anything else. All you need to do is pack a change of clothes and you're all sorted.'

Luna asked if she could bring Bonzer. Izzy gracefully covered by pulling out the koala toy that Freya remembered seeing at Sittingstone. From the smile on Luna's face, it was clear she knew her daughter very well. Freya had a proud mum moment when Regan put her arm around the little girl and promised to look after her. Luna smiled at her as if she were a princess.

'What about you lot?' Monty finally remembered to ask. 'Don't you want to come, too?'

'Oh, no,' Freya said, putting her arms round Charlotte and Izzy's shoulders as Emily propped her chin on Freya's shoulder. 'We're going to stay here and drink wine.'

'Frey?' Emily held the bottle aloft over Freya's cup. They'd polished off the Pimm's an hour or so ago and had, on Emily's lead, moved on to Prosecco with strawberries.

'Yes, please,' Freya grinned. The day was feeling deliciously sinful, but her family seemed to be happy, if the selfies she'd just received from Regan were anything to go by. Plus she'd eaten some melon and remembered to take her turmeric supplement earlier, so – balance.

Freya took a swig of the icy-cold Prosecco. It was from one of the gorgeous bottles Emily had brought. Miles better than the stuff she'd got from Aldi. Not that Aldi was anything to sneer at. They had all sorts of brilliant things, it was just . . . Oh, who was she kidding? Her principles were dear to her and, given their finances, of course they didn't need fancy fizz in their lives, but it would be nice to splash out on indulgences every now and again. Shop at Waitrose, like Charlotte! It wasn't as if Bob Geldof lived in a hovel and ate gruel to maintain his moral integrity. Maybe if she stopped washing her hair and held a globally lauded couture event to save the rainforest, she could start paying the mortgage again. Sting might come. Or Bono. Gisele Bündchen should, seeing as she was Brazilian.

'So . . . Charlotte.' Izzy, characteristically, didn't bother beating around the bush. 'What happened with Oli?'

Three sets of eyes trained themselves on Charlotte.

'Oh, we're having such a lovely day,' Charlotte put her cup

into the special compartment in her chair and scrunched her nose. 'Do we have to talk about this now?'

Emms gave her the type of nod Freya imagined she would give a patient who was in denial about a hip replacement. 'Yes, you do. C'mon. Rip off the plaster. The sooner you talk, the sooner it'll all be over and done with.'

Charlotte started to protest.

Emily cut her off. 'You know how I am about feelings.' She shuddered to illustrate her point then said, 'But until we know what that husband of yours has done, we're just going to sit here and stare at you . . . *wondering*. Your call.'

Charlotte squirmed in the limelight. 'I'm not sure what you want me to say. That I'm furious? Heartbroken? In pieces? All of the above?'

'If that's what you're feeling.' Izzy was clearly much more *au fait* with the American style of spilling one's guts freely and openly to anyone who would listen.

'Oliver wants a divorce,' Charlotte said simply. 'And he's fathering a child with his lover. Xanthe.'

They all repeated the name like it was a bad word. Then Charlotte, mysteriously, giggled.

'Shithead,' Emily added.

Izzy was looking bewildered. 'I thought at your birthday you said he wanted to make a fresh start.'

'He did. *We* did.' Charlotte worried at Bonzer's forehead fur, which kept flopping back over his eyes. 'I carried on as usual . . . no.' She corrected herself. 'That's not right. I took up Lady Venetia's suggestion to apply myself to something outside the home. Build up a bit of confidence.'

'The Sittingstone Larder,' Freya explained, when Izzy and Emily looked confused. 'Charlotte's turned it into quite a money-spinner for the estate. Waitrose featured it in their weekly magazine!'

Freya hoped she didn't sound jealous. It wasn't as if Waitrose would ever feature a woman who made 'I'm a Polyamorous Unicorn' T-shirts for a living. A woman who made honeysuckle ball gowns to save the rainforest on the other hand . . . She forced herself away from the insane daydream and tuned back in to Charlotte.

'As wonderful as it's been, the truth was it was helping me turn a blind eye to the fact that Oli had never stopped seeing her.'

Izzy sucked her teeth.

Emily muttered something in Mandarin.

Freya gave Charlotte a sympathetic nod. 'Did he tell you as much?'

'He told me he was trying to end things with her, but that with the baby situation it was a delicate matter and that he needed to tread carefully. Then a few days ago, Oli came home from the office, I'd cooked us both a nice supper and, over pudding, he announced he was leaving me.'

No one said a word.

Charlotte leant back in her chair, a philosophical look replacing the lost, hurt one. 'The funny thing was, I wasn't even surprised. I was just waiting for it really. I'm not sure who I feel more sorry for.'

'Not him, surely?' Emily made another round with the Prosecco bottle.

'No, but . . . I'm not entirely sure this is what Oli wants. I think he feels a bit trapped by the situation.'

Freya almost spluttered her Prosecco back into its glass. 'Charlotte. You shouldn't be wasting even a moment's compassion on that man. He's lied to you.' So had her husband. 'And cheated.' There. No comparison.

'The guy's a total douche,' Izzy said. 'Throw him to the sharks, babes.'

'Let Charlotte speak, people.' Emily held up her hand to quell their babble and they instantly fell silent. Mrs Cheung was right. Emily definitely could've been the UN Secretary-General if she'd wanted.

Izzy clapped her hands for Bonzer, who boinged over to her and engulfed her lap. Dumbledore wandered over and took his place by Charlotte's knee. She was clearly sending out dog-cuddle vibes.

Izzy asked Charlotte, 'Do you know what you're going to do?'

'Not really. It's obviously all very new, but . . . of course there are the children to think about.'

'Are they okay?' Freya's children would murder her if she left Monty. They adored him, with a capital A. There was a good reason for that.

'They don't know. Oli intentionally waited until they'd gone on their school trips to tell me.' Her eyebrows lifted. 'He's asked me to come up with a "party line" for their return.'

'He did not.' Freya wished she'd thrown all three cakes at Oli now.

Charlotte nodded then admitted, 'I actually agree. The children don't need to get caught up in all of this. They'll be off to boarding school in the autumn anyway, so it won't be as if the whole sordid mess will be playing out in front of them, but . . .' She pressed her fingers to her mouth as if stemming a silent sob. 'But they are getting older and we mustn't treat them like small children.'

'How do you think they're going to take it?' Emily asked.

Charlotte tipped her head from side to side, as if letting each of her children's perspectives slip into place. 'Well. Jack is a typical boy and rarely externalizes any of his feelings – but he worships his father. Poppy is a different kettle of fish. She's been quite withdrawn lately. Ever since she's been boarding. I'm worried about her and yanking the one stable thing in her life out from under her . . .' Her voice caught in her throat.

'Hey.' Freya gave Charlotte's knee a rub. It was awful knowing your kid was hurting. Doubly so if you were the reason why. Well . . . if your jackass of a husband was the reason why.

Charlotte teased the hair away from Dumbledore's eyes, the way she might have her daughter's thick fringe. 'I've always hated sending the children to boarding school. I wish I'd made that clearer. Pressed my point. Especially in Poppy's case. They're my children every bit as much as they're his and if I thought for one minute being there was hurting them, I'd—' The sob that had been trying to work its way out finally came.

Her friends instinctively reached out to her, Izzy putting her arms around her in an uncomfortable hug, Freya stroking her leg; even the usually undemonstrative Emily patted her hand a little. They all made soothing noises, assured her that her kids loved her, told her how brave she was and that she was holding it together brilliantly.

'I'm not so sure about that.' Her face crumpled again. 'If you'll just . . .' And then she bolted off towards the campsite.

'Hey! Lotts!' Emily had to run to catch up to Charlotte. 'Hang on.'

Charlotte didn't say anything, her eyes glued on an unveering path towards the compost loo hut.

Emily tried again. How the hell she'd ended up being the only one running after Charlotte was beyond her. 'Do you, um, want to talk about it?'

Charlotte wheeled on Emily as if she were brandishing pepper spray against a rapist.

They stared at one another, panting. It felt like a scene from a Western, but one in which painful, core-deep emotions stood in for bullets. Ridiculously uncomfortable terrain.

Charlotte jabbed her finger into the air between them. 'Do. Not. Be. Nice. To. Me.'

'Okay. Well. In that case . . .' Emily countered, 'Stop crying.'

'I'm *not* crying,' Charlotte said, swiping away about a million tears. 'I'm fine!'

'No, you're not!'

'I am. I'm fine.' She swept some more tears away and inhaled deeply. 'Look. Obviously life isn't ideal right now, but the last thing I need is to have the most put-together person in the universe offering me advice. Okay?' She turned to go.

'*I do Nordic cuddling!*' Emily shouted.

Charlotte stopped. If she'd been a dog, her ears would've twitched upwards. 'I beg your pardon?'

'Nordic cuddling,' Emily repeated, suddenly feeling as if the admission had cut the restrictive ribbons of her emotional corset. 'I pay someone money, cash usually, to hug me.' She shrugged. 'They also take PayPal.'

Charlotte digested the revelation in her usual way, silently, and then, rather unexpectedly, began to laugh.

'Why didn't you say if you wanted a hug?'

Yuck. No. 'That's lovely, but – it's not about that and anyway – just . . . no.'

Charlotte's tear-flow increased. Nice one, Emms. First her husband, then her children and now Emily was throwing her love back in her face as if it were useless.

'It's nothing to do with you Charlotte. It's my weird upbringing, parental expectations and . . . other stuff. Besides. I was hardly going to confess to *you* – the person *I* think has it all together – what a shambles of a life I lead.'

'But . . .' Charlotte looked genuinely shocked. 'There's no need to impress me. Or pretend. After all, I was pretending *my* life was perfect.'

Emily couldn't bear it. Charlotte didn't have to take the fall for her. Had this been what her marriage had comprised of? Taking the bullet for everyone? 'Okay, look. I was being an idiot. You, on the other hand, were making the best out of a very bad situation. How many people go ahead and have their birthday party when they've just found out their husband is cheating on them? You should win a prize. You are *awesome* at pretending your life is perfect.'

'Thank you!' Charlotte looked strangely pleased. 'You are, too.'

Emily made a face. They were at risk of going overboard here.

Charlotte squinted at Emily then did one of those awkward forward-backwards moves that meant she was thinking about giving Emily a hug.

Emily raised her hands. If they started hugging this out, who knew where it would lead? 'No consolation necessary. I'm not telling you this for sympathy. I'm telling you because I want you to know there's no one out there who's perfect.'

Charlotte didn't look entirely convinced.

Emily tried to pull a leaf off the hedge and ended up pricking her finger. She sucked the blood off it and stared at the minuscule puncture wound. It would most likely go septic and require amputation with the luck she was having this week. 'Lotts. Look. I am truly sorry things didn't work out with Oli, but . . . he didn't adore you. You deserve to be adored.'

'I don't think my children like me very much either.' Charlotte sounded as if she was admitting to mass genocide of baby bunnies.

'Lotts! I'm sure they love you.' She wasn't. They seemed like unappreciative little shits, but . . . she was trying to be nice. 'Look. They probably don't know you. The *real* you that we know. They're kids. Teens. Their worlds revolve around hormones, acne and growth spurts, not being besties with their mum. Whatever it is you think you've failed at – it doesn't matter. We're all a jumble of imperfections. And there are people out there who will love you anyway. Like us! So, how 'bout we concentrate on that, instead of shitty husbands who impregnate their secretaries.'

'She's a junior partner.'

'Whatever. The point being, you're free to live your life on *your* terms now. All you have to do is pick what it is you want to do and go for it.'

Charlotte smiled that gentle costume-drama smile of hers that made you pray for her happy ending.

'Right then,' Emily pointed up to the campsite. 'Shall we

go and give your face a wash then head back to the beach? Get something to eat? We could ask Izzy to make her gooey grilled-cheese sandwiches.'

'Oliver hates cheese sandwiches.' Charlotte's lips were beginning to twitch into a smile.

'All the more reason to do it!' Emily grinned.

'Do what?' Freya, Izzy and the dogs came up behind them on the path, arms and shoulders weighted with towels, bags and the huge frying pan that went atop the tripod.

'Make grilled-cheese sandwiches,' Emily said, as if it had been the plan all along.

'Grilled-cheese sandwiches!' Izzy crowed, as she did an about-face then began whistling the seven dwarves song as they all headed back to the beach.

'What you really need is to get a good lawyer,' Emily said, polishing off her sandwich. 'I hope you're taking him to the cleaners.'

Freya was about to throw out an 'amen' when Charlotte shook her head. 'Anything like that leaves me in a cold sweat. The whole idea of having to negotiate . . . No. I couldn't do it. I don't want to do it.'

Freya shot *help!* glances at Izzy and Emily. Charlotte didn't have anything. The last thing she should do was leave her 'departure package' up to Oli's discretion.

'I've got some good contacts. Let's talk when we're back home.' Emily had her 'I'm not taking no for an answer' face on.

'Please, let's talk about something else.' Despite the cheese sandwiches and supportive chitchat, Charlotte suddenly looked ground down by it all. Freya gave her knee a squeeze. Oli certainly had a lot to answer for.

'No Callum this weekend, Emily?' Freya proactively changed the subject for Charlotte.

Emily waved her hands. 'No. Nope. I don't want to talk about him either.'

Charlotte looked confused. Izzy was about to answer for her, but Emily put a hand over her mouth and explained: 'Callum's just asked me to move out, so I'm a bit stressed.'

A chorus of 'What?'s and 'No!' circled round their group.

'Look, it's not what you think. I'm okay.'

Freya threw a look at Izzy, who arced an eyebrow. Perhaps she too had had suspicions about Callum. Whose team he was on, and all.

'I'm so sorry, Emms. Have you split up?' Charlotte asked.

'No!' Emily floundered. 'It was never like that, we were just . . .' She struggled to find the words.

'Friends with Benefits?' offered Freya.

'FBs,' said Izzy, more mischievously.

'FBs? What's that?' asked Charlotte.

'It means Fuc—'

'It means none of your freaking business!' Emily interrupted, before Izzy could articulate the ruder version of Friends with Benefits. 'Look, it was never like that, we were just friends. The man is as gay as Paree.'

'I knew it!' Freya crowed, then remembered they were meant to be upset because he'd just asked Emily to move out.

'Is it a recent thing? Since the bank holiday?' Charlotte looked utterly befuddled by the revelation.

Izzy drowned her sniggers in Bonzer's furry bonce.

'What are you sniggering about?' Emily snapped at her best friend.

'Sorry!' Izzy put up her hands, not looking all that sorry.

'Anyway,' Emily jabbed a finger at her, pulling a classic turn of the tables, 'you need a plan to get out of that hellhole you're in, missus.'

'What's wrong with your cottage, Izzy?' Charlotte asked. 'You got in so late last night I didn't get to ask.'

'It's falling down around my ears and full of toxic mould,' Izzy answered easily. 'That, and Luna doesn't seem to be fitting in at school. I can't find a job. Plus we've got no friends anywhere near us, it's a forty-minute drive to the nearest town and I can't even get a signal on my mobile. Other than that?' She flashed a bright Izzy smile. 'Life is peachy.'

'It sounds like all our lives are a bit pants,' Freya said.

'Cheers to pants lives!' Emily slopped some of her drink onto her wrist then sucked it off.

'Cheers to *good* lives!' Izzy countered. They all toasted to that.

'Okay.' Freya stuck the flowers she'd been weaving together into a bouquet atop a stick, as if it were a magic wand, then fastened them on with a hairband she'd had around her wrist. 'I grant each of you a wish.'

She waved the wand at Emily. 'Go. Make a wish.'

'I wish . . .' Emily looked as if she were going to say something flippant, then suddenly turned serious. 'I wish I had more time off to see you all more.'

Izzy grabbed her heart and made an 'awww, that's sweet' noise.

'Charlotte? You're next.'

'I wish . . .' Charlotte scrunched her eyes tight, as if she were a little girl about to blow out her birthday candles. 'I wish I could leave my marriage without taking any of Oliver's money.'

'It's not about taking Oli's money, though,' Freya jumped in. 'It's about fairness. He should be made to pay!' Why couldn't Charlotte see this? Emily was right, she needed a good lawyer.

'It's her wish, not ours,' Izzy reminded them.

Izzy was right, of course. Charlotte was finding her voice. It was hard to hear . . . but it was in there. They all told her that it was a very good wish but Freya was pretty sure they were all thinking the same thing: *Fleece him till his bank account bleeds.*

Charlotte took the wand from Freya and put it on Freya's shoulders, as if she were knighting her. 'What's your wish?'

'I wish . . . so many things.' Freya looked at her friends' expectant faces. What she was about to say felt like a confession. 'I wish I could make a living out of the clothes and art I really love making.'

Everyone cheered and told her it was a fabulous wish. Freya's heart skipped a beat. Awwwww.

Charlotte swished the wand in Izzy's direction. 'Just you left, lovely. What do you wish?'

'I wish . . .' She hesitated. 'I wish . . .' She made her decision then said, 'I'm gonna keep this one to myself for a bit.'

'Hey, that's not fair!' Freya said.

'Wishes *are* meant to be secret until they come true,' Charlotte pointed out.

'Exactly, I don't have to tell!' Izzy gave Freya a Meaningful Look then, as a concession, 'I'll tell you when it happens.'

Freya said sorry, silently irked that Izzy always had to be so bloody mysterious.

Out of the corner of her eye she saw Charlotte drumming

her fingers against her lips. You could almost see the wheels whirling behind her green eyes.

'Izzy . . . it's going to take time to sort the cottage out, isn't it?'

Izzy shrugged, 'Probably.'

'Then why don't you and Luna come and stay with me?'

Izzy froze, then abruptly, like the sun coming out from behind a cloud, beamed. 'Seriously?'

Charlotte's smile widened with Izzy's. 'Absolutely. There's a granny flat above the garage next to the pool house. You and Luna would have plenty of room there. You're completely welcome to stay in the house of course. It would be lovely. Especially with the children away and, you know, other things.'

'Well, then,' Izzy's grin actually reached her ears. 'I suppose that's part one of the wish taken care of!'

'What's part two?' Freya couldn't help herself.

Izzy tapped the side of her nose. 'That's for me to know . . .'

Chapter Fifteen

Charlotte gazed at the stars and then back down at their cosy little sprawl of people, blankets and dogs round the fire. For the first time since she'd arrived in Wales, she felt genuinely capable of facing her future. Emily was right. She'd been hiding behind her 'everything's fine' mask for too long.

She'd been treating the seaside cove like a cocoon. A place to shelter from the myriad of pragmatics that lay in wait. Lawyers. Joint bank accounts being cleaved in two. Telling her children their parents were no longer in love.

She wasn't entirely sure the news would come as a revelation. Whilst she hoped the children took her love for them for granted (she'd been sending largely unanswered texts all week), she was afraid Oli's behaviour had coloured their opinion of her. And not for the better.

'Marshmallow?' Freya held out a banana-leaf plate.

'I'll have one.' Emily took a marshmallow.

'I miss my kids,' Freya said.

'I miss Looney,' Izzy buried her head in Bonzer's fluffy coat. He twisted his head round and licked her hand.

Charlotte missed hers too, but she was definitely enjoying this little beach bubble away from real life. Precious days away to absorb the fact her marriage was well and truly over. She loved the children. Of course she did. Would throw herself in front of a car for them. She'd fed them, clothed them, put cool cloths on their heads all night long when they'd needed it. Driven them to the A&E at all hours. For broken arms, asthma attacks, a sore toe. Made birthday cakes, catered to rounds of veganism, nothing but pasta, a raw food diet that had lasted half a day. All of which added up to a love that simply transcended anything she'd ever known.

She patted the Deluxe Folding Chair pocket for the phone. She'd been planning on sending a pair of 'thinking of you' texts to her two. Nothing too sentimental, just . . . letting them know she was here for them. 'Why don't you ring them?'

'No.' Izzy shook her head, looking about as old as her daughter. 'I want to hug her. Have you smelt my daughter? They should bottle that.'

'We can video-call them.' Freya pulled out her phone again.

'Oh, for god's sake!' Emily threw up her hands. 'You know there's a way to fix this.'

'What?' They all looked at her.

'We join them in the morning for the zip wiring.' She threw a naughty look at Charlotte. She'd confessed earlier that she had always wanted to go zip wiring. See if she could get an adrenaline buzz from anything apart from calling a code red.

Charlotte shook her head in an 'oh, you' smiley way. It was fun having secrets with someone. Especially Emily. She'd always been such a dark horse and now they had a secret!

Izzy sat up and beamed. 'That's a *genius* idea. Frey?'

Freya looked round the group, clearly lifted by the growing buzz of a most excellent idea. 'Sounds good to me.'

They all turned to Charlotte. 'You up for a bit of an adrenaline rush, Lotts? Get those cobwebs loose for the next chapter in your life?'

The idea of zip wiring filled Charlotte with absolute terror. Then again, so had going to a party dressed in a frock made entirely of Cheerios, but she'd done that.

She was surrounded by friends. Friends who made her feel safe. Loved, even. 'Yes,' she said, her own smile broadening along with everyone else's. 'I think that's a brilliant idea.'

Chapter Sixteen

Luna ran so fast and hard into Izzy she had to windmill her arms to keep her balance. 'Woah! I missed you, too.' She looked up and saw Monty jogging towards them. 'Everything all right?'

Monty nodded, leant in for a kiss on the cheek. 'She had some growing pains last night. Said she felt a bit achy and sore.'

Izzy's brow instantly furrowed. 'Is she all right?'

'Don't worry. She's good. Felix and Regan used to get them all the time at that age. So we knocked them out with some Calpol and a bit of stretching, didn't we, Luna?' He grinned down at Luna who nodded and smiled shyly, but tightened her grip on her mother's waist. Izzy's mama-bear claws retracted.

Monty had a way of putting people at ease. Even after their silly fling in uni, she'd still valued his friendship.

Izzy dropped down to her daughter's eye level. 'Hey Booboo. Mama's going to go zip wiring, too. What do you think?'

'I've got dibs on Looney!' Regan bounced over and lightly patted Luna's hair as if she were a favoured doll.

'What about your old dad?' Monty pretended to look offended.

Regan rolled her eyes. 'You're in charge of Felix.' She mimed holding a huge book in front of her. 'I've got, like, twenty more chapters. Just . . . wait . . .' And then she pretended to die. Everyone laughed, even more so when Felix, who was sitting over at a picnic table, looked up from his book, saw everyone was staring at him, gave them all an eye-roll, then went straight back to reading. He still had some blue paint on his left cheek.

'You good with that Looney? Zipping with Regan?' Izzy gave her daughter's cheek a pinch and Luna twisted out of it which meant, yes, she was good with it.

'Right then!' Izzy rolled her shoulders back then took a sharp breath in.

'What was that face for?' Emily appeared by her side exactly when she wished she hadn't.

'Nothing. Just my shoulder giving me gyp.'

'Your shoulder,' Emily repeated, as if she'd just asked her to go and fetch a baby dragon from Charlotte's Land Rover.

'Yup,' Izzy said and rolled it again, fighting to hide her grimace as her muscles spasmed behind her boobs. Ugh. It was really beginning to hurt. She probably shouldn't have moved the couch round the other day. She probably shouldn't have done a lot of things.

Emily did her peering thing, as if Izzy's head was actually a Magic 8 ball and it was going to reveal all the secrets Izzy was hiding. Then, unexpectedly, she backed off, smiled and pointed at the zip-wire launch, 'Wanna do a double with me?'

Emily looked at her as if she was insane. 'No.'

'Ohmigawd. You're a scaredy pants, aren't you?' She

whacked her arm round Emily's shoulders and began to baby-talk, 'Have I just found the one thing widdle-biddle Emms is afwaid of?'

'What are you two up to?' Freya bounced up, tugging on a fleece. She was looking less stressy than she had the other night. Good to see that furrow smoothed out of her forehead.

Izzy grabbed Freya with her other arm. 'Emily needs a bit of group hugging. Don't you, Emms? A bit of courage from the girls before her big jump out into the great beyond.'

'Get off!' Emily growled.

'Are we group hugging?' Charlotte appeared from the toilets. Her hair was redone in two adorable Heidi plaits. No make-up. She looked about ten years younger. She was wearing a cute T-shirt (a T-shirt! Charlotte!), with a raccoon wearing a cape. It had to be one of Freya's. She looked nervous, but excited.

Izzy widened the circle so Charlotte could get in but Emily couldn't get out. 'We're definitely group hugging. Little Emmy Wemmy's got the jitters so we're going to hug her better.'

Emily urghed and arghed her protests. Charlotte kept suggesting they let her go, that was probably enough now, while Freya seemed to be the only one who actually wanted a hug. 'Resistance is futile!' Izzy shouted.

When they eventually freed Emily, she grumbled, as expected, then grinned. Izzy loved Emily. Didn't know what she'd do without her. Before Charlotte had saved her bacon, she'd almost suggested that she and Emms should move in together, but there was no way she could get a job that would earn her enough money to pay London rent. This way she could keep Emily's barrage of 'why haven't you done that yet?'s at arm's length.

'So are we going to do the zip thing together or what?' Emily asked Izzy.

'Sure.' She gave Emily's kiss a cheek and grinned as Emily wiped it off as though it was green bogies. That done, Emily said, 'Which leaves the all-important question . . .'

It appeared none of them knew what the all-important question was.

'When shall we four meet again?' Emily asked in her Shakespearean/you're all village idiots voice.

Charlotte's eyes lit up. Izzy shrugged but was excited that Emily was even asking.

'I can't believe you're the one who wants to know.' Freya looked shell-shocked.

Izzy threw out an option. A fictional option, but it was an option. 'Luna and I were hoping to go glamping in Devon next spring. Check out the surf.'

'That's months away.' Charlotte's eyebrows templed. She was clearly hoping to meet up sooner.

Living in her swish granny flat wouldn't be that bad. Izzy could go swimming every day. She'd pay rent. Definitely. When she got a job. There were jobs in East Sussex. Had to be. She'd find a quiet moment, like the hours' long drive back to Cardiff, and say yes.

Freya's brown eyes widened as an idea struck. 'What about the farm? Up in Scotland. At Hogmanay. Why don't you lot come up just after Boxing Day? That way you can do whatever it is you do over the hols, then come up to Scotland!'

'St Andrews?' Izzy said the name as if it was Brigadoon.

'Just outside, yeah.'

'Will Rocco be there?' asked Charlotte, a bit of a spark in

her eye quickly replaced by embarrassment. 'I mean, we wouldn't want to impose on any family traditions.'

'Are you kidding? It's going to be the first Christmas without Mum, so, honestly? It'd be bloody brilliant if you all came.'

'The kids normally go skiing with Oli and his parents around then . . . but things might be different this year . . .' Charlotte's eyes darted between them. 'Would you mind if I brought them? I mean, I could always not come.'

'Don't be ridiculous,' Freya batted away the suggestion. 'There's room enough for everyone.'

Just then they heard the first of their names being called for the zip runs. Freya said she'd go last as she wanted to pop her tote into their car. As she headed towards the car park, they saw Monty take off after her in a run.

Right! Izzy jogged her shoulders up and down. Let the fun begin!

'The car is where?'

Monty couldn't even look Freya in the eye. 'Bailiffs took it.'

'How?' As if it mattered.

Monty looked as though she'd just asked him to explain nuclear fission. 'I don't know. They have remote disablers and keys and . . . I don't know, Frey. I came out this morning to put some stuff in it and there they were and there it went and now it's gone.'

'But it's on a lease! The payments should be on . . .' She stopped herself. Direct debit. Just as the council tax payments should have been. Freya could hardly breathe. She couldn't tell if her heart was pounding so fast that she could no longer track it, or if it had stopped altogether.

Their car had been repossessed while they were on their family holiday.

'At least you had all the camping stuff, right?'

Oh, please tell her Monty was not trying to put a silver lining on this. Blood roared between her ears as she tried to figure out how to handle the situation. Normally she would've torn into him. The children were nowhere in sight. They had the car park to themselves, apart from a solitary security camera that wouldn't catch them if she were to lunge at him and choke the living daylights out of him.

But she couldn't.

Couldn't say anything. Move anything. Think anything.

He'd actually turned her into a zombie.

'What do you want me to do, Frey?' Monty was tugging at his hair, shifting his feet back and forth, peering into her eyes, waiting for an answer. She was always the one he came to for answers. Only this time . . . this time she had nothing.

At least there was an edge of desperation in his voice. That was something.

'I'll talk to Charlotte.'

'And say what?'

Oh, she didn't know. Maybe that her fucking idiot of a husband was proactively trying to make them homeless. That her children would have to nourish their growing brains with gruel. That the Burns-Wests were heading towards becoming a 'more families than ever have been struggling to meet basic bill payments' statistic. That was an option. Slightly inaccurate, self-indulgent, and verging on histrionic, but . . .

'I'll ask her if she can help us get a hire car.' Heaven knew there wasn't anything left on the credit cards. She'd checked last night.

'What? Say ours broke down or something?'

Tears she refused to cry backlogged behind her eyes. The pressure was overwhelming. She blinked, then suddenly saw him afresh, as if a filter had been removed. Here he was. A forty-one-year-old man who'd wanted to be a human rights lawyer who'd ended up a stay-at-home dad. A stay-at-home dad who also did the family accounts. Badly. Unbelievably badly. 'Hide the empty bottles behind the books on the shelves' badly. Was this his fault or hers? They were meant to be a team. If she'd known things were this bad, she would have never, ever . . . No. For what felt like the first time ever, she stopped herself. If she let her temper flare now, there'd be a wildfire. So she walked away. It was the best she could do in a very, very bad situation. What happened next was anybody's guess. Who knew? Maybe she and Charlotte could share a lawyer after all.

Somehow they'd managed to leave the car park together. A combination of numbness and disbelief that any of this was real, she supposed. They were back up near the launch pad, trying not to look as if their lives depended upon Charlotte wrapping up her phone call so that they could ask for yet another favour. She'd thought of asking Emily but as they'd need Charlotte's car in the first instance . . . Yet another swell of nausea churned the remains of her breakfast. Freya wasn't sure she'd ever felt more humiliated.

Emily and Izzy were halfway down their zip line. You could still hear Emily screaming.

Screams she couldn't wait to unleash once it was their turn. Perhaps the ride would whip away some of the truly vile thoughts she was having. About herself. About Monty.

The weight of shame on Monty's slumped shoulders doubled the load on her own. He did genuinely seem to have finally understood just how bad things had become because of his inability to tell her what a shambles he'd made of things. Like a gambling addict at their lowest ebb. She felt like the survivor of an explosion – a bomb built by her very own husband – and was desperately trying to make sense of it all. At the heart of it was one solitary question. Why would he compromise them like this? He'd not only vowed to love and cherish her for ever, he'd done the same for the kids. Right there in front of everyone they knew. Her parents. His parents. All their friends. Promised to care for them. Shelter them. Feed them. Clothe them.

As, she reminded herself, had she.

She had, after all, taken on the mantel of chief breadwinner not out of necessity but by choice. And she was failing at it. On an epic level. It didn't excuse Monty making such a hash of things, but if she'd worked a bit smarter, grasped the need to be stronger about their online presence, maybe none of this would be a problem. Or maybe it would. Perhaps no matter how much money she made, Monty would spend it all. Right now, she simply didn't know. Didn't want to know.

Charlotte walked a bit further away, her expression impossible to read as she talked and listened to whoever it was, Oli maybe, her gaze pinned to the huge slate monument atop the hill. A list of the thousands of the men who'd worked in the quarry back in the day. Many of whom, she supposed, had sacrificed their lives to put a crust of bread on their families' tables.

'Freya, please.' Monty reached out a hand.

She tucked her hands tight beneath her arms, her shoulders

cinched up around her ears as she avoided Monty's bright, blue-eyed gaze. She shouldn't have totted up her business taxes this morning. Adding the app to her phone had been a mistake. Especially when she'd gone on to include the council tax and the arrears on the mortgage. Oh, yes. And the home insurance. She'd had an email confirming that that had lapsed, too. It had been a ridiculous thing to do, but she'd wanted to see Monty again, knowing she had a clear picture of what they'd be facing together. As a family. She'd got that all right. And then some. Emily, who'd been out for a morning run, had found her on the beach and had had to find a paper bag for her to breathe into. Then, of course, been sworn to a vow of silence. Maybe she should ask Emily instead of Charlotte. How bone-crushingly mortifying that she had to ask at all.

Monty tried to pull her in for a cuddle.

She shook her head and very quietly, very firmly said, 'No.'

He huffed and pointed to the quarry. 'No way am I going out there attached to you wondering whether or not you're going to unclip it the whole time.'

They stared out at the zip line they'd chosen. It was an almighty drop. Together, they would step off the wooden platform at the top of the massive quarry. Hanging from nothing but a single wire, they'd career out and over the bare, stripped-out hillside down and over the quarry pond and then into a small woodland.

Monty changed tack. 'Aw, c'mon, Frey. This is our last day of hols. We should enjoy it!'

She stared at him in utter disbelief.

'It's a few thousand pounds. We'll sort it.'

She actually saw red. No they wouldn't. It was a few *tens* of thousands of pounds. Tens of thousands of pounds they simply did not have.

For once Monty's sheepish 'forgive me' smile failed to tease at the edges of her fury. If possible she was even angrier. She didn't want to be this person. Constantly nagging. Raging at the flip of a switch. It wasn't fair to her family. It wasn't fair to her. Freya used to be the fun one!

She looked at her husband. Smiling. Pleading really. He looked lost. Her very own Peter Pan about to walk the plank. *She'd trusted him.*

She remembered her mother once saying a strong marriage was strong because of all the little chips and nicks it had endured through the years. That somehow, with trust and love, those chips and nicks healed and grew stronger.

She didn't want her family to be destroyed because of money. So. 'You'll be more honest in the future? Talk to me. Properly?'

Relief softened Monty's anxious features. Eased the hunch in his shoulders. Glassed over his eyes. 'Absolutely. With every fibre of my being.' He craned his neck, looking past her to where their children had just disappeared down the zip line. Her eyes snagged on his profile.

Monty was the love of her life. She didn't want to hate him. But there was an increasingly large chance they would be homeless if things carried on as they were.

'C'mere.' He took her small hand in his big old wide ones. The hands he'd used to build all of the cupboards in their kitchen. Her shed in the back garden. The one who kept everything going while she went on research trips to meet new suppliers. The ones that had bathed the children while she sat late into the night making new designs. They were softer now than they'd been back when he'd been their resident Monts the Builder. He'd been happier then. More charged with purpose. He led her to a weathered picnic table that overlooked the sprawling vista. They sat down, side by side, both of her hands in both of his. He kissed her fingertips then put them back in her lap.

'I know I cocked up. I should've been honest with you. I should've got a job years ago when the kids started school. Used my degree. Sold some photos. Sold that bloody microbrewery kit. ' He pressed his hands between his knees and they both stared as the blood drained from his thumbs. Then he looked her straight in the eye. 'I was ashamed, Frey. You work so hard for us. I know your dreams aren't being fulfilled, at least in the way you thought they might be, but I guess I just . . . I'd hoped having the kids and me was enough. And we're all so used to you being the capable one. The one who sorts everything out. I'm not like that. I don't have it in me to do what you do.'

Freya wanted to protest. Wanted to remind him how bloody brilliant he would've been as a lawyer. He was so passionate. So intelligent. So caring.

Was that what he was doing now? Laying out his case before her? Both judge and juror of how their marriage would continue?

'I'm going to talk to my parents,' Monty said. 'See if I can get a loan.' He held up his hands because he knew how Freya felt about borrowing money. Especially from his family. 'And I'm going to get a job.'

Her eyes popped wide open. 'Seriously?'

She'd heard that one before.

'Yes. Absolutely. Let's make some changes. The kids are

old enough to start helping out round the house a bit more. I can dust off the old CV. We'll all muck in. We'll do this. Together. As a family.'

She wanted to say yes. Wanted to believe him. But . . . 'I just . . .' Oh, blimey, it was so many things. Trust. Fear. Control. They were all big issues with her. Holding them tight was so much easier than letting go. But had that been part of the problem? Had she held so tight to her dream of running a shop that she'd cornered Monty into being something he wasn't? What if he'd taken that law job? Or a corporate one like his mum had wanted? Would she be the stay-at-home mum? Buying bits of fabric with her pin money, trying to steal the odd free hour to put together a frock to sell on Etsy? Perhaps that's why all of Monty's projects had gone wrong. He was so busy looking after them, he genuinely had no time to make a success of himself. Who knew? They both might be where they'd wanted now if they'd chosen his path and not hers.

Was there not one path wide enough for both of them?

'C'mere, babe.' Monty pulled her into his arms. Arms she had always been powerless to resist. Today she sat rigidly, desperately counting down the seconds until he let go.

'We can't live like this any more,' she said as she eventually extracted herself from the never-ending hug.

'I know, babe. I know.'

Their names were called to go up to the zip-line platform.

She knew he would try to change. He always did. It never worked but at least he tried. Had she? Or each time something like this cropped up, had she simply popped on some blinkers and soldiered on, waiting for him to one day catch up with her vision of who she wanted him to be? The male version of a power woman.

Maybe being strapped to him for a kilometre-long zip ride would do the trick.

'You two ready for the ride of your life?' the guide asked enthusiastically.

'Bring it on!' Monty rubbed his hands together and held out his hand. 'Ready to hurtle yourself out into the great unknown with me?'

Freya thought for a nanosecond then said, 'No. I think I need to do this one alone.'

Charlotte was a bit shell-shocked at how swiftly her real life had pierced through the new-found strength she thought she'd channelled over the past few days.

They'd lost signal for a bit on the drive up, and here, at the top of the quarry, a flurry of messages had pinged in. The first one was from Oli. He'd been held up getting the paperwork together but it should be with her in the next few days. One from Jack with a solitary question mark. Then seven from Poppy. All asking to come home.

They knew about the divorce.

Oliver had told them. By text.

He'd not waited for them to come home. Not rung to form a 'party line'. Nothing. So she did something she hadn't done in a very long time. Followed her instinct. After a tearful 'why is this happening to me?' talk, and a lengthy conversation with Poppy's head of year, Charlotte had booked her daughter on the next flight home. If all went according to plan, and there was no reason why it shouldn't, Charlotte would be holding her baby girl in her arms by the end of the day. Half of her was terrified she wouldn't know what to do, the other half was desperate to reclaim the love and respect she feared she'd lost.

'You all right there, love?'

She looked at the safety instructor and, for one mad moment, considered saying, 'No. No, I'm not all right. My husband's left me for another woman. She's pregnant. By him. At least I presume so. He's also told our children we're splitting up, which he'd promised not to do. I think my daughter's being bullied and that my son's respect for me is subterranean, but other than that . . . things are tickety-boo, ta.'

She didn't of course. She smiled, said she was fine and watched as the lean, corded muscles of his arms stretched and lengthened while he triple-checked the multiple ropes and clips she was attached to. His arms reminded her of Rocco. Freya's brother was a much larger man, of course. Taller. Not fat. Not at all. Just . . . *capable*. One of those men who, given a few minutes, could tinker about with anything and fix it. A tractor. A cow with a dislocated shoulder. A broken heart.

'Safety's off!'

She bent her knees and felt her weight being taken by the double sets of cables and the thick harness. She barely heard the guide doing a swift countdown as he eased her towards the edge of the platform, her heart pounding so hard she couldn't make out what he was saying to her. It didn't matter now. She was flying!

Arms spread wide, she was soaring towards the woodlands. For the first time in she didn't know how long, she let all of her thoughts and worries glide away.

Her broken marriage. Her children's swithering loyalties. The fact she didn't know how long she'd be living in her house. There was nothing she could do about anything over the next ten minutes. No cakes to bake. Shirts to press. Appearances to maintain. It was an extraordinary feeling. This, she thought, was the sensation she wanted to capture as she set off on the next phase of her life. Liberated. Powerful. Free.

Chapter Seventeen

'Mum! Get out!'

'Sorry, darling.' Charlotte made a beeline for the washing basket. 'I was just checking if you had anything that needed urgent washing before your ski trip tomorrow.'

Poppy glared at her then burst into tears.

Charlotte took some tissues off her daughter's bedside table and carried them over to the beanbag, where Poppy had buried her forehead against her knees after flinging her phone to the floor. A lame joke about Boxing Day not having anything to do with tissue boxes briefly flared then fizzled.

A fortnight into the winter holidays, Charlotte had grown accustomed to expecting the unexpected when she dared open Poppy's bedroom door. For the first few days she'd written off her kaleidoscoping moods as exhaustion, hormones, and the fact it was to be the first family Christmas without their father. Though Oli and Xanthe's baby wasn't due until mid-January, Oli had made it very clear his calendar was blocked out. Xanthe had put him on call for emergencies. Emergencies, Charlotte presumed, like proposing to his girlfriend before his divorce had gone through. Not that there'd been an announcement. A trip to Paris and a surprisingly large diamond had made an unexpected appearance on #CheekyLawGirl's Instagram account a couple of weeks back. Izzy had since banned her from the site.

Now that they'd stumbled through Christmas Day (thank you Izzy and Luna for making Wii fun again!), Charlotte was acutely aware that there was definitely more to Poppy's moods than her parents' looming divorce. Unlike Jack, who was constantly out with friends or making plans with friends or gaming over his headsets with friends, Poppy seemed to be increasingly isolated. If she wasn't reading, practising her flute, or thumbing through heaven-knew-what on her phone, she was rewatching *Gilmore Girls* with a near feverish dedication. She'd never once suggested inviting a friend over or going out.

Whenever Charlotte braved suggesting they watch television together or, heaven forbid, talk, there was either a total shutdown or a whirl and strop – Poppy's new signature move. It had swept into their lives after this summer's disastrous divorce announcement and showed few signs of departure.

If it weren't so heartbreaking – the glare, dramatic whirl of hair and rapid-fire departure – it would be funny. 'Classic teenager', Izzy had laughed when she first bore witness to one. *Hilarious!*

If only she knew. She had a little girl who still liked holding hands.

In truth, the only time Poppy seemed truly at peace was when she was playing with Luna. Izzy's ten year old absolutely adored her. Followed her around the same way Bonzer, the not-so-puppy-sized puppy, loped after Luna. She was always trying to copy her hair, giddily accepting hand-me-downs, absolutely loved being experimented on with Poppy's increasingly large eyeliner collection. The genuine smiles and occasional laughs that Luna elicited were just one of the many pluses of having Izzy and Luna living in the granny flat above the garage.

They were just the injection of energy she'd needed to keep the huge family home from feeling like a mausoleum to a failed marriage. Selling the place and moving closer to the children's boarding school had occurred to her more than once, but Jack hadn't spoken to her for a week when she'd suggested as much. Poppy had given a world-weary shrug and said, 'Whatever. It isn't like we actually have a choice, is it?'

At this point, there was an element of truth to it. The past few months had been lived in limbo as the lawyers dug their claws into Charlotte and Oliver's marital history. It was just the sort of thing Charlotte abhorred. Luckily, Emily had found Charlotte an extremely confident lawyer called Hazel Pryce – a quirkily dressed, rainbow-haired woman – whose sole remit seemed to be nailing Oli to the cross. *All good things come at a Pryce!*

The intensity of her crusade against Oli made Charlotte squeamish. She was, after all, entitled to stay in the house until the children were eighteen. She was earning some money of her own (who knew so many farm shops would pay her for her advice?). And there was the monthly direct debit Oli continued to pay into the household account. (*His lawyers probably told him to do that so we couldn't take him to the cleaners, Charlotte. Stay tough. Stay focused. We won't stop until the Pryce is right.*)

Normally she found speaking with someone who regularly referred to herself in the third person tricky terrain, but on days when her daughter was falling to bits in front of her? She was a card-carrying Hazel fan.

'Darling,' Charlotte rubbed Poppy's back and gently wiggled the tissues in front of her. 'Anything I can help with?'

'Look!' Poppy grabbed her phone and virtually flung it at Charlotte before hurling herself across the room onto her bed and curling into a small, weeping ball. Charlotte's favourite cushion, one Freya had given her years ago, absorbed her daughter's tears.

When Charlotte looked at the phone, her frustration with not being able to stem her daughter's histrionics instantly shifted to pain.

CheekyLawGirl's Instagram page.

Charlotte ran her tongue along her upper teeth as she flicked through the images. She wasn't a vain woman, but she certainly wasn't succumbing to lip wrinkles because of her husband's pregnant lover.

Ah.

The chronicles of 'Bump in the City' had gone on holiday. '*Le Bump dans Les Montagnes*' was the latest instalment. A swish chalet in France or Switzerland, from the looks of the gooey cheese she was selflessly forgoing. They must've taken the train as Xanthe wouldn't be allowed to fly this late into her pregnancy. *Honestly.* Did the world really care if Xanthe and Oli were 'seeing out the rest of the year *à la française*'? Charlotte wasn't even sure that was a thing. Unless, of course, you were talking about peas.

As she absorbed the picture, the comments, the time, the date, the penny dropped.

Poppy and Jack were meant to be skiing with their father. Tomorrow. In Austria.

The plan had been to drop the children off at the airport with Oli before she, Izzy and Luna headed up to Scotland.

It was the one bit of normal the children had planned for the holidays. The annual Mayfield Family ski trip: new country, new pistes, new year. Oli's parents, sister and her family went every year and had done so since the children were little.

They hired a huge chalet. The children took overpriced lessons, chased up by insanely priced cake and hot chocolate sessions. The adults had ridiculously boozy lunches. Everyone ate too much, drank too much, stayed up too late and annually declared New Year's Eve *the best time ever*. Charlotte had never really taken to skiing, or the pressure of having *the best time ever*, so was 'given a few days off to pamper herself at home' every year. No one ever noticed that the house was always immaculate when they returned. Regardless, it was the one thing Oli had vowed would stay the same.

It appeared Oli had lied.

Charlotte scrolled down and saw yet another post.

Xanthe gazing thoughtfully out into the middle-distance. A mountainscape at sunset glowed beyond the gauzily curtained window, her diamond-ringed finger held just so . . . Her hair was down, she didn't have on make-up and she was . . . oh . . . she was wearing a hospital gown.

And then the telephone beeped.

Emms: Happy Après Christmas from Ward Seven. Feasted on Twiglets and Christmas cake that tasted of old boot.

Lotte: I would've paid handsomely for some of yours. Next year can you do mail order? How boozy are they? #Askingforafriend

Izz: Hey woman! I'll see if I can bring one up to Scotland with us tommoz. I'm sure there's one kicking around Charlotte's mahooosive pantry. You still taking the train?

Emms: Yup. Surgeries through the rest of today and tomorrow, then off midday on the 27th. See you at cocktail o'clock?

Izz: Deffo. Total chaos at Charlotte's. Looney and I are hiding in the granny flat. ()£&%)ing Oli's bit on the side has gone into labour! In FRANCE!

FREYA: Wot??????

Emms: Way to bury the freaking lead! More deets please, Detective Yeats.

Charlotte: Poppy and I are at Sittingstone delivering cakes. Will hold one back for you Emily. Izzy . . . perhaps it's best to let the dust settle a bit before we air the details on Oliver's situation?

Izz: Sorry, Lotts! My bad! I just thought as skiing was off and we're bringing Pops and Jack up to Scotland it was open news. *zips lips until further notice*

Freya: WOT?????????

Freya put her phone down with a weary sigh. She'd been so excited for Izzy, Loons, Charlotte and Emily to arrive, but Charlotte's children as well? Obviously it wasn't nice to dislike other people's children but *plfffttt* . . . they were just so . . . *bleurgh*.

She started making a mental list for extra bedding, pillows, hot-water bottles and whatever else the over-privileged little so-and-sos would be used to at their fancy boarding school. Chocolates on their pillows at night? A butler?

Freya caught her sourpuss expression as she passed the entrance hall mirror, backtracked then stuck her tongue out at herself. She was being envious, spiteful and ungracious. The perfect trilogy of holiday cheer!

Not.

Her shoulders sagged as the last twenty-four hours swept through her afresh. This wasn't her. She loved huge, boisterous, holiday get-togethers. She loved Christmas! More to the point, she loved coming home. Her annual top-up of 'Burns juju'. Her mum had always made these sorts of unexpected arrivals an adventure, not a burden. Besides. What were a couple of bratty teens when the whole rest of her life was a shambles? She pressed her head to the cool front-door window.

She still couldn't wrap her head round how her childhood home looked the same as it had last Christmas, but felt completely different. The tumbling remains of the stone tower still stood to the side of the huge old house. The cowsheds still circled the yard abutting the back of the house. The grazing and fodder fields still sprawled on for acres and acres until they eventually dipped into the River Tay. Yes, it all looked the same, but none of the comfort or beauty of her childhood home had distracted from just how tough Christmas Day had been.

In keeping with the Scottish style of not acknowledging

the blatantly obvious – everyone desperately missing Freya's mum – they'd all tiptoed over every scrap of minutiae instead.

We're totally happy! We just thought we'd get pyjamas is all. We normally – doesn't matter. Last year's onesie was super big so . . .

If that look's to make sure I kept the receipt—

No, sis. The turkey wasn't dry, I just wanted more gravy is all. Is this a new recipe?

Are these chestnuts in the stuffing? No, no. They're fine. Different. *Good, but different.*

After they'd slogged their way through Christmas dinner and retold all the jokes from the Christmas crackers, they'd retired to the sitting room to play a game. Everyone had been over-polite. Then snappy. Then wildly apologetic. Or, in Monty's case . . . downright childish.

It turned out teasing him about bunking off paying a household bill so he could get her the rather lovely charm bracelet he'd given her had been exactly the wrong thing to say.

How was she meant to have known it was precisely what he'd done? The bracelet was nice, but it was hardly 'The Gift of the Magi'. And it wasn't as if she'd *actually* meant him to bugger off and give her space to think.

Driving through the night to his parents or, more likely, his brother's as it was nearer to the pub, had been yet another show of Monty's emotions outweighing his ever-decreasing common sense. It was taking what little remained of her fortitude to keep the terrifying thought at bay that her marriage may have absorbed its final blow.

She was so tired of it all. The fighting, the worrying, the fear.

She plodded back to the mirror and gave herself a wan smile. As much as she hated him leaving in a roiling cloud of hurt and fury, with Monty gone she had a few days to wrap her head round where they were as a couple and, more pressingly, where they stood as debtors.

Right now, both were looking grim.

They might have their car back, but chances were high it would disappear again. It turned out that Monty had put the debt collector's fee on one of his secret stash credit cards. At least the regular minimum payments explained where the money had gone for the council tax, the water bills and the mortgage. She swallowed down the increasingly familiar tang of guilt, knowing the shop should've really been raking it in during the lead-up to Christmas, but . . . it was as if all the stress had tamped out any sort of creative fire that still might be flickering somewhere deep within her.

She stared at her phone, willing a message notification to ping up.

Nothing.

She supposed she could always text him. Find out if he was lying in a ditch somewhere.

No. She stuffed it back in her pocket. She wasn't ready. The chances of a phone call degenerating into something she well and truly regretted were too high.

So here she was, listlessly making faces at herself, when a normal Boxing Day wouldn't have seen so much as a moment to loiter. With Christmas over and done with, Freya's mum would've roped her into some project or other (baking, sewing, painting name tags for the cows). The children and Monty would've been put to work, too. None of them would've had a moment to think about how awful it had truly been. Then again, it wouldn't have been awful because her mum would have been alive, full of practical advice she would no doubt have followed, and everything would have been less . . . different.

She put a few stray ribbons back into the wrapping paper box and set it at the foot of the stairs along with Monty's favourite jumper. The one with the worn elbows. He would be less than pleased when he realized he'd forgotten it.

She pulled her phone out again, willing a message to ping up. One full of misery and woe and, of course, fathomless apologies for being such a class-A twat on her first Christmas without her mother.

She sighed heavily and dropped onto the cold, stone stairwell. She hoped he felt as miserable as she did. There'd been no need to take the dog. Dumbledore adored it here. All of that cow poo to roll around in. New things to smell. But no. If Monty was miserable, everyone else had to be, too. Score one to Monty!

Freya's eyes drifted round the sitting room while she waited for her father to make up his mind about tea. The Christmas tree was glittering away in the corner. The stockings had been hung by the vast inglenook fireplace. Half the children's presents were still strewn around the place. Books, of course, for Felix. Not the latest and greatest gaming console he'd been hoping for, but . . . Regan had been delighted with her stethoscope and veterinary dictionary. She'd been even more over the moon when she'd unwrapped her nan's pedal-operated sewing machine. Freya wished she could've given her a few bolts of fabric to play around with. She smiled, remembering the endless trips her mum had made to the charity shops for old wool coats, satin dresses, cotton prints. Then on to the woollen mill, where they'd picked up reams of odd-shaped ends going for next to nothing. Their booty was the inspiration behind Freya's first-ever pair of homemade throw pillows. She'd given a set to Charlotte for her wedding. Butterflies, if she remembered correctly.

'Dad, would you like a cup of tea?' she asked again. Normally she didn't ask him. She just made one and he would scoop up the mug in one of his big old capable hands and give her a wink of thanks. This – the asking – was part of a series of cognitive tests she was trying to slip into their day-to-day chat as suggested by her own GP.

'Aye,' Freya's father said. Then, 'No.'

Crumbs. This was exactly the sort of thing Rocco had mentioned. Uncertainty in a man who never dithered. He was a doer. A farmer, first and foremost, but in whatever capacity, he was someone who always knew what to do. Rock solid. Vital. Even at the ripe old age of seventy-three which, suddenly, didn't seem that old. A shiver shunted down Freya's spine. This couldn't be the beginning of the end. Even though it had been almost a year, it felt as if they'd only just lost her mum. She wasn't up to losing her father, too.

She tried again, with a brighter smile this time. One she might have used for the children when they were toddlers.

'I'm making one for Rocco and me.'

'Sit down, love. Freya'll do it. She's probably got the kettle on already.'

Bollocks.

Chapter Eighteen

A niggle of guilt had been needling through Izzy since they left for Scotland. She'd yet to register at the GP's in Sussex. She'd told herself she'd put it off because Charlotte had mentioned, more than once, the possibility of selling the house and moving nearer to the children's school, but honestly . . . ? The last scan had been fine; she'd wanted to focus on that memory rather than facing a new one and the possible nightmare that would ensue. The whole idea of having to go through everything again and then, perhaps, *again* had . . . well, it had given Izzy the excuse she'd wanted to put it off. Who wanted to find out if their cancer had come back? Anybody? Anybody? Yeah. Thought so.

She stuck her face to the spare bedroom window of Freya's family farm.

Some fairy lights were twinkling away on the rowan tree in front of the house. It had been planted a couple of hundred years ago to keep the demons at bay, according to Freya's brilliantly Scottish father. She pressed her nose even closer to the window then screamed. 'Looney! It's snowing!!!'

Izzy did a little happy dance. This was well worth the hours in the car with Charlotte on the journey up with Jack blithering on about how wretched Scotland was going to be when Austria was, obvs, going to be *the absolute best time*. Never mind the fact that Jack and Poppy were the ones who had refused to go with their grandparents. They were both obviously hurt, and vetoing the trip was their only means of sticking it to their father, but even so . . . Poppy had really hurt Luna's feelings when she'd refused to sit next to her. Izzy had been impressed Charlotte hadn't lost her temper or left them at the services. Her mother would've gone ballistic if she'd behaved so rudely. Theodora Yeats did not take to ingratitude. It was one of her mother's perennial life lessons: *Be grateful for what you* do *have, child. Not waste precious time aching for what you don't.*

Which was how, a year ago, when she'd had absolutely nothing, she'd forced herself to look beyond all that she had lost and ended up back here in the UK. It was amazing what looking for the good in life revealed.

Packing up their few possessions and moving back to the UK was probably the scariest thing Izzy had ever done. And that was saying something, considering her history. She'd naively thought what she had dubbed the 'Nr Cardiff' cottage would provide her with the most comfort. Solid evidence that her mother and father had shared something beyond an impassioned one-night stand. Proof family was the foundation of everything, even if it did come in non-traditional packaging.

It wasn't the house, in the end, that had provided the comfort. It was her friendships. She'd been terrified that spring day, showing up with a child she hadn't told anyone but Emily about. Holding so many secrets close to her chest. Apart from a bit of a catch-up, it had been like no time had passed at all. Everyone was exactly as she had remembered them. Emily, still sharp as a whip and scratchily caustic. Freya, able to turn her hand to anything and make it more beautiful. Charlotte was still the cake-maker. The organizer. The fixer.

Which was ultimately why she had accepted Charlotte's offer to move into her granny flat, even after the 'deadly mould' in the Nr Cardiff cottage had turned out to be not so deadly. The black splotches had appeared courtesy of a dodgy bathroom fan and the damp Welsh weather. Emily had helped her sort an electrician and some hardcore cleaners. Freya had sent her countless emoticon messages and hilarious GIFs whenever her spirits had sagged, and Charlotte had organized for Izzy's flat to become a holiday let, administered by a well-established company that had already booked several couples in for a 'magical Welsh getaway'.

'Look Mummy! Towels!'

Luna ran back into their room from heaven-knew-where with a set of well-worn towels. She placed them on the bed then dived straight into tidily unpacking her things into a heavy wooden chest of drawers. Luna was the nester of the two of them.

The niggles came back more powerfully. She really should reach out to Looney's father. If Charlotte sold the house, there was no guarantee they'd be invited to move to her next place. Izzy's house style (slob) was the total opposite to Charlotte's (immaculate). Charlotte had been lovely about helping them out in a crisis, but they were out of sight in the granny flat. If she had to downsize and the Welsh cottage had already been let, then Izzy might well have to find yet another place to live.

Oh, well. There was nothing she could do about it right now, and Charlotte had said she wouldn't think about selling the house until the spring if at all, so . . .

Izzy did a slow twirl in the centre of the room, soaking in the antler lighting fixtures, the dozen or so individually framed pressed flowers, the hand-carved lampstands shaped like owls. 'It's like staying in a quirky art museum.' She shivered. 'A museum without any heat.'

Charlotte, who'd just walked through from her room, tugged her gilet a bit closer round her. It was a lovely shade of maroon that really made her green eyes ping out against her pale skin. Pale skin made paler by the cold? Or worry about Freya, in the wake of Monty having buggered off to his brother's place. Or was it to his parents'? Somewhere near Bristol anyway.

'I suppose it must cost quite a lot to heat the whole house with only Freya's father and brother here on their own.'

'Good point.' Izzy nodded at the four-poster bed. 'I thought Freya was the only arty-farty one, but you said her brother *made* this bed?'

Charlotte nodded, a slightly wistful expression softening her features. Was it for the bed, or Freya's hunky brother who had helped them haul in their nine thousand bags?

Izzy ran her hand along the thick silver birch tree branch that made up one of the four posters of the huge, fairy-tale bed, then pounced on the squeaky mattress, beckoning for Luna and Charlotte to join her. 'Did you see these cushions? I bet Freya made them. They have that Frey-Frey touch, don't they?'

She made fancy hand gestures round the flannel and wool throw pillows, as if she were a model on the shopping channel. They really were spectacular. Ink and tartan cut-outs stitched onto all sorts of different fabrics, with the odd embroidered embellishment. Red deer. Otters. Highland cattle. All of them anthropomorphized to look as though they were at some sort of Highland Mad Hatter's tea party. They were wonderful. The embellishments showed off Freya's amazing skill at capturing the tiniest details. A miniature kingfisher dipping its beak into an exquisite cup of tea. A stag, with its head cocked, as if it were listening to the sounds that the wind beyond the window was carrying.

Luna, who hadn't taken up the invitation to jump on the bed, was still exploring the room. Opening doors and drawers, oohing and aahing as she went. 'Mum! Look! It's a secret passageway!' She held open a door that Izzy hadn't spied, took a step in then hesitated. 'Can you go first?'

'Of course, Booboo!' Izzy bounced over to the door. This sort of bravery she could do.

She dramatically tiptoed along the short corridor and tried to open the door at the end of it. 'Nope. Locked. Maybe it's one of those olden days passages where the rich people snuck into one another's rooms without the servants knowing.'

Charlotte laughed, 'Izzy, your imagination is about a thousand times more fertile than mine. I would've thought it was for the servants to carry wood to each of the rooms for the fires in the morning.'

'Do they still have servants?' Luna was wide-eyed with wonder.

'Fraid not, Booboo.' Izzy fluffed her daughter's billow of ringleted hair. 'There aren't many folk who have a fleet of servants to light their fires these days.' Or men to sneak round and have secret affairs with, for that matter. Although if this led to Rocco's room and she switched with Charlotte . . .

Izzy jumped when someone knocked on the door then opened it. Freya's father. 'All right girls? I was just wondering if you fancied me lighting the fires in your rooms? Take the edge off.'

Izzy and Charlotte burst out laughing. Charlotte instantly fell over herself apologizing, saying, yes, absolutely, that would be wonderful, but would it be a waste seeing as they were all going to be down in the kitchen soon enough?

'Fair enough, then.' Lachlan Burns, who still had a full thick shock of white hair and bright, engaged blue eyes, started to walk away and then doubled back on himself. 'I think there are a few of those electric bar jobbies – you know, the heating elements. Any chance you fancy following me up to the attic and seeing if we can't unearth them?'

'Absolutely!'

Izzy, Charlotte and Luna trooped behind him as they worked their way round the twisty-turny corridors to yet another door at the far end of the house.

'Where does that go?' Luna asked, clearly in awe of Lachlan who had a vague resemblance to Sean Connery.

'Up to the attic. Untold treasures up there.' He wiggled his eyebrows to great effect. Luna, it was clear to see, was smitten.

Charlotte whispered something about how Freya had wanted them to pay attention to whether or not he remembered things. Judging by Lachlan's chitchat as he led them round the attic, he had all his marbles in the right order so far as she could tell. One thing, at least, she could stop worrying about.

Would that Izzy could do the same. Maybe if she just told everyone, they'd take over like they had with the Welsh cottage. Make her appointments, nod wisely and ensure her daughter was always loved and secure and never once had to worry about being anything other than being a little girl . . . Maybe the consultant would give her the all clear? Maybe he or she would playfully chide her for worrying about the tickly little cough she'd felt developing. Or the achiness that seemed to be creeping into her bones and would smile and say, 'This is Britain! The symptoms you're experiencing are caused by the *cold*! Not cancer.' Then they'd laugh and hug and never see each other ever again.

Izzy forced herself to tune into Charlotte, who was nattering away to Lachlan now, telling him he would just love Lady Venetia. That the two of them should meet up one day. They'd really hit it off.

'Oh, no,' Lachlan waved her off. 'There was only one woman for me and she's alive and well in here.' He patted his heart, then busied himself with handing them each an electric heater.

They paused when Freya rang the bell hanging just outside the boot room to signal it was time to do the milking. As they followed Lachlan down the stairs, each of them went quiet, lost in their own thoughts. For the first time ever Izzy wondered if she would ever love someone – apart from Luna, obviously – as much as Lachlan had clearly loved his wife. Would Charlotte? Emily? She guiltily threw Freya into the mix then pulled her back out. From the fleeting explanation regarding Monty's absence, she seemed to have enough on her plate.

Surely to god one of them deserved a happy ending.

*

Charlotte jumped. 'What was *that*?'

'Front door,' explained Rocco.

'Goodness. That's . . . loud.' Charlotte didn't know if her heart was beating so quickly because of the sudden noise, or the way Rocco had passed the butter to her. Just one brush of his fingertips against hers and . . . goose bumps. Who knew that making garlic bread could be such a sensory experience?

Thunk. Thunk. Thunk.

'Coming!' Freya called as they pushed back their chairs and went to the door. It had to be Emily. She'd texted about an hour ago saying the train had just left Edinburgh.

Freya pulled the door open.

'Wooooot! It's time to par-taaaaay!' Emily hoisted two clinky jute bags full of booze up as far as her arms would permit. 'Guess who made friends with the serving chappie in the first-class carriage? Beverages,' she explained, 'come free.'

Her friends were staring at her. Izzy broke the silence. 'Wow! Emms. Look at you. You've . . .' Izzy floundered as whatever she was going to say was lost in a cough.

'I have cut my hair. Thoughts?' Emily quipped in her inimitable, 'this is entirely rhetorical, feel free not to answer' style. Or perhaps she genuinely did care and was masking it. She handed Izzy one of the clinky bags and shook her head to realign the choppy pixie cut. She looked like an anime character. With an eye-twitch.

Oh, bless. She did care. She also didn't bother waiting for a response. 'My mother abhors it. And you know what? It shouldn't really matter what she thinks, but what do you know? It does.'

Charlotte gave her arm a squeeze. Emily appeared to have taken advantage of a few complimentary beverages prior to arrival. Talking about feelings straight off the bat was unusual for her, to say the least.

'When does it stop?' she wailed, dropping the rest of her bags to the ground. 'I mean, how many forty-year-old orthopaedic surgeons worry what their mother is going to say after they have their hair trimmed?'

'Emms,' Izzy gave her a wary grin. 'Are we actually talking about hair here?'

Charlotte looked between the pair of them. How had Izzy made that leap? The haircut was a significant change. Charlotte's mum probably wouldn't have noticed if she'd shaved her head, but from everything she knew about Emily's mother, she would care. And comment. Apart from which, Emily was a bit off-base calling it a trim. It was, Charlotte believed, what they called a 'statement cut'.

'Of course we're talking about *hair*,' Emily self-consciously tweaked her fringe. 'What else would we be talking about?'

No one answered. Emily was very much an enigma to Charlotte, who was still processing the revelation that Emily occasionally paid to have 'Nordic cuddling' therapy.

'I think it's fun,' Charlotte finally said tactfully. 'It suits you.'

The style was actually not anything at all like the Emily she thought she knew. But life was making it abundantly clear that things she thought she knew weren't always as they seemed. Her (almost) ex-husband, for example, had just named his brand-new daughter Olive. A name she knew he loathed, because he had regularly mocked a little girl in Poppy's nursery who bore the same name. Wasn't life – or Instagram – just full of surprises?

'You're quiet tonight,' Emily observed, as Freya inched round her to try and shut the door.

Izzy hip-bumped Emily further into the hallway. 'Move woman. It's bloody freezing. Freya's trying not to heat up the whole of Scotland. Any other big life changes you want to tell us about?'

'No,' Emily intoned, 'unless you're talking about the bliss that is being a forty-year-old woman living in her parents' basement flat.'

Izzy grinned. 'How is the bliss?'

'They're in Islington right?' Freya asked, as she took Emily's knee-length puffer jacket from her.

'You might want to keep that,' Izzy said. 'It's freezing. Soz, Frey.' She rubbed her hands together and coughed again.

'Healthy as ever, I see,' Emily observed, frowning, then continued in a falsely bright tone. 'Perhaps we need to go and see the doctor?'

'Perhaps it's nothing to worry about,' Izzy mimicked Emily's tone and won herself a glare.

'I'll make her an appointment with my GP when we get back.' Charlotte took Emily's overnight bag off her shoulder and put it by the stairs. 'I've been meaning to register her for ages—'

Emily cut her off with another pointed question for Izzy. 'You should be the one registering. What's wrong with you? You should've done it months ago. It's a simple phone call.'

Before Izzy could answer, the children ran in with Bonzer. There was a fresh chorus of hellos, awkward hugs, and *you remember Emily don't you*s for Poppy and Jack who hadn't seen her since May.

As Emily gently extracted herself from a particularly

loving Luna embrace, she looked round and asked, 'Where's Monty?'

Freya's shoulders zapped to her ears.

Charlotte caught Izzy mouthing *tell you later* when the kitchen door phwapped open.

'Right you lot!' Rocco was wielding a spatula. 'Lasagne's up!'

Charlotte was struck anew by just how vital he was. The man didn't do anything by halves. When he laughed? It was a belly laugh. Smiled? It was ear to ear. He was entirely present in whatever he did. Settling his father into his chair in the kitchen. Milking dozens of cows. Handing her the butter . . .

An hour later, the moreish lasagne had been demolished. When Charlotte asked after the recipe, Freya said it was her maternal grandmother's. An Italian. Lachlan had them all in stitches as he described the 'wiry, weasel-eyed woman who'd run the best gelateria St Andrews had ever seen.'

'Do you ever make ice cream with the milk from the dairy?'

Rocco shook his head. 'It all goes to the milk board. Mum had always wanted to. We even registered with the council a couple of years back as vendors, but . . . Right!' He clapped his hands together and pushed back from the huge old pine table. 'I'd best get out to the barn and see how the girls are getting on.' He flashed them all a smile. 'Anyone up for freezing their nuts off with me?'

Chapter Nineteen

'Well, hello there.'

Charlotte nearly leapt out of her skin. It wasn't often six foot three, twinkly-eyed men appeared in the kitchen predawn. Particularly ones who had been, *ahem*, the main character in a shockingly naughty dream. So *vivid*. And now here Rocco was in real life, sending a rather vibrant surge of butterflies winging round her body.

'Are you all right, lassie?'

Definitely not.

Rocco stomped his feet on the stone flooring of the boot room and swirled his thick winter coat off onto a nearby antler hook in a well-practised move.

'Goodness,' Charlotte finally managed. 'You start bright and early.'

'Aye. The first milking's at four, so.' Rocco's green eyes travelled from her bunny rabbit slippers, up along her skinny jeans, swooping up and over the pinafore covering her sage green jumper, and stopped when he met her eyes. Had she noticed just how green his eyes were before? Again she thought of the heather.

He pulled off his knitted cap and scrubbed the back of

his head, his smile not quite as bright as it normally was.

'Everything all right?'

'Aye. No.' He laughed at his own dithering. 'The milk truck's late. They got stuck on someone else's farm track a-ways down the road and are refusing to do any more collections until the snow thaws, which has a knock-on effect.' He saw she had no idea what that meant. 'We only have so much milk storage here on the farm. No collection? Nowhere to put the extra.'

'Oh, that sounds . . .' Totally outside anything she might be able to help with.

'Ach, it's happened before. And they'll probably be here later, but it's a spanner in the works I could do without.' He winked at her. 'Who knows? I might have to get my finger out and do what Freya and Mum have been suggesting for years.'

'What's that?'

'Specializing. Setting up a wee shop here on the farm.'

'Oh, that sounds interesting.' Charlotte was on firmer ground here. Ish.

'Mum dreamt it up back when . . .' He waved his big old hand towards the past. 'We're registered with the council, but it's a lot of work and would take a lot of time I don't have.' He didn't say it as though he was angry about it. It was just the way things were. Busy. Which would go hand in hand with Freya's thoughts on why he'd yet to marry. Too little time. So much to do.

Rocco's eyes abruptly dropped from her eyes to her – *oh my* – her chest. Had he been having confusing and startlingly explicit dreams as well?

'What's that you got on there?'

Her thoughts were muddled as she stared down at the pinny. It wasn't strictly Agent Provocateur, but . . .

'Oh this? I found it in the pantry.' She smoothed her fingers over the hand-stitched goldfinches and thick cotton fabric that had obviously been through the washing machine more than a few times then threw him an apologetic smile. 'I hope you don't mind.'

'No, no.' He narrowed his gaze. 'I think it's one Freya made Mum quite a few years back.' He looked up and met her eyes. 'It's lovely.'

Something flickered deep inside Charlotte that she hadn't felt in years.

Oh, sugar plum fairies.

Raw, unabashed lust was tripping the light fantastic through her nether regions. How *embarrassing*. Was this what happened when you were an *almost* divorcée? According to the latest letter from her solicitor, All she and Oli had to do was sit back and wait for the decree absolute and then they could all get on with their lives. Oli had obviously jumped the gun in that department. If the past few months had taught her anything, it was that *their* lives – Oli's and the children's – had been her life. Developing a sideline with the cakes and revamping the shop with Lady V had been a huge help. As had driving out to see the children in their West Country schools when they'd forgotten something at home, or going to see Poppy's school play, but really? They were time fillers, not soul satisfiers. Would she ever have the courage to make one of her own dreams come true?

Her stomach flipped as Rocco closed the gap between them, her heart pounding so hard she could feel its beat at the base of her throat. Every single cell in her body was on high alert.

Was this what happened when you met the person you were meant to have been with all along?

Rocco put his hand on her arm and gave it a squeeze. 'You all right, darlin'? You're looking a wee bit pale.'

Rocco's voice was like warm butter. Better. Syrup. It trickled through her body in all the right places. Could crushes really last twenty years?

'I understand things at home have been, ah, tricky for you.'

Oh. He was just being polite. Well, in that case she may as well be honest.

'Yes, mostly for the children. I was shocked at first, of course, *and* upset. But now that I've had some time to think about it, I sometimes wonder whether we'd known one another at all. Our interests are – *were* – so wildly different. Anyway. I'm presuming it's all happened this way for a reason.' Her voice was getting higher pitched as she spoke, 'All that's left for me to do is work out the silver lining.'

Rocco nodded, sat with what she'd said for a minute then said in a rush, 'I'd always meant to come down to London to see you – and Freya of course – back in the day, but . . .'

Her eyes caught with his again. He had felt it, too? The connection.

'That summer you spent up here was memorable.'

'Yes,' she said, her voice almost a whisper. 'Yes it was. I would've loved to come back, but . . .'

He gave the back of his neck a rub, eyes still glued to hers. 'Funny how life gets in the way of living sometimes, isn't it?'

'Yes,' she nodded and they shared a smile so full of meaning that she suddenly felt less alone in the world than she ever had. Rocco seemed so confident, but perhaps he too had an insecurity that he had yet to overcome. Perhaps he lacked confidence on the romance front. It couldn't be easy getting away from the farm. Maybe he thought women might want something different to what he had to offer. She remembered how he used to joke that she and Freya were taking a step up on the social ladder thanks to their degrees. Did he think she wouldn't have considered him an option because he couldn't break down the finer plot points of *Ulysses*? How ironic. Charlotte Bunce of Sheffield's least plummy tower block, too high-falutin' for the most honest, kind, man she'd ever had the privilege to meet. Her mind reeled as she absorbed all the things their lives could have been if just one of them had *said* something.

As if by internal conditioning, she stepped back, unable to be quite so close to him any more, her nervous laughter filling the space she'd just been standing in. Rocco probably wasn't even flirting. He was simply being kind. Asking after the poor divorcée in the wake of her husband's latest reminder that neither she nor the children had ever been his priority. How was it she could no longer read a simple kindness?

Fifteen years of marriage to someone who never entirely approved, perhaps?

'What's that you're doing there?' Rocco's dark curls piled onto his forehead as he leant in to inspect the huge mixing bowl Charlotte had unearthed from the pantry.

Rocco was about to plunge his finger into the batter so she reached out to stop him – almost short-circuiting at the electricity that shot from his hand to hers.

She said the only thing she could think of, 'Just knocking up some pancake batter.'

'Pancakes?' Rocco looked delighted, eventually extracting his hand from hers and running it through his hair.

'The American kind,' she clarified, just for something to say.

Rocco tapped the side of his nose. 'You know those "American" ones were originally called Scotch pancakes?'

She liked how he said American. It was about nineteen syllables and sounded utterly erotic.

Charlotte! she chided herself. *The poor man is not flirting with you!*

'Scotch pancakes,' Rocco sighed. 'I haven't had those since Mum died.' His expression softened. 'Thank you Charlotte. That's really thoughtful.' He tucked a lock of her hair behind her ear, his hand lingering ever so slightly before he took a brisk step back and rubbed his hands together.

Oh. Maybe he was flirting with her.

'Right. I've got a few more things to see to out in the cowshed, but you can count me in if you're making enough for everyone.'

'It shall be done.' She waved her mixing spoon at him as if it were a magic wand. A ridiculous thing to do really, but he smiled and gave her the thumbs-up.

She would've made ten more batches there and then if he'd asked. And every day after if he'd asked again.

When the door shut behind him, she had to press her hands together to stop them from shaking. Ridiculous! Getting all giddy at the first male to show her common courtesy after all of the fuss with Oliver.

Fuss that involved lawyers, dates for selling the family home, spreadsheets of joint assets, only to see in black and white that all she had contributed to the marriage had been herself. And, of course, the children.

It was all so crude. Putting a price tag on the emotional devastation Oli had wrought on her and the children.

She poured a bit more flour into the batter and slowly stirred the pancake batter, watching the little clumps of flour dissolve into the milk and egg mixture. It was like bearing witness to the slow and subtle elimination of her own hopes and dreams. The ones of having a big, happy, bustling family, then, one day, starting up a little business of her own. One of those kitchen-table businesses she'd read about in *Waitrose Weekend*, where a bad situation had brought about something good. Gourmet crisps from a beleaguered potato farm. Insanely expensive scented candles from an abundance of lavender.

She saw Rocco passing from the cowshed out to another, smaller barn. He looked over to the kitchen window, stopped and waved, then headed off again, that lovely smile of his playing upon his lips.

Would he whisk her away from all of this 'real life' business and show her what it felt like to experience genuine pleasure?

She laughed into the empty kitchen.

This wasn't *Madame Bovary*. It *was* real life, and she needed to start seeing it as such. Rocco was a very kind man. That was all.

A couple of hours later, the huge kitchen table teeming with three generations' worth of pancake fans, and Charlotte was back in her element. This was what she'd needed. To be part of a busy household again. She had been born to organize. To pick up Granddad's dropped serviette; to pull out the extra tray of bacon no one had remembered was in the Rayburn. Wash it all up. Put it all away. Then start all over again.

That said, she didn't mind that each time her eyes just happened to meet Rocco's, he dropped her a little wink.

Yes. That was nice. That was very nice indeed.

*

The kitchen was the warmest room in the house and, as a result, where everyone was congregating.

Izzy had made herself quite at home on the lumpy old sofa by the fireplace. Freya was strangely comforted to see she and Luna had tucked themselves underneath one of her mum's old patchwork quilts, reading trashy magazines they'd picked up at the services.

Emily was not so subtly playing cognitive games with Freya's father. She'd unearthed an old Trivial Pursuit game and had challenged him to a quick-fire game with Felix and Regan. Jack and Poppy had yet to look up from their iPads. Didn't even ooh and aah when Charlotte pulled two trays of the most beautiful-looking scones she'd ever seen out of the oven.

Charlotte was on some sort of baking mission. She'd found Freya's mum's old pinny this morning. The one to which Freya had added goldfinches swirling round a mixing bowl when her mother had wondered aloud if her new purchase – a light blue checked affair – was a bit plain.

'Course it is, Mum! You never go flash enough for yourself,' Freya had teased. She pressed her fingers against her closed eyes to stop the tears coming. It was nice, she told herself, to see the pinafore being put to use.

What would their marriage be like, she wondered, if she'd spent more time complimenting Monty for the things he did, rather than snapping at him about the things he didn't? She was so hard on herself, she supposed she thought he was getting it easy, but really? Being on the wrong end of her half Italian, half Scottish temper was very likely less than pleasant.

Freya checked her phone for the nineteenth time that morning. Though they'd agreed to a 'news blackout' when he'd *finally* rung, she was still hurt there weren't any messages.

Apologies more like. When Monty had stormed out on Christmas night, her gut instinct had been to jump into her brother's scrappy old Land Rover, chase him down and scream it out on the side of the M6. Tell him to take his ring and shove it where the sun didn't shine. This was her first Christmas without her mother and he had made it all about him. The niggling possibility that she'd contributed to the drama was something she wasn't quite ready to confront.

Her mother was never coming back.

The blunt truth of it had hit her like a lead weight when they'd pulled into the farmyard four days ago and seen none of the usual Christmas decorations. Rocco had tried his best with the tree, and her dad, well . . . he was struggling to hit the keynotes of his daily routine, let alone remember that they always had cock-a-leekie soup on Christmas Eve and smoked salmon with their breakfast eggs.

She should've known it was up to her now to do all of the things her mother had done, but . . . the whole prospect of being responsible for more things when her business woes were eating her brain alive had, she supposed, made her rather miserable to be with.

Now that she knew Monty was safely at his brother's, Freya was quickly coming round to his proposal that they should spend some time apart to think about things. He was right. She needed the headspace to try and figure out what exactly it was she wanted from herself and husband. That idealistic dreamer she'd fallen so very much in love with that first day Izzy had brought him home.

How had it come to pass that the precise attributes that had drawn her to him were now the repellents? Could she fall in love with them again? Or had she become the one who'd become impossible to love? Her brain began to short-circuit with the flood of questions that followed. There was an awful lot to think about.

'Who's up for a bit of Scottish raspberry jam on their scones?' Charlotte asked.

Rocco was clumping the snow off his huge feet in the boot room. The man had been in and out of the kitchen like a yo-yo. He squinted when his eyes lit on Freya. 'All right, sis?'

Once again she ached to tell him everything. How she was making a right hash of her life. How she didn't even begin to know where to start fixing things. The business? Her husband? Her dad? Charlotte appeared in the doorway. 'Everything all right?'

'Yup! Absolutely. Come!' She hooked her arm into her brother's, knowing the physical contact would be enough to see her through for a bit. 'Sit, you restless beast!'

The name Rocco meant rest. The last thing on earth her brother did was rest. Never idle. Always something on the go. And always so *happy*.

None of which they were achieving right now because of the financial sinkhole that Monty had led them into, but . . . people fucked up. She certainly had. No one had forced her to make clothes that made her miserable. Charlotte had tried to say as much when she'd come up to London a month ago. Freya had moaned endlessly about pulling her eyes out if she had to draw one more unicorn. After a thoughtful pause, Charlotte had pointed out that it was always possible to trial-run one or two items that didn't savage her artistic integrity quite so violently. There were, after all, about fifty other stalls selling unicorn T-shirts. Or, she'd quietly suggested, how about Freya consider getting a day job. Teach maybe. Or work at a Sainsbury's and enjoy the staff discount. Anything to take the pressure off art having to cover her financially as well as fulfil her emotionally.

The truth was she was terrified. Terrified of financial ruin, of having nothing practical (like a law degree) to fall back on. Of her family falling apart. But at the centre of it all was a young, dreamy-eyed teenaged Freya desperate not to let her parents down. She'd promised them that if they were happy for her not to help out on the farm, she would never, ever ask them for help. Unicorns meant money. Her own art? At this rate, she might never know.

Freya took the jar of jam that Charlotte had set on the counter and was about to crack it open when she realized it was from the last batch her mother had made. She debated a moment before opening it. This was exactly the sort of moment her mother would've opened it for. A normal moment.

What's the point of keeping it for special? she would have asked. *Life is special!*

Freya dolloped spoonfuls of the glossy red jam into a pair of bowls, wondering if she'd be able to taste her mother's touch in it. She always added a bit of something extra 'just to liven things up'. Lemon zest. Vanilla. Whatever was to hand, really.

'Shall I be mum?' Charlotte heaved up the huge teapot and carried it over to the table.

Charlotte's son, Jack, made a *gahh* noise. 'What else would you be? That's what you are.'

Rocco shot him a look. 'And you should count yourself lucky to have one of the finest.'

Jack looked shocked. As if no one ever dared to correct him. He quickly regrouped with a charmless laugh. 'Thanks Mum, for being so perfect that Dad had to go find a new version.'

Freya did an actual double take. Emily choked on her coffee. Izzy forgot to stop pouring water into her glass until Luna pointed out it was overflowing.

Charlotte looked as though she'd been punched in the stomach.

'Right, laddie,' Rocco's chair scraped against the stone flooring. 'That's you and me away to have a word in the cowshed.'

Charlotte shook her head. 'No, it's all right. He's just—'

'He's being bloody rude to his mother is what he's being. Forgive my French.' Rocco's eyes narrowed at Jack who, extraordinarily, was looking about the group, apparently waiting for some positive response. He'd be waiting a ruddy long time if he wanted it from Rocco. 'C'mon, laddie. Get your gear on. We've got some calves that'll need destoning.'

Freya pressed her fingers to her mouth to stem an inappropriate cackle. Jack wouldn't have a clue what destoning a calf meant. She wondered if Rocco would do the age-old trick of offering him the bullock's testicles for his tea.

'But . . . Mum's just made the scones.' Jack suddenly looked like a little boy. A spoilt little boy. But a little boy just the same.

Rocco gave him a polite but firm smile and pointed towards the boot room. 'Not for you she didn't. Not until you learn how to respect the work that went into making those scones.'

'I . . . Mum?'

Funny how a fifteen year old full of bravura could turn into a mummy's boy at the drop of a hat.

Charlotte very deliberately settled a tea cosy the shape of a hedgehog onto the teapot then, after a quick glance at Rocco, turned to her son and said, 'We're guests here, Jack. I think you should do as you're told and help our host.' Before he could respond, Charlotte busied herself gathering together a bunch of mugs onto a tray. Poppy made a move to start clapping but quickly stopped when she saw the sober faces around her.

'Are you talking about those bull calves I forgot to ring, son?' Lachlan asked.

'Aye. That's right, Dad.' Rocco shot a quick look at Freya to see if she'd react. She decided not to. Too much going on. 'All right then, Jack. You heard your mother. Let's get off to the shed, then.'

They all sat silently while Jack miserably pulled on his immaculate sky-blue Arc'teryx jacket and even more miserably agreed to wear the oversized, dun-coloured wellies Rocco told him he should put on so he didn't ruin his 'posh kicks'.

A swell of pride warmed Freya's chest. It was never nice to see a child punished. And it was extremely rare to see someone sort out another person's child, but somehow . . . this seemed right. Charlotte was the one who had made the call in the end.

Once Jack and Rocco had left, everyone extra politely asked for jam and could they please have some of the home-made thick cream? They all told Charlotte how lovely the scones were and ate them silently, the sound of her father masticating the living daylights out of Charlotte's lighter-than-air scones their only soundtrack. As they finished and Charlotte began tidying everything away, the uncomfortable atmosphere became too much for Freya.

Lounging around didn't feel right. Her mother would've fed them the scones then fully expected everyone to get back to work, not slope off to the television. Freya put down her mug of tea and licked a bit of errant raspberry jam off her little finger then said, 'Right, you lot. We need a project.'

Chapter Twenty

Izzy triple-blinked at Freya then eyed the 'wee project' again.

No one looked particularly keen apart from Freya, so Izzy started pulling melodramatic 'Oh, I see!' faces. She put her hands up like a film director would frame a final, crucial scene. 'So, the plan is to turn the tower ruins into an outdoor picnic-slash-bonfire-slash cocktail area?'

'For Hogmanay. Yes.' Freya's determined expression spoke volumes. She'd do it on her own if she had to.

Izzy quietly dropped her plan to vote for an indoor adventure, clapped her hands together and whooped. 'Let's do it.'

Freya looked so grateful it almost brought tears to her eyes. Izzy got it. Freya was going through one of the worst of the firsts without her mum. A season laden with ritual. Izzy's own mother had adored ritual and made loads of them up. Called them her and Izzy's 'little secrets'. Three smiles at a stranger per day (*Bringing joy never hurts*). Eggs before and after but never at Easter (*Why kill a beginning when you are mourning an end?*). Pudding before starters when eating outside (*You never know what the weather is going to throw up*, or, as her cancer progressed, *if she* was going to throw up). Up until the day she'd died, Izzy had thought her mother insisted on the rituals because they'd never had anywhere permanent to live. *Ritual,* she used to say, *is what makes a soul flourish. Ingrains it in your body.* Izzy felt the opposite was true. Losing the person she did her rituals with had drained her of the very essence of who she thought she'd been.

Emily pulled her gloved hand out from her armpit long enough to flick it towards the low stone building next to the tower. 'And you want the hovel to be a shop showcasing the milk?'

Freya's eyes lit up just as they had in uni when she described making something like a bodice out of buttercups. 'No. Better. I think it should be a milk bar. Not like a tuck shop. More . . .' She drummed her mittened fingers along her lower lip then abruptly pointed her index finger in the air. 'A place where milk and booze and Hogmanay all come together for one perfect night.'

Izzy pressed her own mittened hands to her chest and smiled. She wasn't up for much hard labour because of her silly cough, but she loved watching crazy ideas gain traction.

Freya was totally into it now. Nodding, walking round the site with one of those intensely earnest expressions worn by the cash-strapped builders on *Grand Designs* who were going to give it their absolute best even if it meant crying on national television.

Emily muttered something about it being too cold to breathe properly. Charlotte wondered aloud about alcohol licences while Izzy tried to remember if she'd packed thermal underwear.

Freya opened her hands in appeal, her accent thickening with every word. 'The poor wee barn's stood empty for nearly five years so Mum could have her shop in it. A shop she never got to have because we were too busy doing other things that were "more pressing". She stomped her foot on the thick layer of snow that had settled overnight. 'There's permission from the council. We can sort the other bits and bobs. C'mon, guys. How long are we going to let this shop cry itself to sleep at night wondering if my mum's hopes and dreams for it will ever come true?'

Luna made a sad face. She liked hopes and dreams to come true. So did Izzy. Oh, hell. They all did. Except perhaps Emily, who would've been perfectly happy watching B-grade movies and drinking hot toddies for the rest of the day.

Surely Emms could see that this was a daughter trying to make her mother's dream come true. Izzy answered for everyone. 'I guess we'd better get to it.'

Freya did a happy dance. Her hair was sticking out at all sorts of crazy angles from the tweed and lambswool headband she was wearing. This atop a surprisingly trendy ensemble of boiler suit, hot-pink Dickies gilet and thick leather workboots. With her cheeks all pinked up from the cold and eyes alight with excitement, she looked exactly like she had whenever Monty used to appear, unbidden, at their front door back in the day at uni. A girl who believed dreams really did come true.

Izzy hoped they worked it out. Monty and Freya were one of those couples who'd been made for each other. Shared causes, hopes and dreams. Raising children with social consciences. Freya making her artistic mark on the world. Monty doing . . . whatever it was Monty had pictured himself doing, which obviously wasn't practising law. He would've actually been super-handy for a job like this. The man was like a carpentry savant. One of the fruits of being the son of a builder, she supposed. As she watched Freya take stock of what they'd need, Izzy smiled at the memory of Monty's 'Jesus phase', as he'd been fond of calling it. When they'd first moved into their house he'd not only looked after the toddler twins, but had constructed tonnes of built-in bookcases, side tables, and a rather awesome kitchen peninsula.

'C'mon everyone.' Freya beckoned for them to join her outside the stone barn, its slightly wonky slate shingled roof glinting in the watery winter sun. 'We can do this. It doesn't need to be perfect, just in line with the vision. Dad and Rocco will muck in. I'm pretty sure Dad put a load of shelving in before Mum . . .'

Izzy's heart squeezed tight. She'd found it completely impossible to say 'when my mum died' for years after the event.

'We obviously can't get it *entirely* fancied up to be a proper shop, but what if we prettied it up with some fairy lights and . . . ermm . . . there're some frames up in the attic I can pop something into. Then we can sell the milk and cream.'

'That'd be a real crowd-pleaser,' Emily deadpanned. She popped on her best Mary Poppins accent, 'Glass of milk to see in the New Year please, guv'nor!'

'Eggnog?' Charlotte suggested more helpfully.

'Does anyone actually drink eggnog?' Emily obviously had yet to harness any dairy-based enthusiasm.

'Americans *love* eggnog,' Izzy said pointedly, ignoring Emily's stink eye. American eggnog was usually non-alcoholic, so she used to spike it with rum. Perhaps . . . no. Scotland was all about whisky – Izzy held out her hands. 'I've got it! What about "malted milk"? You know. Whisky shots in warm milk with honey?'

Freya made 'ding ding ding you've won the prize' sounds. 'Totally works with the milk-bar theme. And, as we know, there ain't no party—'

'—like a theme party!' the rest of the girls joined in. They'd been rather good at theme parties back in the day. The 'Come As Your Favourite Canadian' had required quite of lot of research, but they'd done pretty well channelling Avril Lavigne, Celine Dion and Pamela Anderson. The maple syrup crisps might've been a step too far, but . . .

'What kind of nibbles go with malted milk?' Izzy asked.

'Cake,' they all said, then looked at Charlotte.

'Do you want a break from cake baking?' Freya asked in a voice that made it super-clear she hoped Charlotte wanted the polar opposite. Charlotte said she was more than happy to make lots of cake.

Freya chewed on her lip for a second, then, 'What if we get the other farms between here and St Andrews to come along and set up stalls? There's a beef farmer on the other side of us with Belted Galloways who's always doing farmers' markets. Maybe they'd do some burgers. There's a sheep guy further along the road. He could make—'

'Posh kebabs?' Emily mimed eating a tiny kebab, finally making an effort.

'Posh kebabs!' Freya shouted joyously. 'And there's a tattie and turnip farm nearby. Maybe they'd do jacket potatoes and some sort of neeps thing? Neep curly fries? Is that a thing?'

They all agreed it could definitely be a thing.

Izzy hopped from one foot to the other. She was absolutely bloody freezing. Once she got properly moving she'd be fine, but *wow* did the Scottish cold go straight through to her bones.

Freya's face went a funny combination of hopeful and anxious. 'If we could make some money for Dad and Rocco out of it, it'd be brilliant. I've been trying to get them to do something niche for ages, but they say it's easier to supply The Man.'

'Isn't that a good thing? Supplying The Man?' Izzy asked.

Freya looked horrified. 'Not when The Man doesn't pay you what your product's worth. Do you know how many small dairy farms go out of business each year?'

Emily stepped between Izzy and the inevitable Freya speech. 'No one's going to show The Man anything if we stand around talking about it. Can we get moving please? Izzy's turning blue.'

'All right, ladies? What's brought you all out here into the elements?' Rocco appeared behind them with Jack in tow.

'Rocs,' Freya put her hands on her brother's shoulders and stared at him in the way a coach might before giving an inspirational speech about commitment and risks and laying everything on the line for just one victory. 'Whaddya think about letting us use the milk from today?'

'What for?' He flashed them a sly grin. 'Are you lot planning on bathing in it for some Wiccan ritual?'

No one missed the wink he threw a furiously blushing Charlotte.

Everyone started talking over everyone about The Big Plan.

Rocco put his fingers in his mouth and made an ear-piercing whistle. 'Right. Can we go back to the part about you lot needing my milk? Charlotte?' He made a courtly half-bow to open the floor for her.

Bless her. You'd have thought he'd just laid his coat over a puddle for her to daintily tread across from the beam of gratitude she braved in his direction. How often had Oli asked her opinion, Izzy wondered. Probably never.

'Freya had the lovely idea of opening up the shop on Hogmanay to remember your mum by. A sort of milk bar.'

Rocco pulled off his knitted cap and gave his head a scratch. 'That's a lovely idea, sis. But you cannae sell raw milk in Scotland.'

Freya looked absolutely stricken. No one said anything until Rocco got that same glint in his eye Freya did when an idea struck. 'You know . . . we do have an old pasteurizer gathering dust somewhere in one of the sheds. It'd do maybe . . . a hundred litres? We got it from Dougie Stewart when he sold up. What if I dust that off and you do some eggnog, eh?' He rubbed his tummy. 'I love a proper eggnog.'

'I suggested eggnog!' Charlotte beamed.

The smile the pair of them exchanged was so sweet Izzy nearly caught diabetes. *Awwwww.*

And then the chaos began.

Luna volunteered Bonzer's services as a stand-in reindeer.

Regan volunteered to play her violin if she could find sheet music for 'Auld Lang Syne'. Poppy offered her services to unearth the pasteurizer.

Emily put her hand up for booze questing at the local distilleries and added holiday bunting to their list of things to do. Wherever Charlotte went, Emily said soberly, bunting must follow.

Izzy volunteered to do anything so long as it involved moving. Frostbite was settling in. Her lungs actually *ached*. She really would have to register with a new GP the minute she got back to Sussex, get her regular check-ups back on track.

Rocco clapped his hands together and cracked that huge,

lopsided, sunbeam of a smile of his. 'A proper project for the hols, eh, Freya? Mum would be very, very proud of you.'

Freya batted at the air between them and, when he saw her eyes mist over, he pulled her into a bear hug, his chin easily resting atop her curly brown head, then grinned at the rest of them. 'I guess we'd all better get to work then. Operation Milk Bar is under way!'

If it weren't so blinking cold, Emily would have taken her hat off to Charlotte.

She was the only one of the four of them who could discreetly stage-manage an entire operation and still make everyone else feel as if they were the ones running the show. They were all beavering away like the seven dwarves in the diamond mines. Singing. Clearing things out. Unearthing unexpected treasures (several boxes of mismatched china teacups and jam jars for the drinks which they agreed should be paid for by donation). Laughing. *Sneezing*.

Izzy was definitely getting a cold. Emily was just about to break her promise to herself to not nag her again about staying warm when Freya's dad appeared by her side. 'Well, hello there, Mr Burns.'

'It's Lachlan, dearie. I think you're all old enough to call me by my first name, now.' He was dressed in work clothes, too. Well-worn work gloves holding a rock in one hand as he deftly scooped up another. For someone who was allegedly heading down Alzheimer's Alley, he was unbelievably fit and present. 'Thought I'd lend you girlies a hand.'

'Want to start here?' The stone she was trying to relocate wouldn't budge.

'Hey, Dad.' Freya bounced over to them with a couple of

sloshing buckets in each hand. She was in full Tigger mode. 'What are you doing out here? You all right?'

His eyes flicked over to Luna who was skipping from the house to the low barn. 'A wee birdie told me you were going to get your mum's shop up and running. Thought I'd lend my daughter a hand.'

Emily didn't miss Freya's eyes going all watery as she nodded along. 'Thanks, Dad. Ummm. Maybe rather than hauling the loose stones out one by one, we should get some of the wheelbarrows over? D'you think Rocco'd mind if we used the big red ones?'

'I'll do you one better,' Lachlan deftly dropped the stones into place at the fire pit. 'We'll get the mule out.'

'You have a donkey?' Izzy dropped her rock and clapped. Izzy had always fostered a strange affection for donkeys.

Lachlan laughed. 'This one comes with a bit more horse-power.' He made a vroom-vroom noise then said to Freya, 'I'll get the digger in first. We can drop the rocks you don't need into the mule to haul away, unless you're wanting the extra stones for something else.'

Freya narrowed her eyes. It was a look the Holly House girls had grown used to over the uni years, but had faded out of use. It was like watching a disco ball light up inside someone's head then morphing into an epic To Do list. The end result was always worth mucking in for.

'Dad, could you scrape all the stones out and then maybe make a path with them. A footpath up from the yard where everyone'll be parking?'

Crikey. Emily's dad was thrilled if he got through his morning t'ai-chi session in one piece. Did Freya know her father was over seventy?

'Don't see why not.'

Ooo-kay. Apparently the Burnses' idea of what could be done in a few days was very different from the Cheungs'.

An unfamiliar niggle of guilt wormed into Emily's conscience. She should spend more time with her parents. Take her mother up on the frequent offers to play mah-jong with her old biddy friends. They wouldn't last for ever, her parents. Acting like they would rarely made it so.

Freya wagged her finger at her father. 'Don't let the lads drive off with the mule, all right? It's too icy. And no digger lessons! Remember what happened last time with Monty.'

Emily followed Freya's eyes to a patched-up corner of the barn. Ha! She could totally imagine Monty having an absolute field day on a digger. Bless him.

Lachlan tugged his fingers through his thick shock of white hair. 'Shame we've not got Monty here. He'd make short work of all that shelving I bought for your mother. Remember the year he redid her pantry? Wonderfully patient lad, your Monty. He must've changed the design a dozen times before your mother deemed it perfect.'

Emily didn't miss the hit of guilt in Freya's eyes as Lachlan gave a little sigh, then briskly rubbed his hands together and gave them all a broad smile. 'Right! If we're going to get this done by Hogmanay, I guess we'd better get cracking.'

Chapter Twenty-One

The farmhouse was virtually vibrating with excitement. Everyone had worked so hard the day before, they'd all slept like logs then risen early as the countdown to make the milk bar a reality continued. Charlotte had volunteered to do all the cooking so that Freya could focus on the shop. When she wasn't preparing a meal, she was experimenting with new cake recipes. It was such fun she even occasionally forgot about Xanthe's photos of Oli changing tiny nappies. Oli giving foot rubs. Oli doing any number of things he'd never once done for Charlotte, apart from crowing about the fact she'd done a 'proper Diana' by giving him an heir.

If he'd been bothered enough to ring and ask how his children's 'ruined' holiday was going, he'd find out his heir had just learned how to give CPR to a calf. Charlotte had never been more proud of her son. He knew how to do a *thing*, and had asked to do it *again* if possible to make sure he'd got it right. Such a change from a boy who, if she was honest, was not the finest of pupils.

Poppy had come out of her shell as well. She'd volunteered to help Regan make signs to post out on the road and had even started a small #HogmanayMilkBar buzz on

Twitter, with a terrifically clever video she and the other girls had made last night. They'd unearthed some toy carts and horses from the attic, piled the carts with miniature whisky bottles, then rigged them up to look as though they were gliding up the farm track to the theme song from *Chariots of Fire*.

Charlotte scanned the kitchen. Experimental rings of sponge cake were cooling everywhere. She'd not yet made the boozy buttercream, as Emily still hadn't gone on her 'Rocco-chauffeured booze cruise'. Rocco was so busy with calving, gritting the drive for the milk lorries, and doing heaven knew how many other chores on top, at Freya's bidding, that she daren't press him. She'd never known a man to be so generous with his time. And so *patient*!

Charlotte tutted to herself. She was being silly about Rocco. The winks. The moments when their hands brushed. It felt nice to know the shine she'd taken to Rocco back in the day may have been reciprocated, but he lived up here and she lived down there, and soon enough this whole fluttery-tummy business would be but a distant memory.

It needed to be. Given what lay in store for her when she got back to her real life, romance should be the last thing on her mind. The children's cancelled ski trip was very likely the first of many disappointments she'd have to smooth over. Even before he'd left, Oli had been unreliable. Regularly missing Jack's electric guitar recitals, Poppy's choral concerts. Client dos. Dos she'd never been invited to because 'she'd find it all dreadfully boring.' Perhaps Xanthe had been his 'plus one' at those events all along. His #CheekyLawGirl.

Anyway.

She glanced out the window to where most of the group

was busily whitewashing the new shop (Jack had actually volunteered!) and then picked up the freshly cleaned manual butter churn she'd found in the pantry. When Lachlan had seen her washing it, he'd choked up. Said he'd got it years ago at a farm sale for Mariella, who had used it nonstop for about a month before it had faded out of use. Put aside for another project, no doubt. Lachlan had noisily blown his nose then gone out and joined Rocco in the barn.

'How many of these labels did Freya want?' Emily, who had point-blank refused to go outside, was cutting labels for the old-fashioned bottles they had yet to sterilize and fill with the newly pasteurized milk. Freya had decided everyone who came to the party would want to buy some milk for the inevitable gallons of tea and fry-ups they'd need in the morning.

'I think she wanted about twenty. She said if they got enough donations it would cover the costs for the missed collection from the dairy distributor.'

'She thinks that many people will come?'

'If the children carry on with Twitter and Instagram as they have been . . . Perhaps you should make a few more, just in case.' Charlotte ran a finger along her lower lip.

She wondered what it would feel like if Rocco ran one of his rough fingers over her lip.

She dropped her hands to her sides.

Naughty Charlotte.

Emily held a cutting board out in front of her. 'Right. I've got the labels cut and found some potatoes to carve for the stamps. Do you think we should wait for Freya?'

'Probably best, seeing as this is really her project.'

The back door blew open and in came Rocco and Jack,

his new little shadow. If a five foot eleven gangly, teenaged boy could be considered a shadow.

'Something smells delicious!'

Rocco pounced on the cakes then pulled his hand back as if he'd been burnt. 'Sorry. Any spare cake for two hard-working men?'

'Of course, please! Help yourself. You too, Jack.'

Jack professed to hate her cake but, much to her astonishment, he took a wedge, and both of them made appreciative *nom nom* sounds.

It was nice to see the glow of hard work on her son's cheeks. And, of course, on Rocco's.

'Looks as if everything's moving along quite nicely here.' Rocco licked a few crumbs off his fingers then spied the butter churn on the draining board. 'Ha! Where on earth did you find that?' His voice softened as the nostalgia hit him. 'Mum had insisted on making her own butter for tablet. Do you know tablet?'

Charlotte did. 'It's a bit like fudge, isn't it? Sugar and butter, basically.'

Rocco laughed. 'That's about right. Mum made it solid for about a month until Dad accused her of trying to give him a heart attack and get rid of him. She never made it again. Daft woman.'

Charlotte had never heard the words 'daft woman' sound so tender.

She loved Rocco's . . . *Scottishness*. There was something so genuine about it. Raw. A bit untethered, maybe? *Honest*. Yes. That was it. Everything about Rocco Burns was honest. What you saw was what you got. No games. No lies. No second-guessing if a compliment was actually a cleverly disguised insult. A ribbon of something rather delicious swirled round her belly. She saw Emily pointedly staring at her.

'Goodness! Is that the time? I'd best get lunch on.'

Freya zipped her fleece up to her chin. 'I thought the attic would be warmer than outside, but look!' She blew out a breath. Izzy and Charlotte leaned in as it crystallized on the small window.

Late afternoon on the second day of their pre-Hogmanay mission and they'd already achieved much more than Freya would have believed possible.

The shop was whitewashed. Her father had done his magic with his digger and fashioned a stone-lined path up to the bonfire area. Rocco had saved Charlotte so much milk from the afternoon to make her butter that they'd all had to have a go at the manual churn.

Freya's dad had put it out on the 'geriatric grapevine' that they were showing some Southern Softies how the Scots celebrated Hogmanay and already had two offers of stalls. One doing slow-cooked beef-cheek rolls and another doing sausages. They were also going to bring pre-packed sausages and bacon to go with the milk for breakfast bundles people could buy to take away.

The children were still volunteering for jobs instead of having to be cajoled into helping. It was particularly gratifying to watch Charlotte's lot get stuck in and, as a result, become utterly filthy.

'What do you want me to do, Frey?'

Freya couldn't resist poking her finger into Izzy's multiple layers of clothing. She made a gurgling sound.

'Water bottle,' Izzy explained.

'Are you sure you're all right, Izz?' Charlotte twirled Izzy's scarf round her neck so that it went right up to her chin. 'You've been looking a bit off colour today.'

'Why don't you head back down to the kitchen if you're that cold?' Freya suggested. 'Here's a quilt if you want an extra layer.'

'I'm fine. Just – get off me, all right?'

Charlotte and Freya exchanged a look. Izzy didn't bite people's heads off over a bit of fussing. Quite the opposite, in fact. She usually adored it. That whole 'why haven't you made an appointment at the GP?' thing between her and Emily suddenly began to change hue.

'As long as you're sure.' Freya patted the quilt so that Izz knew where it was if she wanted it, then looked round the bare-bulb-lit room. 'Right!' Freya scanned the attic then pointed at a huge old wooden dresser. 'Izzy, why don't you start over there? I'm pretty sure that's where Mum put the old kitchen stuff.'

'I thought you'd already found loads of teacups.'

'We did, but I was hoping for more jam jars. If people are pished out of their heads, I doubt they're going to be delicate with Mum's china.'

'Good point.'

Charlotte opened a box and peered inside, as if something might jump out at her. She'd expressed reservations about going through other people's things, but when the first thing she unearthed was one of Rocco's old rugby jerseys, her features softened.

If Freya wasn't mistaken, Charlotte was a wee bit taken with Rocco. Perhaps the pair of them could do with a good old-fashioned holiday shag. No remorse. No ties to worry about. A bit of an ego boost.

She was a bit jealous actually. Not of Charlotte shagging her brother, which was a whole set of images she never wanted to think about in any detail whatsoever. It was envy over that intoxicating flush of a new attraction. Similar, she supposed, to the charge of energy she'd felt since they'd begun doing up the shop. The thrill of coming up with a new design. It'd been some time since she'd felt that high.

Charlotte neatly folded the top and closed the box. 'Would it be all right if I went through the paintings? You said you wanted some things for the walls and – ' she pointed at the box – 'this feels a bit intrusive.'

'I love nosing through other people's stuff.' Izzy, now draped in the quilt, happily pawed through box after box.

Freya nodded Charlotte towards another corner of the attic. 'If the art history graduate in you can bear it, there's a stack of old paintings and prints that Mum and Dad used to hang in the barn. They called it the Parlour Gallery.' She laughed at the memory of her friends' wide-eyed expressions whenever they came along to see milking (which wasn't often) and saw the wall of art. 'Most of the paintings were bought at boot sales. Things that cracked my mother up.'

'Why aren't they still hanging in the barn?'

'Food hygiene regulations.'

'Ah.'

'Rules and regulations,' she sighed. 'The squisher of dreams.'

'Since when did you let The Man get you down?' Izzy sat back on her heels and blew on her hands. 'Why not paint directly on the wall? A mural or something?'

Freya looked out of the window towards the milking parlour, then back at Izzy. She was right. Why not? The art might have been banished, but that didn't mean it spelled the end of creativity. A fresh ream of ideas began pouring in. Sprawling murals. Paintings of paintings. An enormous set of black-and-white markings to match the cows. A single, beautiful buttercup.

'Izzy? You're a genius.'

Izzy turned back to her box with a quiet smile. 'Finally! Taken you long enough.'

A few minutes later, Charlotte called Freya over to look at a painting.

By the time Freya absorbed what Charlotte was showing her, she could barely breathe.

'Dad?' Freya called his name loudly and urgently. No one expected him to hear it, but after she'd called for him a couple more times, he appeared in the attic doorway.

'Yes, darlin'?'

Charlotte beckoned for him to come and see the painting.

'Is this a Jack Vettriano painting?'

He was Scotland's most famous contemporary artist. His iconic paintings sold for tens of thousands. Millions even. Well. One million. But that was a million more than any of Freya's T-shirts had sold for.

Her father took off his glasses and squinted at the painting. 'Aye.'

Freya's whole body felt as though it had received an electric shock.

'Ummmm . . .' The picture was highly stylized. As if it were set in another era, but . . . 'Is that you and Mum?'

Her father cleared his throat.

'Aye. And your brother.'

Together they stared at the painting. Charlotte and Izzy backed right off, as if the power of the painting had pushed them.

It featured the reverse view of a young woman leaning on an iron railing, arms stretched to either side. She was looking out onto the beach at St Andrews where a little boy was playing in the sand. There was a man on her left with his arm casually draped along her shoulders. He was looking away from her. On the right side of the woman there was another man's hand reaching across the railing, a few electric centimetres away from her mother's outstretched fingers.

'What's it called?'

Her father looked up and to the left then cleared his throat. '*Choices*.'

'*Choices*?'

He pointed to the hand that wasn't his and started untying a bit of twine that was hanging from a rafter. 'Aye. *Choices*.'

'What does that mean? *Choices*.'

'Well,' her father's voice changed as the memories flooded in. 'When we said yes to posing for the young man who painted it, we hadn't quite realized what we had got ourselves into. He wanted a house cow, see? He was struggling. Trying to make ends meet by living off his paintings.'

Freya could relate. She'd lasted a sum total of one month trying to sell her more stylized designs at a pop-up café. They'd eaten a lot of beans on toast that month.

Lachlan looked round, found a chair and sat down heavily. 'Anyway, your mother said, why don't you do us in one of your paintings? She'd just found out she was pregnant with you, you see.'

Freya fought the sting at the back of her throat as she looked back at the painting. That was her mum pregnant with her?

'She wanted a family portrait. There was no chance we'd ever be able to afford one on what the farm was bringing in, especially with you on the way, so Mariella thought she'd barter.'

'Wait. You traded a cow for this painting?' Technically, this made her parents patrons of art.

'Aye.' Her father stared blindly ahead of him. 'Petunia, I think that one was called. A bit on the mature side, but we didn't think he'd manage with one of the younger girls. By all accounts he took good care of her. Jack.' He didn't look as if he knew how he felt about it all.

Freya frowned at the photo. 'I don't get why he put in the other man's hand. Why it's called *Choices*. I mean, obviously as an artist I get it – but if this is a family portrait, why does Mum have another man's hand reaching out to her?'

Her father's eyes clashed with hers so abruptly she almost lost her balance.

'I suppose it's a commentary on marriage. Your mother was young and beautiful. I wasn't the only man who had wanted to marry her. She chose me, but it didn't mean her other suitors gave up hoping. When she fell pregnant with you we were dead broke. I wasn't sure we could afford another child, and it hadn't been too long before that she'd had an offer from another gent, so . . . she had choices.'

Freya dropped from her squatted position in front of the painting onto the floor.

Charlotte looked as shell-shocked as Freya felt. Whether it was the fact that there was an unknown Jack Vettriano lying about in their attic, or the fact that Freya's mum had had *choices*, she didn't know.

Was Freya even her father's child? She stared hard into his face and saw elements of her own. The same nose. The same stubbornness. The same drive to make his business work, no matter what.

Yes. She was her father's daughter. And her mother's.

If they sold it, she and Monty could be debt free. Rocco could update the milking parlour or, even better, afford an extra pair of hands to help on the farm and her dad could have nursing care if he needed it in future . . .

It was her mother.

Her brain fizzed and popped. Too much.

The only thing that fell into place were more questions.

Her mother had had *choices*?

She tried the head-clearing thing the grief counsellor had suggested all those months ago – swooshing the conflicting thoughts away.

Freya had had choices, too.

When she'd been putting together her soft-furnishings collection and scraping a living from her upcycled charity shop skirts, she'd crossed paths with Monty at an anti-war demonstration. She hadn't seen him since the last house party they'd thrown at uni when he'd tried, unsuccessfully, to have a 'snog for old times' sake' with Izzy. He'd exchanged numbers with her and said he'd ring for a drink. He hadn't, so she'd rung him. Chased him up until he'd finally met up with her on an art gallery crawl around various galleries who offered free drinks and nibbles to art enthusiasts and, after an abundance of mojitos, they had finished with a drunken shag at her sparsely furnished studio. A few more

Freya-inspired evenings out and they'd become a couple. Two years later, when she announced she was pregnant, he'd freaked. Disappeared for a few days. When he came back she'd tearfully promised him that having children didn't mean pursuing the path towards commercial property law his mother had pinned on him. Before their wedding he'd looked so ashen she'd promised him she would never pressure him to do anything he didn't want to. That their lives together would be about the higher things in life, not the tedious logistics of survival.

What a numpty.

It was increasingly likely that everything was falling apart around her because she'd spent the past twenty years of her life trying to bash square pegs into round holes. Whether she was the peg or the hole in this scenario eluded her, but she could see now that if she hadn't actively pursued Monty, both of their lives would have been very different. He would probably be saving the disappearing tribes of Ulan Bator about now. She might be debt free and selling the type of quirky couture she'd always dreamed of making. Donating dresses to the Victoria and Albert. Championing charities that celebrated peace and nature and an end to microbeads in the world's waterways.

She could be also be single, childless, and living in a garret somewhere, convincing herself that her 'masterpieces' weren't bad, just misunderstood.

'Freya?' Charlotte touched her arm. 'Are you all right?'

No. She was having a meltdown.

Freya forced herself to focus on what was in front of her. A painting by a famous artist stuffed in her parents' attic that could change their futures.

'Dad? Why is the painting up here?'

Her father scratched his head. 'Oh, she didn't take to it in the end, your mother. Said it wasn't the sort of portrait she'd been after, but thought it'd be rude not to keep it after all the effort the young man had put in. You're more than welcome to it if you'd like it.' He glanced out towards the barn. 'Rocco didn't express an interest when we were up here a while back looking for something for your mother, and from what I've seen in the shopfronts up in St Andrews, the lad's doing a fair trade now. Perhaps you can get a few bob for it.'

Uhh . . . Jack Vettriano's career was insanely fabulous. He was an OBE, had his own publishing company, not to mention regularly selling more prints than every other British painter, even if he was sneered at by the *Establishment*.

He'd stayed true to his vision and ultimately been rewarded for it.

Oh, bums. All of this was striking a bit too close to the bone.

Her father abruptly pushed himself up and out of his chair and ruffled Freya's hair as he had when she was a child. 'It's nothing to worry about now. Your mother chose me and we never once looked back.' He popped on a happy, contented smile. 'Now, then. When are you girls coming down out of this attic for some hot chocolate? Izzy here looks as though she's on the brink of a cold.'

'Soon, Dad.' Freya watched him go, feeling aftershocks of the discovery rippling through her. The world looked the same, but it felt completely different.

When he'd gone, Izzy joined her in staring at the painting. 'Should we hang it out in the shop?'

Freya and Charlotte turned to her as one and said, 'No.'

*

'Would you like to try the gin infused with salted caramel or the pink peppercorn vodka?'

Emily stared at Tansy, the sylphlike micro-distiller, and nodded heavily.

'Yes.'

Tansy – because beautiful micro-distillers of distinctive spirits wouldn't be called Ethel or Madge – smiled at Emily. Emily hoped she was smiling back. Chances were high that if she ever got off her stool, she wouldn't be able to walk in a straight line. Rocco, on the other hand, was completely sober. Fair enough, as he was driving, and Scotland was very, *very* strict about obeying rules and sticking to the Letter of the Law.

Why were all her thoughts happening in slow motion?

'Can I get you anything else?'

Tansy again.

She was insanely beautiful. A sheet of luminescent red hair rippled down to her bum. Dark brown eyes. They actually looked like chocolate. From Ecuador. Or . . . Zanzibar.

Rocco waved his hand above their empty glasses. 'I think that'll do us. Anything take your fancy, Emily or are we sticking with the malted milk?'

'You sell malted milk?' Tansy perched a hand on her hip and grinned.

'Why, yes we do!' Emily enthused, ignoring Rocco's bemused look. 'We sell *boozy* malted milk. It's milk . . . with malt. Whisky, vodka, rum, all sorts. There will be cake. There will be . . .' She swung her eyes to Rocco for help. She'd run out of things to dazzle Tansy with.

Rocco quickly explained what they were doing; that there'd be a party at the farm on Hogmanay with milk-based cocktails, cake, sausages, burgers and all sorts. Donations gratefully accepted to make up for a missed milk collection. Tansy, he added, was most welcome.

Tansy's brown eyes lit up. 'Why don't you take a couple of bottles on the house? We've got an Amaretto vodka and a coffee gin that'd be absolutely brilliant. If they do well it's good for us too, yeah?'

'Us?' slurred Emily.

'Me and my partner.'

Partner?

She slumped at the irritating word. It was so . . . vague. Business, romantic, dance . . . which was it?

Tansy waved down the hippest hipster of them all. Above the requisite ensemble of charcoal skinny trousers, black turtleneck jumper and a leather strapped apron, he was wearing a pair of Fair Isle knitted antlers. Bah! Freya could make *much* cooler antlers. She'd call her immediately. Say the party simply couldn't go on without kick-ass hipster antlers.

'Brodie! C'mere, listen to this.'

Emily fuzzed her lips. Was no one in the trendy booze world called Bob? Derek?

'Ooops! Easy there, girlie.' Rocco caught Emily as she slid off the stool towards the stone floor. 'Looks as if we'd better make our way back to the dairy and get some tea into you. See you on Hogmanay?' That part was for Tansy and *Brodie*. The *partner*.

'Absolutely. It sounds a cracking good time. What's the name of the farm?'

'Burns' Folly.'

When Rocco got her back into the car and buckled her up, Emily swivelled her head round to him. It took some effort.

'Did I disgrace myself?'

'Nah,' Rocco grinned that sweet grin of his that actually made her believe him. 'While you were in the loo, she double-checked the address with me. I think you're in with a chance.'

Emily instantly felt very, very sober.

Charlotte dried a serving dish and handed it to Freya to put away.

'I think – ummm . . .' *Ooof.* Freya was actually feeling pretty emotional. 'I think for the first time ever, I'm properly scared.'

Charlotte nodded. She understood the complexities of marriage more than most.

'What scares you the most?'

'Today? Being tempted to sell a painting of my newly pregnant mother.'

'Do you have to?'

'It would solve a lot of problems.'

On the flipside, clearing their debts wouldn't change Monty. Already, Freya could feel a growing rage that his idiocy was forcing her to consider selling a family treasure to avoid declaring bankruptcy. That's how broke they were. She didn't even know how she was going to get the children back down the road and yet . . . selling the painting would be like selling her mother's ashes.

Impossible.

The truth hit hard and fast. They were going to have to find a way to do this on their own. It was time for both of them to grow up. Face facts. They were in debt, limiting their children's futures, and needed to make some fundamental decisions about how they wanted to proceed because, at the end of the day . . . ? No amount of money was going to change the fact that their marriage was failing and neither one of them was doing anything to fix it.

She and Charlotte walked upstairs together, each lost in their thoughts, barely remembering to say goodnight when they reached their bedroom doors.

When Freya crawled into bed with her hot-water bottle, she picked up her phone and pressed the icon for favourites.

'Hi,' Freya whispered. Which was stupid, seeing as she was alone in bed with thick stone walls between her and everyone else in the house.

'Hi,' Monty whispered back.

'It's me.'

'Hello, you.'

Freya's heart did an unexpected flip. Monty hadn't said plain old 'hello, you' in just about for ever.

'I miss you.'

'I know,' he sighed. 'I miss you, too.'

Chapter Twenty-Two

The attic had once been Freya's favourite place. Her escape zone in which to read, sew, paint and dream. It had been her magic place. Now it felt like a creepy Narnia.

Just knowing *it* was here. The solution to all of her financial problems, or the most beautiful reminder that her mother had chosen her.

Not just Freya. Mariella had chosen *family*. This family. The people who had cocooned Freya through a thousand different knockbacks. Scraped knees. Torn dresses. Failed exams. A bloody nose. Her first school disco. Her first rejection. A skin rash so embarrassing her mother had let her stay home from school for a week.

Had Monty left her because of the mistakes he'd made? Or had it been her mistake to give him the job of household accountant? She'd genuinely thought he'd liked the job. Her stomach churned as another wave of guilt swept in. Perhaps doing the accounts had been like becoming the house-husband. It was something he'd had to do because she hadn't been around to do it.

Freya ached for her mother's advice. She wouldn't dare ask her father. Or her brother. They worked so hard on the farm, the last thing she wanted to do was to admit everything she'd worked for – with their blessing – had gone horribly, terrifically wrong.

She checked that Charlotte was busy at the far end of the long room, then uncovered the painting, her eyes arrowing in on that mysterious male hand reaching out to her mother's.

People had choices.

Of course your father drives me mad, child, but he's part of my fabric now. If I pulled that thread out, it would affect, you, Rocco, the wee bairns you're expecting . . . Ach, child. It's not worth thinking about. C'mon. Show us how your new quilt's coming along, then. Let's focus on what can change.

Her mother's words were, as ever, wise and practical. Life wasn't always sunshine and lollipops. Besides. It wasn't as if she and Monty were getting divorced or anything. This was a blip. A painful blip, but a surmountable one. They were *not* Oliver and Charlotte.

That's what she'd keep telling herself anyway.

'*Oh!* Look at these!' Charlotte – who had stoically endured a FaceTime call from Oli during which he promised the children a 'monumentally epic' sailing holiday over Easter, which virtually no one believed he would honour – held up a cushion cover she'd found in a black bag marked *Don't Let Freya Bin.* Her mother's handwriting, of course. 'Frey, I think rather than decorate with these, we should sell them.'

Freya snorted. She'd been down this road before. No matter how much her mother had loved them, her quirky sofa cushions did not sell. 'They'd sell as well as T-shirts with Wookiees and leprechauns, I expect.'

Charlotte looked confused. 'You've done leprechaun T-shirts?'

Freya was about to tell Charlotte to use them as fodder for the bonfire when she stopped herself. Her shy, quiet, unassuming friend had, in the midst of an awful divorce, single-handedly turned a shack with a few jars of question-able honey into a *Waitrose Weekend*-featured success story. Surely to god she could give her cushion covers another shot.

Rocco stuck his head through the door. 'You ladies coming down? I expect we might be getting our first guests soon.'

Charlotte's cheeks pinked up.

Oh, for heaven's sake, would the two of them get on with it and bonk? The energy between the pair of them was humming with pent-up lust. It was ruddy annoying.

'I think Freya's cushions would sell in the shop.' Charlotte held up another. It featured a Highland cow knitting an Islay scarf. 'You could get forty quid for this. Easy.'

Rocco's guffaw was as disbelieving as his sister's.

Charlotte pursed her lips. 'When I go into a farm shop, and I go into *quite* a few, customers don't just want fresh tomatoes or a fennel bulb with a bit of earth still clinging to it.' Her eyes took on a dreamlike quality. 'They want the upper-middle-class *lifestyle* that goes with it—'

'A *fictional* lifestyle,' Freya cut in.

'An aspirational lifestyle . . .' Charlotte countered. Firmly.

'It's up to you, but . . .' Charlotte looked as though she was about to give up the fight then, after a nod from Rocco (!), carried on. 'The thing is, Freya, the type of people you want buying – or in this case making donations for – your brother's milk are not your everyday punters. You want people willing to spend two pounds on a pint of the beautiful, organic milk, mostly because there's a picture of a buttercup on the bottle. A bottle which, by the by, should warrant a fifty pence charge and ten p credit if it's returned.'

Freya and Rocco gawped at her.

She thought for a moment then said, 'If you won't sell the cushions here, with your permission I'll bring them down to Sittingstone. I guarantee you they'll be gone by the end of the week.'

'If we get two pounds for each pint of milk, we don't need to sell the cushions,' Rocco laughed in disbelief.

'Of course you do!' Charlotte chided, already stacking the covers in a tidy pile. 'You'll have to factor in the bottles, the cleaning, the staff you'll need to hire. The profit will obviously be larger than if you sell to the bigger retailers, but you'll definitely need second-tier customers buying higher-end items like the cushions to boost your profit levels. Those mismatched china teacups you found would sell for a small fortune.' She laughed as an idea hit. 'If you filled them with artisanal butter, you could double the price and call them butter cups!'

Freya could hardly believe the woman standing in front of her was the very same Charlotte who'd been unable to speak up for herself while her husband humiliated her in front of everyone she knew. If only Charlotte could take some of this confidence and use it to hammer Oli to the wall.

'And you think all of this is genuinely possible?' Rocco leant against the doorframe, genuinely engrossed. All their lives they'd milked the cows without so much as a second thought about anything beyond ensuring it was ready for the milk distributor. There was just too much work involved in doing anything apart from that. Freya's eyes flicked towards the Vettriano. If Rocco sold it, he could make the shop a proper concern. He definitely deserved some cream after all of his years of hard graft keeping the farm afloat.

Charlotte glanced at her watch. 'We'd best get down there, but if you help me with these, I can explain on the way.'

An hour later, the shop looked as if it had been plucked out of a 'Fabulous Farm Shops of Fyfe' newspaper spread. Rocco had given Charlotte free rein to put suggested donations on everything. It was an impressive spread. The bottles of milk stood in a glass-fronted mini refrigerator that Lachlan had unearthed. There were gingham-cloth-wrapped Breakfast Bundles (milk, a small disc of butter, sausages or bacon and a few rolls from a local bakery). Freya's cushion covers were tagged at an eye-watering forty-two pounds. (Freshly stuffed after an emergency trip to a craft shop which had opened its doors after Emily had threatened to throw herself through the window.) Something had really got into Emily over the past couple of days. And, of course, there were Charlotte's cakes and the malted milks. A huge Kilner jar marked 'Donations' had a solitary pound coin in it courtesy of Lachlan 'as a primer'.

Four farmers who regularly sold their wares at farmers' markets pulled up with portable food trucks and trailers. The air smelt of bonfire, sausages and baked potatoes.

Emily had augmented her standard black ensemble with a tartan scarf that Lachlan had insisted she wear, and a knitted hat decorated with a bauble that Freya had taken from the Christmas tree. Izzy had necked a bottle of Day

Nurse, put on one of Freya's old snow suits and kept insisting she was ready to parrrr-tayyyyy before dissolving into more worrisome coughing fits.

The children were all wearing silly Christmas jumpers, apart from Jack, who was refusing on the grounds they were for children. Fortunately, Regan and Felix were perfectly comfortable with looking ridiculous. Monty had fostered healthy levels of silliness in them to make this sort of thing fun.

Freya was tempted to make a video call and show Monty the shop, but thought it best to leave it, as they'd promised, until midnight.

'Right!' Charlotte clapped her hands together, as she so often did, in prayer position in front of her lips, as if she were holding in everything she actually wanted to say. She dropped them to her chin. 'What do we do now?'

They both looked out to the road where the odd car was passing by but not turning in.

'Well . . .' Freya crossed her fingers and held them up for Charlotte to see. 'We wait!'

Emily wondered if this was what partying in Lapland would be like. Berloody freezing, but utterly hedonistic. She kind of liked it.

There were flames and dancing and drinking and singing. One man had been tossed into a frozen water trough and pronounced it 'ab-so-lute-ly *legendary*'.

It looked as if the entire Kingdom of Fife had turned up. Cars had long since filled the extra field they'd earmarked for an overflow car park and were spilling onto the road. They'd run out of booze ages ago, but it hadn't been a problem as word had gone out on the Twitter-sphere that it was BYOB at Burns' Folly. Apparently it was traditional to show up with a bottle anyway, so . . . these Scots could *cane* it!

The milk and breakfast bundles had been snaffled hours ago, as had the cakes. Every time Charlotte emptied the donations jar, Lachlan shook his head in wonder and said he always knew the Scots were a generous sort but not this generous. The last of Freya's cushions had just been snapped up. She was compiling a waiting list of would-be buyers for more. Rocco's chest was so puffed out with pride, he genuinely did look fit to burst.

Even Charlotte had let her hair down. She was wearing one of Freya's woodland crowns atop her neat, ash-blonde mum do – a whorl of tiny pine cones sprayed gold, interwoven with holly berries and multi-coloured silk flowers that someone had found in the attic. She was glowing.

There was no sign of Tansy, but . . . it wasn't as if Emily would have anything to talk to her about. That was what had struck her the most as the evening had progressed. Emily couldn't do chitchat. Izzy, who looked like death warmed up, could jabber away with anyone. And was. Freya kept flinging herself into people's arms, talking and laughing. Friends, no doubt, from the olden days. Even Charlotte was chatting with ease to total strangers. Emily simply didn't have it as a skill base. How could she when her entire life revolved around the hospital?

'Sausage?'

Emily blinked as a sausage was put directly in her eye line. Behind it glowed a crown of shiny auburn hair.

'You came.'

Nice one, Emms. Stating the obvious.

'How could I not?' Tansy revealed her freckly nose and smiley lips. She made a tragedy face. 'I can't believe we missed the butterscotch gin cakes!'

Emily shrugged and said nothing. Her insides were doing all sorts of weird things. Like swooping.

A skinny-jeaned, antler-wearing, sausage-eating man emerged from the crowd. 'This place is absolutely amazing.'

Emily's heart dropped back into place. Lower probably.

Brodie.

Brodie the 'partner'.

Brodie the Partner stuffing a sausage into his smug beardy face. Emily decided against telling him he had onions stuck on his chin.

He whacked a possessive arm over Tansy's shoulders. 'This place is brilliant. Mind if we talk to the big man about doing a partnership with the malted milks? A little "I scratch your back if you scratch mine" action?'

Bleuuurgh.

'Please. Be my guest.' She pointed towards the bonfire where Rocco was putting another huge log on amidst a shower of sparks.

'Mint!' Brodie pulled Tansy in for a greasy, sausagey cheek kiss. 'Catcha later!'

Emily needed a drink.

'SEVEN!'

Being one of a hundred-odd people round a bonfire counting down to the New Year was sending fireworks through Charlotte's bloodstream. Or perhaps it was the fact that Rocco had his arm casually slung over Charlotte's shoulder. He'd been telling someone how helpful she'd been, given her a half-hug and then . . . simply left his arm on her shoulders.

He'd been so busy all night. Talking about the farm, his cows, the milk, his (new) plans for selling artisanal butter. Apart from the days her children were born, Charlotte had only felt more proud once in her life. The day she'd graduated from university.

'SIX!'

'Lotte!' Izzy danced up to her and squeezed in between Rocco and Charlotte. 'There you are, woman! I wanna sneeze in the New Year with my girlie girls!'

Charlotte and Rocco's eyes met over Izzy's head. A feat, considering Izzy was both tall and wearing sparkly reindeer antlers. Rocco looked perplexed. Charlotte didn't know what she felt. She wasn't divorced yet. Or ready to date. But . . . she had fancied Rocco Burns from the first day she'd laid eyes on him all those years ago. What would her life have been like today if she'd said something?

Izzy launched forward as another violent sneeze took hold of her. Charlotte scooped an arm round her waist and shifted her to her far side. The one not next to Rocco. His arm slipped back into place across her shoulders. She didn't dare meet his gaze.

'FIVE!'

'*Where's the best big brother in the world?*'

Freya was high as a kite. It was nice to see her letting go after all the hard graft she'd put in over the past few days. She dance-walked to them, wielding a half-empty bottle of red, her lips and tongue stained a dark purple. '*Iloveyoubothsomuchithurts!* Physically.' She thumped herself on the chest. '*Ithurtsmyheart!*'

281

Izzy raised her own bottle for a clink. Prosecco, from the looks of things. 'Amen to that, sister! Feeling your love pain!'

'FOUR!'

'Where's Emily?' Izzy suddenly looked mournful. 'And Booboo. I want my little Booboo by my side when the bell strikes.'

'THREE!'

'In the cowshed.' Rocco said so that Izzy could hear him above the crowd noise. His hand slid along Charlotte's shoulder to her lower back as he moved. 'She and Dad are showing the other children the calves.' His hand moved back into place on her shoulders, a bit more snugly if she wasn't mistaken.

Izzy hiccoughed. 'I can't see Emily anywhere!' Izzy cupped her mittened hands to her mouth. 'Emmilly! Booboo!'

'TWO!'

Freya was jumping up and down. 'Bring. It. On!'

'ONE!' The crowd went berserk. 'HAPPY NEW YEAR!'

Roars and whoops surrounded them. Couples drew together. Friends kissed cheeks and laughed. The children danced around the crowd like lunatics, with poppers and environmentally friendly confetti. Izzy and Freya clinked bottles again, lurched forward, conked foreheads and dissolved into hysterics as the crowd consumed them.

Charlotte felt Rocco's hand shift from her shoulder to her face. She turned to him. His other hand cupped her bare cheek. He tipped her face up so gently she felt like a baby lamb. Delicate. New. Surprisingly lusty. So perhaps not like a baby lamb at all.

The moment their lips touched, Charlotte felt such an explosion of pleasure she literally lost her balance. Rocco moved his arm to her waist and pulled her in to him, deepening his kiss as he did so. Charlotte had never felt safer or more desirable in her entire life.

'Happy New Year, Charlotte,' Rocco whispered against her lips.

'Happy New Year,' Charlotte breathed back.

'MUM!'

Charlotte turned so quickly she pulled something in her neck.

Poppy was staring at her in horror. 'What are you *doing*?'

Rocco dropped his hand from Charlotte's cheek and took two large steps back, hands raised up in surrender position.

'I'm sorry, I . . .' Charlotte sought out her daughter's retreating figure in the crowd.

'You go on and find her,' Rocco looked as deflated as Charlotte felt.

'I . . .' She wanted to apologize. To explain. But nothing would come out.

'I know, lassie,' Rocco stuffed his hands in his pockets. 'I know.'

Chapter Twenty-Three

The cowshed was surprisingly warm.

Izzy wiped at the sheen of sweat on her face. She felt very, very peculiar. Emily would probably give her a lecture about mixing booze with cold medicine but . . . She wanted her Booboo.

She walked heavily, a quilt draped over her shoulders, an empty bottle of Prosecco dangling from her fingers as the cows looked up with only a vague interest as she passed.

Izzy made her way down to the far end of the shed where Rocco had built a crèche for the calves who had been rejected or, in one case, orphaned.

'Oh!'

Izzy dropped the bottle, hands flying to her mouth. She felt like a clumsy wise man discovering baby Jesus, but perhaps a bit drunker. And, of course, a few days early.

Regan was leaning against the wall of the barn with a beautiful calf in her lap, both of them sound asleep, whilst Luna, Bonzer and the other calves were all curled up, asleep as well, in a huge whorl of fresh straw.

Izzy patted her sides for her phone. Nope. She obviously hadn't transferred it to the snow suit.

She considered whether to wake the children and bundle their inevitably grumpy little selves into the house or just to leave them here. It was warm enough. A bit pooey, but . . . Would children's services have her for neglect if she left them?

'Looks like we've got ourselves some extra calves.'

'Oh! Rocco. I didn't even hear you come in.' A mix of relief and disappointment yanked at her chest. She had happened upon the world's best tableau and now it would change, but . . . Rocco would make the decision about the children. Izzy suddenly, urgently, wanted nothing more than a big brother just like Rocco to make decisions for her. Emily was great, and obviously knew medical stuff better than she did, but she didn't want Emily to have to take on the role of carer. She just wanted Emily to be her friend. A person with whom she could escape from the harshness of reality. Not inspect it in painstaking detail.

She gave Rocco a heavy nod. 'What does one do in a situation like this, farmer man?'

Rocco smiled that kind smile of his, the crinkles by his eyes raying out like sunbeams. Charlotte should fall in love with him and marry him. They could all live here at the farm happily ever after, selling cake and milk. Then Izzy wouldn't have to worry about waking Luna up and telling her that Mama wasn't feeling so well.

Rocco shifted a pitchfork that had been leaning on the side of the pen to the wall rack.

Bonzer opened one eye, then abruptly sat up. He was wearing a rather striking holiday vest. A chunky-knit, cherry-red number with a gold star on the centre of his chest. He was going to be the size of a moose when he grew up, and the one constant in Luna's life, if Izzy's hunch about the pain in her armpit was anything to go by. He nuzzled Luna who blinked open her eyes, saw her mother and smiled. She did a luxurious little-girl stretch and yawn. 'Did you make your New Year's wishes?'

Oh, what a loaded question.

She tapped her head then her heart. 'Got 'em in here.'

Regan woke up, then her calf and, mostly thanks to Rocco, they bundled the humans and the dog back into the house and up to their rooms with hot-water bottles and a reminder that they were heading back down the road to Sussex in the morning. Both girls, who'd asked to sleep together in a Bonzer sandwich, were too tired to protest.

With no Luna to cuddle up to, Izzy felt unexpectedly bereft. Her one resolution had been to tell the truth. She didn't want to tell the truth because it meant being honest with herself. So she did what she'd always done when she felt this way. Made a pillow person and cuddled up to it. Maybe Emily would come and check on her later. Sniff. That would make her feel better. And then, perhaps, she'd be brave enough to tell everyone her news.

'All right there, Mr Burns? Enjoyed your New Year's party?'

Emily had enjoyed hers. Sort of. At midnight, Tansy had stuffed her number into Emily's pocket and given her a delightfully lingering kiss on the cheek then *ping!* disappeared.

Lachlan looked away from the television where the revelry had passed its peak in London and moved on to New York. He said he'd been outside for a bit, but when things had got a bit overcrowded he'd opted for the comfort of the cosy sitting room.

He smiled and stroked his chin. 'The children certainly enjoyed it.' His gaze shifted to the window, where Rocco was gently encouraging people to find a new place to see out the rest of their Hogmanay. 'It was good to see a smile on Mariella's face tonight.'

That got Emily's attention.

'You mean Freya?'

'Eh?' He looked perplexed.

'Tonight. Smiling. It was good to see a smile on *Freya's* face.'

He looked at her as if she'd gone daft. 'Aye, lassie. That's what I said.'

Hmmm.

'I'm heading off to bed,' Emily told him. 'Anything I can get you?'

'No, thank you, darlin'. I'm a contented man.'

He looked it, too. Flanked by a Christmas tree and a modest pile of Christmas presents that he had yet to put away. A tin mug with Scottish birds on it. A sweater Freya had made. A book on whittling.

'Made any resolutions?' He pressed up and out of his worn armchair with a chesty groan.

'Who? Me? Nooo.' It wasn't her thing. Emily's entire life had been about hitting goalposts. She'd balked at adding extra pressure to the New Year when her parents had already meticulously crafted her life to perfection in spreadsheet after spreadsheet.

'You?' She remembered to ask. It was something her professional cuddler had taught her. To ask a person the same question in return, even if you weren't that interested.

'Aye,' he said, then smiled mysteriously and tapped the side of his head. 'The main problem is remembering what it is.'

She was about to launch into a list of memory aids he could put to use, but stopped herself. He was a happy man. Why complicate things when there was no need?

Once in bed, Emily lay awake, staring at the ceiling. She was a grown woman, long since free of her parents' spreadsheets. Why not make a resolution?

She thought of that tingling feeling she'd had when Tansy's kiss had lit upon her cheek and the envy she'd felt when Brodie had swept in and pulled her into a conga line. If she had any sort of skill base in being footloose and fancy-free, Emily would've simply joined in with them. She was silly with Izzy, and had been known to fling the odd boa about with her former flatmate Callum. See? Silly. She replayed the scenes in her head then corrected herself. She had basked in the glow of their silly. Silly by proxy.

Which is why, no doubt, she'd not bothered to find Tansy again.

She stretched, then curled up into a ball under the covers. She knew what her resolution was. Find a way to feel comfortable enough in her own skin to let someone know her. Really know her. Like Izzy did. But different.

She squeezed her eyes tight until the little white dots appeared. When she opened them, her life appeared before her with crystal-clear clarity. She wasn't silly because her parents had raised a little grown-up. Made a mini-them. Two earnest, hardworking academics whose sole quest – after recovering from the disappointment of having had a girl – had been to devote themselves to ensuring Emily excelled. At everything. They hadn't done it because they were mean. Or horrid. Or masochistic. It was what they had been programmed to do. *Muchos gracias*, China.

Apart from failing to get married and give them a grandson, she'd done everything perfectly. Okay, she could've pushed it on the violin front, but they were happy enough with the focused, career-obsessed surgeon they'd made. The one whose goal in life was to do better than they had, to make all of their sacrifices worth their while.

Perhaps this was why Emily loved Izzy so much. Adored, really. Izzy was her polar opposite. Absolutely carefree and the least judgemental person she'd ever met. She never cackled at Emily's stiff social demeanour. Never mocked her solemnity. Or teased her when she stuck her foot in it with Charlotte or Freya. She accepted Emily 'as is'. You couldn't really ask for more from a friend. She loved Izzy. At the beginning probably more than a friend, but that jagged path of unrequited never-gonna-happen had softened over the years into a deep, abiding friendship. Or maybe it was the fact that Izzy had lived in Hawaii for the last ten years and Emily hadn't had to think about it.

She froze when she heard a cough at the door, then the creak of hinges. The Burns' house could do with a bit of WD-40.

'Emms?' Izzy hissed from the doorway. 'You awake?'

Emily faked being asleep. Thinking all of that mushy friend stuff about Izzy and then having her appear was too much.

Izzy tried again. 'Emmillyy? Wanna cuddle?'

Emily held her breath. Izzy used to do this in uni before exams. She'd done it a lot more when her mum had got ill in that first round of breast cancer treatment. Emily had never slept a wink on those nights. Izzy always wove her limbs around, across and through Emily's, as if she was in a pile of puppies.

Izzy tiptoed over to the bed, eased up the covers and spooned up against Emily. She was all warm and snuffly and a little bit squirmy.

It felt so nice.

Would this torture never end?

Once Izzy's breath softened and slowed, Emily inched her telephone off the bed stand. She scanned the train times out of the nearest station, then sent an email to her registrar to let him know she'd be available to be rostered onto the surgical schedule by the afternoon. Work always made not thinking about personal stuff so much easier.

She stared out into the darkness.

She made a resolution to play mah-jong with her mother before the year was out.

She made another to bring her father to a karaoke bar over the Chinese New Year.

She made another she couldn't quite articulate about Izzy.

She looked at her watch.

Only five more hours of not moving to go.

Freya looked at her list of resolutions and sighed.

It was more like a To Do list rather than something she could attack with zest and verve. Normally, she loved making resolution lists. Loved crossing things off. Revisiting lists of days gone by. Seeing how much she had or hadn't achieved.

It was weird, doing it on her own. She and Monty had always done them together, no matter how blotto or exhausted they'd been. They would find their notebooks, curl up wherever and write.

His list would be full of things like 'Do Parkour with Felix',

'Teach Regan how to make a kite', 'Run a 10k for a hedgehog charity'.

Hers were always a combination of artistic goals and practicalities. Strive for greater creative fulfilment. Change savings account. Try new colour scheme for woodland creature prints. Switch mortgage to fixed rate!

Her phone rang. She rolled over to Monty's pillow, where the phone was lying, and smiled.

When the video call pixelated into focus, he still looked a bit bleary. There was a poster of a snowboarder behind him. He must be in one of his nephews' bedrooms.

'Hey, babe. Happy New Year.' His voice was a bit scratchy. If he was here she would've instantly made him a hot toddy. Or at least told him to make one. Instantly.

'Happy New Year to you, darlin'.'

'Cameron and Marnie send their best. Did you have a good time?'

He sounded properly emosh. Was he regretting not coming back for Hogmanay?

'Brilliant actually. We sold out of everything. The donations more than make up for the milk run the distributers couldn't do. Rocco's even got a couple of micro-distillers interested in doing a deal with him to make vodka. Apparently milk vodka is a thing.'

'Great!' Monty wasn't enthusing with his usual verve.

'I sold all of my cushions!' She made a happy crowd noise.

'Oh, love. That's wonderful. The wildlife ones with the . . .' He mimed pouring tea.

'Yeah. The tea-party ones. Charlotte charged over forty quid a pop and got it!' Freya was still in a bit of shock. They were time-consuming, but if she could make a few each month, it would cover the minimum payment for the council tax. It was on her list, of course. Chipping away at the council tax.

'Did you make your resolutions?' Monty swept a hand across his face.

Was he sweating? Cameron always kept the house warm, but not sauna warm.

Freya held her notebook up so he could see the list. 'You?'

'Mmm. Yes.' Monty looked terribly serious. And epically sad. She suddenly wanted him to be here in the bed beside her so much it physically hurt. Could a person who drove you mad become essential to your wellbeing if you loved them enough? That critical thread that held your proverbial cloth together?

She resolved then and there to tell him about the painting. She would talk to Rocco about selling it. Even if the painting wasn't worth tens of thousands, it would help. She had brainstormed some great ideas with Charlotte about making tweaks in her shop and, of course, if Rocco could keep the farm shop open he might be able to update his clanky Land Rover one day. Or, at the very least, afford to take a day off and shag Charlotte.

'Want to hear my resolutions?' Freya asked.

'Frey – I need to talk.'

His face was going a peculiar shade of red.

'Monts, have you drunk too much? Are you going to be sick?'

'Yes. No. Freya. Listen to me.'

Everything in her stilled. In a bad way.

'I have to tell you something.'

She forced herself to stay quiet. Surely there could be

292

nothing so bad they couldn't fix it. Especially if they did it together.

'I told my parents and Cameron about the credit cards.'

'Everything?' she whispered. They were cash only people. Like her family. Buy what you can afford and don't if you can't. They would have been horrified.

His forehead crinkled in on itself. 'Everything. They wanted to know what the hell I was doing leaving you and the kids . . .' He faltered then sobbed, 'I'm not like you. I can't turn ideas into money. I can't juggle nineteen things at once. I tried so hard to make the money stretch out and I just . . . I can't, Frey.' He raked a hand through his hair as he choked back another sob. He looked a peculiar combination of young and old. But mostly he looked spent. 'I told them everything. I told them about maxing out the credit cards. I told them about taking out more to pay off the maxed-out ones. I told them about emptying the children's bank accounts.'

Oh, *gosh*. She hadn't known about the children's bank accounts.

She stopped hearing the details. A loud buzzing filled her head with the odd word popping through. Arrears. Bankruptcy. Collection officers.

'They asked how much we owed and I told them.'

It was roughly equivalent to what they had paid into the house. This, after years of scraping and saving and economizing to get the deposit, whilst also supporting Monty through law school.

He sucked in a jagged breath then began to openly weep. Through his snot and tears and gasps for oxygen he confessed his fears about telling her. The anxiety about having let her down. The children down. His parents, his big brother;

everyone he'd ever met or who had, for even the tiniest of moments, believed in him.

It was like watching someone have a breakdown. Actually. That was precisely what was happening. She was watching her husband have a breakdown and all she could do was sit there and wonder whether or not her phone service would last long enough to see it through.

His brother, he eventually explained, would sort it. The money, the loans, the debt – but on one condition: Monty would work for him as a carpenter. Which, he added eyes glued to hers, would entail staying in the West Country.

Freya realized she'd forgotten to breathe.

She pictured that anonymous hand reaching out to touch her newly pregnant mother's hand. She remembered how frightened she'd felt the day she'd told Monty she was pregnant, only to have her worst fear come to pass: him leaving. She forced herself to remember how all of that fear and pain and anxiety had been swept away not when he'd come back, but when she saw the pride in his face as he held his infant children for the first time.

Choices.

Everyone had choices.

She looked down at her resolutions. It was such a long list.

Would any of this have happened if she'd stepped away from the shop when she started noticing things simply weren't working any more? They could've switched roles. She could've sold things online from home while Monty saved the world – or at least part of it – and got a steady income. She could know where Felix's kilt pin was.

'Freya?' Monty sobbed. 'Say something. Anything.'

This was her fault. Her gorgeous, beautiful, generous

husband was falling to bits because she hadn't reined in her need to prove to her parents she had what it took to make it in the fashion world.

Then again, she hadn't been the one to take out six secret credit cards, max them all out, then drain what little they'd managed to save for the children's uni fees, freeze the mortgage and leave untold number of bills unpaid.

Could all this have been fixed if they'd trusted one another more? Believed in one another more?

'Give me a minute, love,' she managed to say. Her mind was reeling so fast, nothing would stick.

'Please Freya. I love you. I will do anything in the world so long as you forgive me.'

He sounded as though he meant it. Monty always meant it when he apologized. It was follow-through that was his problem.

It takes two to tango, darlin'.

There was a knock on her door. 'Mum?' Regan slipped in, wiping the sleep out of her eyes. 'Are you talking to Dad?'

'Yes, darlin'.' She waited until Monty swept away his tears and blew his nose before handing the phone to her daughter. She squealed with delight when she saw Monty making a silly face at her. They gabbled on a bit about the party and how much more fun it would've been if he'd been there. Regan wandered to the next room so Monty could wish Felix a Happy New Year. A moment later, she heard them all burst into gales of laughter.

She began gouging thick, dark lines across each of her resolutions. The good intentions. The minutiae. The broad strokes. It all boiled down to one very simple choice. A choice that would stay with all of them for ever.

Would she spend the rest of her life resenting her husband for all of the things he wasn't – or love him for all of the things he was?

Charlotte's massive platter of pancakes had been demolished. The bacon had long since been eaten and one sad little remaining sausage had Bonzer's name written all over it. The children had begged an unusually quiet Rocco for one last trip to the barns for calf-cuddles, and Lachlan had excused himself for a wee lie-down before everyone set off on their travels. It was just the girls left at the table, finishing the dregs of their coffee before Emily's taxi arrived. Izzy steeled herself. It was now or never.

She tinged her fork against the side of the syrup bottle. 'Announcement time!'

Everyone turned to her, foreheads lifted in curiosity, mouths tweaked into intrigued smiles.

'Let me guess?' Emily, who was unbelievably grumpy, said, 'You made an appointment at the GP's.'

'Oh, I was going to do that for you, Izzy,' Charlotte rushed in.

'Why can't we all let Izzy look after Izzy?' Freya asked. Freya clearly needed more sleep, but it was precisely the point Izzy was going to make. She was a grown woman who needed to both look after herself and ask her friends for help.

'I have made an appointment,' she said a bit more grandly than she'd intended.

Emily raised her arms in a 'finally!' gesture. Izzy reached out and clasped Emily's hands in her own. 'With the oncologist.'

Everyone exchanged confused looks, apart from Emily, whose face was impossible to read.

Charlotte was the one who finally managed to ask why.

'I had breast cancer back in Hawaii. I think it might be coming back.'

'Granddad's car smells like moss and cow poo.'

'It does, doesn't it?' Freya was refusing to let herself be annoyed by the fact that she and her children and all their bags were jammed into her father's tiny little two-door tin bucket.

Her husband was having a breakdown. They were subterranean levels of broke. Her business was crumbling to bits. She didn't have the remotest clue what to do about any of it. Or whether or not things could carry on as they had been. (Actually she knew the answer to that one. No. They couldn't.)

All of which was neither here nor there, because the one thing not on her list was cancer.

Izzy's news had hit them like an atom bomb. She'd not gone into great detail, but she'd had a single mastectomy, chemo and radiation. Owing to a domino effect of cock-ups between her hospital in Hawaii, Wales, and the one she'd yet to register with in Sussex, she was three months late on her annual scan. She'd had one shortly before she'd moved back and had been clear but, as of late, she hadn't been feeling quite herself and, no, she wasn't just talking about the head cold.

So for today? It simply didn't matter that they were in a cramped car reeking of teenaged boy socks and cow dung. Not when the one thing they didn't have to worry about was dying.

*

Poppy climbed out of the car and closed the door quietly behind her. 'All right, Mum?'

'Of course, darling.' Charlotte wasn't. She was absolutely heartbroken for Izzy. How they'd managed to pack the car, get the children in, particularly with Jack taking up his status as resident moody teen again, and hit the motorway was beyond her. She'd driven in a daze and, it appeared, pulled in for coffee in much the same state.

At least Izzy (doped up on cold medicine) and Luna (in the back row with Bonzer) were asleep. The last thing they needed was to realize they were being driven down the road by a woman in shock.

Izzy was the most exuberant person Charlotte had ever met. It was impossible to imagine all of that energy being savaged by cells, uncontrollably dividing again and again with the sole intent of malevolence.

Mercifully, any animosity Poppy had felt over seeing her and Rocco kissing had vanished. Jack, on the other hand, was re-harnessing his surliness with each passing mile. Whether it was the absence of cows to tend to or the Instagram pictures she could see him thumbing past – well, she had her guesses. The past few days had been a little bubble of perfection. A bubble now slit wide open with the blunt reappearance of reality. A reality that included a message from Hazel hoping to discuss 'the assets situation' sooner rather than later.

'Mum.' Jack tugged her phone off the charging jack, glared at it then climbed out of the car and handed it to her. 'Dad's sent you something.'

Irritatingly, her fingers shook as she pressed the download button. The attachment – there was no note – was from Oli's divorce lawyers.

Something about this being the busiest time of year for divorce lawyers sprung to mind then faded as she began to read.

She scanned the document, doing her very best to keep her face neutral as she absorbed the full brunt of the blow.

If she was interested, Oliver had a buyer for the house. If Charlotte wanted to stay that was, of course, her legal right, but . . . benefiting both parties . . . expediting the proceedings . . . would have to be sold eventually . . .

She pinched her fingers to the bridge of her nose.

'Is he coming back early?' Jack asked, his ever-deepening voice tinged with hope.

'No, darling. I'm afraid it's to do with the divorce.'

Jack swore. Poppy told him off. He bit her head off.

'All right, you two. Why don't we go in and get something hot to drink, shall we?'

As they walked towards the services, Poppy quietly asked, 'Is he going to, like, totally forget about us? I mean, he still loves us, right?'

Jack told her not to be such an idiot; he'd offered to let them stay in London instead of Sussex, hadn't he?

Poppy snapped back at Jack that she was *only asking, gawwwd*, then slipped her hand into Charlotte's.

Charlotte didn't know whose hand needed holding more. Oli had said they could *move in* with him?

'Of course he still loves you, darling,' Charlotte said. 'Life's just a bit complicated at the moment.'

And there it was. The complexity of divorce in a nutshell. A beeped-out word one minute. A father his children couldn't bear to lose the next. A wife who'd thought her family's world revolved around her, only to discover it didn't.

'Should we get Izzy some more cold medicine and Luna a hot chocolate?'

'Good idea.' Charlotte gave Poppy's hand a squeeze. 'I just need to run to the loo. If I give you some money, why don't you and Jack get some hot chocolates for everyone.'

After a quiet weep in the cubicle, Charlotte pulled herself together and went to the sink to give her face a quick wash. As awful as it was, she couldn't help but appreciate how the divorce had thrown a spotlight on how she'd lived her life. The wallflower who'd been so busy running around trying to make everyone else's lives better, she'd nearly faded out of her own. She washed her hands, eyes locked on the long mirror as busy, tired travellers shuffled in and out of the cubicles behind her. So many lives.

She hoped she had what it took to be a good example to her children. She hoped she had what it took to look after Izzy if, god forbid, her suspicions were true. What scared her the most was facing so much loss. Her children. Her dear, sweet friend. Her marriage.

Well.

She thought of Rocco and that wonderfully perfect kiss.

The marriage was becoming easier to live without.

Izzy and the children?

She'd fight tooth and nail for them.

She gave herself a determined nod, then headed out into the world to get on with things.

Chapter Twenty-Four

Whatsapp Group: Happy Glampers

Charlotte: Good luck Izzy! We know we promised not to text after you and Emms left this morning but Luna and I wanted you to know we think you're amazing. Luna also wants to triple check that Emily has downloaded *Moana* and *Point Break* for you and to assure you she's done the 'Crazy for Swayze' dance several times. Apparently it was a good luck thing back in Hawaii?

Freya: Throwing my bushel of luck into the ring, such as it is. A bit of pre-Easter mania at the shop (thank god it's come early this year). Monty sends his love. Apparently the house they're working on is coming along blue blazes so he might be coming home to see the kids this weekend. And me. Obvs. Big love Izz! #

Charlotte: Hi Mummy!!!! It's me. We're making lemon drizzle! Done the dance seven times so far. Seven more to go! ♥ xoxoxo Booboo

Charlotte: Apologies if she wasn't meant to see that. Just nipped to the pantry to get some fondant. Will be more careful.

Izzy: Luna's heard it all before. Not to worry.

Emily: Izz just done blood tests etc., and is at gift shop stocking up on *Heat* and *Grazia* (exact same gossip as last month when she had scans, dunno why she bothers). Doctors didn't like the sound of her never-ending cough/temp. If bloods are bad I'm betting it gets called off.

Freya: Sorry, Izz. Hope all goes well. Sending lots of love.

Charlotte: Shall I hold off on telling Luna if it's cancelled?

Emily: That child is hard as nails. She can take it. Izzy, however, may not.

Izzy: Ta very much, Emms. You're a dumbass.

Emily: No you are.

Charlotte: You're both wonderful. Either way, we'll be here waiting for you with bells on unless it's around 5 as have to nip out and pick up Pops from a friend's. xx C

Charlotte and Luna sat back and admired their handiwork. One extra-large, extra-squidgy lemon drizzle cake decorated with a blue wave (fondant), a surfer (Lego) and a pig (Moana Adventure Collection).

'Do you think she'll like it?'

Charlotte pulled Luna in for a one-armed squeeze. 'I think she'll love it.'

'What if she can't eat it?'

'Oh, I'm sure she'll give it a try. It'll keep for a couple of days if she's not up to it today. We'll make her a fresh one if it takes longer than that.'

Charlotte had, of course, prepared for that option. Since the New Year's revelation that Izzy suspected her breast cancer had returned, Charlotte's bedside reading had shifted from book club to cancer survivor memoirs. She'd steered away from the books where the women died in the end as she wasn't quite up to facing that option. She'd also become a bit of a voyeur on the breast cancer patients' forums as Izzy point-blank refused to enter 'that sort of community'. Between that, looking after Luna, Poppy, and doing the odd farm-shop consultancy, she'd barely had time to obsess over CheekyLawGirl's Instagram updates on Baby Mayfield.

Sorry.

Olive.

She only wished the children would stop calling the infant 'the pit of despair'. It was difficult to keep a straight face.

'Charlotte?' Luna moved the pig so that it, too, was riding on the surfboard.

'Yes, love?'

'Thanks for letting us move into the house.'

'Of course, darling. We love having you here, Poppy and me. Jack, too, of course. When he's home.'

Luna gently patted her on the arm as if the tables had suddenly switched and that the whole reason they'd moved in was for Charlotte's benefit. She flashed Charlotte a bright smile. 'I'm going to check Mummy's vomit bins are ready.'

Charlotte tried and failed to swallow the lump in her throat as Luna and her billow of hair 'Crazy for Swayze' danced into Oli's repurposed office. Jack had been furious when they'd cleared it out for Izzy (no stairs, *en suite*, very practical for a woman going through chemotherapy). She knew it was difficult but, quite frankly, cancer trumped philandering fathers who wanted their almost ex-wives to sell the family home.

As it was, Charlotte was still wrapping her head round the fact that Luna was the seasoned caretaker of the two of them. Luna had been eight when Izzy had gone through her first round. She would've been seven, but Izzy had delayed the treatment so that she could send Luna to a surf camp. *Wouldn't go in the end*, Izzy told them with palpable pride. Luna had insisted on staying and helping the local hospice workers. *Saw me through the worst of it. Helped remind me what I was doing it all for.*

Charlotte thought of her own mother's quick and fatal journey through lung cancer. Into hospital one day with what they thought was pneumonia, and, bar the cigarette breaks, out eight days later in a casket. Swift, brutal, and utterly of her own making. A line of thought that suggested Charlotte had yet to forgive her mother for looking after herself so poorly.

Anyway.

She briskly set about tidying up the kitchen for another round of cakes. She was experimenting with some gluten-free Italian-style Easter cakes to try out at Sittingstone. Lady V had begun loudly expressing her doubts as to whether or not 'the girl' would be returning from her maternity. Charlotte was confident she would, but the last person she'd leave in the lurch was Lady Venetia. Particularly with Oliver dropping increasingly persistent hints that his mate would buy the house any time. The new house *he'd* upgraded to must have cost much more than anticipated. Shame. It looked as if Oli would have to work that little bit harder for a bonus this year.

With things as they were – Izzy's treatment finally under way, Poppy settling into the local grammar school and Jack back to his fractious *why is this all happening to me* self – she wasn't going anywhere. She hadn't been blind to the spike in film and game downloads on the family Apple account during his 'Dad weekends'. Or the rather expensive noise-cancelling headsets. All of which, at Hazel the Lawyer's recommendation, she documented in a little notebook. She was particularly proud of the graph she'd made to monitor Oli's hint-dropping about the house. It seemed to spike with each of CheekyLawGirl's mentions of #desperateforananny or #MaternityLeaveForever.

There was, it turned out, a pinch of time in every day for Instagram.

A picture of several women holding up infants and Buck's Fizzes slid into view. #BabiesWhoBrunch.

As if on cue, a text from Oliver pinged in. *Hello, love. Any chance you'd join me for lunch at The Four Feathers next week? Would love a bit of a catch-up. x Oli*

The Four Feathers? Oliver only took her there when he'd well and truly stuffed something up. Goodness. He really must want to free up some cash. She was about to answer that she was very busy, but thank you for the kind offer, when the crunch of gravel on the drive drew her attention.

Izzy's van with Emily at the wheel and a raging Izzy in the passenger seat pulled to a halt.

Oh, dear.

'Darling! Your mother's back a bit early. What do you say we put that posy of sweet peas in her room after all?'

Freya Burns-West
15 Canter Lane
Balham, London SW12

9 April

Dr William Clarke
Headmaster's Office
Thamesbank Comprehensive School
11–27 Oakbank Road
Barnes
London SW13

Dear Dr Clarke,

Please accept this letter as confirmation that my son, Felix Burns-West, and daughter, Regan Burns-West, will not be continuing their education at Thamesbank Comprehensive this coming autumn.

We would like to thank you for the excellent level of education they have received during their time with you. If it is possible to pick up their academic records on the last day of term rather than having them posted, I would be most grateful. Apologies for any confusion regarding addresses. Monty and I are still very much married. Business has kept him in the West Country for the past term.

If a set of records could also be forwarded on to Cottleston School (address below) so that Felix's admission records will be complete when the new term begins, I would be grateful.

Thank you for putting the children at your school first. Felix and Regan have formed some incredible friendships and, of course, we are grateful for the academic foundation upon which the rest of their scholastic journey will depend.

Yours,
Freya Burns-West

FELIX'S NEW SCHOOL:
Cottleston School
Cottleston Square
Bristol BS10
AVON

TO: NHS GREYSTONE HOSPITAL TRUST, HR
FROM: Dr Emily Cheung
RE: Osteopath Consultancy Snafu

To Whom It May Concern in this Vast NHS Beast of a Machine Because There Was No *Human Name* on the Job Offer

Yes please. I would like to accept the Surgical Osteopathy Consultancy with the title of Consultant Osteopath. (Can we blame typos or autocorrect for the position offered in your email: Sultan Osteopath?)

(Apologies for any misinterpretation of the term 'suck it' in previous communication. In certain Chinese cultures, it is a very good thing, particularly when in reference to fish heads.)

Special interests include hips, knees, feet, ankles and lumbar spine pain. I also am looking into sciatica but best not to make a thing out of it just yet. And yes. The hours of nine to five (Dolly Parton withstanding) sound most excellent.

Yours,

Dr E Cheung

NB: My preference is to remain *Dr* Cheung on all relevant paperwork. My parents didn't immigrate halfway round the world to write home about their daughter, Miss Cheung. I think you'll agree it lacks gravitas.

TO: Devon Surf Co
FROM: Isabella Yeats
RE: Administrative Error

Dear Ashley (and Kai – Aloha Kai, if you're reading this),

Thank you for the (second) letter and follow-up phone message confirming my appointment as Surf Instructor at your new venture within the National Trust. I know it sounds like a lie, but the dog did genuinely eat your first letter!

I'm afraid I've hit a little blip in the health department and am stuck here in Sussex for the next couple of months, so a recce isn't possible over the bank holiday weekend as I'd thought.

As previously mentioned, my daughter is in school until 8 July. I'm not sure how much they actually learn in those last couple of weeks (LOL), but I do know she is looking forward to participating in her first-ever British school sports day (she is a gifted runner) which is on 7 July. Is there any chance the June start date could be a bit more . . . elastic?

Yours sincerely,

Izzy Yeats

Surfer

Dear Headmaster Lindley,

Please accept my apologies for writing to you on informal notepaper. I'm afraid I am 'between' printers at present. I was terrifically embarrassed upon hearing about my son, Jack Mayfield's, role in that dreadful prank. More than embarrassed, frankly. I am truly ashamed to have raised such an unkind young man.

Though you are generous in saying that boys will be boys, it is absolutely no excuse for tying another student to a lavatory in a disused outbuilding. It was a cruel, cruel thing to do.

Obviously, we are well beyond the days of corporal punishment, but I agree that working in the dining room throughout half-term for the overseas boarders would be a better option than mucking out the horses in the stables. As you noted, he's a bit obsessed with horses right now and would more than likely see it as a reward rather than a punishment. If his riding privileges could also be revoked I would be most grateful.

Jack's father is tricky to reach at this time as he is

balancing work with the arrival of his new daughter. I can be reached at all times on my mobile.

Please note, for future communications I will be using my maiden name, Bunce.

Yours sincerely,

Charlotte Mayfield née Bunce

Freya Burns-West
15 Canter Lane
Balham, London SW12

2 May

Camden Market
Shop Letting Unit
Camden
London NW1

Dear Barry,

I never thought this day would come! As per your instruction, please accept this letter as three months' notice on my shop, Tee-Boned (why did I ever think that was a good idea?).

If there is any way the committee could allow me a bit of leeway and 'forgive' the balance on the final month's rent (July), I'd be eternally grateful. (Still waiting to make my millions! Ha ha.)

As it is prime market space, perhaps some pop-ups could fill the void if you don't find a permanent vendor? I hear the hubcap chap is branching out into lightbulb art?!?!

As you know, Monty has taken up his brother's offer

to work full time. As such, the children and I will be moving to Bristol when this school term finishes (end of June, the cheeky blighters!), so if any post could please be forwarded to the address below, I would be grateful.

Thank you for many years of happiness at Camden Markets. It is an extraordinary venue. Perhaps I'll be applying for a pop-up over the Christmas hols with my new venture: Animal Accents (name still a work in progress! LOL).

All the best, yours sincerely, big hugs etc., etc.,

Freya

Whatsapp Group: Happy Glampers

Emily: Thanks for coming up to the Dragon Boat thing with me and my parents, Izz. You showed real chutzpah as the Senior Sultan Osteopath would say. My parents were impressed with how well Luna uses chopsticks. GO TO THE EFFING DOCTOR IF YOUR RASH PERSISTS. NOT NORMAL.

Izzy: Have lotion. Will apply.

Emily: Hey ladies – any chance you could nag Izzy about going to the doctor? Maybe Lady V could bully her into it next time Luna and Bonzer go for Sittingstone playdate?

Charlotte: How did interview go? Everyone: LMIRL before Freya heads to Bristol.

Izzy: Why are you convinced I can't see the messages you send about me? You're not typing them in invisible ink, doofus.

Emily: You're a doofus.

Freya: You both are. Izzy – go to the doctor. Charlotte, the Surrey farm-shop launch you oversaw sounded epic. Soz couldn't make it. Packing up fifteen years' worth of things that spark joy is a bitch!

TO: Oliver Mayfield
FROM: Charlotte Bunce
CC: Hazel Pryce
RE: Lunch at Four Feathers

Dear Oliver,
    After discussion with my lawyer, Hazel Pryce, I will meet for lunch on one condition:
    No talk of the house.
    Sincerely,
    Charlotte Bunce

TO: Devon Surf Co
FROM: Isabella Yeats

Aloha Kai!
    Thanks so much for talking admin into delaying my start date. I appreciate you can't offer the same instructor's fee as before seeing as I'll be on shore duty, but staying in the geodome will more than make up for it.

312

Result, my friend. MAHOLO TO THE HIGHEST!!! Thanks for pulling strings. I promise to give your clients their money's worth.

Might need to beg for some work in the autumn as things gone a bit woo-woo at this end.

Aloha, my friend x (you remember it means hello and goodbye, right? Or is that wo-mansplaining?) ;-)

PS – You wouldn't happen to know if there's a medical clinic or anything nearby. A hospital? Asking for a friend. LOL

TO: Monty
FROM: Wifey
MONTS! WE DID IT!! WE HAVE A BUYER FOR THE HOUSE!!!! BRING ON BRISTOL LIFE!!! Xoxoxooxxooxoxox

Dear Headmaster Lindley,

Please accept my heartfelt apologies for my son's behaviour.

However painful it is to admit, I agree that expelling Jack is the only course of action.

His father, Oliver Mayfield, will be collecting him at the end of the week, as discussed. Using drugs, even soft ones like marijuana, is entirely unacceptable. I suspect disruption to Jack's home life hasn't been helpful in offering him the sense of security any child (teenager) requires. He may have mentioned the sale of the family home, which, of course, I am not offering as an excuse, merely an explanation as to why he may be acting up.

I shall be writing to the other parents as well and accepting full responsibility for my son's actions. The other boys would very likely not have taken the drugs if he had not supplied them.

Please note, for future communications I will be available on my mobile telephone. I'd appreciate any written communication to be held until I am able to provide you with a new forwarding address. As mentioned, we are in the process of selling the house and have not yet bought a new property.

Yours sincerely,
Charlotte Bunce

TO: Devon Surf Co
FROM: Isabella Yeats

Aloha Kai!

Really really sorry, buddy. Things are f***ing complicated. 'Fraid I'm going to have to leave you in the lurch. I can send word out on the surf web that there's a kick-ass job going. Would still like to help out at some juncture. Good news is, I'm moving closer. Bristol! Any possibility of keeping me in mind for the autumn?

Aloha on the other end. x Izz

Chapter Twenty-Five

'Darling, you wouldn't mind doing us another, would you?' Lady Venetia held her empty martini glass in front of her face and grinned through it. 'Just to top me up before I head down to the kennels.'

Charlotte didn't think Lady V needed another martini but, as their Sunday Sundowners would be drawing to a close . . .

'You know, dear . . .' Lady V accepted her fresh martini with a demi-bow of the head, as if it were she and not Charlotte who was the recipient of great largesse. 'I think you've ruined me for ever.'

'What do you mean?' Charlotte hovered above her usual perch, a rather fetching eggshell-blue courting chair, until it was indicated that she'd done nothing wrong. Quite the opposite, in fact.

'I know *the gehl* will work out just fine, but it won't be the same, will it?'

Charlotte tried to explain that Lucy was every bit as dab a hand at the cakes as she was, but Lady Venetia wasn't having it.

'She's young and not terribly interesting.' Lady V gave her

fingers a bit of a flick as if the matter was settled. Poor Lucy. 'She doesn't seem to see things the way you do. It's little wonder those Bristolians snapped you up for their new venture, precocious talent that you are.' Lady V laughed, but there was no mistaking the strain it took her to do so.

Charlotte looked down at her lap, still shy of basking in the light of a well-deserved compliment. In all honesty, she was still in shock. And not a little terrified. She'd just signed a two-year contract with one of the country's most prominent visual merchandizers. They were building seven brand-new motorway service stations, all modelled on the farm-to-fork aesthetic she'd developed at Sittingstone. *Boutique rustique*, they called her style. Loved it, apparently. Her new boss had been flexible about the start date, but the first shop would be opening in late September. *In keeping with the harvest*, said the man eating out-of-season raspberries at the morning meeting. Freya would've had him for breakfast.

Lady V tapped the side of her glass with an olive to draw Charlotte's attention back to her. 'I wanted you to know it's been a comfort having you keeping an eye on things here. I shall miss our Sunday evening business chats. They save me from my increasingly tedious son.'

Charlotte smiled. Their 'business chats' were very rarely about business. Lady Venetia, she had long suspected, was actually just lonely.

Her mentor recrossed her legs and arched a solitary eyebrow. 'You won't forget me, will you darling?'

The lump in Charlotte's throat quadrupled. 'Of course not. You're my mentor, my inspiration . . .' She debated for a nano-second over whether to say the next word then threw caution to the wind, 'You're my friend. I will never forget you.'

Mollified, Venetia threw her the most heartfelt smile they'd ever shared. 'Darling, come.' She patted the sofa. 'Sit by me.'

Charlotte joined her, surprised at how papery and soft Lady Venetia's hands were. 'Is everything all right?'

'Yes. Perfectly, it's just that . . . saying goodbye to you is a bit like sending my favourite child out into the big wide world.' She dropped Charlotte's hand and drained her martini.

Charlotte couldn't meet her eye. She didn't know if she'd ever been paid such a high compliment.

Life, after all, had cornered her into choosing this new path.

Hazel the Lawyer had put it quite simply. Charlotte could either be entirely dependent upon Oliver until the children were eighteen (living in the house, bickering about which schools were right for which child, endlessly debating who cared for which child when), or she could take the reins of her own life right now and get on with things.

After a rather painful lunch with Oliver, she'd chosen the latter.

'How's your friend receiving the treatment getting on?' Venetia's tone suggested Izzy had been receiving weekly facials instead of chemotherapy. 'And that fabulous child of hers?'

Charlotte didn't take offence that Lady V never asked after her own children. Everyone had a child they adored, and in Lady V's case it was most definitely Luna.

'I think all of the skipping about with schools has been a bit much, but hopefully the move to Bristol for Izzy's new treatment will be a good thing.' It was strange to be breezily discussing an experimental treatment that could kill Izzy as easily as it could cure her. Then again, what choice did Izzy have? The first round of chemotherapy had had no impact on her tumour at all. It had taken some doing, but Emily had finally convinced her that moving to Bristol where they were trialling some intensive new treatments was the best course of action.

Lady V cut into her silent musings. 'Did you know Izzy sold her surfing company to one of those child television stars? You know the one I mean. He played an adorable child prodigy lawyer but grew up to look like a thug and – ' she made a pinging noise – 'career over.'

Charlotte did know that. She'd sold it to pay her hospital bills in Hawaii.

'And her little one will be staying at your new place in Bristol?'

'Yes, that's right. Izzy says she has some sort of job lined up in Devon come autumn, but it all sounded rather vague. I thought I'd check into getting Luna registered at Poppy's new school just in case.'

'She's always welcome to rattle round Sittingstone with me. Especially if she learns how to make martinis as well as you do.'

Before Charlotte could come up with an appropriate response, Lady V rose from the sofa. 'Be careful how you tread, darling. Make sure Izzy has some proper plans in place – legal forms and such – in case things don't pan out for her. Some friends,' her tone turned ominous, 'remain a mystery on purpose.'

True, but, everyone had a set of cards they played close to their chest.

Charlotte thought of Rocco. The kiss they'd shared. The

warmth that still flared inside her when she thought of the moment when he had held her in his arms. The scant contact they'd had since then. She'd sent a thank you card. He'd sent one back. She'd not come up with a reason to thank him for his thank you card without sounding ridiculous, so it appeared that was that.

He'd be letting the cows out to pasture soon. At least according to *Countryfile*. She'd taken to watching it on catch-up after her talks with Lady V. It was terribly informative.

'What is it, darling? You look wistful.'

'Oh, it's nothing.'

'Don't be obtuse. I can see with my wise old lady eyes you are lost in a romantic thought.'

Charlotte's eyes widened.

Lady V gave a victorious laugh, then pulled Charlotte in for a brisk farewell hug and kiss at the door to the kennels where they always bade one another adieu. 'Why don't you stop torturing yourself and ring him . . . your farmer.'

Charlotte flushed. 'I don't know what you're talking about.'

'You're the worst liar I've ever met.' Venetia mimicked Charlotte, 'Freya's brother would have had those shelves up in less than an hour. The milk Freya's brother's cows produce is superb. And the butter. Did you know he's been selling kilo upon kilo of butter?'

Charlotte flushed. 'Well.'

Lady V's eyes glittered with delight. 'Well, indeed.'

'Where are the kids tonight?'

Freya handed Emily a small vase, which she dutifully rolled into a sheet of newspaper and stuffed into a box. The vase certainly didn't spark any joy in her, but . . . she lived on a futon in her parents' basement so it wasn't as if she had much room to argue.

'Staying overnight with friends. They're binge-socializing. Felix has been out three nights on the trot.' Freya almost sounded proud.

For some reason it made Emily cranky.

She'd thought of Felix as a kindred spirit. Someone who merely tolerated human company. It looked like everyone was changing apart from her.

Other than her weekends in Sussex to see Izzy through her chemo (utterly worthless), Emily's life had fallen into that same, tedious, endless cycle of work, eat, sleep, repeat. The nine-to-five consultancy job meant far too much free time. Free time she'd slavishly applied to Netflix, volunteering for surgical shifts at the hospital, and a rather consumptive obsession with the bonsai crab-apple tree her father had given her for Chinese New Year. With any luck it would flower soon.

Freya handed her a screwdriver set. 'Don't bother packing this. Monty'll want it straight away. D'you mind popping it in that box over there?'

Emily dumped the screwdrivers into the box, then dug into a bag of vegetable crisps Freya had unearthed then immediately wished she hadn't. It was possible the crisps were potpourri. 'Do you think Monty's taking this whole carpenter thing a bit seriously?'

'What do you mean?' Freya snapped open another bin bag. Number thirty-nine by Emily's last count.

'You know. The whole falling on his sword thing.' Freya tensed but Emily powered on. 'Becoming a carpenter to show his love for you.' She put on her earnest voice. 'Moving into a *church*. It's all a bit Jesus-y. Is he on a twelve-step programme or something?'

'There's absolutely nothing wrong with twelve steps,' Freya snapped defensively.

So, that was a yes, then. She said nothing as Freya ploughed on.

'There's a lot more going on than simply falling on a sword.' She started ticking things off on her fingers. 'A. He's not sacrificing himself. He may have started working for his brother as a means of getting through this rough patch, but we made the decision to move as a family.'

'I thought you said Cameron was a twat.'

'He is, but . . .' Freya glared at her then ticked off another finger. 'B. Selling the house repays a substantial amount of Cameron's generous assistance which means we only have to tolerate him lording it over Monty for another year or two rather than eternity. C? Monty's working on the Hawkesbury development because he *likes* it. He's an excellent carpenter. If you remember, he did most of the work on the kitchen.' Freya flung her arm out and cracked her knuckles on a cupboard door that was sagging on its hinges. She shot Emily a look that dared her to say anything. 'D, E, and F? They've deconsecrated the church, god is a myth created to bolster the patriarchal hierarchy and none of it matters anyway because you know as well as I do that Monty and I are agnostics.'

Emily tapped the side of her nose. 'Best to keep that quiet when you move into the house of the lord.'

Freya scowled and swept some of her curls back from her forehead. Emily could see at least an inch of grey working its way into Freya's hairline. It was the first time she'd known Freya not to have kept up with her appearance. Money must be extra tight if she was forgoing her trips to the hairdresser's.

'Anyway,' Freya sniffed. 'By doing the townhouses, Monty and Cam are preserving a "building at risk", not a church.'

Oh, *honestly*.

'When Prince went by a symbol and Kanye wanted to be Ye, they were still Prince and Kanye. It's a *church*, Freya. You're going to be living in an as-yet-to-be-built townhouse in a *church*. With a massive loan hanging over your head. It's hardly the philanthropic preservation of an old building. It's survival. I thought the whole point of the move was to start being honest.'

Freya gave the tiniest of nods, a muscle twitching in her jaw as she flicked her hair back into submission. Again.

'Like I said, Monty's working on the townhouses. The bulk of his salary will go towards the situation with his brother. I'll be building up my business in the artist's co-operative—'

Emily cut her off. 'Freya! If this whole thing is the fresh start you claim it is, you may as well start calling things by their actual names. Debts. Loans. Churches. What Monty is doing is virtually indentured servitude. What *you're* doing is . . . I don't even know what the name of it is. Madness? Insanity? I know you love him, but letting Monty put you all at risk a second time? Bonkers.'

Freya lashed out. 'I've taken over the finances again. I'm dealing with all of the paperwork. I'm finding schools for the children. Giving up my shop. I'm changing everything so that our *family* can find a way to work to the best of all our abilities. I'm not kicking him out the door just because he cocked up. We both did.'

Emily gave Freya her best 'I'm saying this because I'm your friend' face. 'It seems to me, you're the only one making sacrifices to fix what Monty's done.'

Freya lost her cool. 'I thought you came over here to help, not rip me to shreds. The house is sold! The deal's been made. I'm trying to keep my fucking family together, all right?'

Emily stuffed the healthy crisps/potpourri into the bin bag. Freya was right. It was her decision to make. Even if it was completely mental. 'Hey. As long as you're happy.'

'I *am* happy,' Freya ground out. 'I have my husband back. The children are looking forward to us all living together again . . .' And then she burst into tears.

Uh-oh. This was unusual. There was obviously more going on here than Monty being an eejit with the joint account. Emily steeled herself and asked, 'Want to talk about it?'

Freya sniffed and wiped her face on the sleeve of her T-shirt. A plain green one. 'No.' And then, 'It's all my fault.'

'What? Don't be ridiculous. You didn't not pay the bills. Monty's a lovely man, but the ball is in his court on this one, lady.'

'No, seriously. It actually is my fault. Or a lot my fault,' she acquiesced when Emily tried to interrupt her. In a steadier voice she explained, 'The business hasn't been going well for ages. Instead of facing up to it or changing tack I've just been barrelling on hoping it will all come good. Monty's been struggling to pay whatever he could with less and less and I guess, in his own fucked-up way, taking out all those credit cards and ignoring the mountain of debt was his way of making sure I didn't have to worry about it so I could focus on the business.' She swiped away a fresh wash of tears. 'I was going to talk to him about making some changes a while back but then Mum died and Felix needed braces and . . .' she threw up her hands. 'Life.'

Emily nodded. It made more sense now. She still wasn't sure miring them in massive debt was something she'd forgive quite so easily, but even with her heart of stone, she could see that the pair of them had been trying to do what they thought best. Poor Freya. And, she supposed, poor Monty. The phrase 'clouded judgement' sprang to mind. A mental pea-souper more like. 'Is Monty still seeing the counsellor?'

Freya shook her head. 'It took a couple of goes to find one who was a good fit. I'm seeing one too and, of course, we've still got a few more sessions with the debt therapist, but . . .' Freya made a noise that was hard to read. Did she actually want out but felt duty bound to stand by her man?

'A lot of people would've left him.'

'I'm not a lot of people.' Freya knotted the bin bag tightly and marched off towards the hallway.

Emily looked round the large open-plan kitchen/living space she knew Freya loved and tried to see things from her perspective. If she stayed in London she'd be facing a life of endless penury and, most likely, bankruptcy. Being a single mother would be exhausting. Freya's art embodied joy and whimsy. She wouldn't feel either of those things if she tried to press on through. She supposed she could always move back to Scotland. Her brother and father would be over the moon if she moved back.

Freya slammed the door shut then stomped back into the room.

Uh-oh. She had her lecture face on. Emily took a swig of lukewarm wine. It too had a tang of potpourri.

'Monty is brilliant.'

'Okay.'

'Don't make that face! He loves the kids. He loves me!' Freya poked herself in the chest. Too hard from the looks of things.

'No one's saying he doesn't love you.'

Freya took in a deep breath. Then another. After the third she began in a more measured tone, 'I was every bit as responsible for this mess as Monty was.'

'Fine. You were an idiot, too, but that doesn't mean you have to tie yourself to Monty for the rest of your life. So he's doing some work for his brother. Fab. Don't forget that that work is to pay back debts *he* accrued. Not you. And how is working and micro-managing the family finances going to work out? Will Monty love being on the end of a string for every penny he spends? Will it give you more time with the children? I doubt it. And don't tell me that's what the counselling is for because what he's done – what you've *both* done since you're so keen to share the blame – is break the foundations of your trust in one another. Is that something that can really be fixed by moving?'

'It's something that can be fixed by talking.'

Emily barked a laugh. 'What? Because the pair of you have been doing that so brilliantly.'

Freya glared at her then spat out, 'You're just jealous everyone is moving to Bristol without you.'

The words hung between them like little razors. Little razors of truth.

Izzy needed the treatment, so her move was a no-brainer.

Monty had work there.

Charlotte did too.

Everyone was moving onwards and upwards, apart from Emily. Well. She was a Sultan Osteopath. That was something.

Before she could respond, Freya began backtracking. 'I was superimposing a patriarchal system on Monty that spoke to a preconceived and archaic notion about marital expectations.'

Right.

'Oh. My. *Fucking god*, Freya! Drop the lingo will you? Speak-a da English!'

'You can be such a bitch sometimes, Emily.'

'So can you, you sanctimonious granola-eating do-gooder.'

They glared at one another. Emily pushed the bottle of wine across the counter. This was possibly the most honest they had ever been with one another. 'Drink. Speak normal words to me.'

Freya defensively crossed her arms. 'You know what your problem is, Emily?'

Oh, this would be rich. 'No, Freya. I don't know what my problem is, but I bet you're going to tell me.'

'You're jealous. And I'm not just talking about Bristol.'

Pah! 'Of what?'

'The fresh start Monty and I have chosen to take. *Together*.'

All right. No need to freaking rub it in. So she was married. Whatevs. Not everybody needed a cottage with roses bedecking the door.

'You're unable to trust people and you're jealous because we *do* trust one another. Trust each other enough to take a risk. Follow our hearts. You are so risk averse it's no wonder you're stuck living in your parents' basement. Just like they'd always planned.'

'Ooohoo! Touché!'

And then the words sunk in.

Oh, shit. She was right. Emily took a swig of wine.

Freya took advantage of her silence to push the knife in further. 'And whether or not you care to admit it, I think you *are* jealous that Charlotte and Izzy are coming to Bristol as well. Foolhardy or not, we're all proactively changing our lives, when all you're doing is playing out the script your mum and dad wrote for you the day you were born.'

Emily grabbed her coat, fully prepared to storm out f-o-r-e-v-e-r when Freya hoinked her shoulders up to her ears then heavily let them drop. 'I'm sorry. That was really mean. I'm too tired to argue. Can we be friends again?'

They stared at one another.

Emily didn't want to fight either, but she wanted Freya to admit she had a point. Following their hearts wasn't fool-proof. Freya wanted her family to be whole again. Izzy wanted to live. Charlotte didn't want to stay in a house suffocatingly full of memories of Oliver, even if it legally was hers (score one to Hazel the Lawyer!).

But Emily felt as though she was the only one dealing with the practicalities of making each of those dreams a reality. She'd been the one to get Izzy into the trial when it became apparent the chemo wasn't working. She'd hooked Charlotte up with Hazel the Lawyer when Oli was primed to steamroller her into a divorce on his terms. Okay, she hadn't done much for Freya, but she was helping her pack. That was something.

Her chest began to constrict as Freya's accusation took root.

She wanted her friends to be happy but they weren't *all* meant to move on without her.

She thought of Tansy's number stuffed into her purse, the ink fading with each passing fistful of coins.

'C'mon, Emms.' Freya pushed the wine bottle towards her. 'Let's be friends. I don't want to move with us being all . . .' She waggled her fingers and made a *plerfzzzt* noise. 'Let's make up?'

Emily shifted her hip so that she looked super nonchalant, but her insides were vibrating. She'd never had a fight like this – if you didn't count the time she smashed her violin in front of her mother. 'Dunno.'

'Hug it out?'

Emily made a face.

They both started giggling. Nervously.

'You'd let Izzy hug you.' Freya didn't sound cross about it. It was just a fact.

'Izzy's—'

Freya waved her hand between them. 'I know. I know. You and Izzy have your thang. C'mere.' She opened up her arms. 'I'm gonna hug you anyway.'

Emily didn't move. She hadn't finished being furious yet. But when Freya wrapped her arms around her, she did her very best not to squirm.

Who'd forgotten to tell Bristol it was summer?

If only Izzy could find a way to blast the vicarage's central heating without banjaxing Charlotte's bill, life would be perfect.

As it was, layers would be the name of the game. Izzy tugged up the zip on the puffer jacket Emily had bought for her in the sales. A thick neck-to-knees number with built-in pocket warmers. Cosy toasty. Most likely she'd be tearing it off in a few minutes when yet another hot flush hit, but for now? Perfection in a down cocoon.

'Just pop that one over there, Izzy.' Charlotte put down her own box then frowned. 'If it's too heavy, leave it.'

'I'm perfectly capable,' Izzy groused as she went to pick up the box and couldn't courtesy of the pins and needles in her hands. Unwilling to admit as much to Charlotte, she sat down and unpacked it where it sat. Inside was a jumble of books and framed paintings that looked very much as though Izzy had packed it. Nothing like the neat and tidy boxes Charlotte had put together. She picked up a loosely wrapped object. Sugar and *spice* she was tired. She'd finish this box then sneak away for a nap in her lovely quiet ground-floor room that Charlotte had insisted she accept.

After Charlotte watched her for a bit she put on her 'let's talk positive' voice. 'Did Luna tell you what was on her programme today?'

Izzy had to laugh. 'Combat archery chased up by street dance and Parkour, if memory serves. There might be some maths in there but I'm not one hundred per cent on that.'

Charlotte shook her head. 'Honestly. Schools these days.'

'No, Charlotte,' Izzy corrected. 'Very fancy school summer camp which Luna and I shall be eternally grateful for. Thank you.'

She meant it. From the bottom of her heart.

The chemo had ended just over a month ago and when the scans had come back? Virtually everything had changed in the blink of an eye.

Freya had given up her shop and was already working

as an office manager at an artists' co-operative here in Bristol.

Emily was working all hours at her very grown-up sounding job.

Charlotte sold the Sussex house, not because Oli had pressured her to but because, in her words, 'There was simply no way the children could move on if they were living in that pristine shrine to what didn't work.'

And Izzy still had cancer.

In fairness, she felt a million times better than a few weeks ago when she was a vomiting, aching, crippled chemo mess. But now that she was about to go into the clinical trial? Bit of a yo-yo.

Unlike in Hawaii, when her doctors had whipped off her breast and taken nearly all of her lymph nodes along for the ride before the standard rounds of chemo and radiotherapy, the team in Sussex felt she should have the opposite protocol. Chemo first. Lumpectomy second. This, of course, was dependent on her tumour shrinking.

Not only was her disturbingly large tumour still very much in place (evil, deeply burrowed beast that it was), it had decided to forge new frontiers threatening encroachment on her skin, her lungs and her brain. Score one to tumour.

All of which made agreeing to the clinical trial Emily had wormed her onto a no-brainer. Six to eight weeks solid in hospital that would make or break the cancer. Which was where fancy summer camp came into play.

After selling her house for quite the breathtaking sum, Charlotte had asked if Luna would like to join Poppy at Badminton's summer school. It was lush. The girls swotted in the morning then threw themselves into archery, swimming, riding, flute (Poppy), and ukulele (Luna). They even had a special week of survival skills in August. All this and the girls could return home every night to the vicarage.

Izzy absolutely loved the house and, more to the point, so did Charlotte.

It was already completely different to her marital home. The sitting room was strewn with brightly coloured throw pillows. Soft blankets were invitingly draped over sofa arms. Verdant houseplants gave the whole place a vibrant, botanical flair. Not a grey thing in sight.

It was, effectively, an homage to everything Oliver had disliked. Joy, mostly, if the report on their lunch was anything to go by. How had the man only just learned that babies were peeing, pooing, barf-monsters? And what was he doing whining to Charlotte about it? She didn't knock Xanthe up. Izzy had loved seeing Charlotte's mouth twitch when she showed her the latest Instagram post from CheekyLawGirl. The kitchen looked as though a bomb had hit it and, more astonishingly, Xanthe had appeared *sans* make-up, hair like a rat's nest and bags under her eyes. #mumslife #needamanny

'Thank *you*, by the way,' Charlotte gave Izzy a gentle pat on the shoulder, wary, as ever, of hurting her.

'For what?'

'Helping with this. I know the children should be giving me a hand with it all, but . . .'

'Don't worry,' Izzy waved her off. She got it. Jack was always in London. Poppy was struggling to make yet another set of friends. Oli was a wanker. Divorce sucked.

Izzy unwrapped a small painting and held it out at arm's length. The gilt-framed canvas was quirky. And strangely moving. 'Is this yours?'

It wasn't at all like the art that had been hanging in the Sussex house.

Charlotte knelt beside her and took it in her hands with a soft *ohh, I remember you*. The painting featured a cuckoo clock but, instead of a wooden cuckoo, there was a little girl in a suit emerging from the tiny door.

'Goodness,' Charlotte pressed her fingers to her mouth as she put the painting down then unwrapped a second one. It was plainly framed and had a much more modern aesthetic than the first. There was a girl falling from the sky in the foreground with some cotton wool clouds far out of reach. You couldn't see the girl's face. Just her hair. From the looks of things she was falling at an accelerated rate. Izzy knew the feeling. Some birds were swooping in. To the rescue maybe? 'Are those goldfinches?'

'Yes,' Charlotte answered distractedly. 'Yes they are.'

'I'm going to guess these aren't Oli's.'

'Mmm. No.'

'Poppy's?'

'They're mine.' Charlotte sat back on her heels and smiled. 'I bought them before I met Oli at an Affordable Art Fair. They were going to be the first things I hung up in my art café.'

'The one you always wanted to open?'

'Yes.' Charlotte beamed at the paintings. 'The one I always wanted to open. You know, Izzy?' She gave Izzy's shoulder another light squeeze. 'You've just given me a wonderful idea.'

Freya had been right not to let Monty and the children stay. They had protested. Said they should do the reverse of a ship's christening and perform some sort of silly ritual to bring good luck along with them to Bristol. But something deep inside her had needed to do this on her own. So she'd told them not to be ridiculous, it was just a pile of bricks. Their *future* home was where their energy should be spent. Besides, she pointed out. Who else was going to drive the removal van to Bristol?

It had been a lie, of course.

She wasn't meant to be attached to material things but now that it was no longer theirs, the house symbolized much more than she had thought. Their hopes and dreams as a family. Goalposts they had hit. Shelter in good times and, more recently, some very bad.

Mostly, though – now that she was calling a spade a spade – it had been a drain.

Up until now, she thought her adult life had been devoted to her family, her business, her principles, her moral core, the *stand* she took. On everything. But in reality? Her entire adult life had been devoted to buying, then keeping the house. Saving for the deposit. Paying the mortgage. Financing repairs. Remortgaging for the extension. Scraping together more money to cover the drains being refitted, the bathroom retiled, the boiler replaced. Doubling her efforts to pay the catapulting interest rate. Negotiating a mortgage freeze. Deciding to sell.

And now it was all over.

The hopes. And the dream. All to make way for new, more realistic ones.

Somebody else would live here from tomorrow. They'd have their own rose-hued vision for the future, no doubt. And she could, at long last, look towards the future clear-eyed.

She walked through each of the bare rooms, scooping up a final set of memories as she went. Felix's broken tooth. Regan's 'incident' with the candle. Monty's height chart for the kids and Dumbledore. When she hit the landing, the woman that the estate agency had recommended 'to guarantee that "ready to move in" look' appeared at the foot of the stairs.

'You want anything else? Last chance.' The cleaning lady looked at her expectantly.

Yes, she did. She wanted her family.

And they weren't here.

It was all a bit of a shambles really. This great denouement. What had she expected? To be handed a prize for having bought a house? People did it all the time. The same way people changed the goalposts on what was important.

The cleaning woman eventually made her mind up for her, shooing her out of the hallway and onto the frayed welcome mat. Freya watched as she mopped backwards down the corridor, out of the front door, put the mop in the bucket and, in one swift move, closed the door for good.

In that moment Freya felt an instant, blissful sense of freedom.

Chapter Twenty-Six

'Hey! Look at you with the new hair!'

'Yeah.' Emily touched her slightly mellowed avatar look, equally surprised by the changes in her Nordic cuddler. Well, not *hers*, but . . . 'I thought it was time for a change.'

'Nice one.' Noomi the Cuddler put her hand out for a fist-bump.

Emily didn't want to fist-bump. Nor did she really want to be hugged by Noomi now that she was here. Perhaps it was time for another change.

'What do you think of *my* new do?' Noomi tugged her hair out of the high ponytail.

Not much if she was being honest.

'Nice.'

It wasn't.

Rather than the whimsical 'I'm half butterfly' effect that she presumed Noomi had been going for when she'd requested blue hair, the dye job made her look more . . . mortal. Which was a shame. The whole reason Emily had entertained this whole 'money for hugging' thing was because Noomi had seemed other-worldly. The golden hair, the willowy limbs, the whole lemon-verbena vibe. A vibe that came with a price tag, obviously, but at least it had allowed Emily to kid herself that the sessions were not part of her real life.

Noomi shook her head. 'I can't believe how *different* you look. Any other big changes in your life?'

Apart from the fact that all her friends had moved to Bristol leaving her to wallow in an ever-deepening pool of self-pity? Nope. Nothing new to see here. Apart from the hair. Obvs.

Emily looked down the street and saw a smattering of normal people doing normal things. Taking out the rubbish. Waving goodbye to a friend. Talking on their mobile phones. Laughing.

She would bet any amount of money that none of them had ever paid a person to cuddle them.

'Emily?' Noomi swept her My Little Pony forelock up and out of her eyes.

What on earth was she doing paying someone to hug her? It wasn't fulfilling. It wasn't *real*.

The revelation hit her like whiplash.

It wasn't an absence of cuddling that was creating that vast, gaping, black hole in Emily's soul. It was proactively closing herself off from everyone she cared about.

Her parents. Izzy, Charlotte, Freya.

It didn't take a shrink to point out that she hadn't needed pound-a-minute cuddling when she'd been whizzing back and forth to Sussex for Izzy, helping Freya out with the move, meeting Hazel the Lawyer to hand over documents for Charlotte. It was, she believed, what most people called Having A Life.

Once they'd all headed to Bristol, she'd withdrawn into the same ol' same ol' patterns. Work, sleep, repeat.

She'd not seen Callum for months. Well. They'd met once for brunch with Ernesto and she'd faked an emergency surgery page halfway through. (A trick she'd learnt from Callum, so the ruse was short-lived.) All of those gooey doe-eyes had felt like lasers obliterating the remains of their friendship. On reflection, she hadn't been annoyed; she'd been jealous. Just as she had been when she'd helped Freya pack up, watched the Sold sign get nailed up outside Charlotte's and packed Izzy off in her new coat. It had been like sending everyone off for a grand adventure on the Yellow Brick Road while she stayed behind to toe the line because *that's what she did.*

But why?

Because it seemed easier than jumping into the roiling pit of emotional chaos they were all battling their way through.

Noomi held out her hand.

Emily didn't take it.

Freya was right. She was a dried-up, bitter prune of a tiger baby who'd never learned to connect the emotional dots.

She was brilliant at telling everyone else how fucked up their lives were, but if she ever bothered to turn the mirror on herself? She knew exactly what she'd see. Abject, bone-deep terror that Izzy's new treatment wouldn't work. Same again when she told her parents she was never, ever going to marry The Wang Boy, no matter how many flipping degrees in biochemistry he had.

Noomi waved her hand in front of Emily's face. 'Sweetie? Should I call someone? An ambulance, maybe?'

'No. Thank you.' Emily had trains to book. Parents to sit down. A life to live. 'I've got to go.'

She turned and walked straight back to the high street, picked up her pace as she hit the stairs into the underground, then, when she arrived at her stop, she hit the ground running.

'Mum? How long do we have to stay?'

Charlotte put her finger to her lips. Surely Jack knew it was rude to speak during a recital. His own sister, no less! Never mind that Poppy didn't appear to be exactly gifted with the flute, but . . . she showed mechanical flair.

'See you outside.' Jack climbed across her and into the aisle then sloped out of the auditorium.

Honestly. Where had his manners gone? His father, from the sounds of it, had been letting him run feral. Not that Oliver had been all that explicit about his parenting regime when he'd 'returned' Jack for a bit of 'quality time with his mother'. (*No. He hasn't run away, Charlotte. He just wants to see his mum.*) At least Jack had actually come to Bristol and not swanned off to Magaluf or wherever it was boys on the edge of making some very bad decisions went. He seemed to have an awful lot of spending money for a lad whose summer internship at his father's law firm had ended in the space of a day and a half. (*Not for me, Mum. Bunch of tight-assed know-it-alls.*)

The moment Poppy finished, Charlotte too sneaked out, nipped round to the stage door, whispered something vague to the music teacher about a family emergency, and marched out to the car park, only to find Jack stubbing out a cigarette round the back of the Land Rover.

Rather than tell him off for something he clearly knew he shouldn't have been doing, she thought it best to bring the entire matter home where they could discuss things sensibly. They'd have the house to themselves, as Luna and Izzy were in Devon for a bit of mother-daughter time before Izzy went into hospital.

'Jack? Poppy? In the car, please. It's time to go home.'

'Mum!' Poppy was indignant. 'I told Riley and Teigan I'd go to the village for ice cream after and Teigan still has to do the a cappella choir. Can't you pick me up later?'

'Just leave her here,' Jack sneered. 'It's not like she's sided with Xanthe or anything. I know I'm a bad influence.' He made scary monster noises that, in the circumstances, were rather disturbing.

'Mum, tell him to stop it. I want to be with my friends is all.'

Jack gave a mean laugh. 'Friends? Is that what you call them? How stupid are you? The only reason they're nice to you is because you spend your allowance on them, idiot.'

'Jack! That's enough.' Her son's indifference to his sister had developed into a rather vile disdain since he'd arrived. She knew staying with his father might cause a bit of a divide, but nothing like this. Before she could intervene he started poking Poppy in the arm.

'What's Dad giving you to buy your friends now, hunh? Fifty? A hundred? More?'

Poppy swiped at him, only to stumble into the car when he dodged her hand, her flute case cracking against the immaculate finish. 'Asshole.'

'Poppy!' Jack mimicked Charlotte's shocked tone perfectly, and then, 'Language!'

'All right, you two. Why don't we all settle down?' Charlotte opened the passenger door. Neither of her children moved.

Jack pressed up to his full height. He was over six foot now. Intimidating when he wanted to be. And right now he wanted to be. 'Did you know that, Mum? That Dad's been paying Poppy not to come for her weekends in London? That he paid me to come out here? I guess now that you've got your big job and "Saint Luna" hanging onto your apron strings you'll be paying us to stay away as well.'

In that instant her heart broke.

The anguish morphed into a white-hot rage that Oliver had led their children to believe her love for them could be monetized.

'At least I don't have to buy my friends with drugs!' Poppy snapped.

The pair of them went wild. They hit screaming level just as pairs of hand-holding parents began to wander out from the concert hall. Lovely.

'Right!' Charlotte pointed at the car with a level of authority she hadn't realized she possessed. 'Get in the car. The pair of you. We're going on a little trip.'

Freya had only been to a handful of suppers at Cameron's over the years. Living in London was very useful in that respect. Not because he was unpleasant – actually, he was unpleasant – but up until now Freya had always felt slightly sorry for him. Whatever he did, no matter how grand the achievement, the poor man's feats never outshone the fact that Monty had a law degree. The fact that Monty had never actually *used* his law degree seemed to be irrelevant. And, whilst a Tory-devotee and a bit of a boor, poor old Cam worked hard. He'd turned his father's two-man building business into a company that employed over fifty people.

They developed entire communities where once there had been a neglected field. He re-envisioned old buildings. Re-purposed newer ones. Was sending his own children to university. And still, Monty remained the family's golden child.

Until now.

Being indebted to Cameron was turning out to be a real bitch.

Twenty minutes in and she was ready to gouge her own eyeballs out. Sure. Cameron had helped them out of a particularly tough spot, but there was no need to talk to Monty as if he were a thicko. He'd had a breakdown, not a lobotomy. And if she had to coo over Cam's pool house/lad's pad one more time . . .

Would this be their lives for the foreseeable future? Kowtowing to an aspirational lifestyle they'd proactively sought to escape?

When talk shifted to the twins' academic ambitions, she smiled tightly throughout Marnie's – Cam's wife's – pontifications. 'As I understand it from *my* boys, most young people who want to *succeed* in life are doing something *sensible* in university these days. Something like engineering or computer science. You know. *Useful* degrees for *useful* jobs.'

Marnie had never once bought one of her T-shirts so she knew it was a dig. But now the woman was insulting her kids.

Did she not know that applied mathematics was the *foundation* of those *useful* jobs? Like cement to a builder. And hello? Veterinary science? That was useful. Especially to that overweight chocolate lab of theirs. The type-2 diabetes would strike any day now if the titbits from the table were anything to go by. Or a coronary. A malicious urge to call the RSPCA kept her smiling through the non-native prawn cocktails.

Penance was what it felt like. Penance for every wrong she'd ever done. Which was fitting, she supposed, now that they were living in a church. (Deconsecrated as of 27 June, though Izzy claimed she could still feel the presence of 'a higher energy'.)

She choked her way through Marnie's dry rib roast and Cam's talk of the new Tory town councillor they'd held a drinks do for. She drank glass after glass of artisanal water from Fiji (the air miles!) despite having insisted that tap water was fine. She needed it to choke down the endless *sycophancy*. Her own children, who were normally eye-rollers at nouveau middle-class excess, were all, 'Thank you so much for giving us the opportunity to live in the church' this and, 'Oh my goodness we think your house/car/pool/shed/Magimix is amazing' that. Regan even performed triage on Trudy, their Persian cat, when the fur ball's claw got snagged on the floor-to-ceiling scratching tree after Dumbledore may have accidentally on purpose chased her up the thing. A nail clipper would've done the trick back home.

A home, she reminded herself, they'd had to sell to begin to pay back Cameron for digging them out of an epically bad hole. And the Fiji Water had been irritatingly refreshing.

After the obligatory hugs and kisses goodbye (of the pat-pat, air-kiss variety that suggested her in-laws couldn't wait to close the door and talk about them), Freya and her family got in the car to go home. They'd been unable to resist a 'playful comment' on the diesel fuel she was gobbling up in the old Volvo estate she was driving these days. She'd bought it for a snip from a friend at Camden Market who'd given up cars for public transport. When she scraped some change together she'd donate to her favourite CO_2 emissions charity. Or sell it and insist they ride cycles everywhere. Bristol wasn't *that* hilly.

Once they were heading back into Bristol, Monty gave his nonexistent belly a pat and sighed. 'Oh, it's good being so close to family, isn't it?'

Freya kept her eyes on the road. He'd *never* spoken about his family like this before. He'd always preferred her family to his. They didn't give a monkey's about his law degree. It was the bottles of homemade beer, the flirtation with cheese making and the thousands of other experiments he brought up to the farm each and every Christmas that had dazzled them. They liked him for him. End of story.

He slipped a hand onto her leg. 'I was thinking, Frey . . .'

'Oh?' She glanced at the rear-view mirror. Felix was reading a book and Regan was unsuccessfully plaiting her hair into a fishtail. He squeezed her leg. She and Monty hadn't had sex in a while. She could do with a bit of intimacy. But where? The 'house' was a vast, stripped-down church with a few bits of scaffolding marking out the future townhouses. Privacy was not an option.

'What would you say if we branched out from the townhouses?'

She laughed to hide her disappointment. 'Monty, you've barely started *our* townhouse, let alone the other three.'

'Yeah, I know, but . . . I've been doing a bit of blue-sky thinking. You know, inspired by working on the church and seeing it come together.'

What was he talking about? There were a few chalk lines etched out around the apse, but that was it.

'I was talking to Cam about it before we left. There are so many interesting buildings out there. And not just in the UK. There's France, Croatia. Italy! I was flicking through Cam's *Telegraph* and it had an amazing article about these abandoned ghost villages. Entire villages just dying to be turned into boutique hotels.'

Freya's toes begin to curl in her sandals.

Not again. She couldn't do this again. It had taken nearly every fibre of her sanity to make it this far.

Monty nattered on and the kids joined in with *ooo, that'd be cool*s as the white noise of blood roaring round her brain drowned him out.

Emily had hit the nail on the head. Monty wasn't depressed or scrabbling to make up for her shortcomings in the bringing-home-the-bacon department. He was living in cloud-cuckoo-land. So was she, come to think of it. She'd fallen for all of this – the church, the 'potential big income' if they wanted to flip theirs and do up another big project further down the line. Watching a man who normally flipped pancakes put his newly lean, fit body to work at a table saw with a sheet of double ply had blinded her to reality. Her husband was no longer the man she'd married.

Just as she was gearing up to remind him about the money they had not yet paid his brother and the *four entire town-houses* he had yet to finish, she had an idea.

She pulled into a lay-by, took off her seatbelt and twisted round so they could all see one another.

'I know we've gone through some huge changes lately, but how about we all take a page out of the Franciscans' handbook?'

They all looked at her as if she'd just told them they should become Scientologists.

344

'Look. I know things are tough right now, but we don't need more stuff to make us happy, do we? Or more projects. We have a roof with a spire over our heads. Almost two full months to explore Bristol. Pretty cool schools to go to in the autumn. The best cake baker in the land living just a few feet away.'

They all smiled at this. Charlotte, despite her new work-load looking after Izzy, Luna, Poppy and, periodically, Jack, still managed to drop cakes off just when they needed them most.

'However much I'd love for you to buy a ghost village, what we really need right now is each other.' She looked her husband in his sweet blue eyes. 'We need *you*, Monty. The real you. I need you. The children need you. Don't we, kids?' She opened up the field. 'Tell him. We love him, don't we? Tell your father something you love about him.'

The children squirmed. 'C'mon,' she coaxed. 'I'm not asking for deep stuff here. I'm talking about the way he always makes the best popcorn when we watch a film. Or how he makes homework fun.' They nodded. He did make homework fun.

'I love it when he does my hair. The twisted plait ponytail, especially,' Regan shyly volunteered.

'Don't tell me, tell him! He's right here. Tell your father how much you love it when he does your hair.'

'I love it when you do my hair.' Regan started to giggle. 'Mostly because Mum's terrible at it.' She shot an apologetic look at Freya.

'Good! This is good. C'mon, Felix. Your turn. What do you love about your dad?'

Felix took off his glasses and rubbed the indentations on his nose. 'Ummm . . . well . . . I think Dad's Thai green curry is really good.'

'I wouldn't want any other dad,' Regan said solidly. 'I mean, no offence to Uncle Cameron, but he's kind of . . . materialistic.' She said it like it was a crime against humanity. Which was good. Because being materialistic at this point and time in their family was not a viable option.

'Uncle Cameron's a bit of a bore about his roast beef, isn't he?' Monty said guiltily. Then unleashed a gleeful grin.

Excellent. This was more like it.

Monty sat back in his seat and rubbed Freya's shoulder. 'Forget I said anything, Frey. I was being an idiot.'

'What? No.'

Oh, thank god.

'Honestly? I don't think I could stand sucking up to my brother until the end of time. More loans means more prostrating myself at the altar of Cameron. I don't think that'd be good for any of us.'

Fresh, clean air filled her lungs again.

He was still in there. Her Monty.

She pulled the car back out onto the road.

'I think clearing my debts is a more realistic goal to work towards. Yeah. Clean and clear. That'd work.'

'Would you still want to be partners with him once you're in the clear?'

Monty thought for a moment. 'I don't think so. I don't think he would really either. Especially if I start pointing out how handy my *law degree* would be.'

The children laughed their socks off.

Monty admitted he'd been thinking of actually putting it

to use by volunteering a few hours a week at the local citizens advice bureau. The children cheered.

Freya smiled, silently enjoying all of the Cameron-bashing that ensued.

This type of guilty pleasure, mercifully, was free.

Oohh, this was nice.

Izzy was so pleased she'd accepted Kai's invitation to come down with Luna for a couple of days. Not that life with Charlotte wasn't lovely or anything, but this was most excellent.

Beach. Fire. Looney running round making mincemeat of the other children with her epic boogie-board skillz.

'Hey, Izz.' Kai handed her an enamelled mug of green/ginger/garlic tea, or whatever it was his hippy wife had prepared. The woman sure did love a tincture. Said it would 'set Izzy up' for her treatment. As if some reduced elderberry juice and honey would prepare her body for the most intensive round of chemotherapy she'd ever had.

She took a sip of the tea and grimaced. Oohh, that was foul. Poor Kai.

'Great kid you got there,' Kai said after a while.

'Yeah.' Izzy was never shy about admitting her kid was one of the best. Mostly because it was completely true. Beautiful, sunshiny, bright. She couldn't have asked for a better child. Wouldn't. She wouldn't ask for a single, solitary thing ever again if this worked.

'Who's looking after her while you're in?'

She laughed. 'You make it sound like prison.'

'It will be a bit, won't it?'

Kai lived in a yurt year-round. Had lived under a

palm-frond lean-to in her back garden when they'd been in Hawaii. He was one of those men who'd hyperventilate if he were made to sit in a sealed office block for more than, say, a minute.

'If the treatment makes it possible to have a bit more of this in my life?' Izzy lifted her mug towards the sky, the beach, the ocean. 'I'm in. Looney's staying with friends. Good friends.' Good friends she hadn't been brave enough to discuss the whole 'what if it doesn't work?' factor with. Or absent fathers. She knew she was avoiding a rather critical decision but even considering the possibility that the treatment wouldn't work . . . nah. She couldn't go there. History simply couldn't repeat itself. Not this time.

'We've got a weekend surf camp. If Luna ever wants to come down and show the rest of the kids how it's done, she's more than welcome.'

'Thanks, man.'

'No worries. Least I could do after all the work you threw my way back in Maui.'

He'd been such a surf bum back in the day. Could barely scratch two coins together, let alone save enough to buy the fancy hybrid he'd picked them up in at the station. A bit like the one Freya used to have. He charged it up with solar panels.

They sat in silence and watched as the sun began its slow descent towards the end of this day en route to the next.

Then the day after that she'd be off to hospital. At least Emily was coming out to Bristol on Sunday night and Monday morning. Her last text said she would've come earlier but there was something she had to do with her parents.

She dug her toes into the cool sand, unable to stop the chill from whispering its way up her spine. Would she ever feel warm again?

Going into hospital felt scarier this time. Make or break of the highest order. The similarities to her own mother's recurrence was . . . well, the apple definitely hadn't fallen far from the tree.

She watched as her daughter rode in on a wave, pulled a triple spin, jumped off the board and ran to the shore with a whoop and a jump.

There she was. Her reason to be brave. Her reason to fight. Her reason to live.

Chapter Twenty-Seven

Both of Charlotte's children had turned surly by the time she hit the exit.

Little wonder given how long the trip had taken. It was getting dark and the satnav had kept trying to drag them onto the motorway, though she knew A-roads would be their best bet.

Despite her children's entreaties, she'd refused to stop for food. Or to get a new charger for Poppy who had left hers in her school locker. Or to drop Jack off at the vicarage, despite his vow to open the car door on the motorway and jump out. It had been a taxing journey, but Charlotte was determined to see it through.

'Gross. Sheffield,' Poppy said in her surprisingly plummy accent. 'What on earth are we doing here?'

Charlotte resisted the urge to respond. It wasn't Poppy's fault she'd been raised the way she had been. It was Charlotte's. She should have put her foot down years ago. Taught them life wasn't about how many things you did or didn't have. It was about character. Something she realized she'd parked at the door the moment she'd agreed to marry Oliver Mayfield.

She crossed over a roundabout and took a left against the

satnav's instructions. Though the cooling towers had long since been taken down and many new buildings had been put up, she knew exactly where she was going.

'Mum. It says the city centre is that way. Are we going to a play or something? Ohmigawd. Are we going to see Miley? I'm pretty sure Miley Cyrus is doing a concert here. Or maybe it was Taylor.'

'No, Pops. We are not going to see Taylor or Miley.' Charlotte's tone stemmed any more questions.

She should have brought them here years ago. Shown them just how much strength of character she had once possessed. Enough to give herself goals. Work towards them. Achieve them. Then set some more.

Jack made a series of noises to show his disgust as the shop fronts began to shift from bright and aspirational to faded and world-weary. Takeaway restaurants, betting shops, laundrettes. When was the last time she'd been in a laundrette?

'What the fuck are we doing in Sheffield, *Mother*?' Jack said the word 'Mother' the same way he'd say 'puce'. 'I thought you were bringing us to see Rocco so he could lay down the law for you again.' He gave Rocco's name a nasty singsong tone. A tone that belied the fact that Jack had definitely liked him when they'd been in Scotland.

Her fingers moved to her lips. She'd never quite been able to recapture the sensation of kissing him. A tingle or two had presented itself when Freya forwarded a picture he'd sent of a cow or the shop, but nothing quite as powerful as being held and kissed by the man himself.

An urge to swing the car back to the motorway and do just that gripped her. She'd felt strong in his presence. Supported. Admired even.

She tsked the impulse away.

She needed to do this on her own.

Besides. There'd been more than enough upheaval over the past year without throwing a palpitating heart into the mix. Apart from her new job and looking after Luna, she owed it to her children to be present for them. Present in a way their father clearly couldn't. Parenting wasn't just about fancy holidays and spending money. It was about being tough when necessary. Giving them boundaries. Guiding them into the future with a strong moral compass and sometimes, like now, facing cold, hard facts. Life wasn't easy. It was also what you made of it. The sooner they realized that, the better.

After a few more minutes of weighted silence, Charlotte pulled up in front of her old home. 'Get out.'

She'd never spoken to her children like that before, so they did.

'Mummy?' Poppy slipped her hand into Charlotte's as they stared up at the vast, brutalist construct that housed not only Charlotte's childhood home, but dozens of other families' cramped, poorly heated, poorly maintained, poorly plumbed flats. A woman emerged from the front door and openly bought drugs from a couple of boys about the same age as Jack. An older bloke, passed out from booze most likely, was slumped against the wall in front of a ground-floor flat that had the television blaring so loudly everyone knew *Emmerdale* was about to start. A half-hour to escape into someone else's misery, she supposed.

The green she'd once played on while her mum smoked fags and drank with 'the girls' was little more than a rubbish tip now. Strange. It had never once occurred to her the place would have got worse. She'd thought either that it might've been knocked down, or tarted up like the Park Hill Estates had been. Listed. Trendy. Desirable.

But here it was. Her childhood home. A microcosm of everything that was wrong with the world.

'Mummy, why are we here?'

'I wanted you to see where I grew up.'

A woman dragged her screaming toddler out of the front door, jammed her into a pushchair and set off down the hill throwing a stream of verbal abuse behind her.

Poppy squeezed her hand. Charlotte's eyes glassed over. She had expected her daughter to let go. But she held on tight. She didn't make gagging noises, or launch herself back in the car, or demand to leave as Charlotte had feared she might. She stood by her Northern mum's side in her pristine Zara dress and held her hand tight.

Charlotte braced herself for Jack's response. A scoff, no doubt. *They got it. She'd grown up poor. They'd grown up rich. They'd learned their valuable lesson about not taking things for granted – could they go now, please?*

Instead he tipped his head towards hers – he could almost rest his chin on top of her head. He took her other hand and said, 'Dad doesn't have a fucking clue about real life, does he?'

Rather than answer, she hugged her children in tight. She loved them so much. This moment – however perfect it felt – would probably not last. There'd be more tantrums, more rage, more fights. But they'd taken this first step towards their new reality together, and that was what counted.

An hour later, after they'd wolfed down gourmet burgers in a restaurant so hip it served nothing on an actual plate,

Charlotte was still feeling brave. Daring almost. As if this layer of motherhood – being amicable and fun with her children – had never been a possibility for her. It had. Of course it had. She'd seen all sorts of mothers at the children's school who were trendy and with it. *Besties with their kids.* She didn't think they would go that route – BFFs – because she wasn't their friend. She was their mum. And the distinction was important.

Saying that . . .

She drew a couple of skinny fries through some ketchup then set them down on the wooden serving board. 'How would you two feel if I were to send the odd email to Rocco?'

They both shrugged.

'You can do what you like, Mum,' Jack said through a mouthful of sweet potato wedges. He sounded like he actually meant it. 'Dad does whatever he wants. Why shouldn't you?'

'How about we agree not to discuss your father's romantic life.'

'I'm in,' Jack said, as Poppy vigorously nodded her assent.

They chatted about the vicarage for a bit. If they wanted their rooms painted anything other than Fresh Cotton – the neutral shade Charlotte had chosen over Magnolia. Whether or not they'd mind if Luna or Izzy stayed on if Izzy needed looking after once her treatment was finished.

'No that's cool. They're pretty fun.'

High praise indeed!

Poppy took a sip of her water then asked, 'Mum? Is it all right if I go to the same school as Felix and Regan?'

Oliver had already put down a deposit at Badminton, but . . . 'We can definitely look into it. Do you mind if I ask why?'

Poppy shrugged. 'Luna probably needs another kid around the house.' Charlotte didn't press. That was good enough for now.

'Do you think they'd take me?' Jack asked, eyes glued to the table.

Now this was a surprise.

'I thought you wanted to go to college in London.'

'Yeah, but . . .' He flopped back into his chair, tracing his finger along the ring of water round his fizzy drink. 'Xanthe and Dad are . . . They don't always get along and the baby . . .' He shuddered. 'I just . . . it might be easier if I stayed with you. You remember stuff. Dad and Xanthe? Not so much. Besides. Bonzer might need someone to walk him with Izzy being, you know, the way she is.'

Charlotte said she'd call on Monday morning.

'Well, then.' Charlotte signalled for the bill. 'I guess we'd better hit the road.'

They all stared at the final skinny fry, then one by one looked away, each of them unwilling to be the greedy guts who took it.

Jack picked up his knife and cut it into three equal pieces. 'There,' he said. 'Enough for everyone.'

Emily poured hot water over the fennel tea leaves and renewed her silent vow. 'This time I will do it. This time I will tell them.'

Over supper she'd done the worst preamble ever. She'd gabbled on about how wasn't it interesting how people were like grains of rice – the same, but different. Her father had lifted his own bowl of rice, greens and char siu up to his mouth, drained the lot, then excused himself from the table.

He had a long day of lectures ahead. Her mother, who worked at the Office for National Statistics, began to talk about how even *thinking* two grains of rice could be the same was ridiculous considering how many variants there were – long grain, short grain, sweet, sticky, wild – all of which culminated in her mother landing on her favourite topic: how 'so-called Chinese' food in the UK was never up to snuff. *Fakey, fakey, fakey, fake*, her mother crowed. *Why couldn't anything be genuine any more?* Honest? *Real*.

Hmmm.

Well.

Emily carried her father's tea into the lounge – one palm under the base of the cup, the other perched atop the lid he liked to slurp the tea out of until it cooled.

She set the ceramic cup down on the small lacquer-topped table beside his straight-backed chair. He was scrawling remarks on his students' papers. Some in Mandarin. Some in English. She wondered what he was teaching this year. Something engineery, obviously. Structural? Civil? He never really talked about it. And she never really asked.

He nodded his thanks but kept on working.

Emily went back to the kitchen and repeated the ritual, but this time with ginger tea. She warmed her mother's red cup with hot water, then put in the dried ginger (from China courtesy of a friend) and poured in more water. Her father had brought the mug back from China after he'd been to his father's funeral. It was embossed with three goldfish and represented family. Her mother had never used another mug since.

Her stomach churned. Oh, boy.

She sought the word for 'lesbian' in Mandarin but still

couldn't remember it. It was one of those words that meant one thing but had been repurposed to mean another. Maybe her parents wouldn't even know the difference. The original word, she remembered, meant comrade. That same Google search had pointed out that – until 2001 – being gay was listed as a mental illness in China. It had been a crime up until 1997.

She stared into the sitting room and tried to see it as a stranger might. It was very sparse. At least in comparison to those belonging to the mah-jong players her parents fraternized with down at the Islington Chinese Association. They tended to decorate their homes in the swirly, opulent old style of Chinese interior decor, whereas her parents were more . . . She didn't know what really. Ikea goes to China?

Simplicity.

What you saw was what you got.

She carried the cup of tea into the lounge, hovering as her mother's tiny fingers spread the mah-jong tiles across the green felted frame she kept behind the sofa when they didn't have a game in progress.

'Put tea here, Emily.' She pointed to a small lacquer-ware side table. 'Sit down. You making me nervous.'

Emily sat down, tucking her knees beneath the wobbly card table, careful not to knock the legs. Her mother got snappy when she shook the table. Or maybe that was just a Chinese thing. Feel it. Express it. Move on. Except for the big stuff, of course. If there was one solitary golden rule about being Chinese, it was never ever talk about the big stuff. Which, up to now, had suited Emily to a tee.

'That better.'

After all these years of living in the UK, her mother still

had that staccato, Chinese immigrant way of speaking English. It used to drive Emily mad, seeing as they had sent her to endless elocution lessons. '*You should sound like Maggie Smith.*' This, though neither of them had ever been able to pronounce her surname properly. *Smiff.*

'I like women.'

Emily's father put down the paper he'd been marking, but her mother didn't even look up from the tiles. 'Yea. Okay.'

'Ma. It means I'm gay. A lesbian.'

Her mother moved a tile then looked at her. 'Yea. Okay.'

'Ummmm . . . and you're all right with this?' She clarified the situation. 'It means no grandchildren.'

Her father started to chuckle. He wasn't much of a laugher, but he did have this great, cartoonish chuckle that occasionally burbled out of him when he'd hit the rice wine over Chinese New Year.

'Emily.' He put his papers onto the sofa. 'We've known we weren't getting grandchildren for a very long time.'

'Oh. Right.'

This was a bit anticlimactic. Did everyone know? Rocco had figured it out after she'd gone all gooey-eyed over Tansy, but . . . it had been a moment of weakness. There'd been gin. Too much gin. Charlotte, Freya and Izzy had never said anything. Then again, they had deemed her the Queen of Detachment back in uni. Perfect, they said, for a doctor. They'd also never said a word during her Melissa Etheridge phase. Hmmm . . . Maybe they did know.

Her eyes drifted to the sideboard, where there was a photo of her in her mortarboard and Bristol Uni gown. Izzy was standing next to her. Emily wasn't looking at the camera.

Ah.

She hadn't realized she looked at Izzy so . . . adoringly.

Emily's mother knocked on the table to get her attention. 'You should talk to Mrs Wang's son if you want tips.'

Mrs Wang of 'my son has nine hundred engineering degrees' fame?

'What? On being a lesbian?'

'Yea. He know all the hot spots. He know Soho like this.' Her mother held up her hand and turned it back and forth.

'He's male, Mom. Boys can't be lesbians.' Plus. Wasn't he the one they'd been trying to get her to go out with?

Ohhhhhhhhh.

'I been around the block more than one time, you know.' Her mother continued to clack the mah-jong tiles into place. She was one of those women who did things when they were happy rather than when they needed to be distracted, like Charlotte. Come to think of it, her mother was always busy. 'Song-Li's son not lesbian. He is one of those – whatchamacallits – drag lady.'

'Drag queen?'

'Yea. He perform at Chinese Community Centre last May Day.'

Her father hooted, then did some crazy arm gestures. 'Gangnam style!'

'What? No. Dad, that's K-pop, not drag queen music.'

Her mother waved her hand at him as if he were going senile. 'He talking about karaoke. He won first prize. Song-Li's son do . . . Beyoncé. Maybe Sia. Can't remember.' They both cackled at the memory. Apparently they'd had a whale of a time.

Emily felt as though she was in a Louis Theroux documentary: 'The Secret Lives of Chinese Parents'.

'So, ummm, anyway . . . I guess we're all caught up with the lesbian thing, then?' Emily reached for her ponytail and, too late, remembered it wasn't there.

'Yea. Okay, fine. You ready to play mah-jong with your mother?' Her mother looked across at her and smiled.

Yes. Yes she was.

Freya glanced up at the Vettriano painting and promptly tripped over a box of pans.

'Careful Mum!' Regan held her hands out to catch the cake, although she was nowhere near enough to help. Living in a building site had a way of turning even the simplest of journeys into an obstacle course.

'I've got it. We're fine.' They were as well.

When Rocco had sent the painting down 'to get rid of some of the clutter in the attic', she'd not been under any illusion as to why he'd sent it. He'd done it so she could get the money. It certainly hadn't been so that she could have a daily reminder that her mother could have chosen another life. Now that it had been hanging there for a couple of weeks, she had a new interpretation of the painting. Life was full of options. There would always be other men. Other careers. Other roads to follow. It was what you made of the path you chose that mattered most. And, of course, whether or not you decided to stay on it.

'What's good?' Monty reached up to take off the tie Felix had wrapped over his eyes.

'No you don't!' Felix cupped his hands over Monty's eyes, even though he hadn't taken off the tie. 'You ready, Mum?'

She was. The cake, on the other hand, was a bit of a shambles. Not a patch on what Charlotte would've whipped up, but she was at the cinema with the kids. Izzy and Luna were due back later and Emily was rocking into town tonight if the WhatsApp message was anything to go by, so, this was the cake they had. As long as it tasted good, she told herself. That's what counted here.

At least Monty had been so distracted by getting the television aerial up in the choir loft that he hadn't noticed she and Regan had been making it. Felix really could do 'tragic son being denied his television rights' when called upon to be a decoy.

Regan lit one candle, then the rest. 'Ready?' she whispered, even though Monty wasn't more than a metre from them. The piece of ply straddling two workbenches that served as their table was diagonally opposite their vestry-based corner kitchen. It comprised a microwave, their bashed-up Coleman camp stove, a kettle and a sink big enough for cleansing a pair of hands preparing to do the lord's work and not much more.

Suffice it to say, the lord's architect hadn't envisioned a family of four eating three meals a day in this room, but needs must, and all that. The basement café kitchen had already been gutted, so it was make do or give up the ghost.

This family wasn't planning on giving up the ghost, holy or otherwise, any time soon.

'All right, here we go. One . . . two . . . three!' Felix tugged off the tie blindfold and they all began singing.

'Happy Father's Day to you! Happy Father's Day to You!!! Happy Faaather's Day dear Daaa-dyy! Happy Father's Day to you!'

Monty looked beside himself with joy. He loved being the centre of attention. The cake was lopsided and the butter icing had already started separating under the heat of the candles Regan had weighted it with, but he looked as though they'd just handed him the keys to a gold-plated Ferrari.

'You nutters!' And by nutters he obviously meant the loves of his life. 'It's not even Father's Day.'

'Yeah, we know,' Freya smiled sheepishly. 'We thought things went a bit pants on the real one.'

More than pants. He'd come into London to stay the weekend. Everyone had been excited and a bit hypersensitive as it was the first weekend the For Sale sign had gone up outside their house. They'd had a fight when he'd found out the reason they had enough money to go out for dinner was because Freya had put his brew kit on eBay. Monty had stormed off in a cloud of 'I thought we were being honest about everything' and taken the train back to Bristol. Freya had stomped off to the shed and made some designs that she ended up hating. The children had unearthed a pizza from the freezer and eaten that instead of going to the gastro-pub on the river that Monty loved as they had planned. It was meant to be his 'farewell to London' tour.

Monty said, 'It's perfect. I love it. Help me?' He pointed at the candles.

They all leant in and, after a swift one-two-three, they all made wishes and blew.

After the children had gone to bed in the side chapels they'd partitioned off (Felix, who didn't care about daylight, in the north-facing transept, and Regan, their early bird, in the south), Monty and Freya collapsed onto the sofa which they'd plonked where the altar had once stood.

'Oh, this is nice,' Monty sighed, stretching out so that his head was in her lap.

Freya curled down and pressed a light kiss onto Monty's forehead. He tasted like sawdust and buttercream. Good thing she liked it, because that would be his man scent for the foreseeable future.

'It *is* nice.' She ran her fingers through his hair and felt that old familiar flutter of frisson tickle through her. '*You're* nice.'

Monty twisted round and pushed himself up onto his elbow at her change of tone. 'You're nice, too.'

Monty had The Look on. The one she hadn't seen in a while. Months, if she was being honest. And, as honesty was the new black: 'Wanna play nice with me?'

Monty jigged his eyebrows up and down. 'Definitely.'

Monty climbed over the back of the sofa and did a slut-drop to the bottom zip of their orange tent. She loved their tent. It was old and barely held the weather at bay, but it held a thousand good memories. And, unlike their London home, it was entirely paid for.

Monty did his best Magic Mike bum gyration as he pulled the zip open and flipped the tent door up and over the roof. They hadn't bothered with the waterproofing. They wouldn't need it. Not yet anyway.

'Your boudoir awaits, madame.' He held his hand out so that she could walk up and over the back of the sofa and straight into his arms. Laughing, she willingly did.

Izzy clonked her head on the sterile hospital mini desk.

So many forms. So many *forms*! Somanyforms.

How was she supposed to concentrate on getting better if everything was written in acronyms?

HRA, REC, MHRA, CTA, R&D, SSA, and the list went on.

FFS.

'C'mon woman.' Emily tapped the stack of papers. 'Sign your life away.'

'Emms!' *Jesus.* It wasn't like actual death was on the line or anything.

'Soz.' Emily pushed the papers towards her. 'It works on hip and knee patients.'

'Not so much with cancer patients.' Izzy gave her a half-hearted poke as she slumped in the squeaky vinyl chair. She'd felt so full of energy at the weekend. The best she'd felt since Sussex chemo. When anyone asked how she was feeling about the treatment, she was all 'Rarin' to go!' or 'Can't wait!'

Now that she was here? Not so much.

When Emily put the next form in front of her, one line blurred into the next, apart from the big X she'd put where Izzy needed to confirm that yes, filling her body full of drugs was perfectly fine and no, she wouldn't sue them if it all went wrong.

As Emily read through the next form, highlighting little bits, circling others, Izzy's thoughts drifted back to the beach.

She and Luna had never stayed in a geodome before. They'd stayed awake late, sworn to each other they'd seen shooting stars even when they hadn't, but you couldn't make wishes on ordinary stars, so . . . She'd done little beyond sitting on the beach, enjoying the campfire, talking nonsense about surfing. Mostly she'd watched Looney, prancing about in her cute little wetsuit, dazzling the other children with her boogie-board moves. Izzy's very own shooting star. And yes, she'd made a wish. Just the one.

Emily tapped the paperwork again. 'C'mon, woman. As your newly appointed next of kin, I'm happy to help you go through all this, but – ' she tapped her watch – 'Mrs Hitchin's knee wants replacing. My train's in two hours.'

'Show me the card.' Izzy knew she was wasting time, but . . . she was building up to a question she should have asked the minute she'd arrived back in the UK. Before, even.

Emily indulged her by flipping the card out of her purse like a secret agent.

There it was:

Emily Cheung: Next of kin.

She narrowed her eyes and pictured another line: Emily Cheung: Adoptive mother.

She lifted her gaze to Emily, her exacting features taut with concentration as she pocketed the card and got back to highlighting and circling. Izzy poked her again, trying to elicit a smile. Emily slapped her hand away without looking.

What if Emily was a shit mum? She didn't want Luna being slapped away if she was trying to have a bit of fun.

And then the tsunami of doubts and concerns that had kept her from asking Emily that all-important question clotted her throat.

There's always Alfred.

She'd googled him again last night after Emily faked being asleep. Alf was married, as suspected. At least she presumed he was. If the Family Business website was anything to go by, he had two children. A boy and a girl. Young. Lots of sun-bleached blond hair. Piercing blue eyes. His. She knew that because she stared into a pair of them every morning she woke her daughter up.

Yachts. His family business. Very posh and very expensive yachts. The wife was never in the photos. The grandparents were. And great-grandparents. Which was a good sign for Luna. Longevity clearly wasn't a Yeats thing. Not yet, anyway.

Would Alf's wife mind adding a mixed-race, half-grown addition to her flock? She'd scrolled and scrolled to find a photo of the wife, but hadn't succeeded. Izzy had concluded that she was either camera shy or the one who took the photos. They were good. Arty. And in Denmark. Would Luna be happy eating breakfast pastries and herring for the rest of her life?

Not a factor if she grew a pair and asked Emily to adopt her.

Or she could always not die. That was a good option.

A shrill bell rang somewhere in the ward. A flurry of running feet and rolling carts followed in its wake. The universe, no doubt, tapping her on the shoulder to remind her of her mortality.

'You should move to Bristol like the rest of us.' Izzy nudged Emily with her flipflop.

'Pah! Yeah right.' Emily tapped another X and Izzy signed it without looking. Emily looked at the clock again. Why did she have to go so soon, Izzy silently whined. They had Big Stuff to talk about.

Emily tapped again. 'C'mon. Hurry up.'

Izzy would ask next time. When she was looking more wan and feeble. Emily could never say no to her when she was weak and frail.

Cheery Oncologist – much more charming/informative/helpful than Stern Oncologist – stuck her head inside the door. 'How're we getting on in here?'

'Great!' Izzy crowed a bit too enthusiastically.

'Any questions with the paperwork I can help with?'

'Nope.' Izzy started scribbling her name on the bottom of the remaining sheets.

'I have one.'

Izzy glared at Emily. Hadn't she *expressly* told her to dial back the 'I'm also a doctor therefore totally qualified to ask irritating questions' thing?

'Go on,' said the doctor.

'I can't see anything in here regarding what we do for Luna if, you know . . .' Emily tapped her pen on the stack of paperwork, as if to garner strength from all the facts lying within. 'What I mean is, is there anything we – and by we I mean Izzy . . . Is there anything Izzy needs to sign regarding what to do with Luna if anything should happen to her?'

Cheery Oncologist's brow furrowed. 'Oh. Gosh. I was under the impression that had already been addressed.'

Izzy panic-laughed. This was definitely not the way she'd planned on asking Emily to care for her daughter if she sparked it. She patted Emily on the head as if she were an adorable schoolgirl. 'It's cool. She's joking. Emily's in charge of everything. Aren't you, Emms?'

She'd clear everything with her later. This was just an unfortunate blip.

Until she saw the blood drain from Emily's face, Izzy hadn't taken on board just how much she'd presumed. What a huge thing it was to ask someone to care for your child if you died.

'Ummm . . .' Emily looked down at the forms.

Izzy's entire body began to vibrate with a year's worth of fear. A decade's, if she were being honest.

When Emily finally met her eye, she saw a reflection of her own terror.

Izzy might actually die.

Luna might become an orphan.

And she'd done nothing to ensure her daughter would be safe and cared for if anything went wrong.

The doctor gave the door a light pat and the pair of them a bright smile. 'I'm pretty sure there are a couple of charities that help in these sorts of situations. I'll see if I can rustle up some brochures. Give you two a few more minutes to talk.'

Chapter Twenty-Eight

Emily glanced up at the station clock. If Freya hurried she just might make it. Mrs Hitchin's hip had a lot to answer for.

Charlotte absently poured milk into her tea, blew some of the steam away, then put the cup down. Far too hot.

She looked as thunderstruck as Emily felt. 'And you're sure you want to do this?'

Seriously?

The only thing Emily was sure of was that she'd gone *completely mad*, but what else was she meant to have said? *Nope. Don't want her. Find someone else to care for your orphaned daughter.*

'Luna and I get along.'

'We know you get along. That's not the . . .' Charlotte paused while an announcement about train delays to Cardiff boomed through the station. When it finished she adopted a new tack. 'Whatever Izzy wants is obviously the right path to choose.'

There were a lot of things Emily could say in response but reading between the lines was pretty easy on this one. *Liking a child was one thing.* Raising *one was an entirely different kettle of fish.* Mahi Mahi and Bigeye Tuna in Luna's case.

Emily scrubbed her fingers into her scalp. Leaving Izzy behind all tearful and anxious was one of the hardest things she'd ever done. 'Look. All of this is completely hypothetical. Luna only needs a guardian if Izzy isn't . . . you know . . . alive.'

Charlotte blinked rapidly as she attempted to take another sip of her murky train station tea. It looked like something out of *1984.* In fact, everything was taking on a surreal tint now that Emily had agreed to adopt a ten-year-old child if her best friend died.

'Have you done anything legally binding?'

'Nope.' It was all she could do to get Izzy peeled off the floor once Cheery Oncologist had left the room, let alone google how to do a custody hand-over. 'We wrote it on a Post-it.'

'You didn't.'

'We did.' Emily showed her the Post-it then tucked it back into her bag alongside Tansy's number. Which of the two would be used first?

'And you think this treatment is the best there is on offer?'

'As far as I know it is, but . . .' *Oh fuckety, fuck monsters.* Nothing was foolproof. Emily held her hands up in the surrender position. 'Nothing's guaranteed. She might live. She might die.'

There. She'd said it.

The words hovered over her, then crashed back down, dislodging her heart as they did. Her very best friend in the world – the one she'd had her first proper crush on, her first hangover with, her first laugh until you throw up in your mouth a little with – had, on her suggestion, walked into hospital today and could very likely not walk out again.

Mercifully, Charlotte didn't try to comfort her. There were no placating turns of phrase to change the fact that Izzy was being eaten alive by cancer.

Charlotte slipped a pile of serviettes between Emily's elbows as she pressed her thumbs into her eyes trying to stem the tears.

When she collected herself, Emily briskly patted the table, pretended she didn't look like a red-eyed demon and announced, 'It's all academic anyway. Izzy will be fine and who will or won't look after Luna irrelevant.'

'Sorry, sorry . . .' Freya rushed in, cycle helmet still on, and collapsed into a seat at their corner table, not bothering with the requisite cheek kisses or hugs. 'I know your train leaves soon, Emms. What's going on.'

'Izzy wants Emily to have legal custody of Luna if . . .' Charlotte's voice cracked as she, too, tried to put words to their shared fear. ' . . . if the treatment isn't successful.'

'I think she wants all of us to have custody,' Emily corrected. Hoped? 'I mean, there has to be one person who sorts out the logistics, but you two are totally going to help. Aren't you?'

Freya gave a vague nod, still trying to catch up.

Charlotte pointed out the obvious. 'It will be tricky with you in London.'

'Sure. Of course.' Emily tried to imagine sitting her parents down at the mah-jong table for this one. *Remember that thing about never having a grandchild? Well . . . surprise!*

'I would've thought she'd have had something in place from the first time,' Freya said.

'This is Izzy we're talking about.' There was no need for

Emily to elaborate. Izzy's modus operandi had and always would be: *deal with it when it happens*.

Well, it was happening. Big time.

Freya took a sip of Charlotte's tea, made a face, then started teasing a serviette into slender strips. 'It makes sense now.'

'What does?' Charlotte began folding her own serviette into smaller and smaller squares.

'Why she came back. I can't believe it's taken me so long to work it out. I just thought: typical Izz. Finally settled, running a great business, then poof! Blows it all to smithereens for a diddy cottage in Wales. I thought she had some weird "face her demons" from her mum's death thing going on, but it was to find a family for Luna, wasn't it?'

Charlotte tucked her quadruple-folded serviette between her saucer and cup. 'And as far as you know, she's not been in touch with the father? What was his name again?'

'Alfred,' Emily supplied then shrugged. 'Not as far as I know. Residency – that's what they call it now.' She flashed them all the charity brochure that Cheery Oncologist had given them. 'I presume residency would automatically go to him if Izzy hadn't made a call. So, she made a call.'

'Are you up for it, Emms?' Freya asked.

'No.' If any situation begged for honesty, it was this one. 'But I'll make sure I am when – *if* – the time comes. Which it won't.'

No one dared disagree with her.

She glanced up as the train timetable updated again. 'Sorry, ladies. There's my platform. I know we have a lot to talk about, but I've got to fix a knee.'

Charlotte and Freya exchanged a look.

'I know, I know. But it's not like I'm adopting her *today*.'

They rose and gave each other quick hugs. Emily made a gesture she hoped they understood meant she'd text them and see them soon and hopefully none of what they had just discussed would come to pass. She crossed her fingers the entire train journey home.

Freya tiptoed up to the edge of Izzy's hospital room and peeped in the window. She was watching a surfing film from the looks of things.

She tapped on the doorframe then walked in with a bright smile. 'You're looking good, woman! I thought you'd be all *bleuuurgh* . . . after last week.'

The second week's protocol had really sucked the beans out of Izzy. To the point she'd only done FaceTimes with Luna, asked Freya not to come in at all and slept during both of Charlotte's visits.

Izzy smiled from her mound of pillows. Her hair positively eclipsed her thin face, but, if Freya wasn't mistaken, that little Izzy glow was back. 'Must've turned a corner.' She held out a bunch of grapes.

Freya did an automatic food-miles calculation, then forced herself to set a 'principles exclusion zone' outside Izzy's hospital door. If she was well enough to eat grapes after everything she'd been through, it didn't matter if they'd been grown on the moon.

She took the fruit then plopped down on the vinyl chair Charlotte had covered with a soft polka-dotted throw. Even if Freya did say so herself, the room looked much better with the smattering of her handmade cushions round the place. Her favourite featured a cow in a hammock drinking a martini. She daren't tell Charlotte it had been inspired by Lady V.

She ate a grape as she inspected the opulent fruit bowl. There were some pukka-looking muffins in it as well. 'Blimey. I didn't think the NHS research budget stretched to muffins.'

'It doesn't,' Izzy gave the fruit a loving pat. 'Emily sent it.' Creep.

Sweet creep.

Emily had morphed into a different human over the past few weeks. Always on their WhatsApp group. Coming down to Bristol every chance she got. Forwarding *joke emails*. Whatever next?

'She's probably spiked everything with steroids.' Izzy grinned. 'Anything to get me out of here so she can go back to being Grumpy Emms.' She put a grape to her lips then pretended to be getting electrocuted by it. This struck Izzy as hilariously funny. So funny her whole body began jiggling away until, too soon, she lost her steam.

Poor Izz. The treatment had clearly taken it out of her. Her spirits, however, remained unflagging. The Netflix subscription, smuggled in soups, teas, tonics and aroma-therapy oils all helped, but it was beginning to look like the cutting-edge medicine did too. Scan after scan confirmed it. Izzy's tumours were finally shrinking.

'Is Emms coming down again this weekend?'

'Nope. She's coming Thursday and Friday. Said she had something on this weekend and Looney wanted to go surfing anyway, so that's the plan.' Izzy plucked another grape from the basket and began to pick at it. 'She and Looney are going to the planetarium after fancy school camp.'

Freya was about to say it sounded like just the sort of outing Felix would love, then remembered that their Vow of Poverty prohibited those types of extravagances. She'd take him up to the spire tonight. See if they could do some star-spotting from there.

'How're we doing today, Miss Izzy?' A nurse with a thick Jamaican accent rapped on the side of the door. 'Time for your daily weigh-in, missus.'

Freya didn't miss Izzy pocketing something from her side table as she slid out of bed.

'That's me done.' Izzy accepted Freya's assistance as she crawled back into bed. Once the nurse left the room, Izzy slipped her hand into her pocket and revealed a fistful of crystals.

'What are those for?'

'The weigh-in.' Izzy's eyes glittered with mischief.

'For good luck?'

Izzy scoffed. '*Derrrr*. To weigh more.'

'Why would you want to do that?'

Izzy gave Freya the sort of look you'd give a simple, but well-intentioned child. 'If I don't weigh enough they won't give me the treatment. If I don't get the treatment, I don't get to live. And this week? I don't weigh enough.'

'But . . . isn't that risky? With the medicine being dependent on your real weight?'

'Not if I want to live to see my daughter become a grown woman, it isn't.' Her twinkly smile spoke volumes. She was going to beat this thing.

'Two more weeks. You can do it.' Freya picked the grapes up again and popped one in her mouth. If whatever was in these things helped Izzy surmount the mountains she'd had to climb, she wanted in on it too.

*

Once she'd handed Oli his coffee and sat down, Charlotte looked down at her bare left hand, a slight indentation still visible on the finger where her wedding ring had once lived. She gave it a rub, willing it – and Oliver – to go away. The children would be home soon and she certainly didn't want them seeing him. Not like this.

Red-eyed. A bit of a paunch she was quite sure Xanthe wouldn't approve of (#gymmumforever). That thick blond hair of his was a bit thinner than it had once been. In fact, he looked so out place in her bright, cheery kitchen, it was almost like sitting with a stranger. And, in a way, this Oliver was. She'd never seen him cry before. Not even tears of joy at the birth of his children. There had been the one time when England did so well at the rugby, but there had been quite a lot of alcohol involved, so . . .

'You won't even consider having me back?'

Before she could say no for a third time, he launched into a fresh PR campaign. He was a changed man. He'd always loved her, just been weak. Dazzled by Xanthe and all of that . . . he struggled to find the right word and settled for . . . *youth*. Xanthe couldn't do things the same brilliant way Charlotte could. He appreciated it now. All the work it must've taken to make their home so beautiful. Raise children without a fuss. *Cook.* God, he missed her cottage pie.

He'd move to Bristol if that was what she wanted. The commute wasn't too bad. Plenty of people did it. With his support, she could travel more with that new job of hers. Marketing was it? Visual merchandizing. Yes, of course it was. He knew that because he'd had one of his mates look into the company's development deal and it had all been very sound.

She'd had a bit of a twinge at this. It was the most protective thing Oli had ever done for her. Perhaps he had turned a corner.

He'd love to move in together, but if she wanted him to live in a flat until she adjusted to having him back in her life again, that would be fine, too. If she'd have him. Which he sincerely hoped she would. Please. *Please, Charlotte.* Please take me back.

A text pinged in. Despite her ex-husband's impassioned entreaty to relight the fires of their defunct marriage, she pulled the phone across and peered at it.

Rocco.

No words, just a picture of a pasture thick with buttercups. He did that sometimes. Took a photo of something he thought would tickle her fancy and sent it.

'Could you put the phone down, Charlotte? I'm fucking baring my heart here.' Oli slapped the table so hard that her coffee swooped up and over the edge of her cup. He went on to detail how difficult it had been for him to wangle the free time to get to Bristol. The lies he'd had to tell Xanthe. The chavs he'd had to endure in the train carriage. The work he definitely wouldn't be catching up on, all because he was effing trying to effing change his effing life here. Couldn't she *see* that? The *sacrifices* he'd made?

There he was. The Oliver she knew.

No, she didn't want that life. Didn't want that life at all.

'I'm afraid I've got a call to make.' She held up the phone. 'Business. I'm so sorry, Oliver. For everything.'

He understood what she was saying.

A very firm and a very resolute, no thank you.

*

FROM: Charlotte Bunce
TO: Rocco Burns

Dear Rocco,

How lovely to receive a 'proper' email from you again. Please don't worry about not getting to a computer with any sort of regularity. I know how busy you are.

I'm so pleased you were able to put my tips for the shop to use. I'm still in awe that you already have someone working there full time. Just an idea, but perhaps some autumn-themed butters would be a good idea. Are you able to get your hands on some rosemary or garlic? It could be easily marketed as something savoury to lavish on your 'tatties'. (!!!) Look at me, pretending I'm *au fait* with the lingo up there. Speaking of which, your email had me in absolute stitches. I never realized someone could sound so Scottish in print. Your passion for 'auld Scots' makes me want to dredge up the Yorkshire terminology I regretfully ironed out of my own vocabulary. Did you know 'nithered' means very cold? Heaven knows why I'm thinking of that in the middle of summer!

Yes, you are absolutely right. I had heard of a clootie dumpling as I do enjoy my cooking magazines, but I had never heard of 'baffies' for slippers. I won't be able to get that out of my head now!

Freya did mention your plans for coming 'down the road'. They will be so grateful to have an extra pair of hands when they put in the kitchen. As they say, every little helps.

You are, of course, very welcome to use the guest room here at the vicarage. Poppy and Jack's father is being rather tricky at present, so having positive male role models in their lives is always rewarding. I do hope this is not too presumptuous . . . but, at present, my focus is very much on my children.

Anyway. We're all over the moon as Izzy's treatment seems to be coming along as hoped. All things being well, she will be home by the time you come down. As will Luna, who has been enjoying surf camp in Devon on alternate weekends. She goes down on the train herself, pops a camera on the end of her surfboard and just paddles out to sea. That girl is built of bravery! If you're happy with it, we'll do meals with Freya and her mob when you're here. I wonder if you are a fan of Moroccan food. I've got a wonderful new recipe for a chicken tagine.

Forgive me for wittering on. I must wrap up and help Jack. We're struggling to find a college round here that suits him. He claims to prefer animals to humans right now, so we are currently looking into agricultural colleges. You made quite the impression over the holidays, so perhaps you could advise him on farming life? My little boy is a towering six-foot-something sixteen year old! Imagine.

Oh, I nearly forgot. That was so thoughtful of you to send the Vettriano painting down to Freya. She's hung it pride of place in their temporary kitchen (although that might have changed as everything is moving along at quite a pace. I've never seen Monty work with such *drive!*)

All the very best and with warmest regards,

Charlotte

*

'. . . and here we have your DNA map.' Stern Oncologist circled a long line of gobbledy-gook then tapped it with his pen. 'This is the change we're hoping to see.'

Izzy stared at the X-rays and the accompanying paperwork. For some reason, she preferred Stern Oncologist to Cheery Oncologist for this sort of thing. Hearing about her body's abnormal cell function didn't seem right coming out of a smiley face.

'So, does this mean we're done? I can pack up and never come back?'

'No. Not even close.'

'Why don't you sugar-coat it for me, doc?'

Stern Oncologist gave her a confused look. He didn't do japey humour. He did facts.

Fair enough.

He grabbed a clean sheet of paper and began to make a list. She was looking at another good six months to a year of treatment. A mastectomy still wasn't out of the question. He wasn't convinced she was strong enough for surgery at this juncture. She needed to bear in mind her body had little to no resilience. There was the winter to get through, pneumonia (should she catch it) to survive, strokes not to have, heart attacks to avoid. He'd lost more patients at this juncture than he'd saved. Just to keep her expectations realistic.

As if weeks of vomiting, shaking, weight loss, nail loss, hallucinations and bone-crushing fatigue weren't little-bitty giveaways.

Bless.

'Right then, doc. I guess I'd better make some phone calls.'

*

'Auntie Emily?'

Emily looked at her handset again. What was Luna doing on Izzy's phone? 'Hey, Loons. Everything all right?'

She doubted it. It was the middle of the night. Well. Ten o'clock. Her eyes shifted from the bedside clock to the bottom of the curtains.

Light.

Hmmmm. Maybe it was the other ten o'clock. Blimey.

'Who's on the phone?'

Emily covered the handset. 'Looney.'

'Tooney?' Tansy nodded sleepily then gave Emily's shoulder a little stroke and pat.

Emily slipped out of the covers, pulled a throw off the end of the bed, wrapped it round herself and padded into the lounge. 'What's up Loons?'

'Ummm . . . could you come out today?'

'Sure. Of course.' She couldn't. Not right this instant anyway. Or could she? She wasn't really *au fait* with the rules as regards leaving one's relatively new, long-distance lover in bed to fend for herself. 'Everything okay?'

'Ummm . . . Sort of. It's Mommy.'

Emily's heart leapt to her throat. 'Tell me.'

When Luna finished, it took her about ten seconds to pull on a pair of yoga pants, a hoodie and order a cab.

'Bristol bound?' Tansy showed no signs of getting up.

'Yup.' Emily frowned at her. 'You okay to see yourself out?'

'Ab-so-bloody-lutely okay,' Tansy smiled and gave her a jaunty little salute.

Emily grabbed her keys off the chest of drawers. 'Do you mind asking my parents to lock up after you leave?'

'No probs.'

They'd met Tansy a couple of weeks ago. Had caught the pair of them sneaking out of the flat as her parents headed off to Zumba Gold. They'd had dim sum and seemed to like her. Emily hoped they weren't going to get all happy families in her absence. Tansy was lovely, but from what Emily could gather, she was also a bit of a directionless slut.

All of which was neither here nor there. She needed to get to Bristol. A quick wave goodbye and she was out the door.

'Do you know what this is about?' Freya, who was convinced Emily always had advance notice for everything, was waiting outside the hospital. She'd downed two cups of awful canteen coffee while she'd been waiting, so was a bit hyped up and hoping for a bit of advance information. Especially if the news was bad.

'Clueless.' Emily did actually look clueless. 'Luna said Izzy had big news and that she wanted to tell us when we were all together. Wouldn't say what it was.'

Charlotte ran across from the car park to join them. 'Sorry, girls. Poppy forgot her flute. She's got one final tutorial at camp and wants to make sure she starts at the new school with a bang . . . a trill?' She dismissed her inability to pin down the best descriptor with a flick of her fingers. 'Any idea why Izzy called us all here?'

'No idea.' Freya spied Luna coming out of the double doors leading into the hospital. She didn't look devastated. Which was good. She did look a bit . . . overwhelmed? Whether it was good or bad remained to be seen.

'Hey, there Loons. Everything all right?'

Luna gave them all half-hugs, doing a rather elaborate 'My Lips Are Sealed' mime as she led them all to the lifts.

A hush surrounded them as they shot one another hopeful half-smiles. Charlotte held up a pair of crossed fingers. Freya hoped she was right. There was no way Izzy would use Luna as a foil to tell them the treatment had failed. Especially now, a mere two days before she was due to come home.

The lift ride felt interminable. When they arrived on her floor, they silently followed in Luna's wake.

When they arrived at the correct door, Luna pushed it open with a flourish and there was Izzy. Hair all big and gorgeously wild. A fetching maxi-dress disguising just how thin she was. There were still shadows under her eyes, but the flush in her cheeks wasn't from a make-up brush.

Izzy put on her best game-show hostess smile and did a little display affair with her hands. As if she needed to point out that a six-foot-tall, sun-kissed Scandinavian god was standing in her room.

'Everyone? Meet Alfred.'

Chapter Twenty-Nine

'Do you think I should leave a review on TripAdvisor?'

Izzy's giggles were infectious.

'Here, Izz.' Charlotte beckoned for her to hand over the unruly pile of clothes she'd pulled out of the wardrobe. Charlotte put them on the stripped hospital bed and began to fold them properly. 'I'm not certain hospitals are the target audience for TripAdvisor.'

Izzy feigned disbelief. 'Wot? It's *great* here. There's room service. An *en-suite* bathroom complete with someone to wash you if you're too tired. Staff on hand to save your life. This place is da bomb.'

They'd definitely deserved five stars for saving Izzy's life. For the foreseeable future, anyway – and for that, Charlotte would be permanently grateful to them. Anyone who pooh-poohed the NHS on her watch would receive stern words.

'Hello ladies.' Cheery Oncologist appeared at their door. 'All ready to get out there into the big wide world?'

Izzy whooped with such exuberance that both Charlotte and the doctor rushed forward to steady her.

'I'm all right, I'm all right,' Izzy protested as she let them accept the bulk of her cloud-like bodyweight and led her to the bedside chair.

She was very, very frail. And incredibly happy. The first phase of the trial was over and had been deemed a success. Two more phases and, fingers crossed, Izzy would have the all clear.

'Good. Well,' Cheery Oncologist flicked her thumb towards the nurses' station, 'make sure you sign out. I would say we'll miss you round here, but . . .'

She and Izzy spoke as one: 'Better out than in!'

A quick checklist of Do This and Don't Do Thats followed. 'Right then! We'll see you once a week for check-ups. More if anything unusual crops up.'

Izzy waved a sheaf of papers. 'I know. I've got it all here. It ain't over till the fat lady sings.'

'That's what I'm talking about!' Cheery Oncologist unleashed a High C and a wave as she left.

'Sweet heavens I need a break from that woman,' Izzy said once she'd gone.

'I thought you liked her.'

'I do, it's just . . . have you ever met someone who was so relentlessly *happy*?'

'You're pretty happy.'

Izzy breathed in as though she meant to protest then conceded, 'Yeah. You're right. I am pretty happy.'

'So,' Charlotte said as she went back to her folding, 'how did the rest of your visit with Alfred go?'

'Good! Fun. It was only a flying visit. He's making lots of promises, but . . . we'll see. It's still early days and he had to get back to Copenhagen, so . . . *yes*.'

'Yes?' Charlotte circled her finger so that Izzy would elaborate.

Izzy tipped her cheek into her palm. 'He's . . . well, he's still gorgeous.'

Charlotte didn't say anything. She'd thought Oliver was gorgeous, but that certainly hadn't made him prime husband material. The last she'd heard from him was a curt email about not being able to take the children this weekend as planned because he and Xanthe were going away to 'put things right'. There was also mention of a new nanny.

'He totally loves Luna,' Izzy said proudly. 'He's already booked another flight so he can see her at surf school before actual school begins.'

'That's good.' Charlotte smoothed her hand along an enormous Sex Wax T-shirt that Izzy had worn for the bulk of her treatment. It might have to go, given that Freya had had to cut it open to put Velcro tabs and string ties along the back. Then again, she would be needing it again for round two.

Izzy pushed herself up with a little grunt and started taking her posters down from the walls. 'He's been really cool about everything. He's offered to pay some child support. Says his parents are delighted. The more children the merrier is their motto, apparently.'

Alf, they were surprised to hear, was the eldest of seven.

'He's been everything I'd want from someone who just found out they had a ten-year-old kid, but . . .'

'But?' Charlotte prompted.

'I don't know. He's still going through his divorce. He's gone a lot for work. I just . . . I don't want Looney to invest high hopes in him and I definitely don't want Emily to think I called him to replace her.'

Charlotte didn't think there would be a problem in that

department. After Alf had filled them in on his children, his divorce, the family business, the family island, the long sailing trips they took every summer, Emily had pulled Charlotte and Freya aside to say there wasn't a chance in hell she was going to let Alfred anywhere near Luna. Not on a full-time basis anyway. Or without a chaperone. 'Nordic Noir,' she'd said ominously, 'was a thing for a reason.'

'What made you call him?' Charlotte asked.

'Ohhh . . .' Izzy's progress in taking down the Luna Picture Wall slowed. 'I guess on the nights I believed I actually might die, I thought about my own father. How I could've met him if I'd wanted to and never did.'

'Why didn't you?'

Izzy shrugged. 'I suppose it was some sort of misplaced loyalty for my mum. She hadn't wanted me to meet him when she was alive, so I thought, why bother when she's dead? But now that it's too late? I thought it was only fair to Luna to give her the choice.'

Charlotte nodded. She could see the sense in that. 'Have you ever thought of reaching out to your father's family?'

Izzy made a noncommittal noise. 'Maybe one day. Right now? I just want to go home.'

Charlotte pulled the zip shut on Izzy's duffel bag. 'Right then. Let's do that.'

Without a backwards look, they left the room, the ward, the hospital and headed to the vicarage.

'Mind the scaffolding!'

The church was so wreathed in scaffolding – inside and out – that ducking had become second nature to Freya and her family. Izzy? Not so much. At least she had all of that hair as padding. Adding concussion to her list of medical woes would not be good. Not that she looked like a woman on the brink, or anything. One week out of treatment and she had already put on weight. Izzy said it was the steroids, but Freya was hopeful it was Charlotte's cooking.

They ducked under another scaffolding tower then walked inside the main church doors. 'So this bit will be the entrance to numbers one and two. Our townhouse and number four will have entrances over by the garden.'

'Graveyard, you mean.'

It had been deconsecrated, so technically not . . . 'Yes. Where the graveyard was.'

'Cool. I like thinking of all of those old souls looking after us.' Izzy carefully picked her way through the piles of plywood and supplies. 'I can't believe how *different* it is.' She brushed her fingers along everything she passed, as if she were trying to memorize all that she'd taken for granted. Even dry wall, from the looks of things.

'It's nice to hear someone sees a difference. All Monts and I can see is all the work that's left to do.' Freya tucked her fringe back behind her scarf. Monty was doing his best, but . . . it was slow going. And Cameron wasn't the easiest of men to work for. If he'd *told* them they'd needed planning permission to change the back entrance *before* they'd knocked it down, Monty would've held fire. Now they were facing a fine on top of everything else.

Big breath in . . .

'Oh my gosh! This is *amazing*. Fluffy!' Izzy dived into their upgraded bedroom (Charlotte had donated her tent when a rather silly tickling session sounded a death knell for the old one) and sprawled herself the length of Freya's airbed. It was covered with a Highland cowhide she and her brother had had tanned 'just to see'. It had turned out brilliantly, was super warm (the church was not) and Freya already had orders from a bespoke furniture shop on the King's Road for as many ottomans as she could make when they had more. It was shocking how much money people would pay for an ottoman. But she wasn't arguing. Each little bit of debt she and Monty erased made more room in their marriage for getting back to normal. The new normal, anyway.

'Do you miss the old tent?' Izzy rolled back and forth on the airbed like a little girl.

'Short answer? No.' It had been fun, but there was only so much cosiness a girl could handle in the end. That, and some summer showers a couple of weeks back had made it crystal clear that the church roof needed redoing. Urgently.

'Is Rocco coming down again?' Izzy gave a naughty laugh. 'Or should I be asking Charlotte?'

'He's definitely coming down, but I'm fairly certain he's been told he's staying in the guest room.'

Izzy made a sad clown face.

'No. Nothing like that. I think with Oliver being such an ass, Charlotte just wants to take things slowly. She's got to figure out how to be Charlotte on her own before she takes my big bear of a brother on.'

Freya was crossing everything that they'd get together, but she knew more than most that slow and steady was a wise course of action. 'Anyway, I don't think Rocco likes leaving Dad on his own, so . . . if he does start coming down more regularly, we might have to see about someone coming in to check up on him.'

Izzy's brow furrowed protectively. She'd really taken to Lachlan over Christmas. 'He's not that bad, is he?'

'No, not at all.' He wasn't. The problem was they weren't really sure what he was. They hadn't yet had an official prognosis because, in true Scottish male style, her father was refusing to go to the doctors. 'I'm old!' he'd crow if they questioned him about forgetting something from the past. 'I miss your mother,' he'd say if he'd had a wee nip or two.

'Right!' Freya clapped her hands together then swooped one of her arms towards the door. 'We better get on. Monty's making us all a curry tonight. Thai.'

They wandered round the rest of the building, Izzy oohing and aahing in all the right places. The bathroom that would have not one but two beautiful stained-glass windows. The kitchen that would be floodlit by a skylight over the apse. Freya pointed towards another scaffold-laced area. 'Through there you can see the new stairs they're putting in up to the spire. That'll be Regan's room when they're finished.'

'Oooops!'

Freya turned round just in time to see Izzy's entire head of hair hanging from a bit of scaffolding.

She looked at Izzy, who was laughing despite having just been scalped. Or had she? Her head wasn't bald. Her hair was short, though. Halle Berry pixie short. It looked cute actually. If not 100 per cent different from Big Hair Izzy.

'Ummm . . .' Freya pointed out the obvious. 'You're wearing a wig.'

'Yup!' Izzy detached it from the scaffolding and expertly whirled it back into place. 'Been wearing one since I got back to the UK. This little beauty is one of three.'

'But it . . .'

'Looks like my hair?' Izzy laughed again and fluffed up her curls. 'It *is* my hair. I cut it before I started chemo in Hawaii. My mum's hair had fallen out and she was furious. It was one of her last poems. "Fickle Follicles".'

'Seriously?'

'No,' Izzy laughed. 'She was just worried all my memories of her were going to be of a bloated, balding, shell of a woman. She was wrong, of course, because beauty doesn't work like that, but . . . Looney was so much younger than I was; I wanted her world to at least look normal. There is so little we are in charge of – not the weather, not the waves, not cancer. I wanted to be in charge of something. This was my something.'

For perhaps the first time ever, Freya thought she would do well to take a page out of Izzy's book. It wasn't being an airhead that kept her positive. It was her deep understanding of how life worked. Some things you could control. Some things you couldn't. Freya had almost let her marriage fall apart over money. Something they could control. Badly. But step by step, they were improving.

'It was clever.' Freya reached out but didn't touch Izzy's wig. 'Saving your hair.'

Izzy snorted. 'It was *vanity*. Pure and simple.' She took it off and stared at it. 'It's only supposed to last a few years, so I might have to go off the shelf soon.' She shuddered at the thought.

'I'll give you mine if you want. There's not a lot of it, but you're welcome to it.'

Izzy beamed that beautiful, open smile of hers, then tucked her hand in the crook of Freya's elbow. 'I know you would, girlfriend. I know you would.'

*

'*Ack!*' Izzy howled in protest as they passed the photo round. 'Why didn't you tell me the Alicia Keys phase was so epically bad?'

'Don't be stupid.' Emily rolled her eyes. 'You looked good no matter what you did.'

Izzy batted her lashes. 'Flatterer.'

'Don't get used to it,' Emily sniffed. 'This is only because you've just got out of hospital.'

'That was over two weeks ago.'

'Well, then.' Emily narrowed her eyes. 'You look like shit.'

'That's more like it.' Izzy planted a sloppy kiss on her cheek. 'I don't like it when you're nice. It's creepy.'

They continued to shift through the photos, pointing out bad outfits, long-forgotten friends, T-shirts they'd long since consigned to the charity shops. They had had an awful lot of parties. It was a good thing the children had opted to watch a film in the other room. Some of the photos were not showing the 'responsible adults' in their lives in the best of lights.

'Oh, my gosh. Emms . . . Izz . . .' Freya held out a photo and they all crowded in to look. It was Emily pointing at a beaming Izzy. She was modelling one of Freya's year-end projects – a party frock made entirely of bluebells. Her hair was absolutely enormous. Wild and free. Her eyes sparked with life. She looked utterly stunning. Emily was gazing at her as if she were Aphrodite herself.

Emily looked away, horrified at her transparency. Did everyone have a photo of Emily looking doe-eyed at Izzy? She was about to make a sarcastic comment, then noticed no one was poking fun. Quite the opposite in fact. Her friends were cooing, smiling, reaching out to the photo, as if touching it would transport them back to that moment.

And then it hit her.

They'd known all along.

'Why didn't you guys ever say anything?' They all turned to look at her. 'You know, about the whole "Emily likes girls" thing.'

Charlotte crinkled her nose and gave Emily a funny little smile. 'Because you're Emily.'

'What does that mean?' She wasn't offended. Old Emily would have been. This Emily was simply curious.

'It means you don't talk about things. You're private.' Charlotte closed the lid on the shoebox and put it to the side. 'We all respect that.'

Freya laughed. 'That. And we thought you'd punch us in the face if we did.' She feinted right and left, dodging invisible blows. Charlotte, Freya and Izzy grinned at each other, did the zipped-lips gesture and threw away the keys. It was a well-practised move. Which kind of made Emily feel good.

'Right! I've got a busy day of vending wares ahead of me. There's an art show at the co-op tomorrow. I've got to stop the watercolourists from going to war with the oil painters. So touchy, these arty types.' She gave a self-deprecating laugh. 'Have a good trip back to London, Emms.' Freya gave them all a quick wave then headed off to her scaffolding-clad home.

Izzy yawned and stretched. 'I promised Looney we'd watch *Gilmore Girls* before bed. Poppy got her hooked.' She blew them all kisses and headed into the lounge where a chorus of 'We're watching that! Mummy! Why is she dancing in front of the tele?' made it clear Izzy was most definitely on the mend.

Charlotte and Emily picked up the handful of glasses and empty cake plates from the kitchen table.

'She seems settled,' Emily said.

'Mmmm.' Charlotte handed her a dishtowel. 'I think the counsellor that Freya suggested has been a real help. Izzy sees her a couple of times a week before she goes into the yoga studio.'

'She's really training to become an instructor?' Izzy had got a job as a receptionist a week earlier and had already decided that yoga was her path to serenity. Said it helped a lot of surfers keep their core balanced.

'Not yet. I don't think she's strong enough. But she says working on the reception desk is "giving her the right vibes". You know Izzy. Once she sets her mind to something she goes for it. Whether or not it makes sense.'

Yes. Emily nodded. True dat. And despite that, she had always loved her.

After everything had been tidied away to Charlotte's satisfaction, Emily turned off the kitchen lights then headed towards the stairs with Charlotte. There was a box room with her name on it and she was looking forward to a good night's sleep before heading back to London in the morning. Charlotte suddenly stopped and turned to her.

'I'm sorry, Emms.'

'For what?'

Charlotte looked down at her hands then met Emily's gaze straight on. 'I feel sad that you didn't think you could tell us earlier. About being a lesbian.'

'Don't.' Emily shook her head, the back of her throat tickling with unexpected emotion. 'I'm the one who should be apologizing.'

'What for?'

'For taking this long to figure out I could.'

394

She slipped her arm round Charlotte's waist as they began to make their way up the stairs. 'Mostly? I'm just happy that you lot don't care.'

'That's the whole point, silly,' Charlotte tsked. 'We do care. You're our Emily.'

TO: NHS GREYSTONE HOSPITAL TRUST, HR
FROM: Dr Emily Cheung
RE: RE: RE: Ten Years of Unused Holiday

Dear Over-worked HR Department,

Apologies for any terseness in my previous emails. I did not mean to imply that I alone have earned a year's holiday. Obviously *everyone* at the NHS deserves a year off. I was merely suggesting some leniency as regards the last-minute nature of my request for personal leave. (Which, if anyone in HR had bothered to accrue it, would total 52 weeks.)

If it suits the powers that be, I hereby request ONE WEEK immediately, TWO WEEKS in October (dates to be submitted when I figure out when the school holidays are) and a list of single dates (please see attached document) that will take us up until the Christmas Holidays which I would also like to take off. And the Chinese New Year. All of it.

There.

Is that acceptable?

Regards etc. etc.

Ms DOCTOR Emily Cheung, Sultan Orthopaedic Surgeon

Daisy Tate

Isabella Yeats
Hawkesbury Vicarage
Vicarage Mews
Hawkesbury Square
Bristol BS10

Dear Headmaster McClintock,

I am in shock. I had no idea there was such a thing as a surfing scholarship at Badminton. Obviously I am prejudiced, but I agree, Luna is very talented and very, very clever.

Would you mind if I asked how you received the videos of Luna surfing? (Ha ha, child protection laws and all that.)

The offer of a day scholarship is very kind, as is the offer of a bursary for occasional boarding. As we have only just moved to Bristol, I do feel a bit bad accepting the offer, so if there is another (genuinely) local student who is equally as deserving I understand.

I am guessing from the subtext of your kind letter you understand that Luna and I may have a complicated year ahead. Given the circumstances, we would be very grateful to accept your offer. Is there any chance you teach Danish?

Thanks again and I guess we need to figure out about uniforms. Do you know Charlotte Bunce? Would it be all right if I cc'd her in on things once we hit the email variety of communication? She's a bit more organized than I am on that front.

All the best and many thanks,
Izzy

Happy Glampers

TO: Lady Venetia of Sittingstone
FROM: Freya Burns-West
RE: Sittingstone Glampsite Expansion

Dear Lady Venetia

(Is that right? I wasn't entirely sure how to address you in print. Scots, eh? Rebellious to the end!)

Of course I remember you, and how very kind of Charlotte to recommend me to you regarding the soft furnishings for your new venture.

The eco-friendly cabins sound delightful. I'm sure Charlotte has conveyed my feelings to you about the hunt, so if you're quite convinced your son is happy for a tree-hugging, animal rights-er to make some gorgeous woodland creature themed soft furnishings for you, I'd be delighted. I would be able to offer a discounted rate for bespoke cushions for each of the cabins. I am toying with the idea of swish ottomans with rare-breed cattle hides and sheep fleeces. Perhaps a Highland chaise longue? Would you be interested in seeing some mock-ups? I think you will find they fit in with the 'rustic luxury' you are aiming for.

Please find attached a variety of cushion designs to choose from. We will, of course, include miniatures of the Sittingstone crest and any other specific items you feel would lend that personalized touch you were hoping for. And yes. You are absolutely right. Tweaking the crest to draw the eye away from the sword plunging into the deer's heart might be for the best. I will sketch out some ideas for your approval.

With kind regards,
Freya Burns-West

TO: Hazel_Pryce@PryceCalthorpeHawton.com
FROM: Charlotte Bunce
RE: Decree Absolute

Dear Hazel,

Congratulations to you as well! Named Partner. That *is* something. And well deserved if your work on my settlement is anything to go by (and I can confirm that it is). The decree absolute arrived this morning. I can confirm that it was, indeed, a wonderful bit of post to receive (though I shall probably not frame it as Emily suggested). How freeing to know this chapter is now well and truly closed.

Thank you so much for agreeing to mentor Poppy one day when she is old enough to have a summer internship. I'm sure she'll be a help to you and, of course, learn a great deal.

All the very best and many thanks for your hard work. I simply could not have done this without you.

Yours sincerely,

Charlotte Bunce

Chapter Thirty

'CAKE!'

Izzy held her hair back so she could tip her head forward and inhale Charlotte's freshly baked creation. 'Mmmmmm . . . lemon drizzle. Charlotte. You are an absolute wonder.'

'Isn't she just?' Rocco carried the teapot across to the table looking just a little bit smug.

Izzy elbowed her in the ribs and murmured, 'Looks like someone got a little action last night.'

Charlotte couldn't hide her grin.

Izzy hip-bumped her. 'You go girl. If anyone deserves a big ol' farmer lover, I'm pretty sure it's you.'

Imagine that. Charlotte Bunce had a lover.

They'd agreed to take things slowly, of course, and with Rocco in Scotland there was hardly the possibility of rushing into anything, but . . . my goodness last night had been delightful.

Freya slid a pile of mismatched plates onto the table. The china teacups that went with them would most likely be going back up the road with Rocco. He said he couldn't keep enough of them in stock. Every farm shop in Fife wanted some of their limited edition butter cups. He'd even had a couple of calls from Edinburgh.

Emily lifted up the teapot. 'Shall I be mother?'

They all laughed. Even Emily. An Emily who could take the mickey out of herself was something Charlotte had thought she'd never see.

Or an Emily who visited so regularly. Down every weekend. Longer when she could. She was also, Charlotte suspected, the secret source behind Luna's scholarship. There wasn't a school event you could keep her from.

Charlotte went to the utensil drawer for the cake slice but, when she'd turned around, Freya had already handed out forks and they were all digging in. Just like the old days.

'*Lotts.*' Izzy was in raptures. 'Did you put in extra drizzle?'

Yes. She had.

'Not on this end she didn't,' Freya pointed her fork at a corner of the cake Charlotte had directed her to earlier. 'Mmm. Springy. It's a perfect bake, Charlotte. You really should copyright your recipe. Can you even do that?'

'You can do anything if you're Charlotte,' Izzy said, not bothering to look up as she teased her fork into the gooiest part of the cake.

'They've certainly got you pegged,' Rocco said in that low, sotto-voce voice of his as his fingers brushed against hers.

As much as she loved her children, it was the perfect weekend for their father to make good on a visit. Apparently he was back in his old room at his parents' house as he and Xanthe were on a break.

'Rocco,' Emily pointed her finger at him while she finished swallowing a forkful of cake. 'You have no idea how lucky you are.'

'Oh, I'm beginning to get a pretty good idea.' The way he said it made Charlotte's tummy do fizzy things.

'Well, if you don't, we're going to learn you up fast, laddie!' Freya gave them both a deeply protective smile. If ever Charlotte had thought she might have a sister from another mother somewhere out there, that smile was all the proof she needed.

Through mouthfuls of cake, they quizzed Rocco about the farm, Lachlan, and the shop.

Great, good and couldn't be better. The wink he gave Charlotte on that last bit made her blush straight up to her roots.

After they'd eaten their fill, Emily leant back in her chair. 'Oof,' she glanced at her watch. 'It's getting harder and harder to leave each weekend.'

'So, don't,' Freya said.

'Uhhh . . .' Emily made her *derrrr* face. 'I have a job, aging parents, a girl—' She stopped herself.

'Why, Ms Emily Cheung. Were you going to say you had a *girlfriend*?' Izzy looked like the Cheshire Cat.

'Maybe I was. Maybe I wasn't.' Emily pinched Izzy's arm.

'Owww! I have cancer, don't do that!' They play-fought for a minute and then stopped when Izzy's elbow cracked against the table and she actually did hurt herself.

She rubbed at it while Emily fussed and Freya talked over them about the healing power of arnica.

Charlotte felt like she was in the world's best time machine. One with a future.

'I mean it, Emms,' Izzy said once they'd determined her elbow was fine. 'You should stay.'

'What? Here? What would I do here?'

Now it was Izzy's turn to make her *derrrr* face. 'Work at one of the hospitals. Work at the University Hospital. That would be hilarious. Get back to the old stomping ground. Show 'em what the old Cheung-meister has got up to in London Town. Can I hear a hells to the yeah?' She lifted her hands up to raise the roof.

Emily made a show of rolling her eyes, but . . . yes . . . they could all see the possibility of a relocation grow.

Izzy clapped her hands again. 'Emily's moving to Bristol!!'

'Am not.' Emily was grinning.

'Are too.' So was Izzy.

Charlotte opened the refrigerator and pulled out a bottle of Prosecco. 'I know it's a bit early in the afternoon, but . . . would it be too early to do a toast to all of us being back in the same place?'

Emily didn't say no, which they all took as a yes.

Rocco did the honours with the cork, but stepped back as Charlotte, Emily, Izzy and Freya all lifted their glasses and chimed, 'To Bristol!'

Yes, thought Charlotte, as she drank her fizz. To Bristol, where it all began.

'To us!' Izzy lifted her glass again.

They all cheered and chimed, 'To us!'

To us, thought Charlotte, and to whatever the future may have in store.

Charlotte's Lemon Drizzle Cake (for sharing with friends . . . no plates required, annotations by Freya)

Cake!

- 175g unsalted butter (organic if poss – remember Rocco) – if you only have salted . . . don't add the salt later on ☺
- 175g caster sugar (FairTrade if poss – looks a lovely golden colour)
- 3 large eggs (free range if poss)
- 1 teaspoon baking powder
- Zest of 2 (to 3, depending upon how tangy you like it) unwaxed lemons
- 175g self-raising flour
- Pinch of salt (squish it well if you're using sea salt flakes)
- 2–3 tablespoons of milk if it's too thick (from your local dairy)

(NB: If you want to do a traybake, double everything except the cooking time!)

The Drizzle

100g soft golden sugar or caster sugar – your call (I do it half and half)

Juice of 2–3 lemons, depending on how gooey you want it to be and how juicy they are. (Give these a roll around with your hand to release all of that juice)

*Go mad and use 150g sugar and 3–4 lemons if you like it crazy gooey

How to make cake:

1) Heat oven to 180°C fan 160°C/gas mark 4
2) Beat together butter, sugar and HALF of the lemon zest until beautifully pale and creamy (with dreamy flecks of yellow zest)
3) Add eggs one at a time, ensuring they are fully mixed through
4) Sift in the self-raising flour, baking powder and salt. Give mixture a few good whizzes with the mixer or your spoon to ensure flour is fully incorporated (but not over-whipped)

5) Line a loaf tin (8 x 21cm) or whatever you have because it's the cake that matters, not the shape, right? Pour in mixture and level the top (but it doesn't have to be perfect)

6) Bake for 40–50 minutes (you know your oven). Thin skewer or knife should come out clean at the end and cake should have a little bounce when you touch it (because you know you want to, right?)

7) While the cake is cooling, mix that lemon juice, remaining lemon zest and caster or golden sugar to make the drizzle. While the cake is still warm (this is critical!), poke holes all over the top of the warm cake (knife, chopstick, skewer, be careful if you're using your finger because . . . hot cake!). Pour drizzle over and wait for cake to absorb before pouring on more (remember – one end extra-gooey for Izzy, one end with only a bit for Freya)

8) Note: If you're short on lemons and rich in friends – use whatever citrus you have to hand. Orange is fab. Lime is a delight. I've never tried pineapple, but there's always room to explore

9) Enjoy with friends

ACKNOWLEDGEMENTS

If this was a pop-up book, at this juncture a very long scroll would unfurl with a squillion names on it going back to primary school. Earlier. Birth. Thank you Mum and Dad for having me. And thank you for bringing us camping. A lot. What a fecund pool of material to draw from. This book has been such a great joy to write for many reasons, not least of which because it rekindled a fabulous friendship with the glorious Jackie N. Thank you for all of your honest insight. Lady W – *muchos gracias* for the fashion advice. You are, and shall forever be, my Coco. Netts – you are, as ever, a wonder. You are made of kindness and all of the other lovely things. Beth – you read the earliest, most painful drafts of this and still had nice things to say, so thank you. Darcy – again, thank you for your honesty and insight. You iz most helpful. JP and Mich – your friendship, that chicken soup and those pickles were a godsend. Never before has shampoo been more gratefully received. Natasha, bless you for the Zencils. They made all the difference. James – thank you for the insight into the amorous tiers of lawful luvvin'. Most interesting. Christine and Pam – you're tremendous cheerleaders. *Mwah*. Sue and Stu! You made real-life glamping extra fun. Sarah L – thank you for lunch and illuminating me on just what it takes to pack a large family up for a weekend under canvas. *Exhausting*. To my agent, Jo Bell, who is not only marvellous at reading small print, but who is tremendously talented at reminding me about which small stuff to sweat and which big stuff to get on with and achieve. A heartfelt thanks to you. To the team at HarperCollins for making this twinkle of an idea a reality, especially that transcendentally superpowered Kate Bradley, my amazing faith-filled, patient, inspirational and acutely insightful editor. Thank you for believing in me. Lucy Gilmour, you certainly know how to polish a rough diamond. *Merci mille fois!* Great love to Grissom and Jorja who began this journey with me and to Skye who picked up their batons. And, of course, to my sweet beloved husband. Without you . . . well . . . that's not really worth thinking about is it? Bring on the marshmallows!